D Y A D

D Y A D

MICHAEL BRODSKY

FOUR WALLS EIGHT WINDOWS, NEW YORK

The author wishes to express his gratitude to Noël Burch, whose *Theory of Film Practice* (copyright © 1973 by Praeger Publishers, Inc. [English translation of *Praxis du cinéma,* copyright © 1969 by Éditions Gallimard, Paris]), suggested a line of thought that is explored independently in some portions of this work.

First edition published by:
Four Walls Eight Windows
PO Box 548
Village Station
New York, N.Y. 10014

First Printing October 1989.

Library of Congress Cataloging-in-Publication Data:
Brodsky, Michael, 1948—
Dyad/ by Michael Brodsky. — 1st ed.
p. cm.
I. Title
PS3552.R6233D8   1989   89-36339
813'.54—dc20   CIP

ISBN: 0-941423-30-1 (cloth)
ISBN: 0-941423-31-X (paper)

*W*here is that grief for which I've sought in vain, I heard myself say for no particular reason. On a particularly windswept day in January, with the heavy snows about to fall on city streets, on the buses uptown, on the ladies who with lipstick stains on the rim of their cigarettes and raspberry nail polish jarring wildly with the hue and cry of official visitors keep watch in hospital lobbies though they are not waiting for word regarding a loved one—as I was wending my way up and down those city streets I stumbled on an older man who quickly began to resemble the father I should have had. I went on walking, looking behind, he was clearly after me, after my commodities. I entered a coffee shop at the corner of Huron and Iroquois. "Coffee," I said to the counter man doubling as cashier. He asked if my name was X—, I nodded, he invited me to the city's museum of modern art, I accepted, all through our talk I strained to see the statues in the garden. But the air was frosty, furry, resisted all my efforts to appraise the dregs suspended in its medium. "You see, I'm dying," he said. "I got the diagnosis yesterday morning." Perhaps to give himself strength he ordered more than tea. Tearing grumpily with a fork at his muffin and the special of the day—a braised concoction of what appeared to be broccoli, cheese, stewed apricots, anchovies, olives, pinto beans and chocolate bars trampled underfoot, as well as breadcrumbs, oregano flakes, and Devonshire cream, he was understandably unable to take note of the fashionable dowagers-in-training who coming and going inevitably went colliding with the immigrant busboys. I was assigned to see what was meant for him and what he would have seen had he been looking. "When did your dad

1

die," he asked. I loathe the word. On and on went the conversation flaunting its breakneck speed for the conversation was an organism with its own lungs, sharp turns, luminescent wastes. I did not know what to answer, never having had one. "Last year," I replied. "On a very cold midwinter night." I breathed deep, dutifully remembering how the breaths came slower and slower, how every now and then he raised his arm high above his head then let it fall as if he was that very minute about to expire. By the same token, I had no trouble remembering how he made life especially difficult for the floor nurses claiming they were not doing their job when in actual fact, like these busboys assaulted by dowager fur, they were doing more, far more. Here I was answering well at last though he wasn't listening very hard. He was still deep in the museum stew picking away at his teeth exactly like dad in the last weeks. I got up to go, offended by this more ebb than flow of interest in a subject that happily no longer concerned me, sternum-deep as I once again was in the heady business of earning my bread. A busboy was accidentally smearing one belle's silver fox with—when you came right down to it any museum program committee disclaimers notwithstanding—Mulligan stew. "You must have been real close to your dad," sniffed the stew man. I couldn't decide whether this was an authentic yokel or one merely playing at being one. His inflection seemed sometimes to say I wish I could recapture somebody's proverbial first fine flutter of disbelief at all this impeccable wainscoting. I made another move to go but I wasn't able to remove my hand quickly enough for he was stroking it. There, there, the stroking proclaimed. "I know what it means to lose a father," he said, "and suddenly to be saddled with all kinds of unwieldy responsibility. Sooner or later my son will be in your shoes but will he be able to fill them." "In and out they came—the neighbors, I mean—using the broken down abode of death as a clubhouse where safe-deposit boxes, canasta, gall transplants might be assessed at length at last in peace and security. They went on to triple mastectomiesa quintuple bypasses, mothers widowed in the bloom of youth and youths carried off by the bloomier bloom of puberty, some scratching their privates as they looked off in the general direction of sunset smearing windowpane above the wretched little ghat known variously to its otherwise optionless habitués as X, Y, and Z street." Almost finished with his dessert dish after patting his lips ("Delightful," he murmurs), "Tell me," he went on "did your dad have a good-looking casket." Exactly the phrase that ought to have been used by dad in the terrible last weeks. Dutifully I described the wooden box and how I came to choose it above all others gently steered by the rubicund funeral director toward this only conceivable fusion of the tasteful and the monumental. "Was oak your dad's favorite wood?" Was the fulvous poppy his favorite woodland bloom? Shelley his favorite poetaster? Did he favor spaghetti over noodles of smugger and more recent vintage? "Some things," I retorted, "I know for a fact. Others I will never know nor do I care to." Where is that grief for which I've sought in vain. He looked me over as — I am tempted to say — dad might have done even though not in the least as dad might have done given his spate of respectful tenderness shorn of all that other's poisoning repudiation of all that reminded him all too irrefutably of a loathed consort's invincible stratagem for holding on for dear life. He rose, stretched toward me and before the eyes of all busboys and inchoate dowagers kissed my forehead as if it burned with a pure preternatural light. "You are a good boy," I shrugged away the compliment. "Am I," was all I murmured. "If I could I would adopt you, make you my heir right here and now." In exchange for such an outburst idiotically I felt I owed him a further description of another's last moments. This is what the kiss demanded. "I don't know if I can go on speaking of the *last moments* as I sat before the bed in the full regalia of my hunger to elude what even then showed no sign of ceasing to impose itself as a total fabrication of his craving to manhandle my availability. In short his dying/death was undergone by me as a saprophyte's ploy to keep on sucking." There was nothing more to say and yet the kiss demanded more, much more. Noting what was desiderated still I surprised myself coming to the rescue with, "His dying was nothing but a constant supersession of imperatives," for wasn't this a little the story of my life, or rather, the failed story of that life. "First we fought, Aunt Glorree and I"—for I saw the busboy fighting with the dowager now—fighting back—refusing to be humiliated and undone by that old crone and its consort with his bleached pate and what were meant to signify designer bifocals—"Aunt Glorree and I regarding whether or not to install his remains in a chronic-care facility conveniently planted across the railroad tracks. But when very considerately he went from worse to appalling, no need any longer to worry about chronic care. And before that there had been the question of how to get him to the local quack for his triweekly dose. But when he could no longer rise from the ashes of his cot and had to piss into a little bucket normally utilized in cleaning out the tub no need to worry keeping him at home about getting him from cot to quack. And last, how we did fight about finding him a nurse for imminent Christmas Day when all nurses are gray but lo and behold when he took or gave his last breath on the day before that special day no longer any need to procure one of those bloody helpmates always in such very short supply. So you can see how dad's dying went on comprising to the bitter end a continuous supersession of dire imperatives owing to unpredictable and always spectacular quantum leaps of deterioration that made the last, imperative I mean, always irrelevant and obsolete—quantum leaps that bred their own imperatives incompatible, need I say, with those that had come before." He did not seem to be listening, he murmured: "I never expected to receive a death sentence. All along I took my submission to the whimsical rigor of the business routine I imposed on myself for some kind of indemnificatory earnest of immortality. In the shadow of that rigor there was supposed to be no danger for its despotism was always such an immediate danger, in itself I mean—rather, such an excruciation leaving little time for danger. And yet," he added, seeming to change his tone, "why so gloomy. You should be delighted by all these imperatives, superseded or not, sketching the curve of a dying that remained, from what I can see, forever true to its essence. So what if the patient raged, gave himself up to whims non-compliance with which obliged him to be incessantly firing his next of kin, so what if one minute he exhorted in the name of a good-looking casket and the next reprobated a glaring failure to shoulder your responsibilities as that next of kin—you should be applauding that all this, latent in the prognosis, was brought dutifully and always at the appropriate moment to fulfillment. Swinging vigilantly above the patient's imminent corpse like a hammock woven of elytra is the prognosis but this prognosis has nothing to do with the measly little rescript delivered, say, one calm—deceptively calm—summer morning by some little quack in some little quack's cell on the margin of a teaching hospital—oxymoron if ever there was one—such as I have received today. No, I recognize even this early that the prognosis—the true prognosis—has nothing to do with its slimy little instantiation such as I have lived through today. In your case, young man, someone or something was all along making sure everything turned out not as predicted—for there was never any danger it would *not* turn out as predicted— dad was a dead duck, after all—but along the lines of the strictest and most glorious economy of means. For there is always, in these cases, and not only in these, where so much imminent putrefaction is at stake, the danger of a too vast prodigality of effects. So you have every reason to be grateful—and proud—for you played your role—of economizer—to the hilt. And I do believe you are proud, and grateful too, though the schema of both is a kind of lumbering truculence transparent only to a trained, that is to say, a moribund eye. Never be ashamed to be grateful for things as they are—as they turn out to be. Now you can understand that I want things to turn out as they did for your dad—a maximization of necessary disease events supervening through the strictest economy of means. This is where you come in. With regard to my son, Jim, I mean.

"You see, Jim likes to think of himself as an original thinker. Not that I ever thought as much. What makes a thinker original. Simply this: the capacity to be forever afflicted by what we may call 'the wrong side of the comparison.' In other words, a great and original thinker is always smelling a comparison of what he is at this very moment undergoing, with something else, something wider, vaster, direr. In fact he lives the direr side far more completely than the less dire yet without being quite able to sniff out and make its contour conform to what everybody and his brother implies—tells him—he is supposed to be living. And out of the disjunction, the non-junction, the original thinker concocts his... prophecy. About the fate of all mankind. Even if I have spent my whole life thinking about making money I still think about all mankind. All mankind is my direr side of the comparison, if you will. For all his advantages the original thinker is a man of the people and never thinks twice about scraping his heel on the manure of everybody's everyday argot—you know, the one big monosyllable parceled out for use by the human race. Clearly my son is no original thinker, never will be. If only some body could go out and talk to him, I want him to come home, let bygones be bygones, you see I'm dying."

I stifled a craving to jump up and denounce him, not everybody can leave his job any time he wants even if, like me, he is on the verge of not having one. "So what do you say," prompted, coaxed, the rich man. "I have to think about it," I replied. "Certain ties," I added, and although there were none, absolutely and resolutely none, nor would there ever be any, I was nonetheless furious at his proposing that I uproot myself in the name of another's retrieval. It was a little after midnight when his chauffeur dropped me in front of the building where I said I lived. When he drove away I skulked off in the other direction, parallel to the dead dark river, and tried to remember all I could about his son, whom only the brashest exaggeration could pass off as my old school chum. Our stark resemblance had drawn us together briefly. In the shabby alcove behind all my tics and flukes redolent, but only to the undiscerning eye, of harsh pride and ascetic frenzy, his, the elder's, dinner invitation for the following night had been gladly and gratefully accepted long before he had even extended it. I noted that not just Mr. Jamms but his lady also looked deathly ill. But as the evening wore on she showed more and more stamina and seemed almost to drink deep from the degenerescence of her consort, whose stance suggested a powerful man—a potentate—well on his way out. At a certain moment, which was also an uncertain one, Mrs. Jamms muttered something I could not decipher but aimed clearly at pleasing, or at least defanging, the unuttered, perhaps unutterable, revulsions of her better half which something he, grimly attuned to the downward passage of his meat and potatoes, made it a point of honor barely to acknowledge. Though the bareness—of civility—of attention—proclaimed not only the official end of her effort, largely wasted, but the discouragement as well of any similar indulgence in future, from lips coquettishly pursed in midair it was evident she was still soliciting some verdict more favorable to the ravages of age or, more simply, hadn't the slightest idea how to let herself down, down, down, loosen the stays of a physiognomy suddenly very inward looking and, given the alternative, working very hard at appearing to be so. But then, either by accident or inevitably if, that is, the inward looking had been a mere stalling for time, her eye caught on the unaccommodating hook of his own as the larger than life reflection of this stranded sense of being left to the vain gyrations of a mere and now obsolete purr whence there was no plausible exit. I pitied her, somberly, for she must have been quite pretty in youth. After the soup a bed on casters had to be wheeled in so that Jamms could be propped up against a few pillows. Every so often he groaned and every groan reduced the missus to the most harassed harassing grovelling interrogation, along the lines of, "What do you mean by that, Jamms." Then she turned to me and said, "Do you know what he means by that." When he farted, which sometimes he did, she said, "What do you mean by that." If he asked for milk, "Maybe some beer," she would say. And if he went on to ask for beer after that though — unrelatedly — independently so it seemed — so I needed it to seem — of her prompting she would say she thought he was better off with milk as if beer had been his idea and only his after all. Sometimes he turned his face to the wall as if it was a window opened too late on life's infinite prospects. No danger. It was only when he simultaneously lifted his arm high above his head that I began to collapse. The ravin of time, I wanted to tell him, the ravin of time you are, time's carcass and time's eunuch, but I held back the dawn of my words and preoccupied myself instead and utterly with the family photographs his wife felt obliged to shove under my nose. Here was Jim under an apple tree, hands folded away from his groin in unintentional parody of the good boy, at least I assumed it was he. There was another Jim under an arcade in the middle of a sun-oppressed park. She told me they had already reserved a first-class seat for me on a Valhalla B-439A' going to wherever it was Jamms was stationed in the name of whatever it was he purported to be passionately pursuing. I murmured that I simply was not ready to make a decision. They listened politely but it was clear I had no value — no meaning — apart from reminding them of how dutiful a courier they very much intended me to become come hell or high water. The stupidity of their stance told me that for them I existed within the confines of a specific class still seeking particular redress for particular injustices perpetrated over centuries rather than redress in general for injustice in general comprising wrongs carried out even against them. No, their stance of stupid seeming to hear told me they needed me consigned to a specific class rather than embodying the dissolution of all classes. Their stupid stance of seeming to listen told me that my discrete existence of smells, excretions, close shaves, and wayward encounters was simply too exiguous to qualify as source even of embarrassment. I noted his breathing growing more and more faint. He raised his arm against the blank wall. Before he had barely completed his course Mrs. Jamms said, "What does that mean. What's wrong." I did not know him but his face seemed involuntarily to be mimicking all those he had mimicked eagerly— loathingly—in health. Perhaps within hours he would be dead and gone and would the assignment then still hold good, would my function, even if up to now tepidly repudiated, still be valid. I turned to the missus and she, guessing my thoughts in the midst of ever more frantic preoccupation with the old guy's ever more widely spaced breaths, shook her head up and down sadly as if to say, Go at any rate. Whatever happens you and you alone are our procurator. For even if you belong to a specific class— specifically, *that* class,—and even if you seek redress for the immedicable wounds inflicted on that class which you will not because, look at you, you are temperamentally incapable of putting the needs of your class above your own—it is after all a particular redress you seek, therefore clearcut and annihilable. If you were to seek redress, which you will not, it would be redress for wounds particular rather than for all wrong, wrongs in general. And if you were to seek a change in status it would be some other traditional status you would seek, a classifiable therefore obliterable status, rather than the human status that is the explosive dissolution of all prior statuses. "So you'll be going," said Mrs. Jamms, in the honeyed tones of a hostess surefooted in her seductiveness. I wanted to leap up and strangle her or better yet, or worse, divest her of everything in her apartment, everything she owned, including, so it seemed, the public park below. Yet I could not begin to think of enumerating her arrogance in assuming without question that I would go. I was afraid to mortify, make her tumble. For such arrogance was somehow too deeply ingrained in the nature of things for her to be singled out and held accountable for one particular upsurge even if she was the universal site of that upsurge. And therefore far more than humiliated and enraged I felt protective and afraid for her. To disabuse her of her vision—even if that vision was of me and of my particular class,—would be too provoking, devastating, imper- tinent, what with her husband dying and all. I was the embodiment of unnaturalness and so any reactions that unnaturalness induced were necessarily natural and beyond correction. What impertinence to begin to feel the stirrings of a craving to challenge the impertinence derived from the very deepest nature of things as they are when those stirrings could never be anything but belated, farcical, superfetatory. Yet I could still smell her loathing me for belonging to that particular class which loathing was of course nothing more than her way of insisting I do my utmost to go on belonging in order that my grievances be instantly reducible to some mite gerrymandering for its own aggrandizement.

I thanked her by rising, colliding with the wispy material that grazed her plump shoulder, and going to stand at the window in what I assumed was an appreciative, even an enthralled, posture. When I got back to my seat I noticed how puffy Mr. Jamms's fingers had become. I could not begin to assimilate puffy fingers to that gauntness by which I was beginning to feel if not comforted then at least unintimidated. Quickly concealing them beneath the quilt he said, "Go to hell, go to hell, go to hell," intoning the phrase in triplicate about forty more times. I looked at Mrs. Jamms who simply shook her head.

The day next when I came as agreed upon the night before to visit the Jamms factory and showrooms in the heart of the downtown area he seemed perfectly well. Almost vociferously he informed me that the missus, the little woman, the old gal, was also well, couldn't in fact be better if she tried. I tried to look as if I could have only the foggiest recollection of any indiscretions committed the night before. "How would you like to come work here as creative director," Jamms said, escorting me from cubicle to cubicle. I replied: "I prefer the privileges that come with being an underdog." Though truth to tell, I was tired of under-doggery. I spent my time among coworkers, not colleagues, taking their ease with my sneering contempt and raging irony as the sign of ultimate revulsion at my failure to move beyond the soup kitchen of contempt and rage toward authentic mutiny. I over and over saddled them with the contemptuous expectation that after so many snarling phrases I would at the very least have the decency to revolt. But wasn't it only in my brain that I was being goaded to imminent ultimate upsurge. These others were clearly content to go on parasitizing my feeble wit forever. Loathing was my real, my only, life whereas for the horde of coworkers loathing was a mere and intermittent perquisite, a makeshift ventilation on their trek through the kiln of days. They did not of course know that I stole office equipment.

Jamms's secretary was fulsomely pleasant only because of my enigmatic relation to the boss. Under other circumstances she would have had no trouble overtly despising me. The sun setting and en route to the apartment (at Jamms's suggestion we stopped off at a liquor store for a little cognac) he announced, "Yes, creative director." As if he was repeating a phrase uttered seconds before and to which he had received no audible response. "What do you say. Hired sight unseen." He waited. "Here's a way out of the division of labor, the way to be shepherd in the morning, mogul in the afternoon, countertenor until three P.M., wrestler till dusk, and evangelist after midnight." As we entered the apartment that admitted little of the dazzling sun I noted the caster bed in the middle of the living room floor. Almost the minute he saw it Jamms approached as if mesmerized. Once he was reclining she cried, "I always knew it would be very grave." Then almost in unison they asked what I thought of the office. At first, at very first, I imagined it was because they wanted to draw me into the family business. But they were only drilling me to make sure I could furnish as accurate, that is to say, attractive, a report as was compatible with their exalted hopes for his, their son's, return to the fold. Suddenly he became quite peremptory and as the last rays liquefied the turreted crests across the park called us to his bedside. As I made a pretense of continuing to be enthralled by their scrapbooks of Jim Jamms now here, now there, he could be heard spitting into an empty tissue box. Disavowing this very gurgle of evening's frailty "Something's bothering you," said the old man, very piercing and perceptive, or at least in the tone of one very piercing and perceptive, or at least in the tone of one whose imminent departure authorizes a long suppressed and long overdue frankness. But this fabled perspicacity of the moribund, it made me want to puke. There was no perspicacity here, no content to the perspicacity. He was simply buoyed up by fable, all he had heard about dying and all he deemed himself entitled to as one thrashing in its robes. Where is that grief for which I've sought in vain.

"The old devil thinks you are Jim," intoned the old devil's wife. "Something's bothering you," he repeated, as if he had known my incompetences a whole life long and this the last straw, as if illness, encroaching death, procured him a no-holds-barred perspicacity that could gnaw through the most castironly of dissimulations. When in fact, at least as far as I could see, illness merely transformed the world into the tumorlike outpouching of his own raging fright. Somehow I felt I should be compassionating, at least if I still wanted the ambassadorial trip to hold good. Instead I edged away, toward another wall, perpendicular to the one along which he groped upward. Instead of warming the old fart in the savagery of my surrogate filial embrace I skirted the wall, noting with neither revulsion nor satisfaction the dried snot protruding from one hairy nostril. Here he was playing at being free with a perspicacity he no longer had any reason to keep under wraps.

"Look at his feet," she said, as he glared at her with powerful rage. "They're swollen." After a long silence he sighed deeply as if the silence had after all accomplished something, far too much to assess. "Look at his forehead. Doesn't it look swollen." I couldn't help feeling mamma Jamms made a vocation of the inessential. "Doesn't it look swollen," she said with an edge of irritated impatience. I couldn't help going on feeling she made a vocation of focusing on the inessential and having focused dragging it to her lair and having dragged hammering it, the inessential, to death, and having hammered to death forcing bystanders, me for example, to do the dirty work of procuring the inexpensive furniture appropriate for a last resting place. As the sky went blueblack, particles that were not clouds floating in its curd, I heard the old woman in another room, probably the kitchen, muttering to herself. Changing my position only slightly I could even observe her: always muttering, throwing out tiny bags of garbage, washing down dull surfaces with shrivelled rags of tissue paper, always discarding, always getting ready to discard in this loathsome borough of eternal night where nobody protested that all was sickness, death, bedtime, dead leaves clogging airconditioner flues, uncelebrated inking of rooftop antenna. I caught his eye. Then he chuckled and said, "Don't get me wrong. I love silence, dusky dark, order, stillness, objects in place, all the scion of a recent jettisoning. But she doesn't create order, only a watery stench. She wears down surfaces." Apparently she had heard for the old girl came charging in. Although his eyes were wide open she spoke as if he was having the audacity to be fast asleep when after so much abstemiousness she was warrantedly, well-nigh meritoriously, venting her spleen at last. "Oh if I were ill I would be very different." Then her eyes grew bleary and pointing a finger at me said, "Don't forget to ask the doctor why his feet are swollen, why his forehead bulges, why he coughs—cough cough cough—oh I can't stand it another minute—why his balls are blue—why he still has his balls—and tell him, oh yes, that I can't remember whether or not I fed him the raw mice, I mean rice, once or twice today. Don't forget." She turned away as if delivered of an incubus. He whispered: "She thinks you're Jim. She preys on you as Jim will someday soon be preying on you." Then he fell back on the pillows. "Get Jim," he whispered. "Here. I wrote a little note on my palm." Looking down he read: "Jim: I need your help, things are going bad with me." Mother Jamms jumped in with: "What do you mean, bad." "Jim boy, I'm dying." "What do you mean, dying," she cawed. "Dying," he said quizzically, as if the word was new to him now, as if he had a right to the pleasure of using it. He fingered it. Meanwhile she was irritated, not, I saw that fast enough, with me and neither with the pretexts for her nursing anxiety not coming fast enough so that at last she could be purged of them but rather with the forever imminent danger of disbelieving in these pretexts yet with all the anxiety they induced to be contended with anyway. When I found him, Jim Jamms, he was somewhat standoffish, to say the least, and I, wanting so much for him to like me. Then I realized he was at war with the world, his conversation reduced everything to excrement, more specifically, to horseshit, even more specifically, to an equine turd enhanced in the noonday sun by a paroxysmal dance of war flies, yea, for this young man being was no more nor less than horseshit electrified by its own nullity and likely to remain so for all eternity, if not a little longer. Trying to soften him up I spoke of how ill both his parents appeared to be. He laughed heartily. "You know, don't you," he sputtered, " the whole mother/son-father/son commodity is a fraud. Nothing more than a pretext for the survival of the greeting card industry." Seeing what I assumed he assumed was my look of horror on he went, bolder and bolder, yet I couldn't help feeling the boldness, divorced from all feeling but the very horror he ascribed to me, or rather, to my look, was nothing more than an enervated spur toward—a clumsy and attenuating plea in behalf of—newer routes of feeling otherwise than horrorstruck. In essence, his words sought not dazzling innovations in feeling but numbness. "Well," he added, offering me a drink, "one advantage of their illness is that they are presumably too ill to go on judging me. If I were there which as you see I am not with sole responsibility for the beds, the bedpans, the funeral arrangements, doctors then at least I would no longer be fearing their jaundiced eye on my doings or absence of same." Something in the vicinity of my own best interest prompted me to add, "You talk about their illness as if it is an impersonation, some fabrication to corral you back into the fold." I shook my head at the drink he offered me, arm outstretched a little to my left long after the offering stopped.

"Where are you staying," he asked. When I hesitated he said: "Don't tell me, not in some ghastly hotel-chain monolith like the one I tried to paint last week from that island in the middle of Broadway between, oh, Forty-third and Seventh." "The elevator capsule rises visibly in gaudy yellow outline." A woman came from the direction of what had to be the bedroom. She looked a little groggy, acknowledged me askew in passing as if used to visitors at all hours. Affected by her presence Jim said, "So what do you do," but from the tone it sounded more like, "Identify yourself." Especially in front of the woman I did not want to depict myself as what truly I was, flunkey and thief, huckster and drifter, especially with dusk falling heavy as rain. I said I was a worker. "Jim is a worker," the woman said defiantly. "And things are going beautifully now: he's found the patron of his dreams." Yet the minute I said I was a worker I began, literally, to stagger. Fortunately I was leaning on the refrigerator and could take courage from its hum, all other details of my life had immediately become unascertainable, randomized beyond decipherability. To say what I was was to operate on myself or, as it had just turned out, on no more than the merest fragment of myself—was to bring that minute fragment into extreme close-up and thereby relegate all other imbricating fragments to extreme and hazy long shot. To clear the air I added, "I have a marked tendency to steal on the job—large business machines are my specialty of the house. I also rob my coworkers when their backs are turned." I waited for some glint of approval, it came. At that very moment another woman emerged from what had to be also a bedroom but a smaller, more intimate, one. She smiled. Jamms smiled at her as he had not smiled at the first or rather whatever he now directed at this other, whose name was Bessy, retrospectively modified, that is to say, called radically into question—in other words, into being—some prior something aimed in the general vicinity of the other other, whose name was Maggy. Quietly Jamms said to the new arrival, "He's been telling me my father is very sick." Immediately as if she must intercept this intercourse at all costs Maggy burst out with, "Your father never listened when you spoke about his changing his diet. And when that friend of his developed cancer of the tongue—" At Jim's quizzical look, for the reference or for the appropriateness of the reference at this time was not clear, Maggy said irritably: "You know, the one who had a cancer growing on his tongue for years and was simply too insensitive to his own body to know he had that cancer growing. At any rate, your dad never bothered to visit him." At first I thought he would jump down her throat. Instead he simply lowered his head in deference to the justness of her observation or perhaps to their tacit agreement that in exchange for keeping the other woman, Bessy, she had a right to hold forth at any time on any subject. As arbiter and theoretician of sickness in others it was clear she—and by extension, they, whatever their internal squabbles— were exempt forever. She, Maggy, now went on to explain why people got sick. Everything, refrigerator included, was chronically coated with the residue of this stern self-congratulation for their way of life, whatever that might turn out to be. They—Jamms, Bessy, and Maggy—were outside the maelstrom and I, despite my loathing of panaceas, found myself hungering after their secret. I suddenly feared less getting sick or triturated than their smug verdict on how such a catalysis might have been avoided. I was immediately convinced the trio, however shabbily, would live forever and now, with the best of all possible patrons on the scene to subserve the needs of this best of all possible dilettantes and his houris—As if to clarify my musing Maggy noted, "Jim has just found a buyer for several of his new pieces—the buyer of our dreams, in fact— not to be confused, of course with the patron of our dreams, who lives just down the street." The other woman, Bessy, was peeling a tangerine. The air tart with the spray she said, "What." When the silence became too unbearable I replied, "I have a tendency to steal big business machines. It's not even for the money. I loathe what business and technology is doing to our country." The pietism of "our country" made me laugh inwardly. Outwardly I felt it had to be corrected: I added the phrase "to our world." "To our world," I repeated. The repetition glued me to what I said and turned me into an object of merciless scrutiny, but not that, fortunately or unfortunately, of anyone present. She went on peeling, hearing the repetition no more acutely, from all indications, than she had heard the original utterance. No, she for one was not scrutinizing. It was the air: the very air was heavy with the hypervigilance whose provenance is nowhere. From that nowhere I returned saying, "You're right," taking my leave, "your father wants you to come back and join the firm." As if he felt he had no choice flanked as he was by two women, that is to say by the expectations of two women, Jamms said, "This positive approach he wants from me nauseates me more than life itself. A positive approach to life, whatever the bloody fuck that is, should never be proclaimed and if proclaimed should never proclaim itself to be anything but the grubby timorous fartlike superstitiously reverent composition with shit that essentially it is. It should go quietly, at dusk if at all possible, in the interstices of being with nobody looking. Waiting for one of the many big breaks with which such an approach proverbially always manages to abound it should of course go on looking out for its own fabled best interest, no, its fabled own best interest, with a smile, with a smile, have a good evening with a smile, but for all that should never speak its name for in point of half-fact it is completely without name, it is foundationless, its stratagem a skewedly panicked sidestepping of the major health hazards, its fabled calm a kind of raving simper, its fondness for the traditional values now in such gilded disrepair a subspecies of moxibustion-proof podagra akin to epilepsy, its ever-friendly smile a bilious ruse worthy of—of— In brief, just keep business, home, kiddies, the Masonic temple, army buddies, army bands, armbands, away from me. Families? Why, the biggest abomination ever perpetrated on the exquisite Neanderthal sensibility of our ectypes. Unless, of course, you are prepared to prosectomize that agglomeration of gutter ontologies feeding the positive approach—ontology of the business trip, ontology of the baby sitter, ontology of the second-car garage, ontology of the summer house by the shore, ontology of the pied-à-terre in the heart—the very heart of town, ontology of the Saturday afternoon foray on the art galleries, ontology of the suburban extramarital excursus, ontology of the corporate roundtable discussion, ontology of the hobby. In short," he went on, grabbing a bowl of rice from the refrigerator, and more I once again felt from his ultimately conventional point of view to dissipate the scandalousness of his outburst than to sustain and enhance it, "keep the blessings of the blessed away from me." I asked if I could use their bathroom. Pointing, the second woman gently belched. On my way I heard one of them—I cannot swear it was Maggy—say, "He comes skulking around, trying to land you as if you were somebody's prize haddock."

Leaving without further ado all the way back to Manhattan I couldn't help feeling disturbed and enraged. Looking for him had seemed heroic, now it stank of more flunkeyism. Then, to cheer myself up and just as we were passing under Wall Street I told myself that being able to look for another—never mind whether or not he was retrieved—was no small feat and that Jim, for example, certainly would never have been able to conceive of looking for somebody else, much less somebody else like me, or rather having conceived of such a one as I would have been starkly incapable of going in search of his target since having conceived why must he be supererogatorily burdened with a need for a quest for retrieval.

In my hotel room I remembered the remark, overheard, about the prize haddock. So they thought of me, this trio, as a flunkey. But perceiving I was about to be straitjacketed as a flunkey hadn't I left with an exemplary brusqueness unknown to flunkeys, who non grata tend to linger indefinitely whether or not it is all in the line of apprising another, well-paying or paying ill, of the whereabouts of some exploitable third. No. Whatever I did was in the domain of flunkeydom. Asking how flunkeyed I had or had not been did not differentiate me from my medium, my sludge, only entrenched me more firmly and deeper to boot. My very conceiving of such a question was simply one more secretion of the entrenching sludge, affirming and prolonging entrenchment. Might I go so far as to say that to conceive of such a question put the definitive bolt on the door of my flunkey's cage. Just before I turned out the light next to my bed I heard myself say, How I envy Jim Jamms. Even if I had felt it I could never have said—as he had said and so aptly: Keep the blessings of the blessed away from me. For I wish to produce a specimen—not necessarily of despair—so pure and intractable nothing can mitigate it. And what are these blessings of the blessed but mitigations of despair. And not even. These blessings of the blessed—timely advent of the baby sitter, timely raise to keep pace with inflationary mayhem—are merely puny stand-ins for some impossible mitigation of despair—in actual fact they incarnate a temporary and purely physiologic attrition of the capacity to undergo disgust, defeat, despair, and at maximum capacity. For I too am not immune to such fluctuation factors as proximity of the long weekend, anomalous generosity of the neighbor or postman, supervention of the wife's—if I had a wife, that is—sabbath favors or her preparation— in return for my proving a good little worker during the work week—of my favorite dish: stuffed calves' brains on the half shell. Jamms was a hard act to swallow.

I was awakened early the next morning by a phone call from Mrs. Jamms, despotic and peremptory now I was in her employ. Now I was on the payroll no reason to tread lightly. She was at the airport, Jamms was getting worse and worse. She explained that she had tried for the hundredth time to get in contact with Jim: he just didn't want to have anything to do with them. She held on to my hand as she led me to the window of their hotel room overlooking Central Park. "I know he never wants to come home and so I have to come to him. But doesn't he realize there is a definite value to be got out of life duties if handled property. He can't come home, his silence implies, because the visits, even if to a dying man, eat up his precious time." She sighed. "If only he wouldn't close his eyes on the way to us so that he could take one big fat look at everything— besides illness and bedpans." A corner of a mattress on casters was visible through the door, three quarters open. "The illness and bedpans that supposedly stand in his way." On the train to Rhinebeck she continued: "The obstacles against which he closes his eyes in advance can engender a propulsion he otherwise might never know he had. Take it from me. In other words, being forced to play the son, do his duty, come time and again, would allow him both to collect the collectibles he discards a priori and in impatiently thrashing past them,—but this time with his baby blues wide open—on the way to something else, something I am the very first— and not simply because I am his mother—to admit might be bigger, far bigger, than a father's dying breath or a mother's lonely prayer—to grow into what he might otherwise not become. Coming to us with eyes wide open would oblige him to thrash past the thralldom of collecting what he mistakenly takes to be crucial to his productions—for once his eyes are open he thinks only in terms of a collectioneering thwarted by the penury of circumstance—into a domain where the demon of collection logic and its measly subreptions are thwarted once and for all. In other words, he would at once be beyond objects yet suffused with their glow—having them—in a way that has nothing to do with rancor, avarice, appropriation, ceaseless inventory. Looking the objects—trees, depots, cows, eczematous earlobes, colloped dewlaps—in the eye he would have them, know he had them, in a way that told him immediately whether or not he actually did need them or parts of any of them for the work to come. For my son is a worker. He works hard at his god-given vocation. If only he would come back, his eyes wide open on the landscape of collectibles, cross from the station to the tiny little county park with its trees in every conceivable posture of decay all the time knowing he had to see me, I mean his father, dying dying dying, he would no longer be tempted either to shut his eyes against one long procession of irrelevances or opening them inventory every single spasm inhering in every single posture but rather without taking note at breakneck speed know he was taking note and by not taking note at breakneck speed wrenching them—the postures—or rather laying the groundwork for wrenching them into authentically new configurations worthiest of all he is striving to be." At that moment, with the train speeding toward Rhinebeck and old man Jamms stretched out on his casters in the back of the car, and at that moment only, I felt a certain, in contradistinction to an uncertain, pity for old lady Jamms, at that moment only, with the sun setting plying parched plazas of ersatz grain. Perhaps I would have felt deeper more abiding pity somewhere else. When we arrived at the station I phoned Jim. Bessy answered and said he wasn't home. Maggy and Bessy were both present, both sullen? I immediately realized my function or rather that I myself was a function assigned to transform—or rather, map—detail into event, story event. But if I was to cavort like a scullion I wanted the story at least to be my story, proximally and ultimately.

Yes, this was what I was supposed to be, a function transforming detail into event. How tell them though that I had not planned on such a visit which is not to say that I had actively thought about visiting Rhinebeck and decided against it or that I had not thought about it at all, no, these are degenerative reductions of what I mean. No, what I mean is that I was not prepared to visit Rhinebeck with the Jammses with the intention of embedding that visit into their—our—story. At the very least

I had no event-inducing thoughts at hand to be played against the emptiness, that is to say, the starkly decipherable purpose, of the visit. The only way to have managed a visit, I saw now, when it was too late, with the visit already visited upon me, would have been to be prepared with event-inducing thoughts incessantly at cross-purposes with the going. Up to now each event had not been a threat to my personal integrity precisely because said events — dinner at the Jammses, visit to the factory and showroom, trek up to Jamms and his houris — were isolated and discrete. All of a sudden threads — fibers and fascicles — of these discrete events were struggling to interweave. And I was to be the site of such interweaving. My story was about to begin and yet I was resisting with all my heart and soul. For it was to be my story as their story. And there was no telling if story, once begun, would remain my story.

    I had no thoughts to play against the visit — against my conception of the visit. In other words, I had no way of wrenching or elasticizing event-to-be in such a way as would allow for, that is to say, compel, its bountiful accommodation of, that is to say, its fatal and prostrated capitulation before inevitable assimilation to, whatever past events plausibilized and vindicated the reeruption of the thoughts I was seeking — thoughts that displace the accent of brute duration with its all too predictable hungers and cravings and dimestore aspirations and cattle car rivalries and beauty salon disquisitions on what just might constitute the only ineluctable priorities between cradle, ladle, and grave. All this assuming that the thoughts themselves, in the absence of events to which they had initially adhered, upon which parasitically they had accrued, would not be sufficiently potent to transmogrify event-at-hand, event-to-be. And where was I most potent or, in the words of the well-fed matron with delusions of philanthropic self-abasement: In what capacity could I expect, legitimately of course, to do most good: narrator, spectator, active participant? I was confused, especially at times like these — like this very moment, with its hyperborean, or was it hypogean, whiff of celestial floes a-thawing — when there was suddenly so much affinity and mutual aid among events and all of it in the service of lampooning obfuscation, of thoughts about those very same events, events in which I was or about to be actively immersed — like a sea-biscuit, and events which I could expect, as with a bag of rock-hard toffee in my already perspiring lap, to merely watch unreeling. As I made my phone call from the station I knew I was wide open to, in, this visit and watched with horror as it began to unfold, fibers from prior events already dutifully interweaving. What was this phone call but a precipitation of such interweaving. Before I hung up, in the damp cold, in the drizzle of late afternoon, I strove to think hard of some past thought or some event from the past that could be made, even at this late date, to yield a thought, something recruitable to be applied salvelike to this anticipated wound of forthcoming predictable event, or rather, to the unpredictability of what was about to unfold, something to the effect of delirious widow-to-be reproaching scoundrel son for everything under the sun in the presence of dying father and pouting concubines. Yes, it might very well be the unpredictability that cried out for suture. Yes, yes, yes, it was terrifyingly unpredictable, this event about to unfold, and left no time for other concerns. Yet the unpredictability was after all too too predictable—conceivable—in the sense that fulfilling the promise of its unpredictability event would be obliged to wend its way with the most pedestrian ingenuity among highly foreseeable parameters (mother/ son wariness of too conspicuous revulsion after long separation; father/son explosion after eternal mutual incomprehension; mother/ concubine mutual paralysis as the son set permanently) choosing equally foreseeable versions of the parametric illumination. My terror had to be deeper than terror over a prospective *coup de théâtre*. My terror was for an ostensibly terrifying *coup de théâtre* ultimately, that is to say, concurrently, resolvable into constituents of the most glaring banality, tributes to the expert gerrymandering of those indefatigable troopers, *déjà vu* and *déjà entendu*. Yet I wanted my story and stories comprise such events. A pen fell from my pocket, red, felt-tipped. As I had once lost or thought I had lost one so could I now turn around, spit in its face as the face of old man and old lady Jamms, and thereby lose this event. Loss of the event. Loss of the event. I was no longer so baldly unprepared for the event. Armed with this phrase—this concept—I was no longer quite so terrified. I had suffered less from loss of the pen than from said loss as token, earnest, handsel, of infinite loss to come. I had suffered less from loss of *that pen* than from that loss as inauguration of diathesis to loss—than from that loss (forget the pen itself) as beginning of the crumbling of so much prior hoarding and inventorying of the hoarding (mostly stolen office equipment) — hoarding and inventorying as the keenest propitiation of time as eunuch- and carcass-maker. Hadn't old man Jamms believed anagogically that the rigors of his schedule would keep him forever immune to decay?

Extracting its essence — its concept — could I now substitute for loss of pen loss of imminent visit with moribund parents to Jim Jamms and his concubines. At some point I might turn around and leave in order subsequently to feel acutely the loss of the event. And would I feel acutely loss *of the event* or rather loss — this loss — as inauguration of a predisposition to loss at all times and in all places? If I did not choose to lose the event at some point in its trajectory I could simply denounce the Jammses to their faces and lose their precious esteem, procuring thereby an opportunity to wonder if what I feared was loss *of their esteem* or rather this loss (of their esteem, highly expendable) as earnest of unstanchable losses to come, as well as whether or not such wondering governed by or governing so bifurcated a view of loss — of event — of being — was compatible with the production of stories — with the farrowing down of stories deep in being's sty. All at once the event to come was a little less predictable therefore a little less terrorizing. The event to come was now indissolubly bound to my thought reserves, event-inducing or otherwise, would necessarily be inflected by prior meditations. I was armed against the event. Still standing by the phone I looked out toward the station platform. An elderly bum had left his corner shelter to advance toward the spotless curb. Immediately I put myself in his position, that is to say I wondered at his conception of encroaching night, whether it was streaked with dread or impatience. Through him — through his movement rather — I underwent the chill of an indifferently suffocating encroachment of dusk, night, even if at this moment I was otherwise engaged, weighted down, as it were, with certain loathsome accessories of an event-situation I had done little to provoke. Through him I went on living my terror of dusk, night, the event to come though not, of course, terror of that latter's possibly "terrifying revelations of human character in extremis," always the same, always the same, always the same. No, I lived in terror of the event to come insofar as the sum or product or quotient of certain reassuring parameters (loving mamma's behavior when confronted with only son's profligacy of artistic pretension, dying father's reaction to said son's indifference to family empire wriggling regnant at his feet) it would not, could not, belong to me, to the story I now hoped to recuperate from this detritus of a retrieval operation boasting Jamms as its target. I lived in terror of the event as anybody's plausibly heartrending and hair-raising hymn to a bumbling pertinacity. But hadn't the bum just entered into the day's trajectory thereby through our memorable communion (so what if one-sided) irreparably inflecting said event. The event, thanks to the bum, thanks to the thought about the loss of the pen as potential loss of the event itself or of the Jammses' esteem, was slowly, slowly, coming into its own, that is, my own, and, so to speak, in its own absence. The event was being incubated as all that was not event.

I was already rich in the experience of applying the concept of loss to this prospective event terrifying in its nudity, that is to say, its super-abundance of event elements already seen and heard too too many times over in other contexts, that is to say, under other pretexts. But it no longer seemed there was much hope of expanding the event along the lines of the loss concept. Still waiting for Jim to pick up the phone at the other end I thought of my forays into the marketplace where the self's escapement had to be very finely honed to catch on the ratchet wheel spun by its dragomen and mufti. And when engagement was easiest then it had turned out to be most excruciating, at least for me. When it seemed, as it so often seemed, all up with me in terms of theft and resale then I had gone to an employment agency, on a lark so it seemed. Sitting down I noticed the counselor was eager to expatiate painting the portrait of my future. Yet minutes after she began, as the overwhelmingly lotic flow-to-come petered out into the lentic flow-that-alas-was-never-to-be I realized that the initial enthusiasm—what I had taken to be enthusiasm, worse, zeal—was a mere formality routinely trained on the eponymous hero of the episode in progress. So in rage I decided to assess her tolerance for forays beyond the ostensible purlieus of the episode. I spoke of my previous employer, now dead, and as I suspected, shock and suspicion were the order of the day, not necessarily because she disbelieved me. This would have been and continues to be the least interesting interpretation of that state of affairs. Shock and suspicion were born because introduction of the subject of death into the domain of the employment-related episode was a lewd solecism. Death was not hygienic. The dead were not in good physical shape and by extension he who spoke of the dead must be in decay.

What episode game was I playing now as the sun fell into the Hudson River. And if I was playing a game how transplant the concept of the game gleaned from my experiences looking for a job to this suburban wilderness of imminent family confrontation. I felt neither insufficiently astute to play nor sufficiently vibrant in my joy at transplanting so much first-rate equipment to the playing.

So the event-to-be was still startling in its nudity. I was waiting for somebody on the other end to pick up. Then I remembered (all the time still waiting for that somebody) — another noxious thought bubbling up from the past's many fumaroles — that my life or somebody's was one long straining to produce a turd of despair intractable to fumigatory mitigation via delusory knocks at the door of opportunity. Here in Rhinebeck I might think of myself in a despair that was still amenable to knocks at the door incarnated, in this case, by the soon-to-be-revealed voice at the other end. But I did not feel particularly despairing and so the concept of a despair fighting against accessibility to mitigation would not apply to event unfolding here. When Maggy's voice was once more audible (I had begun with Maggy and I was ending with her) I heard myself say, "Are you guys at home?" It was unclear to me whether using this reprehensible bit of argot I was expressing my deepest self or performing "as if" for the delectation, or rather the abolition, of that categorizing third person who might classify me either as one more unremarkable specimen of prep school trash or ridicule me as conforming oh so badly and limply and unclassifiably-to the godly archetype. At any event, in speaking so I felt I abolished all chance of achieving greatness in the eyes of Jamms, who quickly became the third person at my heels. Greatness. But in what line and as what. Only later, much later, when I don't know, but much later, would he — he — he — for the thought belonged incontrovertibly to Jamms, the younger sleeker Jamms, was rightly his, even if he never thought it, came near thinking it, brought it to birth through such a white agony as I now was undergoing in a phone booth on the edge of nowhere's pristine somewhere — only later would I — he — he — he as I — recuperate this observed unorthodoxy — this descent into "you guys" — this death's blow to greatness — as yet another and by no means negligible — proof of exactly that most elusive of all states, as

Jim Jamms himself should have said if he had not been otherwise
enmeshed—to wit, greatness, to wit, greatness at its most unorthodox
great in refusing to be inimical to any fodder however ostensibly unassimilable worth its assimilation so that it might become not just greatness but
greatness plus x, y, z,..

Here was another thought bubbling up to help make the event
grow into something other than a predictable and platitudinous sum of
obeisances to the usual parameters (mom's reprobation of wayward son,
dad's attraction to unfeeling concubine, second concubine's prostration
before the dying landscape in the presence of mom, dad, first concubine,
tangerine peel). But were these thoughts in fact conduits toward
somehow creating the event or simply refusing to let it grow. Was this
wondering about the prospective event through the thoughts bubbling up
from multitudinous fumaroles of the hated past—was this wondering in
the service of an event beyond recognizable parameters or an escape from
same. Yet—yet—yet: wasn't this ambiguity of said wondering clearest
proof that I was expertly fulfilling my function of function mapping detail
into event. These thoughts, as potential routes beyond the parameters of
platitude and predictability toward authentic event, were already details
mappable into its world, were already well into the thick of inflecting the
course of events and the grandiose hush before their onrush. These
thoughts were very much on the verge of event through my invocation
and sifting of their applicability to event, or rather, the applicability of
what in another context they had managed to subsume—patch together—surmount—supplant—parody—remedy—reinforce—bone—pith—
geld—cataplasm—saute—prolong—ablate—or summarize in the way
of event. (To name just a few of the facilities of thought as factotum.)
These thoughts of mine already belonged to event in *this* context, event
not in the form of some maidenly recreant uncomplainingly running the
gamut or gauntlet of conceivable, foreseen, and preassigned parameters
but as rough and ready subversion of every such. My relentless invocation and sifting by rendering me inaccessible to the doings (not yet events)
of other spheres—the spheres of mamma Jamms and old man Jamms
and, putatively more rarefied, of Jim, Maggy, and Bessy—thereby
subjecting their residents to the deprivation—and relief—sure to influence all future participation in events was already a strong determinant

of their course. Every one of my thoughts was already—by definition—
a mapping of itself—of the detail it incarnated, that is, collision of thought
with event in some faraway context—into the domain of event. No matter
what I did—even if I was to spit in the face of old lady Jamms and the two
concubines—I was still and always the narrator. And the narrator is
constitutionally incapable of either creating or sabotaging the event in
whose imminent shadow he dutifully trembles. Only a Jim Jamms, lithe
and powerful, understood sabotage and would be sure to instruct me in
the blithe and reckless peripeties of its deployment.

      Maggy told me Jim was not at home and that she had absolutely
no idea when he would return. As we drove out to the cottage I was
axiomatically convinced (maybe the imminence of snow had something
to do with it) that if I could not recruit a thought, a shred of eloquence,
to be applied posthaste to and extracted from the event at hand, the event-
to-be, there would be no event. The event would not exist. All would be
lost, my story would be lost. Once again there was nothing, just
anticipation of an event already dead because already lived—by somebody somewhere—over and over and over again. Yes, yes, yes, it was all
coming back to me from yet another fumarole. Once, long long before, I
had been sitting in a little park. I wanted to take the beauty of the park
away with me, to make its beauty the foundation of a new life. I was
convinced that if I did not acquire and remember the names of the various
alleys and shrubs nothing would be taken away and acquired and the park
would not continue to exist nor would it ever have existed. But then—but
then—or rather now I saw what I should have seen then: All is not lost
from the moment that all begins to be lost. For then in desperation at the
prospect of loss one is forced—as I should have forced myself then to be
forced—to investigate this terror at not losing what have been erected as
the only viable acquisitions. Nothing at first seems acquirable beyond the
pale of what I should have styled—back then, in the little park—first-
degree objects. Yet the minute one wrenches oneself free of the self-
imposed tyranny of this cult of credulity with respect to the only viable
objects one finds oneself—as I should long ago have found myself—
acquiring once more but objects of a more truly viable sort. For these are
objects of the *second degree* thus not really objects at all, rather, shreds and
patches of aggressive understanding regarding why one was once credu-

lous enough to believe only a certain species of acquisition could recuperate the lived object loved, the loved object badly lived. Although nothing in the little park seemed acquirable outside the simple knowing or not knowing of names and terms now I was at last wrenched free of too deferring credulity to—toward—authentic acquisition—of understanding, which was no acquisition at all and forever dissolved away into its own urgency of fulfillment.

As the house rose or dipped into view I was on the verge of transplanting this concept born from the ruins of the little park to the prospective event here in Rhinebeck. The event was about to be lost. I had no names for the characters of the drama, names beyond their given names; no names for the dreary options loaned to their prospective behaviors by haberdashers Parameters , Inc., at large. Yet the event was not lost, would not be lost, because I was making and would go on continuing to make a minuscule effort—in desperation—to investigate, to interrogate this ever more suspect certainty of loss compliments of a failure to bring to the prospective event, as the only way of bringing it to birth, rise, peak, subsidence, detritus of past events. Wrenching myself enough free of despair to investigate the certainty of loss was the beginning of restitution, of event.

At first—long ago, at the Rhinebeck train station—nothing had seemed conceivable, acquirable, apart from a being able to furnish forth this or that shred of gloss on excruciations past. Yet now that in spite of myself I was wrenching myself free of this fixed idea I was beginning to acquire the event-to-come and as something other than a mincemeat of marinated meaning cellules. Now I was on the road to acquiring the event: the siege in the telephone booth, the encounter with a bum a little to the right of Mrs. Jamms's right foot, fashionably shod, the waiting for Maggy to return to the phone, the sense of being hotly observed by Lord and Lady Jamms stretched out in the hack come to take us as far as we wished into the Hudsonian hinterland—all these moments were converging on, emphatically not congealing into, event and nothing but event in its purity whereas a short time before event had been nothing more than dreaded and futile search for the possibility of event, event had been nothing more than its own admission of failed morphogenesis.

The Rhinebeck Incident
The Rhinebeck Memorandum

The Rhinebeck Charism

The Rhinebeck Covenant

The Rhinebeck Barmecide

The Rhinebeck Acroama, or, The tooth escapes from the pallet at
regular intervals

As the landscape receded—we took the hack all the way back to
Manhattan—I could not help thinking that I might have salvaged the
incident, spared it some deeper sabotage, by refusing to recruit my own
detritus of quasi-illuminations past to its nourishment. Yet what was this
postmortem but another butt-end of prefabricated meaning masquerading as authentic physiologic disturbance, one more attempt to authenti-
cate event past through professed perturbation over its integrity. As the
landscape receded I did not want to mean, in the old way.

Back in New York, after the last of the doctors had come and
gone—for Mrs. Jamms insisted on a multeity of opinion, this last being
none other than the family's chief source of medical know-how over at
least seven generations—she said—in a tone that suggested she was tying
up some unfinished business between us, "That doctor." Her tone also
suggested an outcry, an outcry of the kind I had been so hard put to draw
from Maggy or Bessy in the Rhinebeck telephone booth that had not
really been a booth at all but an exposed ledge encrusted with pigeon
droppings. Yes, miracle of miracles, here I was thinking of the Rhinebeck
telephone booth: adversion to the booth implied an undismembered event
replete with limousines, bums, vagrant sons, dervishes in repose (Bessy
and Maggy, Maggy and Bessy, Maggy and Maggy). The event existed,
at least—if only—in retrospect. Knowing she meant the last nevertheless
I said, "You mean the last." And this was exactly what she wanted to hear
for she, in turn, said, "Yes," impatiently, almost irascibly. "Scotoma," she
added; I waited, furious at her tone. Did she instinctively sense my
tightening up and fear my refusal to collaborate any further. More gently,
even deferentially, she said, "Anyway Dr. Scotoma could never see Jim
for beans. Maybe that's why he wasn't there when we went up to
Rhinebeck. Imagine! A son refusing to come out and greet his dying
father. I mean: Now he doesn't see us for beans. For we always seemed
to be exposing him to people who would not see him for beans. His father

shared Scotoma's opinion, still does. I don't know whose opinion I share at this point. At any rate, even if I think Jim a bigger fool than both of them put together there is nothing illogical about my stating that Jim was and continues to be Scotoma's most flagrant...scotoma. Every clinician, however great, even the greatest, has one. But Jim didn't know how to take it, grew more and more enraged, instead — as you can be sure I would have done — of taking a pleasure positively voluptuous in said scotoma as lever, wedge, piton, belay, with which and whence to conquer and overthrow worlds founded on incredulity far vaster than that fueling Scotoma's fly-by-night obiter dicta."

All she really wanted was for me to return, apparently, to Rhinebeck, this time with a gift check, pocket money, and a tennis racket of, I presumed, the highest quality. She said it was better I did not see the elder Jamms given his sudden startling turns for the much worse. I bowed respectfully with, however, a still curious corner of my eye on the protruding bit of mattress. Not knowing what to say as I gave him the check I said, jocularly, for I believed he was fond of this kind of remark, "I wish somebody would give me a check so I wouldn't have to keep on stealing office equipment." He looked at me for a long time as if the interval between saying and not was being devoted exclusively to thinking about whether or not to say or how to say or how I would respond to the said—then said the most disheartening thing about me was my apparent anguish over the thefts, big and small. He looked at me for a long time then said—as if the interval between saying and not had been exclusively devoted to thinking about whether or not to say or how to say or how I would respond to the said or unsaid—the most disheartening thing about me was my apparent anguish over the thefts, big and small. I told him somebody had once told me that if only I could stop my stealing I would finally produce something worth stealing myself. And then it happened again as it had happened with his mother back in the hotel after the Rhinebeck event, that is to say, I was suddenly overcome with a thought that threatened to expand this event if it was already an event, which I doubted, or help create it from scratch.

This being with Jamms in his Rhinebeck abode, the gifts from mamma Jamms handed over, the racket sprawled in the middle of the front room, Maggy and Bessy lingering, loitering, somewhere in the background—was it an event? Did this shocking revelation of the thieving damn me at last in his eyes making all further intercourse between us an irrelevance, that is to say, a simple and forthright confirmation of his worst suspicions, or did it in fact furnish a beginning, a crumbling and unstable yet nonetheless tenacious foundation for the possibility of—of— Actually, this thought, this embodied confusion belonged to him, should have been emanating from him. He, Jamms, should have been asking himself whether the revelation of his failure to greet his dying father and palsied mother did not definitively disqualify him for greatness in my eyes for it was greatness he was after or ON THE CONTRARY mightn't it have put the definitive nail in the coffin of an idiosyncrasy indistinguishable in my eyes from greatness. There was of course no immediate answer to this conundrum. Or rather, the answer was Yes, this conundrum was creating the event before us. The thought's apparent vacillation between two meanings was a pretext for the smuggling in of meaning...as the masses know and love meaning: meaning as a vacillation between two ostensibly substantive possibilities both of which are equally meaningless, that is to say, identical, yet each of which is transformed through the magnetic and magical proximity of the other so that in the shadow of that other's coming into plausibility the other other absorbs a certain death knell potency it would otherwise never be able to lay claim to. In its absence—the absence generated and nurtured by the other's presence—each becomes strong, well nigh irresistible, as irresistible as its isomer about to become isomerically strong. Could I confess to Jamms that I was sick to death of meaning and the creation of event from such meaning, meaning of the form: Does shocking revelation P' induce X or rather does it miraculously effectuate Y. "What did you say," he asked. "That I needed them, all the things I stole, for my work. No matter what anybody says." At that moment Maggy entered and as if she had been all along listening said: "Maybe if you stopped stealing you would be immeasurably enriched beyond the need to produce anything." She sat down at a side table and busied herself with odds and ends of ribbon.

"Don't you see," he suddenly cried, as if belatedly awakened to lucidity by the echo of Maggy's words, "that every calling worth a shit requires ruthlessness, and more than ruthlessness, a truly agile stealth, a stealth preferably in the name of nothing. The ruthlessness you are obliged to show in order to haul those machines out of the office and out of the building into the night is far more potent—far more muscle-building—than the false sense of security produced afterwards by having those machines around. presumably as raw material or as the means ultimately to purchase your raw material but in actual fact as mere decor to lull you to an indefinite postponement of the task at hand. You're acquiring ruthlessness and we all need ruthlessness in order to produce. But you are pissing the ruthlessness away by keeping the booty forever at your disposal. Ruthlessness is the true acquisition and that is why you must be so baffled and annoyed by the presence—persistence—of the ostensible target of acquisition long after the act is over and done with." "There is this nostalgia," said Maggy, no, it wasn't Maggy, it was the other woman, Maggy's rival, even if Maggy had just run to her corner kingdom to kiss and comfort her—it was Bessy, again peeling a tangerine, maybe yestertime's, "to be like everybody else wants you to think they are. To sustain the fiction of behaving just like everybody else. And of course the only way to sustain the fiction that such behavior exists is to deviate incessantly from its possibility so that from the vast distance of your deviation you can regard it, treasure it, long for it." "He must reach the point where he doesn't need it."

The woman—which one I don't know—announced she was going to prepare dinner in a tone that implied preparing dinner was a novelty. After a long silence that only through his sudden shrill outburst became retroactively intolerable he cried, "I can't go back. I can't see them. I'll never see them again. You see, I have a memory of the hospital room where he had some vital organ removed. Scotoma urged it. I remember standing at the bedside and looking out at the railroad tracks that terminated in little dismal depot clusters far below and watching him at the same time through the corner of my eye put out his hands quizzically. I hastily made an inventory of arms, legs, shirt, tie, chin, nostrils, testicles, ankles, feet, clammy hands, calves, in short, my very being. According to the outstretched hands there was a colossal piece of inappropriateness running amuck in the sickroom and it had to be connected with me. Then I realized the target was not this hand, this foot, this green thigh, this orange-plated testicle, this filial offering come thirty years too late, but—at least from his perspective—my very being. That is to say, my very being in the guise of this entry into the hospital room, his hospital room, terribly—unforgivably—inappropriate even—especially—if old dad was at death's door. For he has been at death's door many times. Supererogatory and impertinent. That's what my visit was. And when I returned the next day or night—when I had the audacity to repeat what was supererogatory he turned on me the same sick quizzicalness of bony bloated fingers, as if to say, Was this still me or another. Bad enough I had come the first time, Bessy, and here I was come again, Maggy. And in coming again to my simple inappropriateness was of course added a defiance of his initial revulsion at that inappropriateness. Here I was come back as myself and as other than myself for I couldn't very well be myself—the self he had known and loathed right from the conceptus— if I had managed mightily to muster the requisite audacity for coming back despite his quizzical revulsion at my initial coming and yet I could not very well be other than myself thanks not only to the persistence of his revulsion but also to certain cutaneous markers that even someone roiling in his dunnage of imminent death could smell out. So I had come back as myself and other than myself and courtesy of this supervenient defiance in stealth I had come back purely to disorient him further than death—that old vaudevillian—itself was disorienting him. Even if he was convinced—and wasn't this being convinced the purest proof of his befuddlement—that the imminence of death lent him, how can I put it, a certain perspicacity that had a right to sing its piercingly candid song at last, thereby wounding all survivors to irreparable enlightenment." (So Jamms had had the same impression as I! Yet how could he? How dare? After all, we were constructed to be polar opposites so that the story—our story—might be born.) "At any rate, my very being in the guise of my advent was an absurd premeditated clumsiness—a thorn in the side of that song—the embodiment of all of being's stupid cruelty. And with the first and last nickel I had ever earned or purloined glued to my ass! And a flabby dewlap-laden teratoma it most certainly was, according to that old songbird entranced by his melismatic candor."

I tried not to look him in the eye for there were tears, either in his or in mine. "Oh I see, I see, I see," pouncing on the tears. "You were awaiting something memorable. You expected something along the lines

of a traditional *getting under skin of dying man's confusion*, decked out in
mezzotints worthy of the mature Gorky confirming thereby my compassionating breadth of scope and vice-versa. Yet how this sickens me —
Bessy, quick, a pint of ale!" — Bessy did not budge — "this imaginative
depiction — going right to the heart of the matter so it would seem,
whatever that is. Isn't that why you came up with my parents — to get to
the heart of the matter." He looked to Bessy for confirmation that the
heart of the matter was indeed unlocalizable."This anxiously faithful
rendering stinks to me so much — too much — of tourism, the stentorian
innocuous kind that routs ghetto stenches with the aid of a big bold
itinerary. So I'm incorrigible: I've refused your terror its constitutional
right to volatilize into salvos of admiration, heartfelt of course, for the
way — for the delightful pluck with which — so-and-so set out to capture
and very much succeeded in encapsulating the very scrotum whiff of the
great beyond in the gestureless death rattle of an old fart mistaking his
multidirectional incontinence for the ultimate pandect on mean ways and
wayward means of being. No, no, no, concocting such a picture of things
as they are smacks too much of old Maggy — or is it Bessy? Bessy! — in
the kitchen rustling up a little grub for the proverbial and no more than
proverbial men of the house." We both ate ravenously, I not so much from
hunger as confusion regarding what to do next now that the check, pocket
money, and tennis racket were safely delivered. Surprisingly, seeing I
looked a bit heavy-lidded Jim suggested I stay over.

    We were all seated in the front room when Jim said,"Don't be
sad." As she did not respond he repeated,"Don't be sad." At this
repetition Maggy finally woke up and looked as if desperately trying
within a reasonable interval to retrieve a mode of being — past, present,
future — justifying this snivelling dehortation. After a great many failures
and as if taxed beyond endurance she said,"Yes, it was sad. The day I was
there in the hospital with you. I was with him, standing by the bed, trying
to stroke the old man out of his despairing contempt for his son. His
contempt was his despair and his despair his contempt. I wanted Jim to
stand up for himself, fight back, prove he was not an inept nullity." "Prove
his mettle, dazzle with his competence," said Bessy with a certain disgust,
as if mouthing their mutual — Jim's and hers — reprobation of such
bovine expectation. As if she hadn't heard Maggy went on:"I tried to

shake him into competence. I showed him how to lift the pillow and deliver ice water through a straw into the old man's mouth. But he continued to fail, fail, fail, and thereby win his old addled dad's heartiest revulsion. And there I was forever struggling to wriggle him out of the frame delimited by the old man's contempt but he, Jim, would not budge from that frame and I am afraid, terribly afraid, he will repeat what his father did, not only disappear and die embittered but spend every waking moment training himself toward a comparable apotheosis of loathing. I want to shake him out of preparation for such a final scene. I want him to be able to die the right way." "Die the right way," Bessy murmured to herself. She was afraid, it seemed to me, to look to Jim for conspiratorial confirmation of her revulsion for, like me, she strongly felt his preternatural silence. "But I am not he and I am infinitely distant from where his reproach and his verdict can even begin to touch, much less manhandle, me." Looking at me with an appeal new to his voice and eye:"She imputes to me a being weighed down by dad's verdict when in fact—in fact—" Shyly Maggy said,"Then why did you run away from your dad." The shy sententiousness as if she was aware she was making and gaining a point but trying very hard not to reveal expanding awareness of same made me want to choke her. Shy and sullen she became, sensing he must wish to do the same and be within a hair's breadth of so doing. Though Jim and Bessy seemed to loathe her nothing stopped her from leaping off her chair and smothering Bessy with kisses, inquiring at the same time if everything was all right. Bessy surprised me by jumping up and crying out,"No, everything is most emphatically not all right. You," she began looking at me. "You were here the last time when Maggy spoke about the miraculous patron descended from the clouds. Well, said patron has just absconded with some of Jim's best objects. Well, don't you see," she continued as if an excruciatedly long silence had just tried her patience beyond endurance. "I believed Maggy when she said he was the patron we had all been waiting for. Nobody would make such a statement without its being foolproof, i.e., beyond refutability. And I must go on believing this statement is irrefutable otherwise language loses all its prestige, i.e., anybody can say anything at any time. But what now, now that the fabulous intercessor has turned out to be an *escroc*?" Expressionlessly Maggy said,"What do you mean, What now." I had difficulty

paying attention to what was being said. For it seemed that on some level
the question of the patron turned *escroc* had been introduced to build an
event out of scraps and shards, scraps and shards of the *déjà vu* and *déjà vu
entendu*. And here was Bessy to the rescue with what with all her heart she
believed to be authentic misgiving. "Last time I said the patron was a
saint. Now I say he is a devil. Does this prove my futility. On the
contrary. I—we are simply in a new stage of our evolution. This
statement—to the effect that the patron is a scoundrel—does not contradict what came before. On the contrary it forecasts a completely new
venture for which there need be no excuses and which in point of fact was
sorely in need of its predecessor as a kind of jumping off place. This new
outburst— as you were hoping to put it before I cut you off—is very much
related to the previous but only as widening, never slackening, artistic
omnipotence is at any given moment capable of swallowing up all rival
meanings, devouring its ancestors in the name of its progeny. This new
statement—that the patron is a devil—does not indict our irresponsibil-
ity. My dear Bessy, it is a moment, simply an inevitable moment, in
progress toward the only conceivable omnipotence—that which feeds on
contradiction." Where had Bessy's outburst come from? I did not know.
I knew only that what it engendered was now irretrievably part and
parcel of the event playing itself out before and within us all. If only I had
had been armed with such an outburst en route to Rhinebeck and to the
cottage. Instead of with puny little speculations on loss—concept of
loss—of a green ballpoint pen.

    "Don't be sad," Jim murmured as if nothing had just transpired.
"I was there," Maggy murmured. "Every so often he, the father, woke up,
looked around aghast. Your mother was herself sick, or so she never
stopped reminding us, dozed off, pretended to doze. This was the closest
she ever came to tact. Only I don't want to end up like her." Jim looked
as if he had heard all this before and for once refused, perhaps for the very
first time, to take the bait. He looked, longingly in fact, at the other
women, Bessy, to be exact, as if he would compel her to hold out the
promise of never making such remarks. "But when I spoke up to defend
the staff who were after all doing the very best they could under such
circumstances of being overwhelmed with a floorful of endproducts—
stroked the old boy's feet that were cold, ever so cold, then the relict-to-

be drew bovinely back offended. She controlled herself but you could tell she loathed my compassionating self-assertion, could not quite metabolize it. I could smell her trying to transform it in such a way as would render denigration conceivable, achievable. But at least in the beginning I offered no surface. And I did something horrible to and for Jim, I mean—the Jim, of course, who refuses to transcend his limits, his Jimness, as it were—I stormed off exasperated. And poor Jim was left in the middle, a passive lump of lard, a shit, with my absence aggravating abomination and the relict metabolizing the cud of her resentment toward a future big with innuendo. I could already hear her with appalling calm say, 'Why did she get so roiled?' yet with a faintest strained note of the exasperation of one confirmed yet again in a reluctant verdict. But Jim, do you think she would have relished poor Bessy any better?" Jim disregarding the question said, "I loathe families: with a passion. She came to me after you had the audacity to leave the room in a moment of crisis and said, gyrating a gnawing impartiality—that she didn't understand why you got so upset." "But then I came back." "Yes, you came back. That is how our story proceeds. And you proceeded to stroke and lick dad's feet and tell him how strong and courageous mom had been and was continuing to be. You suggested, pulling down the blinds against the sheaf of depots below, that he try to recognize her courage and you went on enlightening him long after he had called a moratorium on all enlightenment by rolling his eyes and spitting disgust at my inexorable slowness and clumsiness—and her—the relict's—slowness and clumsiness—into still another empty tissue box. For at this point in time he saw us as indistinguishable—two indistinguishably loud and loathsome drain pipes siphoning off his being and achieving their conjoint apotheosis in its craved demise. An undifferentiated mass of shit, we were. Not that I care. I loathed the old bastard as he loathed me. I mean, I loathe him as he loathes me. Only there is perhaps a bit more interrogation in my loathing than in his. And strangely enough I felt no gratitude toward Maggy for defanging old mom. Note: I felt no gratitude toward you, Maggy." Inexplicably this was Maggy's sign to once again slip back to the window seat and caressingly console Bessy. "Don't you see, such extreme kindness, such spontaneous overflow of tact carried to the point of delirium only robbed me of my specimen rage at Maggy's provocation of an almost

relict's smothered blundering cowlike anger and of my specimen shame
for that rage—at Maggy's delicate, fragile and selfless self-exposure
before the gnawing cud of the almost relict's slobbering glowering. For
when Mrs. Jamms treated Maggy cruelly it was rage I felt but not quite
dirigible at old mom, rather at the space between them with rage
circulating like an over inspissated fluid in that space. And sometimes
Maggy became the more competitively permeable to that fluid and
through the enlarged pores of her tact drained it all away from mom.
Don't you see: Maggy robbed me of a specimen, a specimen that at some
future date undefinable promised to free me from the sloth of a story in
which two heady females and an almost-defunct member emeritus of the
male species threatened to over-embed me, no longer a species being. The
specimen! the specimen! was my way out of the story-line and here was
Maggy with her wonderful tact and love of humanity robbing me of that
exquisite moment just before the milk of human kindness gushes in to
tread where rage and pain at injustice had neither feared likewise to tread.
Now I no longer had my specimen— the SPECIMEN—to take back
with me to the lair where I or somebody far more competent could
decipher and in deciphering it render me stronger, stronger, stronger yet
not—never—via anything so vulgar as acquisition of the decipherment.
For an acquirable decipherment remains external to the self deciphered
whereas strengthening—against stories! against families! for there is
nothing I loathe more than families; for there is nothing I loathe more than
stories; for there is only one thing I loathe more than stories and that is
families; for there is only one thing I loathe more than families and that
is stories;—is always internal and leaves no trace of mere anxiety-
numbing acquisition. And of course Maggy did not care to see that—" "I
did see! I did see! But I did not care what anybody thought. Unlike you
I did not care, was not unmanned, undone." "—the appreciation—appreciation in very bold quotation marks, of course elicited from the old
dowager by Maggy's laudatory kindness was nothing more than a
fleeting dissimulation— a kind of tongue-in-cheek playing down to the
other—Maggy's—lowest instincts—what the bulldoggy old dowager
needed to treat as Maggy's frenzied and unholy appetency for the fulsome
and the mawkish." Maggy, by amending her conduct at the last moment,
had robbed him of the specimen that was to have stanched the flow of his

story. He was busy acquiring specimens that would stanch story—event—flow and I was busy struggling to acquire thoughts and concepts that could be depended on to construct and enlarge such events from scratch. This was a clear indication of our polar oppositeness proving we were ideally suited to inhabit the same story. I looked at Maggy and did not know whether to loathe or admire her. She was the woman who had robbed him—my beloved Jamms. At the same time she had robbed him of that specimen of cowardice-shame-rage whose analysis by some adroit and enigmatic third was to have cured him once and for all of participation in a story. So she had done me a favor in behalf of *our* story—Jamms's and mine—my last and only chance for happiness.

"Maggy never realized my father's wife had an unimpeded craving stronger than death to besmirch the compassionation she felt compelled to extract from others as her sole mode of engagement. So here we had kindness and trickling simulated appreciation of kindness and both colluding—here is the tragedy, both colluding—BOTH—against the puny specimen of rage and shame at the rage and rage at the shame secreted from all that had passed before the kindness and trickling appreciation—puny specimen that was all I had to take away as booty from the vast wound in which we were all four embroiled, excluding the nurses of course who were so much window dressing and made off as fast as they could. But what does Maggy care about the specimen shame I need to work at, examine, and perfect so that I am never embroiled and embrangled in too too painful family stories ever again. Maggy loves the story and she loves nothing better than to be in the heart of the heart of the story.

"Oh how I loathe families for families breed stories and stories are loathsome. They are loathsome because you know how painfully—jejunely—they will end yet have no control over the anti-velocity with which they descend on an ending. This is what the presocratics were alluding to as the suspense of banality when they spoke of how we tend to put our smelly feet in the same stream not once but twice and sometimes thrice. Maggy's competent kindness—her veering homeostatically from a situation where she might be reprobated beyond rehabilitation—has robbed me of the beloved specimen, the only manageable shred of a solatium for one who loathes to live smothered and subtended at the heart of the story. Most loathsome of all words. But there is no arguing the point with old Maggy. That is why Bessy is here. Bessy soothes my soul. There is never the challenge of mutilating her consciousness into synchrony with my own. It is already in synchrony and even if it isn't there is no threat that I am about to be overwhelmed by an alien consciousness mewling reproaches for my failure to pursue reasonable objectives in the marketplace or some such drivel." Maggy moved quietly to the window. "There she goes again," Jim resumed, "always trying to carry on with the story and thereby deflect my attention from the only remedy for that disease of diseases: the story—the story—my story—a story of occluded loves and hopes. Don't you see, she robbed me, robbed me of my specimen of shame—shame at a certain moment in the story, upsurge in the story. When she decided to make good on her initial rage the story, from my point of view, took a turn for the worst, though not from the point of view of the story—from the point of view of the story it was a turn for the propagating, perpetuating best. I had risen to respond. But one must endure the story's worst before being stimulated to secrete a toxin powerful enough to obliterate the story. Don't you see—she, Maggy, had grown enraged with the Jammses for utilizing their tumors as a pretext for tormenting the hospital's hired help. And she could not tolerate my passivity, my drugged, as if drugged, refusal to intervene. For I was terrified that his wife would notice and anathematizing store away Maggy's outburst as a clinical datum. And at the same time I felt rage at Maggy for inciting his-my father's-wife to an unjust rage that just or unjust would ultimately estrange me from Maggy. And Maggy immediately scented my susceptibility to mom's upthrust of loathing resentment at somebody's questioning the rectitude of her comportment. For mom her comportment was as ineluctable and as of a piece with all of nature as the tides and therefore completely justified by circumstances whatever circumstances turned out to be. And here was Maggy. So you see, everybody was trying to draw everybody else out to the breaking point, testing everybody else to the breaking point, over my dead body of course or over my body trying too too hard to play dead and bloody well not being allowed to succeed. And if only Maggy's righteous outrage hadn't suddenly prolapsed to kindness I certainly would have raged at Maggy for inducing mom's Jammsian rage, as a result of course of my powerlessness to rectify its unjust upsurge, which would never of course have become a specimen instance of injustice if it hadn't been for Maggy's messianism. Yes, if it hadn't been for Maggy's sudden prolapse to reconciliation with *the old girl* I would have raged at Maggy and of course felt shame in front of mom for Maggy's act and shame of course in front of Maggy for my retreat from the scene of the crime, my retreat of course being both crime and scene of crime. In short, just when I was about to take away this instance of [rage and(shame for the rage)] toward Maggy and [shame and(rage for the shame)] toward mom and (rage and rage for the rage) toward Maggy and mom—just when I was about to take away unscathed and pure of all mitigation this instance of my pathology—hopelessly—blissfully—disqualifying me for all relations past, present, and future—just when I was about to abscond with this instance of despair at the irrevocable—just when I was about to abscond with this instance *of* which if enormous was at the same time enormous enough to swallow and drown once and for all the story of the father, the son, the holy shit, and the holy family, all in one gulp—just when I was about to take away my specimen, my entity, my nugget—my specimen rage and shame indistinguishable from Maggy's revolt and his wife's loathsome tyranny, what did Maggy decide to do but rob me of my specimen—of shame and rage at the shame and shame at the rage and rage at the rage, this last minute change of character serving only to ensure the continuation of the story, the Jamms family story. For overcoming her rage and exasperation because homeostatically attuned through fright to my own simultaneously she made it her business to be overcome with a pristine and crystalline hunger to help, to bring succor to the dying and to the beloveds of the dying, a solatium to his last anathematizing for my dad was—is—nothing if not an anathematizer. And Maggy is nothing if not a champion of the joys and sorrows of the family. So just when I was on the verge of taking away unscathed this yet another instance of horrified and horrifying subjection to Jammsian whims of rage and contempt and recoil—for though they always made it a point to bring out the worst or the beast in others they themselves were rigorously trained as Brahmins to stand back appalled at the frenzied dances of heat prostration performed by those others before *their* beastly worst(as if nobody was around to witness the spectacle they-the others-were managing to make!): just when I was on the verge of taking away this one more specimen of subjection more fetal than filial Maggy took it into her head to turn the tables and become so loving and forgiving and so veritable a helpmate praising mom's devotion to dad that I was robbed of enshrining—and on the very verge!—forever Mamma Jamms's cowlike revulsion at one daring to challenge her own freefall and freeplay, mirroring back her own hysterical exasperation and thereby refusing to furnish—such is the tyranny of catoptrics—a safety, an enclosure, for that hysteria. For Maggy's hysteria, if only she had given way to it at last, would have suggested mom's hysteria was boundless by withholding the limit point which the elder lady was always seeking and for which she was always hungering. Just when I was about to enshrine forever not so much Mrs. Jamm's cowlike loathsomeness in loathing one who dared to challenge her undisciplined domination of the field in which she happened to find herself as my own shamed rage and raging shame at genuflection before that loathsomeness loathing without restraint—just when I was about to enshrine my shame indistinguishable from somebody's cowlike rage at Maggy's helpmately exasperation in time of crisis and from somebody's handmaidenly exasperation at Mrs. Jamm's cowlike rage—she—Maggy— destroyed my target, my final specimen, my ultimate stab at the family story's obliteration—through kindness and compassionation—the despicable sharing and caring of the social workers and corporate psychologists—she destroyed all I might take away of a self extricated at last from the bonds of the story. And so the story went on, the story goes on, in spite of my try at a vetoing absconding with my countervailing specimen of raging shame that threatening promised to call a permanent halt to the story's flow. But here it was—is—flowing on again, or rather gurgling on with dad's grateful loathing for everything but Maggy massaging his ascitic toes. So the story gurgles on compliments of Maggy massaging an old man's toes." He looked at me as if I threatened to embody a further extension of the story. And what vast unappeasable contempt was in his eyes—for story, for story, for story. I think it was only from disgust with the women that he decided to invite me on a little jaunt. When he said, "I think it's only neighborly to show our little friend around," Maggy and Bessy did not respond, both probably feeling that better me than the other accompanying Jamms out into the wilds.

The train ride, even before it began, became one of the most delightful of my life, no describing the luxuriant beauty of the depots en route which this, our manly conveyance, bypassed so blithely. Jim, of course, had the window seat: I gladly conceded in behalf of his need for views for—on—his work. As Jim made a point of explaining, he was at work even now, sitting still, and yet he did not seem quite convinced of what he said and looked as if he dared me to challenge or ridicule this statement. Work or no work *our* story was about to begin and unlike Jamms I was eager for it to begin. I for one had no need of specimens to call a halt to—to call into question my qualifications for—the flow. Though nothing seemed to be happening and though we seemed to coexist, might I say, in total silence, I for one had no doubt that a story was flowing along, parallel with, well in advance of, the tracks. He said, "Did I ever tell you about the first time dad went into the hospital for his tumor." At first I pretended not to have heard, it wasn't even a pretending, rather a strangled wish, born from the depths of being overwhelmed, drowned out of use, not to have heard what I had just heard or that I might be strong enough to undo what had been perpetrated against the silence. Finally I replied that no, I had not yet heard about dad and the very first tumor. At first I felt he was simply trying to sabotage our relation as he had tried to sabotage his relation to Maggy and the sick dad in the hospital room though who had been the saboteur was unclear. Or he might be ridiculing me or something about our inchoate relation. For what else but ridicule would goad him, after connectedness—if one wanted magnanimously to go so far as to call our encounter a connectedness—of such short duration and, at least in terms of what I continued to hope for, generally unsatisfactory character—what else but a highly developed sense of the ridiculous would allow him to presume on the density of that connectedness— to think I might think we had so many incidents behind us as to welcome instinctively one more addition to the untidy sum. So I could only believe he was presuming—heavily—on the absence of all connectedness, all plausible past stage business warranting such an inroad, to relieve himself—to deliver himself—of an ironic commentary on that absence... of connectedness and what more telling strategy, pristine in its virulence, unlocalizable, untouchable, than to launch into a tale as if telling me this tale was the most natural thing in the world given our past life together.

He was launching into the tale not for the sake of the tale — the story — for he abominated stories as he abominated families — but to demonstrate the implausibility — the inconceivability — of launching into the story at this time and in this place occupied by the most unprepossessing of interlocutors. He was unfolding a stark disjunction between his telling and the circumstances that were starkly incompatible with such a telling.

I did not relish the ease with which he seemed about to launch into his story cancelling our burgeoning story. I did not respond favorably to the almost flippant ease with which he mentioned Mick and Bell(e) and Frank and Aunt Pauline as well as Grandpappy MacDoofurs without feeling cancelled or as if he literally gave — volatilized — himself away. Here sat one who did not have to withhold himself in order to feel whole. Not that even when withholding myself I for one necessarily felt whole. Normally I loathed telling stories about myself, sniffed out its inadequacy long before I even began to formulate one — loathed, that is, up until this moment, this moment of envy either of Jim or his stories or the ease with which he promised to tell them or the bland audacity with which he smothered nascent unease. I looked out the window for help: I couldn't decide — and the depot-ridden landscape that only moments before had been so nurturing offered no help — whether indeed I too had stories to tell, fascinating stories, and was simply not telling them in order to deprive my listener of the metamorphosis I would be unable to share — or whether mine was a slab of history simply, utterly, refractory — more than refractory, inconceivable — to a telling. But if refractory or inconceivable or both then refractory or inconceivable or both with respect to the pons asinorum of having to give the names of — give names to — the unlikely participants, to read those names off the slate of their ostensible nativeness — for me, perhaps — but not for the other who just as — even more — natively — could be expected to rear and bristle at being consigned to a momentary disjection and oblivion amid the bustle created by these names. Names are far more potent than things, which they easily and instantly eclipse. Or maybe my story was simply refractory — inconceivable — to a telling only within the framework — the bigger coarser slab — of another's listening and that other, from my or perhaps any vantage, always a hostile listener. Or maybe there was, would always be, no story to tell or a story supremely tellable and therefore not worth telling. As the train speeded earthwards I couldn't decide where my torment lay — in telling the story or in having no story to tell. Did I have a story to oppose to Jamms's? And even if I had a story somewhere on my person I might be so immedicably estranged from that story as to render impossible any future of telling. I was the disjunction between my being and my story.

I conceded, "You never told me about the tumor. I mean, about his first tumor." And once I had spoken I realized I was prompting him in vain for he seemed far from his initial upsurge of what I still believed was completely factitious enthusiasm or rather authentic only if one took as its target the absurdity of any kind of enthusiastic telling in the midst of one so tenuously connected to his likes — his only enthusiasm was for the disjunction between the telling and the situation in which said telling had decided to set up shop — I was prompting him in vain for he seemed to have drifted into a sort of dozing contemplation — not a dozing contemplation but a sort of dozing contemplation of the first houses in the first authentic Long Island town into which we had drifted as if on a gondola. But who am I to say what he was contemplating, dozing or not. Then he turned to me and said, "Tumor. Yes, the tumor."

He said, as if giving me at last what I had all along wanted to hear, "He went in to have his tumor excised but at that point the tumor had already spread far and wide and whatever could be excised reduced only to the tail end of a monstrosity too far gone to be tractable to the scalpel's tooth. Every day I went to the hospital and every day he forced them singlehandedly, doctors and nurses, to come on back over to the bed and see to it that he had enough cold water though what is enough and though there was nothing he loathed more than cold water, that the bed was raised or lowered according to specifications though there was nothing he loathed more than to hear and feel the shaft being cranked, that the tube of oxygen was truly stuck in his mouth though there was nothing he loathed more than being prevented from howling. And I never knew how to react to his refusing to accept what they, the medical professionals, first proposed. I mean, was all this a heroic refusal to be passive in the face of the laxity of those so-called professionals or was it a pure and simple retorsiveness toward things as they had to be. Was all this nothing more than a frantic tantrum-laden wish to place blame where there was no

blame to place or ON THE CONTRARY (phrase beloved of all meaning-mongers) a daring rejection of yet another flagrant synonymization
of laymanship and victimizability. Was he, dad, perpetrating but only in
the domain of his own hallucinations or was this *perpetrating* an authentic
handling of a matter authentically out there. In other words, from a few
gestures, commands, smirks, dereistic shrugs, retorts, had he managed to
create a completely fictive universe amid whose furniture such doings
might qualify as heroic or merely responded heroically to a chaos already
given out there. And if the latter was — am — I then nothing but a passive
grumbler never daring to confront phenomena simply because they have
already been set in motion or are about to be set in motion and therefore
virtually indistinguishable from faits accomplis hoary with the resonance
of an eternity in no need of my gurgled imprimatur." Looking me straight
in the eye though getting no response — needing to caulk the silence yet
impatient to save face to himself — to make this new tack appear to be
responding to a new and unanticipated demur of my own he continued
with "You see I've been trying all my life to extricate myself from them —
from their tumors — and the situations were always so impossible and so
impossibly the same and the hunger to extricate so enormously beyond
my powers at any given moment that it is only recently that I have begun
to begin to admit that I want to tear myself loose. For so long what else
did I do but stand on the sidelines of phenomena and of their response to
phenomena which response always completely overwhelmed the phenomena in question and made my laches lose sight of them — the phenomena — completely. I stood away lest all my efforts to extricate come to
overwhelmingly less than nought." I did not know how to answer and
suddenly I didn't need to know for we had arrived in the town of X—,
noon, both famished, or so I heard myself think, for so we were supposed
to be if stories are to be believed. In a coffee shop right near the station
we had, over ample booths and smooth table tops, a full view of the street
fronting the beach, surely of use to one with his highly developed eye. I,
seated across, contented myself with fixation on the porthole in the
swinging door separating kitchen from dining room. Seated across, I
contented myself with fixation on the porthole in the swinging door
separating kitchen from dining room. There was the usual noontide
bustle, so I heard myself say, most of the eaters local folk to judge from

their casual attire and contented air: they did not take note of us as
intruders, the scrambled eggs were fine, just fine, Jim had black coffee
and cherry-cheese Danish, I made do with tea, then we headed for the
beach, a light wind prompted us, prompted or pursued by a wind, light
or not so light, I really can't say. The more I concentrated on our story the
more it resembled a deadfall of cliché.

As the vast countryside unfurled before us, behind us, to the right
and left of us, I became clearer and clearer about my despair in the face
of his story, that of the rebarbative tumor-laden dad, and of the ever-com-
plaisant hospital staff achieving its most moving incarnation in the figure
of the orderly pushing his car of dinner trays out of the elevator yet away
from the terminal ward with a movement of dancerly pleasure or perhaps
repudiating disgust, who can tell. He couldn't tell, he was too busy
"learning from the experience born of healthy conflict with forbears," too
busy accumulating ambiguities from the fare. In the case of this orderly
emerging from the elevator—taking me completely unawares—he was
promulgating yet another ambiguity, one that might even end up rivalling
his dad's heroic combat against/abject retorsiveness toward other members
of the staff. I had the distinctly uncomfortable sensation that through
these ambiguities he was selling his version of meaning, he was a meaning
peddler, nothing but. An apparent alternation between, among, possible
meanings was his version of meaning, his retreat from and initiation into
meaning. Several times I was on the verge of opening my mouth to tell my
own story, whatever that was—wasn't I the man without a story—but
discovered, over and over there was none to tell, nothing but pebbles,
disgust, excrement of velleity. Even and long before I could begin to
formulate some ostensible subject of telling, a topic worthy if not of me
then of this special occasion to which I was suddenly privy as an outsider
though in some sense deep in its heart—stuck in its craw—even before I
could begin I was already overcome with the outcome that was always the
same beyond its uniquely protean stages—the outcome was obliteration,
massive hemorrhage, the taste of tastelessness. In short, even before I
could begin to tell my story—that is to say, begin to conceive of imitating
Jim telling his—I perceived telling my tale would do nothing to confirm
and everything to deform and destroy me as nothing more than the
bracketed aftertaste of limp strivings, limper fruitions. Whereas off his

tongue words tripped so easily and always in the service of the story—
especially, perhaps not especially, notably then, proper names, so casual,
so magnificently casual was he about his linkage to these Sallies, Joes,
Jos, Mrs. Potterses, dad Jamms, mom Jamms, mamma Jamms, grand-
mamma Jamms, uncle Wiggly, and so easily did he imagine me—perhaps
it was his expensive upbringing—sucked into familiarity with the denizens of this cosmos although at the same time I was of course expected to
know my place and keep it when it came time for such high-priced
puppets as he had seen fit to trot out for my toothless delectation to retire
to or from the drawing room and suck on their knuckles. And in contrast,
in very high contrast, look at me trembling in my boots at the merest
possibility of sprinkling my chatter with wary mention of, in my case,
Harry the Baltimore plumber, Aunt Pearl, who threatened to hack me to
bits with a kitchen knife because I would not leave the apartment long
enough for her to mop the floor and the ceilings, cleanliness fiend that she
was if only between epileptic fits though in other respects she was
extremely, might I even go so far as to say flauntingly, filthy—yea,
trembling in my boots at the merest possibility of sprinkling my chatter,
much less imagining others sucked into the very heart of its story. For a
second I too—especially with, perhaps only because—the train was
moving with such authoritative full speed ahead—wanted to share
confidences yet simply, simply, no stories were forthcoming. No stories,
either because my life did not consist of stories or even if it was literally
teeming with stories or with just one there was a concurrent refractori-
ness due to the premonition that the story would not survive, would
disintegrate in its telling. Story, mine—history, mine—chronology, mine—
was mutually exclusive with respect to its telling. If I was enragedly
envious I nevertheless quickly forgave him his dazzling capacity to make
stories out of his doings or glaring absence of authentic doings for he was
so very much—and indubitably—what is known in the trade, what trade,
the knave trade, as a fascinating creature. And more to the point, there
was our present story, neither his, nor mine, our present story. By riding
out to the Island, especially without Maggy or Bessy, we were enacting
at last a story known since long ago, by me I mean, known without my
knowing and to whose minute efflorescing reconstruction unbidden I
was supremely trothed. There were moments as we rode along, ever so

blithely, at least I was ever so blithe in my equivalent of a seersucker Sunday suit, when I felt that if we did not enact the story and doublequick then there would be no story to be made — ever. In other words, no life for me, for this story, the story I intended to construct with my *traveling companion*, on or off his dad's payroll, was my last and only stab at a life.

As the train picked up speed — and even if it did not in fact pick up speed I needed to believe — for if one is going to live a story one must be yielded up to the ploys of a story — and ultimately, no immediately, from the very beginning, no before the very beginning — did believe it was forever picking up speed for a train's picking up speed is a potent sign of a story's advance — as the train picked up speed it became clearer and clearer that here I was, riding a train, sitting beside a companion I barely knew yet loved according to my capacity and feeling that in the realm of reconstruction, that was in fact a construction from scratch, of our story — and wasn't construction as reconstruction my sole reason for being on the train — I was failing according to every respectable criterion of reconstruction — every criterion — overseeing — overhanging the pursuit of storydom/halidom. Maybe I resented my sense that it was entirely up to me to embody the pursuit. Yet why shouldn't it be entirely up to me. After all, our relation was our story, there was no relation, that is to say, no verification of that relation, outside the story. I said, "Excuse me," and wended my way past slackly sprawled vacationers to the filthy toilet. For now that it was up to me to incarnate story's progress — -now that I was in the thick of its shit instead of on its fringe peeping in, piping in the canned music of my schoolboy infatuation — now that I was chosen both to live and propel the story outside the realm of living into one more, oh, darkly bright — it made me sick, physically sick, not only to be living the story but to be associated with each and every one of its moments, or, in this case, failed moments, for aside from getting on the train/chatting briefly which chatting was more the cipher of its own inanity than a robust collision of two souls/wending my way to the stinking toilet, aside from these orts there were no moments. I was simply incompatible with the continued existence of the story. I began to panic or rather, my bladder began to panic: story was beautiful only as enacted by others, only martyrizingly bypassing me. Could I be of the story only insofar as I was barred from even its chilliest purlieus? Maybe Jim saw how wretchedly pale I looked for once I was back in my seat he said, "Sometimes I get so frustrated with regard to my work. Everything seems an obstruction. Even this train, moving so quickly, obstructs even if it would seem to be bringing me ever more quickly to yet another scene of its—the work's— crime. But at least I don't have to shut my eyes against the irrelevance of the landscape as I did when I used to visit my mom and dad. It was as if the landscape was polluted by their own irrelevance to my project, the project they always repudiated. I hope you understand I will have to spend all my time out there working. This may be a pleasure party for you but for me...at any rate it always seems as if everything is conspiring to obstruct my work. And it is only through my work that I can hope to extricate myself from...them. Not only the 'them' I spoke of before but all the 'thems' daring to manifest the slightest skepticism. And at the same time I fear—I know—that by not coming right up against the obstruc- tions I may miss something—I'm sure to miss something—that will ultimately accrue to the greater grandeur of the work by facilitating its metamorphosis into a higher plane...or metamorphose me to a higher plane whence to look back on the work as blessedly no longer relevant to current objectives." He began to wipe his face profusely with a mono- grammed handkerchief. "Oh God, no, no, no. Though sometimes I wonder if I am secretly or not so secretly in collusion with obstruction yielding to which will liberate me at last from my work. Can I achieve the work faster than I wish to be liberated from it. I don't know why I started speaking about it," looking out the window as if no longer interested in the subject nor, for that matter, in wondering why he had ever started speaking about it. It was as if he was repudiating less his subject than my warming interest which somehow contested—aspersed—it. My interest was clearly incompatible with the subject's continued existence. It was as if he was repudiating less X than Y—never mind, never mind, never mind. This is simply to descend into the cesspools of meaning-mongering. I don't know what he was doing. I don't even know he was looking out the window. Then looking back at me as if I was some verminous navvy, "It's just that the way you keep looking at your watch and the absurd way you mounted the platform as if there wasn't a minute to lose and the equally absurd way you hurriedly made your way down the aisle to—to—" I didn't mind—I told myself I didn't mind—X so much as I strongly resented Y. No, no, no, I will not give in to these fine distinctions that are the unvanquishable bread and butter of meaning-mongers. I didn't mind. I didn't mind. I didn't mind —I told myself I didn't mind—his ridiculing my posture so much as I strongly resented—forebodingly—his relegation of my, and by extension, our, mounting the platform to some nether place. Didn't he understand that in our story there was to be no past tense. I had a premonition that gave way to another cold sweat and a hunger to return to the toilet. I feared, perhaps sensed incontrovertibly, that whatever for me would turn out to be the building blocks of our story for him would be mere fissure. My ashlar was his interstice, simple as that and even simpler since it was my very being at stake here. I was fighting for my life and not, as he believed, for a little pleasure party amid the sheltering sands. We would go along, mounting platforms, descending, sharing coffee and Danish, observations concerning the other passengers, and all of a sudden, at some point impossible to foresee, he would indicate that all these moments, these ashlared moments, were so much slaggy interim. Retrospectively and retroactively condemned these moments would shrivel into the nothingness whence I had come and to which I most emphatically did not wish to return, at least just yet. I suspected it would always be like this, casually he would make it clear there was nothing for him in all this except interim, interim, interim, with a bit of makeshift and shabbiest pis-aller thrown in for good measure before the real life event began, the real story or anti-story from which I was necessarily barred beyond appeal. Interim, interim, interim, whereas for me the mounting of the platform and even the descent of the corridor toward the toilet—because enacted in the shadow of his bluegreen right eye—were moments or widening shadows of those moments destined to constitute our life, better yet, much better, the story of that life. "I only meant," he continued, "that you looked as if you couldn't get things done fast enough and everything was against you and so naturally I was only trying to point out from bitter experience that obstructions per se —" This casual remark triggered my first premonition that he, Jim Jamms, was not so much a storyteller as a... At any rate, I did not want his random observations. The train advanced or made a pretense of advancing even if his little speeches seemed definitely to be beginning to stand in the way of the story's advance over land and sea.

I don't know how I looked but he

But he

I don't know how I looked but he looked

He looked

NOT SO MUCH hurt—he would never give me that satisfaction—AS

AS

AS quizzically annoyed at the thought that I was trying to or
thought I could wound him. "What I was trying to say," he went on,
"culled, of course, little man, from eons of bitter experience, is that
nothing stands in the way of anything else. The wobbling of the train, the
slowness of the wheels, do not stand in the way of our getting there. The
getting there and the ostensible obstacles in the way of getting there—
anything, in other words, that we connect in that way—through anathematizing—to the getting there are part of the work, the task at hand, the
project, the objective, all primary aspects of the same thing. And why are
they all part of the same thing? The obstructions fertilize the ostensibly
primary task and therefore are ostensively bound up with it. If the
ostensibly primary thrust of the work can smell out the potential obstructions and rant and rave over them with such fluency then it proves
incontestably that that ostensibly primary thrust is in fact a ranting and
raving in celebration of the ostensible obstructions as sublime fertilizers
of the primary thrust, indispensable to the primary thrust. In its fear of a
terrible dependence on the indispensable fertilizers, in its pitiable misinterpretation of this fundamental and indissoluble interdependence as a
kind of thralldom to any and every little gust of contingency these
fertilizers might be capable of stirring up, it—the ostensibly primary
thrust of the work—turns to ranting and raving as a remedy for fear. The
apparent disgust that the obstacles do not allow the primary thrust to
fester unfertilized in its purity—as if that purity is anything but deple-
tion—is in fact terror that that thrust might miss or be bypassed by the
obstacles crucial to its cenogenesis. And of course the rage and disgust,
the fearful ranting and celebratory raving, the being kickingly and
screamingly escorted into the future of the primary thrust is also part of
the thrust. The primary thrust is simply inconceivable apart from these
kicks against the prick of its ancillaries. In short, the ranting and raving

is a raving and ranting that nothing, including — especially — the ranting and raving, is outside of or secondary to the thrust of the primary thrust. The primary thrust and the obstacles ostensibly inimical to the successful consummation of its trajectory and the celebratory ranting and raving against the obstacles that is far more stymying than the obstacles themselves — or is this just another example of what you call my meaning-mongering or would it be more correct to call it my moral-mongering — are all manifestations of the primary thrust in its thrust toward eternity but when I say 'thrust' I should differentiate among. Primary thrust 1 and the obstacles ostensibly inimical to its consummation are fulgurations of an underlying substratum (or hypostasis, as the Polynesians say) in incessant turnover known as primary thrust 2. And the rage and horror that primary thrust 2 actually comprises in a fructive self-lubricating manner both primary thrust 1 and the obstacles ostensibly standing in the way of its achievement becomes instantly constituent of and indispensable to the progress of primary thrust 2, and so, likewise, and as God meant it to be, that is, at those moments when he is not doing one hell of an impersonation of a catamenial devil bat, the rage and horror at the ways and means of primary thrust 2 are both — raging horror and thrust — absorbed into their substratum and right honorable hypostasis, namely, primal thrust 3. And so on and so forth. Of course, knowing all of this does not help me, only keeps me from actively utilizing what I know." Here he was, holding forth, when all I wanted was the unfolding of a story — ours — that was — yes, why shouldn't I say it — the very opposite of holding forth. And it was at this point — or, rather, for the purposes of the story whose modest needs I refuse even now to frustrate it appears apt theatrically to contend that it was at this point and no other — perhaps because precisely nothing was happening at this point and inexplicably that nothing, to a meaning-monger, was far more terrifying than at other times — though to say that the encapsulated nothing was far more terrifying than at other times is once again to fall into the pit of exaggeration, theatrics, lying, storytelling — and it was at this point that I suspected Jamms would go on bombarding our story, or rather, the possibility of our story, with such anecdotes, such holdings forth. There was certainly no privilege in being chosen as interlocutor especially since I had not been chosen, I was simply at hand. Maybe he already knew something about story—our story—that I didn't know, namely, that our—anybody's—story was a route to death. So he had no choice—great artist that he was—but to explode our story, the progress of our story, his premonition of that progress, and in the only way he knew how: via sclerosed anecdote, intrusion of the ominously irrelevant, first impressions of mom and dad.

I looked round, at all the other little groups trying and seeming to have no difficulty making conversation, keeping its rhegmas permanently caulked, so what if primarily through seizure and doublequick on some heretofore mutually unsuspected grievance fundamentally innocuous yet under duress suddenly—miraculously virulent enough for all that to render them temporarily connected. And yet so rancidly transparent were these efforts—though not, apparently, to the perpetrators who were from all indications digging in with dour professionalism—though all smiles, of course, all smiles—that I was about to excuse myself in order to go puke some more—not puke but go puke. As if finely attuned to what could only enhance my nausea Jim began making more and more pronouncements. For a split second I thought it was to humor and amuse me. But then, judging from the character of these judgments I was forced to recognize that obviously they were spewed to enable him to keep his distance in keeping with Maggy's probable judgment on my character, more more than my character, my very being, in short, she had, with some assistance from Bessy no doubt, been feeding him lies, lies, lies. So as a compromise with his loathing for this freakish fellow traveler he had decided to feel compelled to vomit forth pronouncements and thereby intimidate the parasite into forever holding his peace and subsiding into the exiguity whence he had oozed. He bodied forth his opinion not only of the stately ticket-taker but of the depots flying wanly by untenanted, the steeples incising the fleece of tenderhearted cumulus, the booklet I had taken along to read. Hastily he put forward these opinions, judgments, pronouncements, slovenly verdicts of an unschooled mind, a little belligerently too, as if afraid, always afraid, of being sodomized by an alien adamancy, at once prior and future. After listening to such pronouncements along the lines of, Beaches are farts, Bathers are smelly dregs, Bikini-clad gals and guys have smelly eyes, Ice cream vendors ought to be castrated before they pollute with their tinny vociferations the less than infinite expanse of blue against greyblue and greyblue against red, it became clearer than ever that their overriding purpose was to let me know he had them, such opinions I mean, and therefore no orifice — every orifice a wound! as Prince Hamlet ought to have said — was in any danger of being populated by organs alien. For every orifice was already news-crammed. On my second trip to the john when he called after me, Trains should be blown up as if they were third-rate frescoes — of course I continued to try not to take him too literally though the evergrowing temptation was always there — I tripped and to steady myself murmured, Get a grip on yourself, for I was on the verge of falling into a fat middle-aged man's lap. Get a grip on yourself, I repeated. But here the literal had no meaning, here in its true kingdom the literal was worse and weaker than meaningless, and it was only by playing back the utterance — Get a grip on yourself — in the key of the figurative — and not by seeking out a steadfast grip on the back of a seat or a jamb — that I began to stop tripping, trembling, tumbling. As long as I heard, Get a grip on yourself, literally, I could not follow my own advice, there was no advice to follow, it had volatilized away into a mockery of itself which mockery smothered all possibility of its simultaneous straightforward and forthright applica- tion to a very practical problem. Now that I needed the literal it would not materialize. YET

Yet

Yet

yet in the presence of the clearly

fantasmatic, namely, Jim's pronouncements, my first and only interpretation was literal.

Yet how I loathe this pretty little study in contrasts, supreme pablum for the meaning-monger.

So what.

But could I hope for a story without these unforeseeable lapses into a meaning determined purely by the ups and downs, ebb and flow, of the telling? I was delighted when we arrived in the little town of Greenback/Hampton, or rather, Greenback-Hampton, or rather, Green- back: Hampton, no, Greenback on the Hampton, and even Jamms, jaded as he was or pretended to be, seemed pleased with the wide residential streets and with the little park overlooking a pond. I had been all along so concerned with the overflow of Jamms's feelings or rather of feelings immediately and thus unlocalizably transmuted into outbursts, boluses — specimens — I had had no time for the examination, that is to say, the cultivation of my own. And here they were suddenly and unwelcomely assaulting my vitals. On the one hand I never missed an opportunity to tell myself that only feelings, properly bred in the bone, preferably compact of jars, could drive our story forward. For feelings breed event and surely our story needed events in order to flourish. But how much feeling was needed to produce an event and keep it moving along? And weren't there feelings that were only obstructive to story flow? And what kind of feelings was Jamms producing in me: feelings in the service of our story flow or those obstructive to that flow? My feelings seemed to be paralyzing me and making it more and more clear how spontaneously I tended, at the height of feeling, to put myself frozenly in Jamms's unsteady hands, as if saying, Do with me as you wish. And at the same time I felt or could feel if I so chose that these very feelings, by and large unspeakable, were developing an urgency positively despotic. Yet I was nowhere near being able to begin to decide whether this despotic urgency expected and on its own steam to do away with the story's progress or whether it was at all times in the service of that story's progress. Could I appeal to Jamms, contentedly eating his ice cream and apparently far, very far, from the concerns of his work, could I ask him either to stop provoking these feelings or if all else failed how to keep feelings and the events they did or did not breed within acceptable bounds. To be with Jamms was to be delivered up to feelings. Then could I get and keep the story going in some other way, keeping whatever feelings arose in transit starkly without the domain of stories. Could I appeal to him now, regarding the virulence of feelings, especially now, when nothing, at least to the naked eye, seemed to be happening. How, with or without his aid, for he did not look as if he was capable of or ripe for giving aid, could I go now about the heady business of encouraging the modest proliferation of feelings — assuming it was doomed without them — crucial to our story's herniation into being. Although at this very moment — it had to have something to do with the almost insolent leisureliness with which Jamms devoured his frappe — it seemed that I could easily beguile myself

unendingly with NOT SO MUCH

not so much X as Y

not so much *a* as *a'*

not so much—no I can't—not so much story *per se* as story's form, story's outright musculature, in which case only a very modest proliferation of feeling—subserving such a beguilement—was needed, was desirable. Only feelings of a modest vibrancy and therefore in no danger of overrunning that musculature of whose apperception they would presumably bring me to the threshold could begin to sponsor the kind of investigation I had in mind. Suddenly I was in no hurry for the story to unfold for what was the story but the deployment of unspeakable feelings inundated with the syrup from his frappe whereas the form—the musculature—of the story, the story within the story of the story was authentic food for meditation. A too rapidly unfolding story could only hinder my investigation of story form, story musculature, story inside the story, which investigation would hopefully—by exposing to view the mucoid slime of which its scaffolding was constituted—cure me forever of the hunger for a story. Yes, my aim was to be cured of this hunger for story. And once I had the story of the story inside the story under my belt, as the saying goes, couldn't I use my by then arrogant familiarity with the archetype among archetypes to generate the story—the particular story—of Jamms and myself but this time according to my own classical specifications without recourse to the wrenching and aleatory puniness of my own unspeakable feelings. For my aim was no longer to be cured of this hunger for story but to come at story, still indispensable to my well being—my very being, as it were—from the direction diametrically opposed to that overrun with the slime of feeling. Need: to stay close to the bone of the archetype. I needed to get a meatier and meatier grip on my feelings so that they were not allowed to sprawl to the point where my only concern became, where I wanted nothing more than, to fix them, give them habitation somewhere, anywhere, in what would immediately be deformed into something like a story. For then I would be no better than Jim, dumping the gruesome details of his dad's first, second, and third tumors or of what might have ensued had Maggy only let him abscond as planned with his specimen of rage or shame or raging shame or shamed rage—with his very own little tumorous outpouching of a father's furious loathing—dumping it all into the latent broth of our story. Unlike Jim, I wanted an authentic story. Unlike Jim—for I was paradigmatically unlike Jim, never forget, otherwise I never could claim to be me or Jim to be Jim—I wanted something more, far more, than a makeshift habitation for unwieldy specimens of feeling—whether rage or shame or hemorrhoidal ecstasy—or of thought unspeakable as feeling with nowhere else to go but quick, quick, once more into the breeches of the failed facsimile of a true story engendered from an intrinsic musculature refractory to twitches plotted in vain via the electrodes of hairy bloody feeling. I wanted an authentic story—when I was ready for it. I did not want to fail the authentic story when its true moment came. And suddenly I knew, as Jim leisurely devoured his second frappe, there was no rushing the story, there was no living the story if I was not willing to coincide with its musculature, the genesis of its form uniquely demonstrating how this the story—our story—was unlike yet so very close to all other stories. No stage of the story's gestation and birth must escape my vigilance. Jim's was a leisurely approach to the pyramid of ice cream. He was not devouring it in one fell swoop. No, no, no, he was taking his time come hell or high water and this was what I had to do vis-a-vis the story, our story. Granted, only feeling could bring me to the threshold of apperception of the story's immutable form. I needed feelings. I needed feelings but not to be overrun by feelings to the point where all I sought to do with those feelings was deliver them posthaste into the mold of, say, an epileptic fit or a letter to Jamms, Sr., if he was still alive and kicking, informing him all was well and that little Jim soon would be coming home from his self-made wars, which casts, which—specimens, would then perforce be relocated and for all eternity in the most accessible story makeshift, stalemate of storylike proportions but in actual point of fact as far from a true story as Hyperion from a satyr. Who needed such makeshifts whose dreary availability served only to obfuscate the most excruciating and lucrative of tasks—investigation of the story's form as one among many possibilities.

Watching him then, watching him so blithely devour his snack, I wanted our story to unfold with the same uncaring blitheness, to develop but in developing give me the opportunity to witness—to undergo—to live—its form, the spread, the slow bleeding of its musculature, a musculature that must divulge both its consanguinity with all other stories and its essential difference. I wanted Jim to go on licking, smirking, purring, in other words, provoking feelings, but not to such an extent that these feelings overran the developing musculature, nourishable, it was still true, only with feelings. I wanted to witness—undergo—live—the musculature evolving with an absolute minimum of obscuration/ambiguation compliments of a greasy surfeit of feelings, worthy and unworthy, thoughts, specimens mixing thought, feeling, and event into a fatal brew, all of them alas, cropping up at every turn.

Watching him eat, lick the cone down to nullity—yes, he was now eating a cone—I was overcome by a plethora of feelings I cannot begin to formulate. And how I hated these feelings. Or rather, the feelings came to me, that is to say, were cut off at the root, in the form of thoughts capturing little of their richness. As thought, that feeling-richness was transmogrified into unspeakability. A minute later, though, I had no feelings, no thoughts supplanting those feelings. Or is this merely meaning-mongering once more: the story, the story-to-be demands *stark contrast* between what happened or failed to happen a minute ago and what is happening, or failing to happen at this very minute. At any rate—at any rate—how loathsome and useless I felt in the sudden absence of those feelings I had but a moment before abhorred so vehemently for their multitudinous excess. So here I was engrossed in a fiction that was not, however, a story to the extent that I was very much in the midst of beginning to love nothing better than the work of exploring its terrain, that is to say, the terrain of our connectedness as the imminence of its story-to-be—blotted thanks to my increasing vigilance by the barest minimum of props, horticultural or otherwise, even if once confronted by said bareness I was the first to flee bawling, squealing, and beating my breasts in quest of its remedy. I want the story to develop, I want the story to develop, I kept telling myself as we wandered through the terrain of our connectedness-to-be, in this case, a simple pretty little Long Island town, meaning I wanted its musculature to lay itself bare before that musculature became the prey of feeling and was irreparably overrun with the fat of those feelings become thoughts become feelings again but warped, altogether different, and the whole bloody brew seeking haven in the fat, however—and now immedicably—purulent.

Yet this fabled connectedness, was it even vendable to the story *as* connectedness. I for one was locked in paralysis and Jamms in the unpleasantness of memory, tumor after tumor. As if guessing the train of my thoughts he intoned, the cone wrapper still sticky between his long YET CURIOUSLY INEXPRESSIVE fingers, "Did I ever tell you about the time they got sick both at the same time, with almost identical, one might say symmetrical, tumors." I did not answer, though already far advanced in cursing him for introducing yet another thought about the past—anything not linked to our story-to-be was classifiable as the past—mom, dad, the flotilla of obese nurslings halfheartedly consecrated to the rehabilitation of this not quite delirious dyad.

And suddenly it came to me, a particularly painful thought. I tried to shove it out of my mind but, as we walked along the beach, to no avail. Here I was trying to advance in my work—the work being our story—by first revealing its musculature—here I was trying to get on with my work by making sure first and foremost that whatever changes were necessary for getting out of the shit and slime of storylessness would be effected *in time*. Yet with his fetid reminiscences what was Jim doing but making all too clear the stark disjunction between time given and time needed to alter the puny fetid course of things so that a story—a life—might be born. There was always, at least when I was with him, too little time to assimilate, store, retrieve, and dehisce the momentum needed to leap out of the pod of days into the glaring sunlight of the story. Always—in the presence of Jamms—these stark disjunctions between what was sought and what was feasible, what dreamed and what lived, to the point that the most intolerable disjunction of all was that between this observation and the incidents undergone to produce, substantiate, and confirm it. So that I now began to wonder whether my task was not to live our story but rather accumulate and animate disjunctions as stark as possible between what was desiderated for the story lived and what was feasible. It was Jamm's presence—being—that made these disjunctions real, especially in the fetch-infested—light of their horrifying participation in some future story, some leering perversion of all I took to be story, from which of course I would be the very first to be evicted forever. I was pledged to the laying bare of a story musculature; Jamms, let us say, to the laying bare of a sequence of stark disjunctions between what at any moment might be craved and what cravable. I sought the story now; Jamms sought, let us say, through the disposition of these disjunctions stretching out beyond the crack of doom some future "story" that would

achieve a parody of all elements except my own eviction from its premises.
I hung my head until I was able to take heart: didn't these polar
oppositions between Jamms and I (my seeking this, his seeking that) bode
well for the story now. Wasn't it precisely upon such oppositions that
stories now famously fed?

"At any rate about the same time they developed this tumor on the
spleen, or was it the kidney. I remember looking down from their hospital
room and noting that the greys of the sky and the filmy water were so
subdued—one of those foggy humid summer nights—that anything re-
flected from a condominium tower under construction or a streetlamp or
a passing tug was immediately perceptible—undergone, rather—as a riot
of brilliance. And at the same time I wondered if I was in fact perceiving
all this or whether words had simply joined together in place of the feeling,
in place of the thought." For the first time—was it in fact the first time or
were words merely joining together to create and stretch the significance
of this moment appallingly like any other—I wanted to leap up and
strangle him, mom or no mom, dad or no dad. Couldn't he sense it was
obstructions like these that obscured my vision of form, the story's form,
vitally and crucially in the service of the story indistinguishable from the
life I intended to live—with him, with Jamms—but as one rid at last of all
I was and transformed at longer last into all I was not—the form that
would shear me of the superfluity that was I and deliver me up to myself
as a completely new package. But here he was falling into the old
pattern—had he ever fallen out—of obliterating the form with all this
mush. "Don't you see," he went on, but less to me than to the wainscoting
that expertly caught the fronds of afternoon sun, "it never occured to me
they could have behaved differently. I took their rage and contempt—for
me, as the embodiment of their life—and impatience with my ministrations as the only conceivable approach to living and dying. It never
occured to me things could be different even if within the swamps of the
quotidian I am always proliferating alternatives..." He drifted off: I
wanted to shake him. Idiot, didn't he see this was exactly what I was
striving for—EXACTLY—to rid our life to come of prostration before
false irrevocability. So what, so what, if this discovery embodied one more
stark disjunction...between the monumentality of discovery and the
laughable exility of circumstances to which this discovery was supposedly

traceable. I wanted our story to be truly unique and contingency-free. And only by traversing its musculature from the very beginning and from all directions could I hope some day soon to wrest that story from its — our — depths. "With them reality always assumed a horribly monolithic color. And in fact this was not a real irrevocability: it was simply the flimsiest contingency sclerosed into a simulacrum of authentic necessity. And so you can understand," suddenly looking pointedly at me, "why I refuse to be gulled by hangers-on." Then he looked quickly away not so much. No. No. NOT SO MUCH to P as Q. Not so much. He looked quickly away not so much to soften the blow as far as my feelings were concerned as mitigate his own embarrassment, especially since this now reverberated as something Maggy might have hoped he would say at last to the shaggy little upstart come New York-wards with no other purpose than to separate them. It didn't matter. I thought back to what I had just discovered: Traversing the story's musculature was a wresting it from my depths. Traversal was a wresting. Getting up to pay the bill and walk out was simply a continuation of this turning away in mitigation of his own embarrassment. As we began walking in town I tried not to be literal in interpreting Jamm's remarks.

Just when I thought we were advancing properly into the future through the more than just good auspices of this sweetsmelling seaside town, centaurlike, positively centaurlike in its fusion of city-and country-best, just when I thought we were at last advancing into the future, ours, a story's future traced by a latent musculature comprising the simplest story elements: "When my father was on the verge of dying — " I stopped and stood still looking at an alley, making the stance or rather the transition to the stance — the stance OR RATHER the transition to the stance — stand for, Yes, or rather, Well, or better yet, So, or rather all of these at once and in sequence. "When my father was on the verge of dying or threatened to be dying soon I paced the hospital room, back and forth, back and forth, or rather, the corridor, or rather the not-so-distant extremity of the nurses' station, or rather the waiting room where the terminally ill in their wheelchairs, to revenge themselves at last on their oncologists, were busy diagnosing the landscape with the same lack of mercy experienced first hand under these charlatans' jowlets by their very own viscera — I paced paced paced searching for the authentic gesture capable of transforming me from imp to man. I clutched my scarf. For a split second I felt the electricity of the authentic running through my body. But apart from whatever was liberated in that gesture I felt no authentic grief for the old guy unless trying to evoke miscellaneous circumstances capable of inducing grief may serve in the last resort as symptom of authentic grief. But I doubt if you have ever been plagued by such problems." Meditation had unexpectedly washed him up on my shores. "You who are, above all, so eager to please."

In the course of the evening as we promenaded from bar to bar I pondered the question, no the theme, of this irrepressible eagerness to please, tried to invoke incidents explicitating so venal a trait. When Jamms went to the toilet I became more forthright with the other drinkers, saying, "Do I strike you as above all a creature eager to please." I was careful not to say man, a man eager to please, for that would have taken a brutal edge off the question and oriented me, mitigatingly, in another direction. No, I was a creature and nothing more nor less than a creature until further notice from Jamms. Yet the more I looked the trait, this eagerness to please, in the eye, for what was asking the opinion of these barflies but looking the trait dead in the eye, it vanished, no longer had any connection with me, it was only within the interstices of active investigation that it, the trait, germinated with any perseverance. Here I am again, trying to induce meaning.

At about three in the morning we left the bar, singing at what Jim wanted the world to know was the top of our lungs. For moments at a time, with the sea only the vaguest palpitation on my left, I was greedily, insanely, happy, hurriedly tried to reconcile myself to the fact that happiness for one such as I was a thing of seconds for which there could be no preparation, no legwork, nor, for that matter, any debilitating efforts to acquire what was too swift even to be undergone. Of course the acquiring, or the attempt to acquire, always came later when happiness had, to judge by the crepuscular mezzotinting of the heap of misgivings it left in its wake, distinctly receded. I strongly felt, again only for seconds at a time, that it was inconceivable he would ever again revert to any of them—mom, dad, the tumors, Maggy, Bessy, Grandfather Smallweed, and Pomegranate Pete, as well as the heap of unfinished canvases littering their apartment. In other words, my ecstasy was contingent on the fantasy of his never mentioning family and friends again . But as we reached a park adjacent to a schoolyard standing absolutely still he said, "I shouldn't be dancing. No, no, no, I shouldn't be *dancing*." At first I thought of saying the obvious but then I remembered the stark disjunctions with which our primrose path was doomed to be littered. So this was to be more of same, stark contrast—the starkest of contrasts—between what there was to see and what was heard. Maybe this protestation simply stifled an access of guilt for fleeting pleasure—detoxified as unlocalizable dancing—taken in the face of another's protracted dying. "You aren't dancing," I finally murmured, as if defending him from an accusation. "I am dancing and I shouldn't be dancing." Before I could repeat my consoling words in more than a murmur: "For when my dad was very ill—the first or second or fourth time—at any rate, *that other time*—the tumor of the moment almost prolapsed into his mulligatawny soup and even the servants—why even—turned from the spectacle with the amused outrage (and what was the target of outrage?) of expert prognosticians who are never—do you hear, never—wrong—when my dad was very ill mother called me up the next day or the day after that to announce, 'He's better. . .he's dancing.' And I instantly pictured, or tried to picture, him dancing. Or rather, his dancing, imposed itself on my field of vision craving approval or verdict YET UNBEKNOWNST TO ITSELF. It imposed itself on my field of vision craving verdict—the imposing itself *was* the craving of verdict— yet unbeknownst to itself. Or rather, I did not so much picture him, or rather, he, or rather his image, did not so much impose itself as I found that I could not quite wed her remark, divested of the usual lancinating ridicule where her consort was concerned, to an image in which patient/ consort could be made to figure prominently. Her comment, either in itself or because it came from her, did not quite glue to what it evoked. It rebounded from what it evoked. The words evoking recoiled from what they evoked or stopped dead in their tracks at sight of what they evoked. And here I am dancing—oh I see, I see," he mumbled laughing at the figure I cut against the backdrop of night. "You thought I felt guilty,with dancing standing in as sign of my having one hell of a good time. But I'm not having a good time, certainly not, how could I with somebody like you, and even if I were, which I am not, I have nothing to feel guilty about. No, no, no, dancing I feel suffocatingly indistinquishable from him—

dancing on his own grave, dancing against a judgement, against judgement day. I am sickened to allow myself to be caught off guard. Perhaps I wouldn't be sickened if all along dad had been a kind forgiving soul who never dreamed of ridiculing—worse, repudiating—the excesses of others. Instead in his own desperation to affirm his being—through dancing—he forgets how ceaselessly he gnawed at and girded the absurd little gestures of his fellow lazars. I am sickened at the thought that impersonating him I am becoming someone who allowed himself to be caught off guard. I prefer anything to this image of myself as him soliciting my judgement unbeknownst to himself—this image of myself as him as, in turn, some contestant blissfully unaware of the moment shortly falling due when he will be judged on, for, his very being. I prefer to remember him, if it comes to that, gasping with disgust at my repeated reappearances in the sickroom at the time of the ninth tumor—you remember, it was the reappearance in the face of his ineffectual malediction that was the abominable slight—I recurring yet always the same, he unchangingly fixed yet somehow always different—more prolapsed, more and more prolapsed, toward eternity, as it were. I prefer to remember him saying, concerning one of the many nurses who did not come up to his expectations, 'I fired that bitch: she refused to massage my groin.' For buoyed up by rage and disgust he does not UNBEKNOWNST TO HIMSELF impose his very self on my judging vision. And not imposing himself unbeknownst to himself he thereby shears me of the suffocation that results when having him at my mercy I am most at his mercy or rather at the mercy of a terrifying freedom in potency with respect to that lovable old codger."

I noted a policeman. Speaking politely, Jim added quickly and in an undertone: "Don't you see: I don't want to impersonate somebody who is now weak and worse, ends up embodying all those *he* ridiculed so mercilessly when they were delivered up to their little dance of hope before the jaundiced eye of his intolerance." We traveled and traveled and when we tired of traveling we traveled even more, forever athirst for new landscapes and in our thirst we ended up staggering back from a bar toward dawn, he cursing our camaraderie and the intermittent signs of irrepressible affection to which it had given rise. A policeman pursued but Jim parried pursuit beautifully I thought by muttering that the man bore no small resemblance to his father, the soon to be late-lamented and a policeman also, of sorts at least, and whom he had always admired far too fervently and to no avail since, here, look at his father and look at him. As we began speaking to the policeman I felt once again that Jim was at last beginning to abandon his easy reliance on reminiscence, or rather, reminiscence specimens, and to confront the bare bones of the form our story might take, policeman or no policeman. We found ourselves seated on a bench overlooking the pond. The pond gave no sign, all was blackness, but I knew the pond was there, I fed on that pond's deepest springs as we sat. The policeman trained his flashlight on us and I was forced to squint away the glare but still I saw no pond nor did I wish to. I trembled to think that Jim might go on to ruin this moment unique in our progress toward pure form by sputtering about dad or mom. Every time I turned around there he was dredging up golden moments of eternal boyhood as if the scene at hand miserably would sputter away and die without a reprise of such living breathing testimony. I tried to close my ears against the possibility of the old reminiscing tactic. But he surprised me. With this arm of the law's beam still upon us he drew his hand deep into his pocket, or, at any rate, into his pocket. *Deep into his pocket* belongs to a fully-formed story, which was not yet the case, our case, no, not by a long shot. I knew it must be wet for mine were wet and Jim had done far more splashing in the public fountains and puddles. Hadn't he been the one to leap after the newt head of a capsized streetlamp as it provokingly slithered up to his outrage and after a particularly scrawny oak leaf that somersaulting and gliding rasping refused to do the wind's bidding by folding up against itself like some lunatic bivalve. The policeman grew uneasy and began to gyrate his beam but something in Jim's distracted expression must have calmed him down for he subsided to a simple standing waiting and not at all in the way of somebody expecting an opposing gun to be drawn. On the back of what appeared to be a torn photograph I read: Dearest Freddie and Fredda: Congratulations. Much much love. Hope you and Patsie are as happy as Mdgy (sic) and me have been. Much love, Briggsy and LuLou. Jim completely disregarding the scrawl made haste to turn the photograph right side up. There was what had to be and therefore looked like mom and dad, momentarily tumorless, affectionately entwined, the sky above (no sky in sight) an incandescent blue. He extended it to the policeman as if there could be no truer asseveration of manliness, rectitude, manly rectitude, unimpeachable virility, and dutifulness, to say nothing of good citizenship, than this gesture. I mean, of course, not the gesture of Jamms, Sr., putting his arm around mamma Jamms for all the world to see, but rather that of Jim handing over the photo in which the exemplary flourish was consummated. Maybe initially he meant the true sign of manly rectitude and virile dutifulness to be incarnated in dad's tumorless thrust of affection and in nothing but, only somehow from its first incarnation it had managed to migrate to his very own gesture of graciously deploying another's—dad's—for the delectation of some onlooker. The policeman shook his head, then inveigled by a corner of his eye, found himself reluctantly raising the photo with his free hand to the level of, say, his forehead. I was not quite sure at this early date if we were once again being weighted down with miscellaneous imagery from somebody's past or whether this in fact was a purely heuristic excursion deep into the perils of reminiscence, a demonstration in other words of what at any cost to forswear in order to promote thereby a wider far manlier cause, namely, that of the story's progress detoxified in the here and now and at last of all detritus. The policeman becoming more and more visibly entranced by the transcendent beauty of this ideal couple I could feel Jim grow fidgety. He looked at or at least towards me as if sensing my intuition of the fidgets that, as the surf rose in our ears, threatened to undo him completely. "So," remarked the cop, "they are a beautiful pair. The mom and dad team, eh?" Jim did not answer. Or at least not in the conventional manner. With a flick of the fingers he whisked artwork out of the policeman's hand, waiting for the upshot. "When I gave you the photo," Jim began, and once again I apprehended we might very well be moving in the opposite direction from an authentic passage toward the story, I mean our story, I mean, the domain of our story, I mean, the form of our story, a story unutterable and unutterably new as a new day dawning on a stretch of suburban beach barren at last of impeccable torsos is new, "I was totally caught up in the offering. I was of course one with the offering and the photo did not exist insofar as it was not an extension of me, of my sinews, and only insofar as I was the photograph was I an irrefragable arbiter of high taste and visual music . But then—but then"—bad simulation of somebody gasping for breath — "as I saw you looking and looking and looking it became clear, Mr. Copper, that you did not or no longer wished to see the photo (or the accursed pair therein enshrined) as an extension, a mere and telling extension, of me, adscititious to my future glory, my adnexa as it were, my privates they, but rather as entities unto themselves with a diabolical life of their own in the last analysis far outshining mine: a dragoman's, a tout's, a pander's. And as I—I mean you—read their unabashed joy and I in turn read your robust deciphering of that joy that in fact needs no deciphering, does it? so pure and plain as day is it — as I read your decipherment I realized I was the mere handmaiden of their lordliness and they the true sovereigns. They were, for you, the heart of the heartland and I their abominable unspeakable purlieus to which only the most incorrigible recreants are consigned once they have run ragged the more inconsequential strategies of rehabilitation." He looked at me as if we were friends, true friends. I looked away from his look not, as he might think, embarrassed at so ravaged an eruption but only mildly irritated that once again we seemed to have lost our last chance to lay bare the musculature of our story. But there was no chance of a story with his introducing once again and at every turn these specimens chock full of turnabouts, torments, regrets, ecstasies. Maybe he simply fabricated these torments in order to kill all prospects for the future, which he saw solely as my future, and therefore worth killing. Our story was my future and so was it any wonder he reverted time and again to an invented past, his own . "She refused to massage my groin," Jim murmured. "Get a grip on yourself," said the cop. I thought he was speaking to me, reminding me of Jim's essential frailty: how could I be so cruel as to berate Jamms for the dissolution he underwent in the presence of the forbears he pretended casually to dismiss, whose relic he pretended even more casually to deface! Didn't I see that this spontaneous prostration before the unholy pair was the most virulent blow he was able to deal those who, like me, made the mistake of craving his presence. So that the prostration was at once spontaneous and constructed. Yet its constructedness was even more pitiable than its spontaneity. Yes, yes, yes, the cop's tone seemed to say, the flaunting of his prostrated frailty—going beyond mere inadequacy into a domain that mere inadequacy was helpless clinically speaking to subsume —is his most potent weapon against those who need his strength but a weapon ultimately most potent against himself. "You made a simple mistake — confiding in me, I mean," said the policeman. "Convert obstacle into opportunity." Jim looked as if this was the kind of phrase he might like to deride endlessly, shit upon with all the nihilistic verve at his disposal, and at the same time squat before in slavish devotion of disbelief stemming from the profoundest sense of unworthiness, saturated with the profoundest hunger to be, at last, worthy. As the cop put the gun back into his belt Jim suddenly came out with: "Obstacle into opportunity. Obstacle into opportunity. This situation — does it exist only because of my stupidity or — and — even so — is it a situation capable of shedding enlightenment. Even if I am rightly overwhelmed by the fatuity of the situation and all it reflects of my ineptitude in allowing it to develop — I'm talking about you, copper, and the photo, and this quasi derelict, and me, not much better, harassing this deserted suburban stretch of beach, midnight, summer; even if the situation redounds eternally to the debit of my futility, rather than compounding mishap — albeit self-induced — shouldn't I — I mean, should I? — try to learn from it, strengthen myself from it. But perhaps its ineptitude and futility are contagious and I am already infected and therefore completely disqualified for learning. In other words, is it — this ground of incident we all three are treading — the embodiment of global mishap anticipatorily canceling out all possibility of transcendence in self-correction or is there room still for the struggle of self-correction and incident-rectification which in turn permits the recapture of self-respect. Or is anything connected with the situation — all struggle in the domain of the situation — even its rectification inseparable from my own self-betterment — by definition a further compounding of what should never have been allowed to occur." The cop shrugged as if Jim was misreading his counsel or taking it far more seriously than he had intended it to be taken, having perhaps spewed it purely as the line to a good getaway.

I marveled at Jim's ability to have come up with a thought in response to the policeman's remark. This was the kind of thought I had hungered for up in Rhinebeck, one capable of inaugurating and expanding event beyond a dependence on units that were already seen, already heard, already known. I tried to focus on the way Jamms had joined his reply to the cop's exhortation as to most resinous wainscot and without subsequent warp. When the policeman was gone—I wanted him to stay—I called him back not once but several times though I had the distinct impression that calling him back into the situation would not be the same as prolonging it until, bereft at last of all props, human or otherwise, to say nothing of the unwanted ballast of reminiscence to which such props, human or otherwise, are prone—under which such props lay prone—until at last that situation disclosed its musculature. Calling him back into the situation would be to create a new situation where neither he nor Jim nor I could hope to be the same as once we were and thus no longer predictably stretching our essences to the breaking point because undistracted by new data. We were in short back at zero point. "I don't want him back," said Jim. "He makes me feel more lonely and inept than I really am." But I shut my ears against this introduction of self yet once more into the proceedings or absence of same as I would have shut my ears against a wavelet pretending to be a tidal bore submerging the local harbor.

A little later, at dawn, I was able to look back on the business of the photograph and the policeman and found myself accepting it less as superfetatory filigree thrown in the face of our story—our destiny—whether by the cop or my irrepressible companion and more as symptom of the story itself, even if of the story gone wrong, perhaps for good. In fact everywhere we went subsequently—to a cheap coffee shop, another, to the depot, to the beach for a last look at the waves and other ventifacts, to the pond now visible in the haze—it became a reference point as Jamms had compelled me to live my version of it somewhere nearby—at a point equidistant, say, from me, him, the policeman and some newt-headed lamppost copulating with a puddle. Now, away from it, as Jamms had lived and made me, differently, I needed to maintain, oh so differently, live it, for my living of the incident comprised in addition to its barest contour of transaction between a mamma's boy and a cop my deductions stashed away in and regarding that transaction's underbelly— now, away from it, it became our reference, our supreme reference point so far and though, strictly speaking, there could be nothing subsequent to—against—which rigorously or not so rigorously it could be applied paradigmatic it had become and a paradigm—universal and irrefragable it would remain.

For example, we entered some dive and before lifting the sugar

to his coffee Jim turned to me though already turned and quite seriously
said, "Do you think the way I lift this sugar is in keeping with the high
standard set by exposure of the overexposed photo—you know the one
I mean—to the copper way back there way back when." And I myself
promptly contracted this tic of referring all events, or rather those
amorphous shreds of vagabondage forever striving with all their absence
of heart and soul to accede to the sovereignty of event, to what was now
obliged to pass between us for event among events. So it will come as no
surprise that when I stood pissing in the back—unnaturally smelly even
for a depot dive—just below the sign—no window but a sign—declaring
that all employees had to wash their hands before returning to the even
smellier—I am sure it was not *even smellier* but the needs of the story—its
needs, that is, as perceived by the story itself—get in the way of truth—
to the even smellier kitchen—it will come as no surprise that I turned to
Jim, also pissing, though into another urinal, and said, "Do you think my
stance, or rather the trajectory of my stance, satisfactorily recalls the
trajectory of your photo as it passed from hand to hand, or rather, as it
went straight from your hands across the penumbra of the copper's steely
gaze?"

     What I really wanted was to inform him that the moment when
the photo passed from his hands to the copper's had seemed unnaturally
long. But I suspected he might retort that given the momentously
heuristic nature of the enterprise whose sole purpose, after all, was to
ensure that unlike him I need never complain of having been robbed and
in broad daylight of that most precious of all talismans—a specimen
conducing to rehabilitation at the hands of some third—given its heuristic
nature why was I complaining if the enterprise's crucial enactment had
been distended unnaturally. But then I could have retorted that I was
never aware—was never made aware—that the enterprise's heuristic
monumentality had been molded solely toward me as spectator, assimi-
lator, witness. I don't how he answered me ultimately for our train was
due any moment and he was clearly eager not to miss it, impatient to get
back to his studio with all these impressions garnered from our meagre
little expedition still intact. The trajectory of his piss seemed to imply that
he was content with the puniest of impressions while I, a mere supernu-
merary, had been vouchsafed the lion's share—a specimen, a specimen,

as it were, against time and place and the luminous yardstick against which all my future pratfalls were to be measured and thereby rectified, enriched. Sometimes, I mean, on the way out of the urinal, he reassured me about my specimen and sometimes, I mean, en route to the depot, he shrugged as if mocking such kindness, such conscientiousness—more than conscientiousness, his very being as ebbing fulguration of that primordial event, itself fulguration of some unlocalizable force fiercely exacting albeit through innumerable intermediaries its ration of awe—more than his very being, all of being, being's all. And sometimes he shrugged as if this ticlike referral of all subsequent events to the event primordial, the event acroamatic and at the same time profoundly fleshly, vulgar even, in its unrelenting allusion to hairy orifices guffawingly, bruisingly, plundered,—as if this tic had not been his invention but was on the contrary and after all an excrescence of my own foisted off with a minimum of preambling at every opportunity to the first comer always him—an almshouse strategy for deforming non-events, the meat and potatoes of my slovenly trek through other people's hinterlands, according to specifications of the same archetypal mould. All I wanted to remark and did not was that in his effort to exalt an idiosyncratic realism with its unnaturally distended enactments in behalf of the leisurely production of specimens that were to procure me, his apostle, a missionary vantage on his being as all of being identical with my own rehabilitation (noteworthy even if enacted at the margin of being)—in his effort to exalt an idiosyncratic realism in the service of specimen gestation, production, and acquisition he had given birth at fever pitch to nothing more than a new baroque of preternatural clarity. He might have believed that through this my ostensible obsession with the conformation of non-events to archetypal specifications latent, for example, in the passing of dogeared photo from hand to hand, I intended to make him ignore their—the non-events—intrinsic nullity as they went on, with or without his cooperation, to sketch the curve of our story. Or did he suspect that these incursions of torment over suspected infidelity of non-events to such specifications were little more than an usurpation of the place rightfully reserved for the priority—more than priority, ubiquity—of his reminiscences, the tumor-laden invocations of hospital corridors, terminal wards. So much for the shrug of a Jamms.

On the road back he seemed abnormally preoccupied. Damn the tumor-laden anecdotes, I muttered. In the phrase I discovered the unity of his anecdotes, I decreed that unity. But its discovery could be peddled — and to whom? — only as a repudiation of, revulsion at, that unity. Otherwise the discovery was not theatrically valid, undergoable to the avidity, or at least susceptibility, of some third, the third in search of, athirst for, our story. He spoke of Maggy and then when he had finished with Maggy he reverted to the fairer Bessy but of neither did he warble with any spontaneity but rather with a truculent challenge daring me to locate the source and target of its coercedness. I suddenly felt I had far better things to do than get to the root of his compulsion and looked to the landscape for succor, to the smokestacks, banks, houses of worship, tiny figures prostrate beneath the flagless flagpoles big with shadow, supermarket carts on asphalt parking patches, all the detritus, in short, of technologically able America: all this served me only too well as an alternative to the chaos Jim induced. Unlike him, I told myself, I was no enemy of what the man on the street rightly takes for progress. The blue and virginal sky of Soho had, in my absence, arrived at an equable living arrangement with the rows upon rows of impeccably reconstituted brownstones that had managed, also in my absence, to appropriate a bit of its pastureland. Jim showed no interest: he was intent on getting back to Maggy and Bessy in Rhinebeck. He looked absently into cafes, birdshops, playgrounds, bookstores, thinking or at least talking only of the two women and of their plans for the winter. It was at the corner of Prince and Broadway — he didn't want to stop in a delightful looking café full, as he made haste to explain, less of artists than of artist-types yet far more interesting did they appear, at least to me, than whatever might be touted as the real thing — as I was saying goodbye that Jamms and perforce I ran into Lou Testic, whose vigorous handshake and clucking jowls claimed him as an old pal. Testic stared at me but with no control over stare's intensity and duration. His stare was more than an appraisal: in his stare he took leave of himself and, unsuccessfully, strove to grapple with the eternal problem of why something, in this case me, from nothing. I bore the stare by not acknowledging, much less returning it. When Testic finally turned away I trained my gaze upon him less in reproach than — LESS A THAN B —

    less in reproach

    than as a

belated quizzical bracketing
of such boorish importunity. It was for Jamms's benefit: to demonstrate
how tactful and astute I could be. He noticed nothing. Although the brief
meeting was torture I felt as soon as it was over that my reversion to it as
torture, pure torture, rang false, was in excess of the facts as retrospect
now defanged them. To refer to the meeting as torture was to defer too
much to the storymaking vein.

We walked a short distance away from the cafe´—its original
habitués preempted by the flabbiest of bourgeois poseurs, as Jim put it
or should have put it—and as we bid each other goodbye something
prompted me to speak with panic of the very real danger of my money
running out. Jim laughed and said, like Lou Testic he had a very safe safe-
deposit up on Seventy-second and Lexington simply bulging with jewels
his mother would never even begin to know she was missing. The key was
on his chain, he added. Just then, at my most despairing and wretched
when I could positively taste self-loathing on the tip of my tongue and
with no Jamms to distract me with his unpredictable shifts in the
inflection of disdain, a man coming up and asking the direction of the
World Trade Center—couldn't he see it looming at the end of the clotted
vista of this—of no doubt any number of sidestreets?—I dutifully
pointed, unsmiling, sublimely speechless, yet in that gesture of giving
solicited help and wanting (needing and demanding) nothing in return
achieved a momentary hopefulness or a calm beyond hope. But after a
certain point—long before—no, not long before even if the story's
publicists are busy clamoring for such—a declamatory—an hyperbolic
emphasis—a little before—long before—the solicitor vanished from
sight—this momentary hum of hope gave way to the old panic for I could
already feel it numbing me—feel it numbing me!—to a thirst for the skill
to win Jim back. Ah! delicate perceptions, ah! delicate shifts as one
feeling breeds its contrary, ostensible contrary. Were these shifts in the
service of the story?

I went into a delicatessen, an old-style delicatessen in the heart of
this heartless Soho, where the fat old server said, "What will you have,
son," transforming through *son*, through *son* transforming my flab of preoccupation into something forthright, buoyishly virile, unintriguing and

unabashedly young and hopeful. So here I was rebounding to hope once again yet debouching on its sunny plaza from a slightly different angle. In brief, the word as applied to the sore that was I—nobody's son—washed away all its purulence engendered not so much by Jamms as by "proximity to the likes of Jamms," a phenomenon of a completely different order, vastly different, vaster than vast. As I began to eat my candy bar at one of three asphalt chess tables adjacent to a playground it no longer seemed a bad idea to ride out to Rhinebeck and tell Jim straight off—now that I was buoyed up by having been called *son* and having given directions without disclosing the slightest trace of my overweening and ubiquitous anticipation of a little something vast in return—that we simply could not continue having me actively wishing to construct our story and him at the merest sign of that activity struggling to make me lap up the detritus of some anecdote. I no longer wanted to be fed these scraps, did he hear. I wanted to chart a scrapless forging ahead. Now even the justly celebrated encounter with the policeman had become a scrap in the flow, in the absence of flow. Perhaps I had overrun it with anxiety before it could develop into something far more than an irrelevance. But it was unclear to me of what anxiety I was speaking—anxiety native to the event itself unfolding or that inseparable from—identical with—though by no means compossible with looking back, or rather—OR RATHER

        OR RATHER—

        , the hunger to look back,
at event over and done with and no longer enactable. Yet I had not been the sole participant in the event and so could not be held solely responsible for having spoiled it or rendered it illegible. Jim after all had also participated, far more in fact than I, to say nothing of that cop forever dwindling into the distance of a job well done. But on and on I went, berating myself for having played so foully for—with—the omnipotence/omniscience granted me and me alone toward its shaping by the event itself. Unlocalizable and supererogatory anxiety during and after and over the event, this was what I eagerly and as if by divine decree mistook for the governing omnipotence/omniscience I now wished at all cost to slough. But omnipotence/omniscience, even the retroactive variety, is no easy thing to slough. If only it hadn't led me oh so rashly to label it, the event, Encounter with a cop, or, The cop's sarabande, and instead

magisterially taking a back seat had permitted it, the event, to furcate, ramify, expand far beyond what it had seemed to comprise as perpetual paradigm even if monumentally and maximally. If only my governing ramifying omnipotence/ omniscience had not been tempted to label it, the event, or rather—or rather—

OR RATHER—

its amorphous fissioning precursor, thereby extinguishing it forever: Perpetual Paradigm. But how could I have stopped, how stop, myself from labeling and thereby procuring two doom-haunted drifters their ration of signpost and fulcrum, foothold and belay, even if one or both craved nothing better than to plunge to their eternal bliss unpivoted.

Suddenly seeing a pimp strut with blond teenage mare into the corner pizzeria bypassed in favor of a candy bar I could not help feeling that whatever had transpired between cop, photo, and Jamms was not paradigmatic at all and could have unfolded in some other, infinitely more forward-propelled manner. Suddenly this was a paradigm that could be applied to nothing around: a host of events had emerged no longer susceptible to its lesson. And so what loosely could be characterized as the paradigm bit seemed, in retrospect, vastly overrated and straightforwardly reducible to our, his and my, way of consoling, more than consoling, eulogizing ourselves, for coming up with something—anything only in the most elementary sense memorable, on frighteningly foreign soil. So much for the paradigm bit between the teeth. As the blond mare disappeared it occurred to me the event might have furcated in such a way as to end up having absolutely nothing to do with such penury-ridden props as policemen, beaches public and litter-strewn, photos, tumor-laden honeymoons. As it stood it, and we, were doomed. Walking a little distance toward the river amid houses (sedate erection-date plaques glued to their ruddy cheeks) looking as if they were positively foaming at their bays to be photographed, front, back, and sideways, I painfully tried to isolate that moment when Jim extended the photo to the cop and the cop in turn became appropriately mesmerized. I called up that moment but it was too too excruciating. For calling up the moment implied that such a moment was not yet a fait accompli. Calling up the moment of the photo changing hands was to toy with the highly serious — might I say even the complex—notion of its reversibility, destructibility.

The photo's changing hands was somewhat up in the air, contingent on a host of factors still to come—to be coaxed forward like reluctant witnesses to arson. Calling up the moment of the photo's changing hands pointed to my glaring fallibility, its lexicon of my ineptitudes, specifically those connected with staving off the noxious, the flagitious. But at the same time—I wanted to take counsel of the river on this matter—so much—too much—anguish had already been conscientiously invested in foreseeing, in other words, ushering in, the interminable catastrophe signified by this event for me to try my hand at eradicating it. I could no longer conceive of eradicating it, the event, I was too much bound to the pain it induced, as much as that pain was unendurable especially when I thought of the chores, tasks, and drudgeries certain to ensue from such a simple fact—that a photo of appalling uniqueness had managed to change hands in the presence of bystanders. As much as the pain excruciated, being suddenly divested of its momentum smelled even more noisome than the event that had unleashed it on my little world.

I stopped in my tracks. I was not far from the river. Where had all this babble about pain come from. There was no pain. Babble about pain stank of theatrical self-aggrandizement. There was no pain: there was only opportunism alert for yet another radical disjunction, in this case between what had been undergone—a perfectly harmless little episode—and the wealth of emotion to which it was claimed that mercilessly it had given rise. There was no pain, there was no suffering, there was no consternation, there was only a harmless little event dehiscing its harmless little packet of meaning or absence of meaning, there was only a radical disjunction—yet another radical disjunction being foisted on the world—between what the event meant or failed to mean and what it was being made, through the ostensible enormity of in fact sleekly synthesized repercussion, to mean. Here I was following in the footsteps of Jamms, casting off story in the name of radical disjunctions. And yet...and yet...mightn't this eagerly lacerating self-exposure camouflage something deeper, more excruciating, than insensibility, namely, terrible pain, terrible agony, *undergone by somebody* , as a result of all that was dredged up by that old chestnut, the photo changing hands.

I tried to abstract from the event of the photo changing hands. I tried to abstract from *the event changing hands*. If only I could manage to excise some sneering condemnatory presence, not necessarily my own, hovering in the background not so much of the event as of my universal passivity in the face of that event's unfolding, then I might be freed at last of the lacerating ambivalence I was loaning more and more ungraciously to this presence, this witness. If only this witness witnessing my witnessing of the photo changing hands would go away, yet where was it located, for it was this witness, this witnessing, that underscored and overran and augmented —yea, augmented—the scandalousness of my standing still and doing nothing in the face of such an event. But of course there was always the very real possibility that in speaking of the event as "such an event"—in peddling so laughable a miniature as "such an event"—I was merely after a radical disjunction...between what the event was and what I was trying to create it as being knowing all the time I was failing yet delighting in the broad farcical starkness of the failing, as proof that I was infinitely superior to the event as target of pain and infinitely susceptibile to its triviality as the stuff of mock-epic, of ventifact decorative to the extent that it was substanceless.

But what did I want with a radical disjunction. I was not Jamms. Yet maybe by saying, I am not Jamms, it will be thought I am peddling a gradual takeover by the spirit of Jamms, resisted because craved and prolific of disclaimers hungry for dismissal. But I am not Jamms—yet. As I neared the street before the river—although it occurred nowhere near the street before the river—it was allegiance to the story that was not yet born drove me to pick up again what I hoped would become its threads— shreds into threads, that has always been my motto, at least as of this moment—as I neared the street before the river it came to me that somewhere along the line—somewhere along the zigzag—I no longer had been talking about the passing of the photo from Jim to cop and back again. Another event still unidentified had taken its place. And so whatever anguish I was now pouring out against the event was not supererogatorily in the service of a radical disjunction aiming at obliterating the story-to-be or on the contrary hoping ultimately to become a humble link in the chain of that story-to-be—whatever anguish I was now pouring out was perfectly congruent with its target, some other event, still to be identified. Perhaps it was the prospect of finding myself soon without money—of which event I had begun to speak on the streetcorner as I bid Jim a fond adieu. But what better way to wreak havoc on a truly terrifying event than to displace the anguish incontestably due to it onto some neighboring event with not the slightest capacity to terrorize. And wasn't I in fact rendering a service since as a result of this dastardly displacement somebody somewhere was bound to feel disoriented beyond the remotest possibility of topographic — signpostly — succor. And mightn't such disorientation for some such somebody somewhere suddenly nowhere be the key to authentic maturation, in other words, a treacly "growing old with the story." The passing of the photo from the cop to Jamms or from Jamms to the cop meant absolutely nothing. I had seized upon it as a screen for deeper considerations less susceptible perhaps to such vivid depiction. And on a suburban beach no less.

In spite of this declaration I could not help going back NOT SO MUCH to

not so much to the beach scene as to
AS TO

the witness invisibly hovering to underscore and overrun the scandalousness of my standing still in the face of so momentous an event. For in the presence of this witness — was it Jamms, Sr., mamma Jamms, his tumor, hers, Doctor Scotoma — what was done within the event, to and beyond the photo, became a doing only to me, a doing unto me, a doing over which I had no control. The more I recoiled the more for this sneering witness I was done to. In the presence of this sneering witness I had no substantive relation to the event and derived no profit from its unfolding — a flagrancy, that, *but only in relation to me*, or rather

OR RATHER

to my standing still — except insofar as to be undone and stripped bare and flogged by its uncanny resonance constituted profit. I dreamed of being free of the witness, of doing away with *it*, though I dimly perceived that having lent it my soul as I had, the soul of torment, of course, surely it would soon enough find some other carnivorous hump on which to alight should this big bird see fit to release it from its beak. In the presence of a witness — on the way to the river, on the way to the last street before the river — the event caught me with my pants down, became those pants down amid so many others bystanding and well-dressed. In the presence of a witness, this thirteenth at table, the caption for the event became:

How could this happen to you, or, Why should this happen to you among so many other plumper victims. This witness clearly had a hunger to beat the dead horse of my having been gratuitously marked for danger. And by an event that was a mere displacement from the true source of truest terror. I wanted to cry out—on the way to the river, always on the way to the river, with Jim on his way back to Rhinebeck and the newly exhumed Testic a seedy searing blot in my mind's eye—this witness—this third, fourth, or nineteenth at table—I wanted to cry out—had simply ruined the event for me, no matter which event, all events are the same but I knew that it was I lending to this fourth, ninth, or ninetieth—this imperturbable witness—the power to hover and in hovering ruin.

I tried to isolate that very moment when Jamms, big with event, passed, no extended, the photo to the cop and the cop had been suitably mesmerized. How it had all proceeded without a lapse! suddenly I needed it to have proceeded without lapse so that I might to the sneering witness, still dogging my steps, oppose this ode to pure continuity, proving thereby—again to the witness, sneering less—that there had been no moment when my vigilance lapsed. Always with my eye on the ball there was no reason I deserved to be punished. I was still not sure I had been punished by this or any event. But the hovering witness on the beach suggested—convinced me—that I had indeed been punished. Somewhere in relation to me the flow of the event, continuous or intermittent, had been—had exacted—a perduring punishment, river or no river. Always I had had my eye on the ball. Or had there been a moment big with pretermission. Still, I could recuperate, omittance is no quittance.

But even if I made up for the lapse in vigilance could the punishment noted and delectatingly abominated by the hovering witness ever be annulled. Unless the hovering witness was not to be taken seriously. Perhaps the hovering witness—the unlikely ninth, tenth, or twelfth—was the being to whom Jim had had every intention of bringing his specimen of raging shame and shamed rage before, that is, Maggy through her squalidly good intentions had robbed him of this quintessential once in a lifetime opportunity to undergo definitive rehabilitation (through vociferous supervised scrutiny of said specimen). Yet I could not help feeling—on my way to the river, on my way to the river—that this conflation of the hovering witness with Jamms's hovering rehabilitator was nothing more than a feeble effort to interweave and reinforce strands of a story that still gave no signs of being on the verge of coming to birth. Allusion to one phantom at the time of another's instauration plausibilized neither.

After the event I had traipsed behind as we made our staggering way toward another part of the beach. Every now and then he turned to stare me down with scorn as the waves hit the pebbles. Yet at the same time I sensed that he was relieved to know I was bringing up the rear of his instability. But didn't he realize that my traipsing behind, always at the same fixed distance, had nothing to do with enthusiasm for him, for his cause, for his tumor-laden mom and dad. Always maintained at the same distance from my wary steps he was quickly cancelled out and all that mattered now — I mean, then — for now I am en route to the river — all that mattered then — for both of us — was the endpoint he was bound to achieve even if there was none in sight as yet. I was tracking behind and ultimately beyond what he took to be his destiny toward — the story that, contrary to the preconceptions of his arrogant volubility, had nothing whatsoever — well, perhaps not *nothing whatsoever* all protests of my story-mongering artisans notwithstanding — to do with moms and dads, hospital rooms, arrogant oncologists, prissy nursemarms, myopic family practitioners. I saw for, beyond, him. All during our journey — before, during, and after the cop — he would typically introduce me to a seeing, war of sand and surf, say, and then just as I was catching on — to the unison of the elements — following the trajectory of a wavelet back to its source as a light went on in a shed somewhere above or below — he would be gone, obliging me to carry on alone, carry on the seeing, that is, that once inaugurating he had disdained to live. For he was always dying, this Jim, this dad's son, to the phenomena he induced. Always dying to the events he either brought to birth or had the perspicacity to catch in their first flush. But in so dying he salvaged those events for me. But what was I doing with those events, even now. So there was Jim, trying to find his way home and scattering story shreds all down the route in the name of our reconnoitering but in fact completely disorienting the needed strict attention to relevant detail that might ultimately serve. When would he learn that these ostensible signposts — wavelets retreating to or from their source, gulls alighting on their own shadows, to say nothing of the

inevitable hospitals, tumors, moms, dads, Maggies, Bessies, space between the Maggies and Bessies — simply did not apply, were not strengthen-
ers of the task then at hand which was to find our way back to the depot
in time for the early morning train — which task only a halfwit like me
would attempt to assimilate to the story-building task — were not prosthetic to our endeavors, were so much sand thrown in the eyes of the true
details, track, story, destiny, which, I might ultimately discover, was
beatifically detail-free. But perhaps this was the function of the scraps,
namely, to throw sand in the face of the real details, the real absence of
details, so that they might go on unmolested in their quest for interrelation. I looked around, down and beyond the street's clogged vistas to the
World Trade Center. Hungrily I wanted to assimilate the space between
me and those woolly mammoths before Jim, for example, could over—
populate it with more family anecdotes. But Jim was nowhere in sight.
Nevertheless I sensed this intervening space would be crucial someday
soon to the story. I wanted to know every crevice and cranny in this
intervening space terminating in the towers. The very air fascinated me.
I wanted to get a head start on assimilation of that space — the space — I
was sure of it — of our drama to come before Jim reintroduced himself or
I managed to have him reintroduce himself into that space thereby
incapacitating me for the stolid joys of inventory and acquisition. I
wanted to get a head start on assimilating that space before incident
descended — was visited — on that space — before I, one of the protago-
nists, was sucked into that space and transformed beyond repair. For I
knew, I knew, I knew, this space of several blocks between the little
playground on Spring Street and the overweening hills of the World
Trade was about to figure toweringly— abominably—in the life to come,
the story life, the life inside the story of the story. Yet stranded with Jim,
even if Jim was not here right now, in the playground of our undenumer-
able adventures there was automatically—I should have known better—
no adequate comprehension of that space officially deconsecrated for the
prosecution of our endeavors prior to the onset of those endeavors. For
this was to be the space of our endeavor, I was sure of it, this patch of turf
bounded roughly by Chambers to the south, Spring Street to the north,
Hudson to the west and Broadway to the east. Nevertheless revelation of
this our space, riddled with caltrops and false starts and miraculous

recoveries, would be simultaneous, alas, only with whatever we were willing in the way of event to enact in that space, fathomable, it was suddenly clear, only through event, say, for example, the transduction of family photo from gift to curse. There was no getting a head start on the shared torments to come by lapping up the splinters of the dormant topography set aside for the deployment of those torments—at this moment dormant even if from my anticipatory point of view ostensta- tiously, even flagrantly, alive with bumps, troughs, sharp edges, riparian laughter. There was no living the space of our story without first colliding with Jim—even if ultimately collision ensued only from his absolute refusal to proceed with, in, the space of the story— and with all the objects he chose to abandon—failed targets of collision to be rehabilitated toward inclusion in our story once he could be made to see things my—rather, the story's—way. So there was nothing left to me for the present but to live out each moment—on the way to the river, on the way to the river—as a void, a placeholder, rebarbative to the simultaneity of space and event, event and space, each feeding off the other, glued each to the other, exhausting each other, wringing each other dry. The space was and would remain unreal for all my seemingly successful efforts right here and now at inventory—here a blackbird, there a playground, here a rind of pizza, there a rump defaced by the capitalistic ethic—here a mother pushing her stroller, there a derelict contemplating the empty squares on the playground chess table. There would always be something to elude me in the landscape until Jim returned and our conflict resumed and that something might very well turn out to be the key, the pivot, better yet the necessary scotoma in the eye of event, of story scheduled for our likes. Under these controlled conditions, inventory could never achieve mas- tery of space, was at best a half-assed dress rehearsal for a beggar's opera of masturbatory prophylaxis. I was tempted not to continue in the direction of the river and run back to the hotel. No, no, no. Even if I could not examine the environs with a view toward mastering their miscellany I could sit still and bathe in that strange protracted glowering twilight of late spring, revelling in my impotence as it were. Sitting still and declaring that I hadn't the faintest idea what objects, what shreds, would ultimately prove crucial to our story—what tenement, if any; what dentist masquer- ading as a consumptive sculptor, if any—I would surely put myself in a strange kind of collusion with the landscape I was no longer attempting to wear down to the sum of its parts. I did sit still, then I walked a little further in the glow, but no longer toward the river, and it is a telling commentary on the extent of a self-loathing that was perhaps my one consuming passion that I took this simple — perhaps the very simplest — affirmation of my being for the most flagrant, unholiest and most arrogant challenge to the well being of all things around me. Simply by refusing — by not feeling overwhelmingly compelled — to add up the landscape I felt as if I was leering at my comrades in being.

I want to say that for the first time I began to understand Jim's hunger for anecdotes capable of sabotaging the story. Only I don't know if it is I speaking or the story-to-be prompting me to so speak — understandably, of course, since stories feed on exactly such meanings as I am sketching — flirting with — when I say, For the first time I began to understand Jim's hunger... For the statement implies that I am slowly turning into Jim, that the collocation of bodies breeds metamorphosis of one into the other, which metamorphosis triumphantly if skulkingly proclaims the frailty of that thing we call identity. So I cannot say that sitting in — colluding with — the glowering twilight I *actually* began to understand Jim's hunger as the beginning of my own infection by that hunger. And even if I genuinely began to understand because similarly infected I don't know if I particularly like this state of affairs and want it to expand encroaching on the story itself.

On a sidestreet I was caught by the slender space between two buildings.

NO.

NOT SO MUCH

No

by that space

AS BY

the almost windowless walls defining that space

NO

OR RATHER

NO NO NO

not so much by the walls (though their texture in waxing sun filled me with undefinable misgiving)

AS BY

NO

one tiny window whose outstretched hinged protruding pane cast a shadow *all out of proportion* (though by whose decree) to its own dimensions.

NO NO NO

I could not help feeling that this attachment to the slender space was being made to serve the same purpose as Jim's monologues in the face of the story. The slender space between tenements is the poor man's wealth of anecdote and yet ON SOME LEVEL I could not help feeling too that this discernment of the space and its doings was infinitely richer than Jim's ostensible plethora. For a split second I was armed with the shadow as with a scythe but then the connectedness died and I was left once again though of course differently with a premonition of the story—perhaps of its emergence, perhaps of its eternal failure to emerge—as embodied (the story, not the premonition, though perhaps that, too) in the glowering twilight. The story was already definitively born, or was to be born, or never would be born. Was there a story already and did it date, perhaps, from that moment when he handed the policeman the photo of mom and dad embracing under the fronds of an Indian summer. And if there was a story was it our story or was it a story that derived most of its strength from bypassing me. And if it was our story did this mean he, Jamms, was in the story. Or was he merely a kind of grey eminence allowing for the possibility of the story's unfolding so that in a sense he was far more crucial to the story than any of the bona fide characters parasitizing its meagre strength, why meagre. Or was Jamms our only representative in the story so dearly bought with me a mere fly on the margin, forever presenting myself as a supplicant to the story's maw, living in the hope of ultimate if belated admission to its penetralia—its naos—its cella— even if that admission meant suffocating immersion in a progression developed and developing far beyond the powers of any supplicant— however consecrated—to assimilate. I sat down near a pizza bone, sipped my soft drink thinking the best thing was to resign myself to the story but as Jamms's story alone—to Jamms's entrenchment in the story as his alone because it was forcing him alone, so he thought, so we both thought, as of this moment, that is, to widen his contours as it, the story, went its

merry way deviating from the all-too-typical story codified by centuries
of large-scale production and to opium dreams of whose unfolding I had
been up to this minute ravenously addicted. So he was knee-deep—or
perhaps only striving to be knee-deep—in a story other than—different
from—the one I had warmly anticipated as my due—our due—though
still with its alternative norms and strictures for surely Jim was not so
benightedly arrogant to imagine that this newfangled contraption into
whose troughs and raphes I was seeking admission in vain could get along
without strictures, without norms. So my life was not coming to an end.
Jim Jamms, as it was turning out here in the glowering twilight, did not
hate stories per se, he simply craved a story managing to devitalizingly
deviate at every turn from those norms and strictures for so long
interwoven into the large-scale production of stories championed by the
likes of me. This was why he had all along been bombarding me with
tumors: fear of the story served up in its mold thickened by centuries. So
that it was now my job to accept him entrenched in his newfound story
while steering him clear of too faithful an adherence to its alternative
norms and strictures which, although giving off an expert whiff of total
absence of norm and stricture, must only straitjacket him as the puppet
of its own whims and quirks. Whether or not he knew it, he, Jim Jamms,
living his story while delectating over my havenlessness, had been visited
with another set of norms. No story without norms. Yet here he was—I
could see him, situated somewhere between the Twin Towers and the
corner pizzeria beginning to fill up—parading around as if straitjacket-
free. Here he was, for all his posturing in defiance of my straitjacketed-
ness, straitjacketed equivalently, even

NO

NO NO NO EVEN MORE VIRULENTLY

even more virulently AS IT TURNED OUT

as I was making it turn out here in the glowering twilight. Was this, the
even more virulently, an outburst chocked full of authentic conviction or the
work once again of the story-and meaning-mongers leaving no stone
unturned in their campaign of old age, for a fastness as impregnable as
death, some machicolated oubliette reinforced with all the twists and
turns of anagnorisis and peripety so dear to their grandmas. So here he
was, Jamms straitjacketed equivalently, even

NO

even

more

virulently. Still I wondered what compelled me to say: even more virulently. Clearly no authentic feeling or datum from abroad nor prompting from evil-minded story-or meaning-monger. Simply the flow of the
thought itself struggling to escape its own desert clarity.

  Jim was, I was sure, convinced that he would never permit
himself to be force-fed meaning by the story of his dreams. In contradistinction to his parasite who surely knew what it was to be force-fed such
chunks of meaning. But to be ably alert in identifying those instances of
encroachment when said mongers were prone to speak through my being
as if it *was* my being thereby mangling thoughts and feelings, feelings and
thoughts, into a sour conformity with what they bluntly deemed good for
the story—good for the business of the story—surely this implied a
reserve of strength and subtlety vouchsafed to very few. The story-and
meaning-mongers had, so they thought, the best interests of the story at
heart but these were, alas, the interests of a large-scale production
accessible and acceptable to the appetites of large-scale audiences absolutely sure even before they walk(ed) in the door and took a seat what
they wanted and were by God entitled to in the way of meaning. These
audiences have a hearty appetite for meaning but meaning of a certain
kind: the lowest form of meaning, meaning whose meaning has already
been wrung dry too many times over by superannuated meaning machines themselves wrung dry by "talk" shows and sciolist tabloids.
Looking back sadly I saw this was the kind of meaning my story would
have been encouraged to absorb at an alarming rate. But now I had a new
task via a new story, a new kind of story—namely, to be Jamm's Palin-
urus,—to steer him clear of imagining he was completely manumitted
from the autoclave of norm-and-stricture engendered meaning and
thereby making the biggest imaginable jackass of himself. As long as he
was alert to the pitfalls of norm—stricture—meaning he could avoid
becoming their slave.

  So exhilarated did I feel as a result of his—his story's—his new
story's—need for my services—my tempering influence—I wanted to
run right out to Rhinebeck in quest of...specimens of that need. All right

he had found a story, a new story, a story that laid the siege of my story to scorn, a story that nourished itself on contempt for my kind of story. However, he could never hope to be—to achieve—anything within the precincts of that story without the ministrations of a tenderness such as only I could furnish and capable of alerting and reconciling him to the serpentine strictures actively circulating within those precincts, ostensibly stricture-free. But something held me back, fear of Maggy perhaps, I knew she loathed me, Bessy too, but differently, less personally, more as she might have loathed—or rather,

OR RATHER

sidestepped—a treetrunk defunct or deformed. In the case of Bessy indifference was stronger than loathing but Maggy truly loathed me and even if she did not necessarily loathe me per se she was still big with loathing—of an adjacent being her jealousy constructed without benefit of raw materials and that was no less real for being her construction.

On my way back to the hotel I, big with meaning, dizzy with the succession of meanings that had assaulted me so superabundantly in the last half hour—the only cure for sclerosis through susceptibility to the meanings peddled by the meaning-and story-mongers, enemies of head and heart, is dizzying acceleration of the pace of the peddling—was accosted, still in broad daylight, by someone trying to sell, or rather rid himself, of a roast leg of lamb still frozen. He obtruded the remains of the beast in my direction, it touched me, in a split second and for the same interval I was convinced of infection. Then I recovered myself. And once again—as with the passing of the photo from hand to hand, which was after all only a displacement from another event, true target of frenzy and horror—I played back the moment just before contamination when it had still been up to me to forfend its onslaught.

The hotel clerk gave me a letter from Mrs. Jamms, her husband was apparently deathly ill yet there was no indication from her vibrant and imperious hand that I was no longer on the payroll or she intent on washing her hands of my well-being since that well-being ultimately was Jim's. I read the letter over and over in the dining room. After a long day's wandering I was sitting high above the city in one of the most expensive restaurants in one of its most expensive hotels. Emboldened by a not quite frantic sense of time running out I managed to muster the courage to ask for a table not quite so near the bar traffic as the one the hostess, more appraising than smiling, had immediately wanted to foist off on what was obviously the quintessential bad investment. In front of me [as if we were all world- , or, to use the expression presently favored by those who must at all cost be thought of as on the cutting edge — of nullity, world-class travelers languorously repaired to the imperial dining car of the Orient Express] sat the obligatory middle-class couple at this very moment in the process of being simperingly solicited by waiter or busboy or maitre d' — at any rate, someone purposefully, emblematically, *of another race* — for their approval [appropriate presentational gesture] of the wine. After monsieur deigned to comply, madame, a hefty article, arising with exaggerated daintiness struggled to dumbshow exaggerated grateful surprise when the adjunct hostess, also of another race, pulled back her chair. Recalling the signs and posters grossly visible in the lobby I realized some recondite medical subspecialty must be holding its sesquicentennial convention here and that no doubt this was the better half of one of its worthies. I paid them no further attention, in order to concentrate on soothingly insentient things. I looked down, down, down, to the city below, past the bar's inflamed zinc and its mirrors, past the fulsome insinuation of the "live," in contradistinction to..., entertainment. Be-mused vivacious thanks of the fat woman returning once more to her seat opposite wine-connoisseur spouse as sub-hostess from yet another other race pulls back her seat. Turning my head slightly — to escape — to deny ever having witnessed the fat lady's return — for hadn't I just vowed to consecrate myself exclusively henceforth to insentient things, the insen-sate ways of the big city in its first tender flush of evening — I observed a door ajar on what appeared to be an exquisitely appointed banquet room where a middle-aged man in T-shirt and jockey shorts was pensively vacuuming under one of its three — four — seven lambrequined tables. I looked away from the vacuum-cleaner wielder but not in the way I had just looked away from the fat lady's dainty return roseate with fake gratitude and fake surprise for yet another unfortunate hireling's bland and expedient surrender to grand hotel protocol. I had just turned from the wielder not in disgust but simply because I had noticed without noticing him — couldn't conceive of him as part and parcel of this land-scape, this scheme of things: he had bodied forth a flash of visual static.

Suddenly there was a rush of blood to my pate, still and stupidly unbald: the meaning-mongers, akin to this group of medical specialists running the hotel staff ragged in their *unquenchable eagerness to be apprised of the latest developments in the field,* were returning to *their* convention site swollen with that penury of insight and imprecation—insight as imprecation—acquirable as a rule only in men's rooms or at salad bars. For it was NO

> NO NO
> clear NO
> it was NO clear NO

at least according to the meaning-mongers and their dainty wives NO at least NO according to the meaning-mongers and their hefty wives that I had always been too busy disqualifying crucial details—specimens— simply because they did not appear to fit whatever ensemble of the moment I happened to be—servilely—investing with more exquisite homogeneity than was, to the practiced eye, warranted. And wasn't this NO

> the case NO
> the case YES
> not only in the domain of decor NO NO NO

but on the moral—the ethical NO—plane as well. Yes, I was failing and would continue to fail with Jim and the Jammses and with the story itself because in my arcane and futile fastidiousness—my cockering credulity with respect to any scene, ensemble, glowering perspective that managed to pander to a well-nigh inexhaustible talent for misjudgment—I was always striving—again in behalf of that scene, ensemble, perspective— to eliminate whatever middens-like intruders could be relied upon to perturb a perfectly celestial consilience of parts more than anything akin to music.

Not true, couldn't be true, had no relation to me even if it was I thinking it, this thought chocked full of meaning, transliterating it for the all too typically indecipherable meaning-mongers and their wives, Beth, Ethel, and Babs. Once again, their gerrymandering meaning prolapsed from primordial garbled emotion to thought—to speech—the speech I bountifully procured them from my dwindling stores—was—again, all too typically—going the way not of emotion but of thought, of speech, of speaking thought and thinking speech, delivering itself up to the japes and jobations—culverts and switchbacks—the laws and maps of that speaking thought and thinking speech. And once again I was being sacrificed to the itinerary: initial emotion transliterated into speaking thought and thinking speech and then given up to their secret and unpredictable syntactic convulsions—taken—once again, all too typically—and via their iters and adits and switchbacks—far from its starting point.

Yet I couldn't help envying the primordial emotion of these mongers, however garbled. Whenever they were sufficiently appalled to give birth to emotion, the thinking speech and speaking thought that evolved as a transliteration—always at my expense—of that emotion very quickly—and as much more than that initial transliteration—came to have a life of their own—very quickly went their own way, which was now the way of the medium of thinking speech and speaking thought [with its extremely limited tolerance for any dutiful transliteration's subsequent ungrateful insusceptibility to modification by the quirks of that medium], no longer depending on the peculiarities and vagaries of a primordial sire. If only the emotions induced by Jim, by the Jammses, could, like their emotions—the meaning-mongers'—induced by me if not about me per se—as quickly prolapse to a speaking thought and thinking speech that wasted no time in delivering themselves up to a rollercoasting metamorphosis far from their roots in the lowly emotion that had first spawned them. If only my emotions could call upon the same dexterity in herniating to speaking thought and thinking speech—medium non pareil for the breeding of phantasms, which phantasms would, I am sure, in turn breed their own reactionary emotion—terror, say, or delight, or the loathing intrinsic to lust—but an emotion engendered now by things not without but within, emotion triggered by those incomparable productions of the labyrinthine vagrancies of thinking speech and speaking thought. If only my emotion could learn—had learned—that same subjugation to the autonomy-inducing meanders of a quickly unalien medium—thinking speech and speaking thought—I would now or soon—would have been—able to construct my story—our story—without so much graded and therefore degraded dependence on slender opportunity—for emotion as thought and thought as emotion and speech as both and neither—charily furnished by Jim's begrudging, rarefied, and all too occasional descents—into event.

I looked down again, grew sad, for what was so terrifying about this city was its similarity to all others: the same pigeons, poplars, wakeless sailboats, same belltower chimes, parksite thighs outspread for solar impregnation in all weathers, same repavemented streets heralding ever more daring feats of smug gentrification in the minutes to come. I looked down: at first the distance—of skyscrapers and a bridge—shimmered. Everything visible was too—beatifically!—far—as if the more proximate urban blight—of pimps, dope fiends, panhandlers—had been washed away forever. Until I managed to look straighter down at—in spite of, what was it, seventy stories separating me from—the rete of familiarly grimy streets I had just been pounding, heroically refusing to repudiate or relinquish my quest—for a story beyond the slime of slime, inside me and maybe without. There they were, the city streets, immensely visible down to the most picayune detail of superfetatory ashcan-fringed handball court, in all their uniform ununiformed nudity. No attempt here at scintillating tricks of light refraction suffused and infused all the same with a preternatural purity of sourceless glow. And here was I, unprompted by the mongers yet staging a discovery in their vein—oozing a mummia of meaning that could only warm their convention-cloven hearts with whose beat mine was, of course, unofficially unsynchronized. To create this sort of meaning—order out of chaos, wasn't this another favored therefore loathsome catchphrase of the lumpen-*bougre*oisie?—when all I really wanted was to immobilize some sublaminar fragment of the chaos so representative yet so fine as to proclaim the sodden superfluity of all else—earth, sky, and beyond—to create this sort—ort—of meaning was to go over to the meaning-mongers, the side of the oppressors, was to convince them I was not at all dangerous since I was spending my invaluable leisure hours not perfecting bombs or bombsites but in turning the tricks of meaning all too familiar and therefore all too comforting to their likes, throwing them lavender-scented sops concocted from the most unlikely and unpromising materials, a medical subspecialist's simpering fat lady, for example, on convalescent leave from the loo, which they in turn could be counted on to assimilate to the exaltation of their deus absconditus and vade mecum: things as they are.

And what kind of meaning was it: why, meaning connected with that old bugbear of large-scale-pig-ironic-story production: overturning all the hero's preconceptions. Here I was lulled, by a vision of skyscrapers shimmering in the distance, to a sense of the disappearance of all the grime and slime of the pavements below. Yet turning slightly not only do I recuperate that grime and slime but I discover strictly speaking it is not slime but the very sleep of reason's usual lamias beneath a hatchwork of preternatural purity. Meaning-mongering is now a Federal offense and, depending on the continuing rate of the general public's willing stultification, punishable by several decades of televised apotheosis.

Yet here NO

here NO

was NO yet another breaker of meaning about to sweep over me

NO

The NO

lights in the skyscrapers and on the bridge were going out while

NO

down below NO NO NO

down down below NO NO

amid the slime and ooze of prior peregrinations

that had seemed so very much NO

in danger NO of never ending

the lights were first going on. Here was but another subspecies of meaning: reversal of hero-ly expectations latent with poetic justice. Skyscrapers—home and workplace of the rich, powerful, callous, and unjust—were now extinguished forever whereas down below—down down below—in a belated assertion of natural sovereignty the alleys and byways of the insulted and injured had become at last seraphically conspicuous in all their transparency of misguided intention. I turned away from the scene without, from this scouring confectioner's vision of a world purged at last of its dissights and "unsavory characters," as they are known to the guidebooks. There was no having that scene outside a system of optics furnished compliments—and execrations—of the meaning-mongers who, as it turned out, were not medical sub-subspecialists but mere lens grinders. I cut into my plate drowned in butter and shallot stubs. I looked up for I could not bear to scrutinize its long rump of undergone and, all things considered, mediocre steak. The remaining guests looked like Lou Testic, refunded to my still vivid discomfiture in multiplicate and in all his furry monogrammed splendor. I loathed them: all these types as a single type. At the very next table: adjacent, far too adjacent, for I was almost rubbing elbows with one of what seemed an inordinately large party, a harmless-looking soul whose bulging stomach kept him further from the table than surely he must wish to be was making a joke about somebody else, maybe one of the wine stewards: the eternal sumpter omnifacient, compliments of the new management, in a hundred guises. Before laughing out loud and patting him on the back, the others of his party felt impelled to appeal to me—the mother of them all!—for actively participating ratification of what required only my imprimatur to qualify as the eternally genial, lovable and astonishing daring of authentic verbal invention. I creased my face to signify plausibly affable acknowledgment of the impeccable credentials of the specimen in question. For at heart I was a coward. But in my bowels I was sure

  surer NO than NO NO

  SURER THAN I HAD EVER BEEN ABOUT ANYTHING
that this fat flailing belly proved and in a manner Euclid himself might have envied that man is no more than the most loathsome subjacent underling of the vilest beasts—their basest hairiest barmecide—consecrated to guttling while all others starve; most rapturous, most euphoric, only during moments of noisiest excretion and only when reassured of everybody else's unconsolable envy of his optimally churning gut; forever writhing in paternal, filial, or uxorious complacency and in the name of such pious filiations casually discounting the dismembered cries of all those outside the immediate circle of flab answering, consanguineous, to flab.

  Only one among the diners seemed distinct from, that is to say, spared the deformities of, the others. Once he had taken the immense liberty of sitting down straight across from me I realized he was none other than the vacuum-cleaner wielder but now spectacularly attired—missing, in fact, only monocle, shako, and calf-sheathed yataghan to make this picture of understated yet militant elegance ravishingly complete. "You loathe them all, I know," he said, fingering what remained of my cutlery and napkins with fingers unsurprisingly shapely. "You loathe all these types. As a selfstyled man of the people you want them eliminated. Yet the more you loathe them the more you subsidize and confirm their necessity—as well as your own: as ultimately just another type among many—far too many, you being the type Parcae-assigned to dutifully recoil from all other...necessary types. No, my friend, you are not as far outside being as your loathing—to judge by your beatific, your almost drugged, expression of a few minutes ago—lulled you into believing. In fact, you are not outside being at all. You must agree that seen from a certain—my...heuristic distance, your loathing constitutes proof of nothing so much as life's unaccountable richness in dynamic equilibrium among an endless proliferation of types proclaiming uniqueness through the ostensible loathing they induce each in the other, the ostensible loathing they undergo each for the other. In short, your loathing demonstrates apodictically how much a part of being—how crucial and distinct yet ultimately predictable an addition to the perpetually self-equilibrating status quo—you really are. You are required the way a flaw is required to affirm the purity of a diamond." In short, he was my first contact: a man, neither young nor old, pretending to be reading a tabloid. There were only a few others in the dining room now, a couple, tourists, obviously *very much in love*, and a few mildly potbellied stragglers whose intricate salute to the salad bar was ultimately derivable from the simple refrain, Never say die. As we *got to talking*, he suggested since it was agreed I was still very much in being a very lucrative sideline to be had for a song, in the smuggling of, as he put it, certain pharmaceuticals. "You'll need a friend for this," he said. Did I have one? "Good." He explained that he had taken me immediately for somebody with a vested interest in overthrow of the capitalist system of so-called free enterprise. He did not know my line but it was clear I was estranged from whatever it was that I produced in my line. And I could only be estranged from what I produced by being so estranged—from myself—in the very act of producing it. After all, my product was only the summary of my producing it. I tried to resist: said I was, it was true, estranged from—in—my activity—but not from the product, which was invariably beautiful and an unfailing source of retrospective reconciliation with the hateful activity engendering it. When it seemed he hadn't heard I changed my tack: I was estranged from my product—beautiful or not it hovered above and beyond flaunting its invincibility in contradistinction to my mortal clay—but with the activity producing it I was in eternal harmony. At this very moment I was deriving benefit from the unlocalizable yet very real aftereffects of that activity. Even if I agreed with him I could not allow myself to succumb to his dogma for it seemed to me there were insidious meaning-mongers at work in its depths, especially there where estrangement from product implied estrangement from activity and vice-versa—where, rather, estrangement from product was poetically heightened into estrangement from activity, and vice-versa. All he said was that since activity was torment for me— one had only to note the way my groin drooped—it must be pleasure and delight—groin-soothing delectation—for another. And was that other, I wondered, the disapproving witness—the hovering fourth, fifth, or sixth—on the beach at Greenback-Hampton. And/or the rehabilitator/ shaman to whom Jim Jamms had had every intention of bringing his loathsome specimen of shamed rage and raging shame in order that he might be cured once and for all of the tendency to dehisce such specimens. Begetting my product as a loss of myself I was simultaneously begetting that delectating other's domination over producer, product, and production. Once again feeling his meaning-mongers were hard at work in their smithies of poetic transfiguration I had no choice but to reply

 NO CHOICE
 NO CHOICE BUT TO REPLY
 THAT

though all along I might have been begetting my own production as loss of myself I was not simultaneously begetting some other's—*that* other's— delectating domination over me, product, and production. Because I loathed my work—any kind of work—did not imply there was another proximately licking his chops over my loathing. Yet I was curious about his other—introduction of this other might make the coming-to-birth of the story—my story—easier. For I no longer believed in Jim Jamms's story without norm and stricture. The only viable story was the one neither of us was yet privy to. Colletti—for this was the man's name— explained that these pharmaceuticals in no way resembled vulgar narcotics. They were bona fide nostrums that were simply too far ahead of their time insofar as this time was smeared with the myopic exudations of gutter bureaucrats. Before I could leave he added that such a sideline was unique in that it exacted no labor from its practitioners. Delivering the

remedies to an assigned location was not so much
NOT SO MUCH
I stopped dead in my tracks at this unexpected parody of the most
advanced techniques of my meaning-mongers.

not so much labor as a hasty retreat into the interstices of labor.
No chance for self-estrangement here.

The next day I went out—was off—to Rhinebeck to speak to
Jamms about this possibility. I suspected that this contact with Colletti,
who was clearly outside the law, might serve as a corrective—a lenitive—
to Jim's disastrous encounter with the cop. On my way to the train station
I passed a small street leading to some tunnel or other, Watt I think. Only
the noise and congestion connected with an unending line of cars did little
to faze the row of houses straining every architectural fiber to make the
street seem as normal and unhurried as a by-lane in the middle of
Greenback-Hampton. At first my heart leaped—at what seemed a way
into the story—my story—or a way out of a visit to Rhinebeck—
amounting
NO NO NO
amounting to the
same thing—
but then I realized this event was meaningless to me, the space was
meaningless. The whole street was but a speck very very deep within a
camera's—a hovering witness's—eye—a veritable scotoma like that af-
flicting the Jamms's favorite family doctor with respect to their boy—the
farthest point on the trajectory of an antlike disclosure of some exiguous
landscape that had not even begun to be born, in short, a hyrmos beloved
and worthy of old Fritz, one of my grandma (Lang's) superannuated
suitors.

So that what now seemed the tiniest crevice in the lowest reaches
of a tenement decayed beyond repair would turn out—once, that is, it was
born through the kind of incident I would have liked to avoid at any cost
and which only connection and collision with Jamms and his concubines
could generate—a monolith beyond repair.

When I reached the house Maggy and Jim were at opposite ends
of a table. Maggy immediately left the room, she obviously loathed me.
"It's never happened before," he announced. He looked laughably,

almost detestably, crestfallen. Dutifully I caught on slowly and once it was plausible and seemly for my comprehension to be unambiguous I took the liberty, as any devoted friend would, of suggesting a few possible causes: his father's imminent death(for I had sent him a telegram upon receipt of his mother's letters a few days before), the excruciatingly slow recognition of his nonexistent painterly flair, ebb and flow, mostly flow, of financial worry, pressure of living near the biggest city on earth even if sublimely far from its outermost inflationary outskirts. But in the middle of my enumeration the wretch tensed his fists ostentatiously and pounded, even more NO NO, them ostentatiously on the table. Bessy peeked in for a moment. Then, a little later, Maggy peeked in, now it was dusk and she was framed by a darkness that eloquently became the texture of her flesh. In spite of her loathing, as if taking pity on my efforts to sew up the wound of his frustration, she said, "He doesn't like when we assign causes to what he calls his . . . downfalls." Her speech irritated nonetheless because it was always writhing, did I imagine it, in the coils of an impossible hunger to do the bidding of an impossibly expressive punctuation. I lowered my head in what could have been interpreted by those inclined to give me the benefit of the doubt as homage to her lucidity. "Assigning him a cause embrangles him still further in the event. He wants it to go away. Yet at the same time he is terrified of an absence of causes through which to exonerate himself." I wanted to stop her—stop my ears against her. How could he—one like him—with this manifest loathing of cause and effect, back-bone of event—participate in a story comprising event and nothing but. And at the same time I couldn't help wondering whether such a doubt was not in fact recruited by the story- and meaning-mongers—at work even up here in Rhinebeck—as *seam*— so that this event—this scene about to unfold—might be joined with events and scenes passed so as to give coherence to my meanderings. In other words, his resistance to cause-and-effect could very well have nothing to do with his fitness or his willingness to participate in a story but compliments of the meaning-mongers this resistance was being made to have everything to do with such participation in order that—in order that—justice might be done. "In other words, for all his loathing of causes assigned you won't be surprised to find him dredging up his own quarry even if on another level he sorely repudiates them as beside the point.

Relieved of causes he can feel like the victim of what others have gratuitously done to make him a perpetrator of his...own downfall. But isn't this what we are talking about when we talk *symptom* — which we do often even if we don't know it — an event where the generator is both victim and perpetrator. And when we talk *symptom* — when we are talking this kind of event — are we talking event or hole in the sieve of event." I listened carefully, my heart was pounding. Jamms's previous monologues on mom, dad, and the terminal ward, what were they but holes in the sieve of event, of story. And yet if only I could — yoke these holes! — to our story in the right way: if only I could go about making him feel consistently that he was the victim of my schemes to make him a perpetrator but this time not of his own downfall but of our triumph. Why, then, I would end up living the real story with Jamms at my side — the real story — the real story — not the story as originally conceived by me nor the anti-story with which Jamms unbeknownst to himself proposed over and over again to mask and smother it and which had already turned out far more tedious than its target — but rather

    BUT RATHER no

    but rather NO

but rather the union/product/intersection of both transcending their mere present being eternally tied together as a two-headed sludge. Her voice was spiralling toward hysteria with an admirable — even magisterial — control and which I tried to match (by rubbing my palms together between my knees) with an air equivalently magisterial of not seeming to notice. "So what do we do," he asked, clearly annoyed at the communal dimension his problem had assumed though just as clearly dependent on a resolution through such exposure. Even if she loathed me Maggy cast a glance my way, as if to say it was in some small measure due to my presence that Jamms was now spurred to go on with the investigation of his problem, I too was pleased though I did not relish the possibility of being in harmony with Maggy on that or any score. At any rate, investigation of his problem was consubstantial with its development — its flowering — as a phenomenon vital to our story. "He hates causes, you know." As I did not respond she went on: "Entrenching him in the real world they deliver up his peculiarity — fruit of nothing more than a lifetime's moment's laches — to a network of interconnections that only reinforce its intelligibility—in other words, its damnability—and condemn it thereby to its own perpetuation. Assigning a cause makes it—the symptom—belong to the real world and if it belongs once it belongs forever."

"Whereas it is just the opposite: non-investigation will only give rise to perpetuation of the phenomenon," I said. "My impotence," said Jim, "is not a phenomenon: it's a hole in the sieve of phenomena." I was not sure if this turn of events—Jim's inability to satisfy Maggy's legitimate needs in the shadow of his father's impending death—put an unexpected let in my plans, especially now, with Colletti looming in the shadow of the hotel corridor. Jim looked resentful, as if he would refuse to budge until this matter of his impotence was resolved even if he did not believe the impotence existed and under no circumstances would he endure having it named. As if I had just spoken the word outright under the ungainly lights out came Bessy, who looked to him with almost too theatrical an underlining flourish so there might be no doubt that she intended to speak and about whom. The flourish was heady, dazzling, underlined nothing so much as its own supererogatoriness stemming most copiously from the fact that its target, Jim, was for the time being a mere bulk that could not be expected to respond—whose bulky inexpressiveness was its own response. "He's always been this way. You look at him as if this is new or novel." Jamms sneered and turned away. "This is an approach to rehabilitation akin to degradation ceremonies as they are carried out in prisons, flophouses, terminal wards, of course. She implies that if I—the patient—am behaving this way even if for a moment then I have always been behaving this way. An unusually strenuous effort is required to submit to the meagre acknowledgment that these are exceptional circumstances. For exceptional circumstances imply the humble recognition of normal circumstances with its peaks and troughs whereas the abysm not so latent in, 'He's always been that way,' wallows in and ultimately sucks dry an undifferentiated broth where nonbeings such as I can no longer be permitted to swim—the medium would be perfectly aseptic if it weren't for our swinish fins—toward an endlessly receding coastline riddled with fanged precipices. In short, she loathes any possibility that this might be an interim state, a state with beginning, middle, and end, a state with contour demanding a contoured if strenuous compassion." One of the two—I can't say with certainty who—recoiled toward shadow. I took this movement for a sign that the phenomenon or this hole in the sieve of phenomena was about to enter a new phase. This was misguided, once again a movement was seeing fit to stand in the way of our story or of my perception of story, throwing sand in its or my thousand eyes. Their recoil, the lady's or ladies', simply meant not that the symptom was over and done with as obstruction on our way ahead even if we were all to be moving in different directions but that all obstruction to its—the symptom's—intromission into the future's furry slit—story or no story—was over and done with. As if aware of my rage and impatience over a definitive answer to give to Colletti he smiled and said, "If I were dad and you had asked me, what was wrong, I mean, why the impotence, what with me having a cock and she a cunt so what are we waiting for— if I had been dad clenching my fists and my teeth I would have said, 'There's somebody who lives down the street, now this bastard...'" He cleared his throat as presumably he wanted me to think his dad might have done preparatory to the long haul of evasiveness he was deploying before us now. Although knowing Jamms I knew this was, once again, a mere playing against the facts of the case—in other words, he was bristling with radical disjunctions. For if truly we had been in for a long haul he never would have allowed himself to clear his throat preparatory to that haul designed to sidestep the true target of torment: he had no plans, then, for recruitment of a makeshift reminiscence about some neighborlike quidnunc and nondescript. Another radical disjunction between what was appropriate and what was furnished. For a moment I thought it might be best simply to lay down my arms before these disjunctions and make them my life's work. He would never be caught dead making form and content coincide. But that was because our approaches to the story were vastly different. Yes, perhaps it was not at all a question of his story or mine—it was indeed our story—only I underwent or hoped to undergo the story by living it and he by presenting it for the delectation of that hovering witness, specimen analyzer, fourth, fifth, and ninety-sixth at table. He could not imagine himself connected to the story beyond a concern with aesthetic drapery susceptible to the various quibbling of its first-night audience whereas I lived only for immersion in that story's warm bath. Surprisingly he went on, "Now this bastard who lives down the street—on the ground floor—with the first nickel he ever earned glued to his hindquarters—insists on walking every morning into the depths of the park and shouting my name and serial number to the four winds of hell, as well as the most personal details concerning my assets and liabilities." He paused briefly: "So there is your answer: *he* is why I am ill, why my tumors tend to enlarge, why my night is your day and your day my night. You see," becoming more conversational, "my dad's radical disjunctions between what he felt—feels—and what he claims he feels are not in the service of a literary enterprise, let us say. They are simply in the service of a vision of himself that allows him to survive: maybe these radical disjunctions provoked his tumor." "That's all very nice," I replied, "but will you be coming to meet our contact." I was speaking illogically for there would be no meeting if he did not deign to come. He jumped up and made as if to punch me in the groin murmuring at the same time, "Yes, yes, I'll come. Of course I'll come." Then he appeared to hesitate or perhaps it was merely the impersonation of simple-minded hesitation, torpor, prompted by a fear of having let out too much heart on daw-pecked sleeve; a playing at calculation. "But then again, whether I come or do not come I still participate. My very abstention in affecting your relation with this imbecile is a form of participation." But I had already lost sight of his act in his words, lost sight of him in his words, of his words in his clenched fist, his fist in that larger gesture neither he nor I could lay claim to having generated but which had just succeeded in sending Maggy for one flailing deeper and deeper into shadow. "Dearest Maggy," he murmured when she was clearly out of sight, "will you be coming with us to New York tomorrow." As there was no response he continued, "I love you, Maggy: at least, I will always protect you. But there is no getting away from the fact that we need money. This man he describes"—not acknowledging my presence—"is just the kind I am drawn to, a man in a fashionable hotel's fashionable dining room with a scheme up his sleeve. I find myself drifting ineluctably toward that man, telling myself of course that I am not participating in that man's scheme, that I am merely on the margin regarding that scheme as visual spectacle only but all along I am participating and just as his chaotic cavorting is the necessary background for abstention as participation so my apparent abstention is the necessary background for his frenzied activity at the very heart of the scheme. And so we all, willy-nilly, participate. So it becomes pointless to pretend I am not participating even if I live in terror of that moment of authentic ungainsayable participation latent in his depictions. For he seems to depict—from what you tell me—in such a way that instinctive bloodlust and greed have no choice but to understand far more quickly and damningly than the stigma of understanding may be shed through simulated obfuscation. I am mystified, my loves, but only by the ease with which I begin to transact though seemingly always on the sidelines. Yes, I transact and love the transactions: the dirtier the better. And perhaps as a result of this little enterprise I will return triumphant in my ability to reach for your breast at a moment's notice without regard for whether or not I feel desire for that breast or whether I can "perform" without desire or whether given a startling superfetation of desire that no gesture however global can hope to contain I should not rather relinquish desire's hold by turning aside from all acts into which it is normally channeled."

There was nothing for Maggy or Bessy to say, I held my breath dreading that Jamms's yeasaying would suddenly—perversely—fold back on itself, though strictly speaking even if the upshot of his speech was, Yes, he would be more than delighted to accompany me back to New York, I was still very very far from the upshot of that upshot. In the kitchen, where we recruited ourselves to wringing the lettuce dry he whispered, "She has to understand I have to go. Though maybe my reasons for going are completely different from yours. Maybe this meeting is a necessary preliminary to some other act that cannot get, be gotten, off the ground otherwise. But maybe I delude myself that my purpose in attending is different from yours. Maybe I only delude myself believing that in the midst of any situation I am always very much dreaming beyond it." "That's to be expected. You are an artist," I said weakly. Reluctantly he followed me into the dining room, loping with hands in pockets, keeping his distance, assuring me at every moment and through every gesture that he intended to have done with this budding relation. My first impulse, quickly suppressed, was to amuse him, or rather

OR RATHER

Yes
or rather Yes open him up to distraction via the contempt he must
necessarily feel for my attempts to amuse him. Finally Colletti arrived,
lifting a celery stalk from the salad bar with even defter fingers than I
remembered. As he equably kept up what he staked out as his end of the
conversation Jamms made it a point to keep turning ostentatiously away.
"Your friend appears very nervous," Colletti noted, when Jim had
wandered off to the steam table in back of the salad bar, simulating, I felt,
more spectatorly awe than he could conceivably feel for a type he had to
have encountered many, many times before. When he announced, somewhat challengingly, that he had to take a piss, Colletti turned to me and
said, "That type—your master, for don't you work for him?—always
seems to be going berserk in the name of creative fulfillment, of course,
but in point of fact his so-called torment, so-called despair, is very
carefully calibrated and at all times against the aliquot of quotidian chaos
to which he allows himself to be exposed at any given moment. He knows
just how far to go in his quest for creative ecstasy, for—for—" He drifted
off and the drifting with its stifled anguish at the absence of some
acceptable way to finish the sentence was exactly the effect he was after.
"Of course, as his flunkey, his servant, most of the burden of this creative
ecstasy falls on you. You supply its foundation. You belong to the class
of flunkeys. Never forget it even if he tries placatingly to stuff your skull
with visions of the species Man. And you will remain a member of the
flunkey class until you or somebody like you is able, embodying the
dissolution of all classes—the dissolution of all classes—to obliterate the
existing structure but not from the standpoint of particular grievances.
Particular grievances are a mere lure that end up guaranteeing the
perpetuation of the injustices they profess to abhor. The work you do for
me—should you decide to do it—is work within a community of souls
dedicated to obliterating the existing structure. Yes, yes, yes, I know, you
feel much freer now working for Jamms than you did when you were an
industrial serf, a corporate slave. But you only seem freer, because your
conditions of life subsist from moment to moment at the whim of chance.
In fact you are far less free because you are incessantly subjected to the
violence of things—of Jamms's creative ecstasies, for example. Even if
this violence of things dulls you to a sense of your own oppression that

oppression is far more virulent now than it ever was before no matter what you were doing. But for you and so many others like you there is no achieving social control over the violence of things. You and your kind are not like the urban burghers of old able to assert their latent property and labor, in other words, their conditions of life, against the landed nobility. For you and your kind have no conditions of life to oppose to the Jammses of the world. For your conditions of life—your labor and its modes—are not a property, a positive force—as they were in opposition to the landed nobility for the burghers of old. Your conditions of life are an accident, a violence that overwhelms you to a delirious delusion of infinite freedom. Your conditions of life are simply a being at the mercy of those you wish to overthrow. How can you organize such a *being at the mercy* into a positive condition of life transformable into a new estate? There will be no new estate for you and your kind. We have something far better in mind." I bowed my head, a gesture I had always liked but never had occasion to use, not that this qualified as an appropriate occasion—say that I was overcoming NOT SO MUCH my fear of the gesture AS my usual intimidatedness at the absence of suitable occasion for its publication. But noting Jamms's return through a corner of my eye I saw that I was now having occasion to publish it in contradistinction to Jamms's perduring—overweening—truculence. "I was explaining to your friend here, Jim, that should this little arrangement succeed—if you and he are able to rescue a little fund of material from a certain boat or train, I forget which, then we might be able to see our way clear to—to—" The waiter arrived. Jamms pushed his stew away in disgust. "So he"— (pointing at me)—"and I do our job and for our labor we are paid. And for this wretched little stipend you expect me to give up my creative work. You expect me to bring my product—the transport of a wretched little bag of laxatives—into the marketplace so that you—the big brown god—may valorize my labor-power—now fiercely independent of me, its subject, reduced in turn to its appendage—its disarticulated carcass—may valorize my labor-power against a universal standard—so that you—the little blue god—may fiddling with that standard come up with an equivalence for the labor-power—now abstracted beyond all resemblance to, connection with, the sinews of its generator—an equivalent peculium capable of sending me on my not so merry way contented and posthaste. If we leave things up to him"—the words seemed directed at me though he did not bother looking my way, looked all the more intensely at Colletti—"our labor-power, yours and mine, what does it become but a mainland to which you and I are fleetingly annexed as mere alluvia to be effaced by the next high tide. Everything that is uniquely best about us comes to naught in the name of the law of equivalences. Our capacity for work— our horizon of infinite capabilities, as it were—is congealed into valorizable labor. Heretofore unlocalizable we are suddenly reduced to a fixed place on a continuum. No, no, no, not we, but the capacity-for-work, the labor power, in whose name—for the greater good—we—you and I—have been abolished. And for all this I am to give up my creative work. The fruits of that work have no value therefore the capacity-for-work, the labor power resulting in their production, cannot be valorized, cannot be sucked into the arena of equivalences. As long as I remain a creator of those works I cannot be transmuted into my capacity-for-work in turn transmutable into a fixed place on a continuum. On that continuum each place—to which once living breathing beings have been smelted down— has an identity only insofar as it is greater or lesser than every other place. I'm talking about the continuum of abstract labor perfected with the blood of Joes like you and me. And don't be so foolish as to mistake that abstract labor for a mere mental chimera: abstract labor is real activity. Do you hear me: abstract labor is real activity. Its reality is the stuff of which dreams are made insofar as those dreams manage to remain the shimmering idealization of the predominating material relationships converting men into purulent outpouchings of their own labor power, insofar as those dreams perfect the delusions of all those who grow rich off such purulence. Don't you see"—once again addressing without looking my way—"one day the fact that we two carried his trash from point A to point B in the name of a hefty stipend will be transmuted into a shred of ideology permitting tens of thousands of similarly stoogelike carriers to carry on the tradition and not even in the name of some vague future liberation. For surely he has dangled the prospect of liberation in your face during my absence." I was about to speak. "At any rate, never forget the abstract labor on which he and his kind feed is not a mere phrase. It exists—out there—a little to the right or left of our future specters. This abstract labor, it does not appropriate the real world the way I do when Maggy and Bessy have the decency to leave me alone in my studio. No, no, no, this abstract labor is busy on other fronts separating me, you, and the lamppost from the most vital part of our-selves—our capacity-to-work; to create; to labor strenuously, gloriously, *in anticipation of no value assignable to the product.* Don't you see *their* abstract labor makes us the premature detritus of our own potency, miraculously, malefically cutting off the capacity to labor *on behalf of* from its subject just before we—the subject—are able to fix on an activity that appropriates the real world so that we—the subject—may return—reinvest—infi-nitely more than we have borrowed and always in the name of an activity and of a product of said activity that anticipates no assignable value. It—*their* abstract labor—cuts us off from the very core of ourselves—the perfectly sculpted armature of our humanity, if you will—and in that hysteresis—no other word will do—between the hunger to create and the need to appease the other hungers so we may go on creating. It—*their* abstract labor—lies in wait until the hunger to appropriate the real world in the name of a vaster reinvestment later—is overtaken by the need to clog or declog our various orifices. So—"turning toward the salad bar "— Colletti wants us to do the job so that a little later we may exchange our products and equalize our labors from which all trace of self—yours or mine—has been beatifically obliterated. Just speaking about this ab-stract labor to come I feel I have been obliterated. I have to get back to myself. I must return to Rhinebeck by the 10:24 express." Colletti laughed: "You are obviously struggling with yourself about whether or not to accept my generous offer. But you are an artist and an artist needs to struggle. So you might thank me for offering you this opportunity to struggle."

"I know your kind, Colletti. As you go on amassing the consider-able scraps of this demon, abstract labor, you preserve a soft spot in your heart for the artist as last outpost against the old demon. You *require* that there be no lapse in my martyrdom, my volatilization. And what amazes me is that there is never any sense of contradiction—disjunction—radical or otherwise—between my necessary abasement and your comfortable little profit-seeking life. According to you and your kind I can tolerate any conceivable abasement because I am eternally warmed by a talent you have been set apart to loftily misconstrue. In a single bound that repeats itself every other minute of your waking life—Satan never sleeps—you feel both cruelly and blissfully bereft of such a talent...for disaster. You undergo just enough of the bliss inseparable from its exercise to feel entitled to reparation for being so cruelly bereft of more than a mere earnest. And it is my duty—a duty far greater in your eyes than that which I owe to my productions—to maximally accentuate and accelerate the radical disjunction between your being spared and my being unspared. You positively revere, don't you, Colletti, my repudiation of all comfort vital to the survival of *your* kind, and at the same time reverence so quickly becomes sultanly proprietorship that before you know it you are convinced that above all others you have every right to dispose as you deem fit of what you have come rightfully and righteously to own. As long as I repudiate all you hold dear yet are not—refuse to be—conscious of needing—need so essential for all the little knickknacks and knackknicks of abstract labor, need that is so much wedded to your viscera it is virtually indistinguishable from those viscera, uncontourable, unspeakable, unthinkable, inconceivable, for such need surely you cannot be held accountable—as long, I say, as I repudiate all you hold dear then I give you something to believe in, my ease in ascesis gives you hope for your own indefinitely postponed. I know your kind, Colletti: Because you think you savor the products of my activity—to which no value shall ever be assigned—you thereby have the right to dictate the multitudinous terms of my abasement starting with the pick-up of some unspeakable items at a riverside pier two? three? seven days from now?" I cursed Jamms inwardly for ruining this chance, for playing the artist when least appropriate. Colletti laughed. "I don't savor your creations. I don't know your creations. What do you create. *Does* he create?" he asked turning to me poker-faced. I looked beyond him to Jamms, once again standing in the way of our story inseparable from its rendition here in space. And what a space it was. One couldn't have asked for anything more lordly, more opulent. What did Jamms care? He had his safe-deposit box and as for me— He was making it so difficult for the three of us that at this very moment we were looking off in three different planes. Had Colletti just said: Wait at the Fifty-third Street pier for a man in a green smock with a greenish paper bag held high above his bald head to walk toward us with the titubating provocation of a derelict or had I simply imagined it.

Jamms did not look as if he had heard a thing.

As we continued looking off, each in his own way, I was sure that by no stretch of the imagination could it be assumed our partial views summated to a totality subsuming all planes. Our views contradicted, overlapped, sabotaged the creation of a coherent and consensual reality. I was beginning to see double, triple, as Jamms's and Colletti's hotel dining rooms intersected with and upstaged my own. In Jamms's there was a little old lady who simply would not fit in mine; Colletti's blithely lay claim to a shred of lettuce similarly unthinkable amid the trappings to which I was now accustomed. I tried to accommodate some of Colletti's shreds by saying: "You have to forgive my friend, Mr. Colletti." I was on the verge of introducing a building block into this site of demolition. I was not sure where it came from: its structure, I knew, conformed to the specifications of some completely different event but also I knew it could plausibly be applied to Jamms and what I was now, to pacify Colletti, constructing as his predicament. "Jim is an artist, Mr. Colletti. A great and radical one. Only the work's radicalness is far greater than his capacity to live out the implications — might I say, the repercussions — of that radicalness in the world of everyday, where — as he so eloquently put it — orifices must be plugged and unplugged. You can understand, then, that Jim will be a little touchy when alleviation of a misery stemming from his radicalness is suggested. Yet there are advantages to his predicament insofar as the misery — or rather its excruciation component — is immediately plowed back into the work. According to a dialectic all his own the smaller the capacity to live the repercussions of radicalness out in the world the vaster and more potent the playing out of those repercussions in the work itself, which playing out engenders further repercussions similarly plowed back." Now that I had inserted my building block — in such short supply up in Rhinebeck — I was waiting for one or the other to fortify growing story structure through addition of another. Jim, surprisingly, came through. "Look at him. He doesn't understand a word you say." At first I thought he would simply fizzle out in vituperation for which display anybody might have been recruited. But then: "Yes, I am an artist." (I was grateful for what retrospectively would prove a reinforcement of my previous building block as well as commencement of his own.) "But I'm sure *artist* as I understand the word and *artist* as a slime like him understands it are vastly different, irreconcilable. But I come to praise Colletti not to bury it. What good is he to me dead? As he himself pointed out, an artist thrives on struggle and the Collettis of the world exist to provoke struggle. When he was throwing his weight around a short time ago daring us to enter the labor market, why—and this is the crucial question—why did I take his rejection of my work as *outside the pale* of the usual philistine antitypy to innovation? Why was his philistine contempt different? Why did I resist, inexplicably in his case, the inevitable classification? For we all know that his daring us to enter the labor market—his suggestion that I work for him—was nothing more than a rejection of my work—my being, a way into rejection, as it were." I wanted to jump up and embrace Jamms. For all his vituperation, he was salvaging the evening, forcing the meeting to continue as genuine story event. He was joining his building block to mine in such a way as to suggest that his act was a mere playing out of the gnawing implications latent in my own. By creating before our very eyes and under our very noses a radical disjunction between what Colletti's job offer had meant to mean—i.e., a job offer—and what his need to fulminate was making it mean—i.e., an assault on the selfsufficiency of his genius—Jamms was permitting the meeting to resonate, that is, continue. Deftly insinuating a second building block into the structure barely sketched by my own he was making it clear to Colletti—or was I guilty of producing yet another radical disjunction between what something meant and what it could be made to mean—that we might still accept his offer, most generous, in my unartistic view. "Instead of seeing him for what he is and doing away with him I insisted inexplicably on prolonging his existence, that is, his capacity for boorishness and malevolence. I drew him out, inexplicably as it were, fixing on signs and traits—that is to say, generously furnishing him with such accoutrements—as proved his kind of drooling incomprehension was triumphantly unassimilable to the usual kitchen garden variety predominating all down the ages. But all I was doing was ascribing to him my own horror of being benighted and not just benighted but with a brand of benightedness exhumed over and over and over all down those ages. But clearly Colletti does not feel stigmatized falling into categories, specifically that of benightedness. Perhaps he believes as I needed to believe—INEXPLICABLY—that his rejection of my works— my slant of vision—was the fruit of a universal knowingness that had successfully absorbed all prior lessons of philistinism foiled and exposed." Colletti smiled his irresistible smile. At first I thought he was going to call a halt to the building I had initiated and that Jamms was carrying on.

"You, Jim, were clearly in a quandary. On the one hand it was enraging to believe that I could dare to reject your work —your slant of vision, as you call it. On the other hand it was terrifying to believe as conduit to some significant improvement in your universal condition that I could dare to reject your work in consequence of a gnosis you could not even begin to fathom and not simply as quintessential facsimile of benighted boors past. Simply you had to choose between your rage and your terror. You settled for rage since your terror was simply too terrifying." I did not know how Jamms was undergoing this diagnosis but I was grateful to Colletti for reinforcing his —Jamms's —building block thereby ensuring a further extension of story. "Do you see what I mean, Jim?" said Colletti, leaning across the table. "You had to choose between solitary enlightenment in a world of thugs like me and solitary debasement in a world of at least one single connoisseuring student of history lessons able to penetrate your fraudulence —once again, me. I'm just pointing out" —at a movement of outraged sneering from Jim —"that giving my philistine contempt for your work the benefit of the doubt was not —as you seem to wish us to think —an INEXPLICABLE largesse —one more symptom —of your trailblazing genius. And I am speaking as one who sympathizes —more than sympathizes with —champions —your effort to transform cringing terror into the inexplicable generosity of genius expansible in direct proportion to your skill in prolonging this specimen inexplicability. In short, I am not fooled nor should your sidekick be by this apparent *discomfort* in the face of the inexplicable. For it is precisely the inexplicable —ostensibly inexplicable —nature of that tendency manifested a while back though first brought to light here and now —or rather, the concocted myth of the inexplicable —that has allowed you to achieve your so what if only partially successful browbeating of one more misguided figure in the landscape. In short, you have a vested interest in not only prolonging but celebrating the inexplicable —the myth of the inexplicable. In short, the myth of the inexplicable —the myth of your inexplicable larghesse in giving my egregious philistinism the benefit of the doubt as something more than philistinism, more than benightedness, since according to you what I most of all dread is being straitjacketed to that philistinism, that benightedness —is being straitjacketed, period —in short, the myth of the inexplicable is not so inexplicable when we consider the alternative: to have accepted and to go on accepting my repudiation of your work —all your work —as the well-nigh thetic consequence of a gnosis so penetrating and so vast you could never hope to pick up a paint brush again. So in terror that I might in fact choose to embody the very opposite of benightedness as my suit of mail you choose to give me what you call the benefit of the doubt, that is, you console yourself that I am indeed a complete and unregenerate philistine who is nevertheless — inexplicably—inexplicably—INEXPLICABLY—to be spared such a straightforward unqualified stigmatic bracketing. And as if this qualification of my imbecility has only my well being at heart. Having established—having managed to lull yourself to sleep with—the certainty of my imbecility—my philistinism—my benightedness—my boorishness— in the large—you are able to make certain concessions—to the terror with which that sleep is too often afflicted—in the small.

"As much as you are repelled by the verdict of my philistinism— as much as my philistinism, my benightedness—brackets me as one inaccessible to your outcries—and not only those attempted by your putative art works—still you prefer rage at the philistinism to terror at an overpowering connoisseurship that could only reduce all your productions, past, present, and future, to some poor relation of horseshit. So whenever you get too close to obliterating me and my philistinism with your rage you homeostatically invoke the ghost of connoisseurship with its universal gnostic acuity, and the salutary terror that invariably rises up in tandem restores you to a sense of proportion. It is this shivering sense of proportion that fringes my infinitely preferable philistinism—boorishness—benightedness—with certain qualifications—with a certain tentativeness—that staves off its assimilation to the kitchen garden variety exhumed over and over and over across the centuries. But once again: for whose benefit all this concessionary tender loving care? Your own, damn it. I certainly don't care if I am bracketed—straitjacketed—and even to the most ignominious philistinism in your or anybody else's boorish eyes."

It seemed to me that Colletti had done enough to prolong the building of our story through plausibilization of this meeting in a hotel dining room. It was time for me to come to Jamms's aid before rage, surely increasing, toppled our edifice forever.

"Excuse me, Mr. Colletti, but what I think Jamms was hoping for in the opportunity you held out was an alternative to that old bugbear, the division of labor, which is of course private property under another name. You see, for all his spouting to the contrary Jamms lives in mortal fear that his product — to which no value is assignable — may turn out not a totality unto itself but a mere moment in a division of labor consecrated to production of a commodity whose value is worn on the sleeve of commerce for mere consumers to peck at. He lives in mortal fear that every time he gives himself to the gravity of the production he

      is NOT SO MUCH

not so much living outside all localizable tasks as tinkering blindly and frantically within the confines of that single task assigned him as one of the myriad consecrated to Ur-commodity production. Ever since I have known him (radical disjunction between the actual niggardly time frame and its implied grandiosity of century upon century) he has dreamed through his work, always through his work, of being a hunter at dawn, a fisherman at noon, a shepherd at dusk, and a duenna at midnight, to say nothing of a flunkey with bellwetherly pretensions under the spell of the wee hours. But more and more and with each passing day he begins to fear that his mighty production binds him more forcibly than any assembly-line piecework. From the beginning Jamms proclaimed that in his case there was absolutely no disjunction between his particular and the common interest. Through his productions he was working for mankind. Yet more and more he suspects that he is part of a vast network of wage-slaves, that his particular line of work has in actual fact been forced upon him without possibility of escape. He who has always loathed striving in the name of commodities suspects that he may be a mere cog in the machine perfecting the vastest grossest commodity of all. At some point along the road this or that glorious creation — fruit of his loins — has been transmogrified into a monolith looking back at him looking back at him looking back at him from the far side of expectation as freest play of the spirit. Somewhere along the road the powers that be got wind of his dexterity, his deftness, his assiduity, and managed without his being in the least aware to transform that dexterity-deftness-assiduity into one more measly though vital attribute in their less than divine plan. And so, Mr. Colletti, it is only natural that he should look to you — to you and men like you"(radical disjunction between Jamms's obvious contempt and revulsion and this constructed bedazzlement—between the Collettis of this world as they mean to be and as, however fleetingly, they are made to mean to be, all in the name of a dire subliminally guffawing poetry) "for a means of escape from this terrifying discovery. For one rare moment—as you described the passage down the gangplank in the dazzling winter sun—" (radical disjunction between paltriness of prospects skirted and this skirting depiction of those prospects now massive with promise) "—Jamms began to hope at last he was on the track of emancipation from the gas chamber where division was labor. As you described the walk from pier to highway Jamms began to imagine at last he might become that shepherd at dusk, that profiteer toward late evening, that butcher at midnight, that barber around four A.M. , that butler toward dawn, that Serbian soubrette at the stroke of midmorning , that physiatrist at any time of day, that fop at teatime." At this moment, when I was putting forth Jamms's case with the most unspeakable eloquence he did not seem in the least to be listening and focused instead on one of the waiters. I myself was mesmerized by the hindquarters of a departing frump, Colletti vaguely amused by a single lettuce leaf limply quivering on the salad frontier a few paces away. And once again I told myself, who knows, unbeknownst to me, to all of us, these partial deliriously random views may be madly summating toward the impossible space vital to the story's prosecution, the story that is ours, rightly ours, earned through our mutual incompatibility: not, never, a space *before*—rather inconceivable to—our eyes and easily nauseated by the slightest whiff of perspectival congruence. How would I know when the space was real. When Colletti offered us the job and Jamms accepted? Yes, for such a course of events would advance and enhance the story as I wanted to know it. I looked around, tried to maintain a civil disinterested air as if it no longer mattered whether or not this crook hired us. He had not been impressed with my having smuggled hundreds of thousands of dollars worth of equipment out of the offices in which I worked. As I went on looking at the frump and all she was leaving in her wake and through a corner of my eye at the lettuce leaf, still limply quivering, this became Jamms's view. And when I sought refuge from Jamms's view in a particularly haphazard couple in the corner—the kind of couple that looks as if it does everything together, or better yet, tells everyone it does everything together—this became—even if—ESPE-

CIALLY BECAUSE—no no no—

NO NO Meaning-mongers go away GO

especially

because he was not in the least aware of its—the couple's existence—this became once again his view. Everything in the restaurant was meant for him—every scrap and spark within the confines of the restaurant—was meant for him—the builder of our impossible story space. The haphazard couple had begun as his view but he had seen fit to abdicate that view even if—ESPECIALLY BECAUSE

especially because—in no way responsible for its transfer or forfeiture to my keeping, to my ken. I was seeing what Jamms ought to have seen on the way toward conflating and constructing our story space—a space derived from but in no way traceable to this cascade of perspectives offered us by the restaurant. I was seeing what Jamms ought to have seen, be seeing, in the name of our story. As repository of all he ought to be seeing I could only curse his negligence. That negligence was costing us the story's prosecution. Only

ONLY

Only

mightn't his blindness and deafness and paresis be either a crucial element of the story or an element crucial to the story—a vital message meant for somebody connected with the story, if not me or Colletti then a hovering witness, *the* hovering witness, for example, who had seen fit to signal over and over that the passing of photo from Jamms to cop and back again had had no other function than to abase and annihilate me. Didn't a story comprise not only

NOT ONLY NOT ONLY NOT ONLY triumphs of potency and manual skill but also

ALSO

spectacular defeats, ineptitudes, untimely recoils, manifest blindnesses, deafnesses, in a word contractions. The universe of our story was to be born, then, from not an expansion but a contraction. I tried reminding myself, let's call it reminding, that even if Jamms's refusal to see—the quivering lettuce leaf or Colletti's *seeing of that quivering lettuce leaf* as "final judgment on our joint incompatibility" with his—Colletti's—best of intentions or the departing frump or the convivial couple wedded into an eternity of pleasure—was *no* message as far as I was concerned, was no mighty harbinger of the plot's thickening, was no story-leap forward—for another, for the hovering witness, for example, it mean might far far more than it could ever mean to me and in a distinctly story-enhancing way. Just as I was about to despair over Jamms's refusal to see—hear—smell—what had been erected for his seeing—and as signs of our rise and/or fall within the domain of the story moving ever onward—just as I was about to despair eternally over this refusal as ultimate and irrefutable proof of the story—our story's—demise—it was occurring to me—thanks to the void left by the departing frump—that was it—that was it—that was what had singlehandedly triggered my anagnorisis—that for another, for any number of hovering witnesses extraordinaires, on and off the beach, for this other, his refusal to read the landscape and my despair over that refusal might very well be functioning as story engine and armature more potent than potent, vaster than vast. Through Jamms's blindness and deafness and illiteracy—messages but only to one capable of treasuring gaps and absences as the true stuff of storydom—the story was advancing in leaps and bounds. Analogously and long long ago hadn't I mistaken acquisition of place names for the only sign and embodiment of lived experience—in place. And hadn't I learned, also analogously—wasn't I learning all over again even if I had never learned—that despair over the failure to conform to such canons of lived experience constituted the only authentic beginning of experience authentically lived—to the degree, of course, that said despair degenerated into a wholehearted investigation of why one had ever allowed oneself to be so biassed and straitjacketed in the first place, before experience began, that is.

So Jamms's seeming absence of a message—to me—to any hovering witness—to space itself— story space, of course—regarding what he saw and what he compelled himself to deduce from the seeing as vital to the story—a message expressible not only in a saying but, for example, in a doing, a squirming, a writhing, and a stammering—and my shapeless despair, also messageless, over that seeming absence—might—I had now over and over to remind myself—turn out to be big with message—for the story—for the space of the story—for some other(s) on the fringe of or deep within the story, yet to be identified or come and gone too rapidly ever to be identified or both. Unbeknownst to ourselves these messages were not only being incessantly born but plowed back into — reinvested deep within — the story and at an alarming rate. Jamms's non-seeing was a message to somebody or something intimately connected with the story and highly influential among the story-and meaning-mongers. And my despair over that non-seeing was a message equally vital to the story's propulsion ever onward. I was both elated and terrified by the axiom that forced itself upon my despair with all the serpentine grace of a wilting lettuce leaf: Postures of despair over story failure is already galvanizing resumption of that story or message to somebody somewhere that story is resuming and therefore part and parcel of that resumption. Typically perverse Jammsian failure to regard dutifully the limp lettuce leaf [meant for his eyes only] did not bring story to eternal halt, merely rerouted story to another track, in this case that of my colorful despair over such failure as ultimate dooming missed opportunity for both of us. Nor could said colorful despair be considered an eternal halt shunting over as it was doing yet once more to the track of messages and message transmittal to one or ones capable of transmogrifying Jamms's failure to respond and/or my despair over that failure as crucial building blocks with repercussions virulent enough to keep the story in business forever. After Colletti left, for the Collettis of the world exist to be gone, Jamms turned to me and over the lukewarm Turkish coffee *men of his stamp are usually so fond of* (to the point where they are willing to sacrifice family and friends for one whiff) said—he was still eating ravenously—"Maggy says it's best we stop communicating. Just tell my dad I'm never coming back...into the family business. I'll indemnify you for whatever loss of wages my intransigence might entail." I betrayed no hurt or outrage but all at once Jamms was pounding his fist on the table and saying, "No, it's not Maggy. Or Bessy. I'm sick of your crawling pusillanimous desire to understand—me, yourself, the surroundings. It's a disease, this hunger to know your own flaws and improve thereby." I could not speak for all the time he spoke my only reaction was astonishment—at how little these remarks, well-rehearsed, sounded or affected me. "In addition, I loathe these little business meetings—How did you ever dare to schedule one without asking me first?—where, as you must have deduced quickly enough, it is very much

a point of honor"—[or of inconsequence and despair at that inconsequence, I was tempted to suggest though not in the least believing in the
suggestion]—"to keep my mouth bloody well shut." [Another radical
disjunction between what an event meant and what retrospectively it
could be made to mean: Pretty much anything. "But I hope you noticed
that once we got over the introductions and all that rot—when that fool
starting pressing me to his flabby little bosom"— [Colletti was imperially,
irreproachably lean]—"I didn't show the slightest sign of relief and
delight at being part of the team and one of the boys at last. Who cares that
he desperately needed to be able to ascribe what he even more desperately"—[even NO more NO NO desperately NO NO NO]—"needed to
be able to perceive as my intimidated horror to a tortured and ever
expanding uncertainty about those team prospects. That's his problem.
The more he tried to coddle and put me at my ease the more solemnly
silent I became. "

It was only later as I walked the streets, colliding with passersby
and being obliged to throw myself, from time to time, on the haughty
magnanimity of dowagers, corporate merlins, and other incurables, that
I began to play back THAT IS TO SAY
        no no THAT IS TO SAY No no
that is to say undergo his cruelty become cruelty when played against the
cruelty of street incident: collision with clerks at all levels of the urban
rung. Up until this moment, sitting with him in the comfortable hotel
dining room, I had deserved that cruelty become cruelty only within the
confines of the rancid quotidian. Provocation of street frustration was
giving me the courage to undergo THAT IS TO SAY *protest against* only
it was too late now—now—now that   raging misery over gratuitous
cruelty [emboldened in the face of daily collisional mishap] was at last
drastically greater than the ubiquitous self-loathing that warms and
welcomes just such—never gratuitous, never cruel, always justified,
always adequate—gratuitous cruelty as Jamms had dispensed. I had
finally reached that level where rage at cruelty is greater than the self-
loathing that invoking blesses it. I thought of him doing the bidding of
Maggy—a woman's flunkey for every great lady demands a flunkey. But
didn't he know that the needs of men and women are irrecusably opposed
and that the men who appear to be attuned to those opposing needs are

not men at all but shabbier versions of the women whose praises they sing. Bleating for Maggy and maybe Bessy too. "What about our trip?" I asked. We had agreed to go out to Long Island again and perhaps hop a ferry, as Jamms put it, to Connecticut. "All right," he replied, "but after that I really have to get back to Maggy and my painting." Where did Bessy figure in all this turning over of a new leaf. I played back what I had glimpsed of his life with Bessy. But there was no point trying to understand Jamms in and out of the drudgery of his life with Bessy and Maggy. There would never be any definitive understanding, at least for me, only an endless oscillation, outside the story, our story, for there was no story without his cooperation OR RATHER

      OR RATHER

        or rather

without at least a recusancy relevant to the matter at hand, namely a story—not necessarily the recusancy of a shepherd at dusk, a music critic at the moment when Alice Tully Hall opens her doors to the brawling bourgeois herds, an ax-murderer at the crack of dawn, no, no, no, nothing quite so fantastical and outside the pale of the capitalist experiment. I craved a simple rearing and champing at the bit equivalent to—perhaps better than—active participation. So there was no understanding Jamms. Of course the story might go on a little longer on its own steam without his powerful presence though not much longer than that and I still might be able to distinguish and decipher him from, within, that steam. But was my aim to decipher or rather live the story with him? Soon I would be alone, I knew that, and though someone else—some hovering witness, for example—might crave the solitude I foresaw as precondition for a reparation vaster than space—unobstructed anonymity deliriously synonymous with unimpeded visibility to the gods grumpily conceding that reparation—I for one dreaded it. I left the dining room and proceeded with my collisions at various levels of that urban rung. Though no Saint Martin my first find was my own kind—a beggar, or rather, a pair of beggars, a mother and her baby daughter crouched in a doorway adjacent to what appeared to be a bustling and newly fashionable Chelsea dive. I gave them, or rather the mother, a five dollar bill, in the hope that my generosity, though hardly instinctive, might numb me to, exalt me beyond, the still lancinating repercussions of Jamm's quickwitted cruelty. I walked away from the hustle and bustle into the pocket of shadow inhabited by...yet another. I looked at him with irritation, with distrust. Surely it was by now common knowledge that I had *already given* and that my fixed income of compassion was consequently exhausted. He moved out of the pocket of shadow into my even shabbier streetcorner limelight. According to a newfound eleemosynary perspective [enhanced by the focus only streetcorners can give] at the moment of stooping to succor the homeless woman and her infant all indigents had been officially and conveniently conflated to that single outstretched quivering palm [her palm had been neither: There had been no sign of a palm] withdrawn then in satisfaction and for all eternity. I crossed to the other side of the street, with its better view of the World Trade Center towers. I looked back to emphasize my distrust: A minute after lending him my aid, a split second after crouching myself to succor him crouched in a trash-flailing doorway he was back again and with no qualms about being back again—popping up improbably—inconceivably—hungry and thirsty and cold and desperate. As he did not flinch I was tempted to cry out, And if you haven't all been conflated to a single palm, a single blind mouth, then there is only one authentic indigent extant and I have already stumbled upon and done my civic duty by her. The rest—you, for example—are impostors mimicking what they perceive to be a highly lucrative, if extreme, stratagem for milking the commonwealth.

I lay in the hotel room for days, refused to eat, the money I still had lay in a corner, enough to get by on for a few more weeks. I made no effort to contact either father or son, grazed Colletti a few, maybe several, times on my way out for bicarbonate of soda but he avoided me as if the glowing possibility of collaboration was now a thing of the remotest past. His real interest had been Jamms and as Jamms turned out to be...I was without name, body, appetency of any kind. Just when I was about to fall into what promised to be a feathery drowse after yet another sleepless night remarkable only for unremittingly strenuous efforts to exhaust myself through self-induced vomiting, the phone rang. He began at once to rant against a film he had just seen, or maybe it was a group of paintings at a gallery, I couldn't make out the target of the ranting but as he went on it became clear he was delighted and appalled by this ability—for though indecipherable it was not so indecipherable as to be unclassifiable

as an ability of some kind — to repudiate — jettison — anything and everything especially those things that could by no stretch of the imagination
be considered in his way. As he spoke it also became clear — or was this
but another machination of the meaning-mongers — that he was not much
of a creator for if truly anchored by, in, the arduousness of production he
would not have had time for such a dizzying freedom of devastation. For
all his arguments against this or that new school of landscape or camera
movement what he was really putting forward was his own appalled
amazement at how easy it was to appropriate and demolish, appropriate
and demolish. For he had just enough sensibility to be able to confuse
somebody else's authentic production with his own. He was at once
appalled and delighted by this lonely ability — into whose confidence he
deigned at least for the moment to want to take me and of which he
allowed even himself to catch only the dimmest glimpse between lashed
outpourings — to make all producers, all creators, the naked prey of his
nihilism. So easy for him to reprobate them all, not only they themselves
but those who might come after, those bred in their bone, those who did
come after, worshipful and competitive. "I loathe these pretenders," not
clarifying who the pretenders were and what made them pretenders.
"And at the same time I felt condemned by them, by their frantic and
vulgar activity. But then I took a walk, into the scummiest heart of Forty-
second Street, in and out of the bookstores, in and out of the fashionable
hotels, in and out of the movie theaters of all persuasions, and suddenly
amidst the ravenous and contemptuous gaze of a cityful of scum, rich
scum, poor, I thought, I think: dad is dead. Oh, didn't mom write? And
all of a sudden I wanted to jump for joy, I did positively jump and threw
my cup of coffee (I was sitting in a fast food emporium by this point,
dehydrated as understandably I had to be from so much wandering)
which I didn't want anyway aside, far aside. For I was set apart by this
caption yet not straightjacketed. Potentiated but not straitjacketed. For
I perceived — underwent — myself that very moment as having lived far
beyond the incident, I mean, the event, I was not wedded to it, I had
transcended it though still glued to it. What had transpired and what I had
transcended constituted part of my mystery. The caption — more the
caption than what it evoked — made me real without — and this is most
unusual — robbing me of my mystery. And this, my good man, is the kind

of story caption and captioned story I like—the kind of story where the characters are always well in advance of—beyond, far beyond—the devastation wrought by the droughts and floods of being, give off the whiff of living well beyond that devastation though mysteriously marked, consecrated, by it. I had come through the event—dad's death—and was therefore beyond it though at the same time identified with it in a way I cannot specify, no, not even to you. His dad died—I was identified with this caption, rooted to what it evoked/invoked, entrenched in it, as in a maimed though not maiming rite of passage. At the same time I was incontrovertibly beyond it, far beyond it. I was suddenly—miraculously—the *disjunction* between what they—the producers—the procurers—of the caption said of my relation to the event—the story—and my sense of that relation, or rather, non-sense. This, then, is the kind of story I like, where the events—incidents—glanced are already far beyond their marveling enunciation, unlocalizable, forever out of sight yet strangely anchored." Although delighted with Jamms's effusiveness I could not help saying, "In other words, you only like stories that are over." In a split second and on the basis of what I construed to be a lurid jettisoning of the father/son relation I knew Jamms would never submit to a story. Not that he knew what a story was. He thought he was talking about stories when he talked about the stories he thought he liked, i.e., those that were over perhaps because they were never begun, or better yet, never continued, never made to manifest the raw sludge of their continuity. But in fact did I really know Jamms would never submit to a story, our story, or was this merely a potential sensational twist in that story furnished free of charge by the meaning-mongers. For Jamms was speaking not of story though he thought he was BUT RATHER

      rather

of fact. Based on Jamms's mingled repudiation and exaltation in the face of fact—fact of a father's death, fact of neighborly murmur of pity and curiosity and awe—I had constructed his relation to story. From his tortured relation to fact I had extrapolated to story. But there was no story here, only sabotage once again, its implements compacted from the memorabilia whirling toward and beyond a father's death. "Oh yes, oh yes, I forgot," he sneered, "you are like all the others, yes, you, at the other end of the line, in the vast hotel overlooking the very districts in which I chose not so much to drown as to leach my despair, and therefore for you as for all the others it's a question of how dare I slur this most sacred of relations. Yet why was — is — this sudden joy at both embodying and superseding — secretly in either case — an event ever doleful, ever unsatisfying, such a slur on this most sacred of relations. Joy is after all the core of this most sacred of relations. My joy then can only batten that core. The dad is the man one as son most wishes unwell. The dad is the being on whom one deigns to lavish the greatest intensity of hate. But don't you see, after being almost annihilated by those swells and by that trash I had a feeling that was almost a thought — a thought that was more than akin to feeling — and feeling/thought, thought/feeling, made me larger, much larger, than the being that only a short time before had been almost triturated by everything around it. A feeling that was almost a thought — the feeling that the event — the fact — the story! — was behind yet very much part of me buoyed me up and made me more, far more, than what anybody including dad — who always managed to see me in one way only: going downhill fast — might insist on taking me for. I had transcended a specific crisis — the caption told me so — I had lived beyond a relation that was no longer a relation — beyond to a certain kind of quizzical unpropagandizing resignation in the face of the crisis — the fact — that had had the decency not to render me overtly — captionably — sadder and wiser. Don't you see: it's my persistent quizzicalness in the face of the life event — the fact — the story — the non-story — the fact — that ground me down into the very anus of being — it is my persistent refusal to be seeking wisdom or torment or experience or posthumous reconciliation with the old guy — it is this mute unimposing expressionless eloquence of acceptance as non-acceptance, wisdom as the stateliness of total confusion but an ordered confusion — it is all this that exalts me, at least in my own eyes. And it is this exaltation that the caption, when uttered, releases. Don't you see: I have absolutely nothing to say about my crisis, nothing to sell, peddle, or vend as a heuristic specimen for others. The heuristic specimen that Maggy robbed me of way back when, well, I never had any intention of selling it; I merely wanted to abscond with it toward the vicinity of some...hovering witness who studying it intently might thereby rehabilitate me beyond all the raging shaming poisons it, the specimen, embodied. But how does all this affect our story for I know you are trying to concoct a story for the two of us. Maybe you must try to have us live beyond—as I have managed to live beyond—the crisis, the life event, you are striving so hard to fabricate." All of this did not seem much different from all prior tumor-ridden ooze of sand thrown in the face of our life together. Yet when he first spoke of his exhilaration at having surpassed yet still being eternally yoked to the life event I did not feel as if he was marring our story BUT RATHER

but rather

NO

get thee behind me, meaning-mongers

No but rather eluding to certain shortcuts or furnishing certain techniques for propelling it forward. For once I did not feel his specimens were competing with and ultimately overthrowing the mother of all specimens—our story. And yet that paltry thing—that thing of shreds and patches—his exhilaration—could it really be held accountable for this new feeling that for all his babbling Jamms was propelling the story forward? Maybe whatever was to be held accountable existed even further outside the story, outside the characters of the story, than his exhilaration ever could, was in every way more refractory to story protocol than his exhilaration could ever be. My feeling, then, that the story was *for the first time* advancing through Jamms's chatter had nothing directly to do with that chatter, which functioned as no more than a grey eminence allowing through its mere and colorless withdrawal for an upsurge with which it had not the least affinity.

At any rate, I did not feel jettisoned nor did I feel our still very inchoate story was jettisoned. I waited, he asked if I was still there. "What about the trip. Still want to go." I did not know how to answer to my best advantage for at this very moment that best advantage was nothing more and nothing less than to preserve the moment by stretching his question—ingratiating, rancorless—out to the crack of doom, so exquisite was its inflection bent for the very first time and even if only for a split second to another's need. I did not care about what came after the question or what might surround it. As nothing as euphoriogenic as the question could ever succeed to the question understandably I wanted to conserve the question, expand its essence on the rack of my content. But I did not know how to contend with my good fortune or the tone of voice necessary to prolong this agony spawned from Jamms's efforts to worm himself into my good graces. "Yes, we are still going." Jamms seemed hesitant, as if I was reluctant and he unsure which of too many rhetorical devices to recruit in behalf of my conversion. He said if we were intending to go I should meet him no later than around noon the day after tomorrow. I spent the whole night walking up and down Forty-second Street. On my way up to my room I caught a glimpse of Colletti emerging from one of many grand ballrooms. He accosted me saying, "A convention for druggists. You and your friend could have come if you had only played your cards right." Something in my face caused him to abandon his solemn tone and add, "A multilevel affair permitting these plumbers to acquire as much new, in other words, free, information relevant to their discipline—in other words, knickknacks for the wife and kids—as is compatible with the girth of their shopping bags—also free. All I had planned for you and your friend was straight and narrow, on the level." As he spoke we managed to make our way into the convention-deconsecrated grand ballroom

    where NO

    where I NO

    where I had first NO

    where NO NO NO

it would redound so conveniently to the story's fabled economy of means in achieving a compulsory interweave of its random threads if I had NO

    first espied him

    first

    espied him vacuuming

    under the seventh lambrequined

    display table.

A few stragglers were still filling their newly acquired shopping bags with what schoolmarms call illustrative material. But what most caught my eye was a poster display in the center of the not-so-vast and chilly space constituting what professed to be a "salute" to the previous decades. Photographs of Kennedy, Monroe, Einstein, their "colorful" juxtaposition professing to evoke a "common past." The pious, nauseatingly glib thrust: Something to the effect that Look: We are all brothers, and sisters: We are all *in this together*: Look at what we've *been through* together.

Without flinching: You, me. Look: our similarities are far greater than our differences. One of the world's biggest drug monsters playing the plain folks game. I could *hardly prevent myself* from extrapolating back to the team of publicists pressured and paid to concoct such an "approach" to seduction of the ever-susceptible public of dispensing middlemen. Though no image came. Disgust intervened every time an image even roughly corresponding to the actual concoction by pressured publicists was about to come to bloody birth.

    I couldn't take my eyes off Monroe; nor could Colletti. Now part and parcel of the "great American experience," which she of course always had been but in a slightly more recessive or menacing key signature, *they* had managed to metabolize and spew her forth spotless and ingratiating—an American symptom devoid of offending, even vaguely disturbing, American content. Because she was desperately needed, almost as an afterthought, to provide some visual and comedic contrast to the ponderousness seeping through the cracks in the other icons. But I refused to be sucked into camaraderie with either the conglomerate or the figures it proposed poker-faced for my—always comradely—always colleague-like—veneration. Kennedy, Monroe, Einstein: We were all *in this together*. Whatever their intrinsic defects these were smelted to insignificance now they themselves had been appallingly filtered through the agglomerative consciousness of some monster exploiter of workers and worldwide consumer public. Their striking, that is to say, almost too schematic, contrasts and differences had been abolished and resynthesized toward some infinitely higher purpose: global pill pushing. "By working for me," Colletti remarked, "you would have been striking a blow against all this." But he refrained from the appropriate demonstrational sweeping gesture.

    Before I traversed the few streets between subway and doorstep—Jamms was staying with a friend in Brooklyn—I sat myself down in a little playground, perhaps to savor my good fortune. I wanted to concentrate on the story, on the story alone, and on nothing but the story for far more important than this imbecilic little pleasure trip was the story bound to emerge from its hindquarters. In a little playground not unlike so many of its facsimiles one naturally dives for the first unoccupied bench. The very word, *bench*, specifically, city park bench, brings tears to my eyes. For what is it to sit on a bench but to affirm one's humanity for all one's prior pullulating pretense to a status beyond same. To align one's buttocks with the slats (sometimes sadly lacking so that the bench fast becomes in fact the sign of—the concept of—itself) is to succumb to one's humanness. At any rate, a man was playing with his tiny son or daughter, before my very eyes, or something neither daughter or son but closely allied to these concepts. At moments

I stopped, tried to stop, dead in the tracks of my seeing. For to go on seeing, wasn't that to acquire an anecdote appallingly homologous with Jamms's tales of the terminal ward.

the man, casually dressed, an unemployed actor perhaps, hid behind a tree, an oak, a maple, oak and maple at once, with a smile ingratiatingly fey for being ironically taunting. He did not appear well-dressed but since I could not imagine anybody physically and psychically fit in sadder straits than I what was I to assume but that this was nothing but an example of italicized

poor dress

and therefore high

elegance indeed. The anecdote was going on and on, sabotaging the story to come. I was as curious about whether his dress was poor or not, or about how I would eventually make peace with the state of confused hope and dread into which this single moot point in the landscape was trajecting me, as I was about his strategy with regard to the child. I was baffled and at the same time I was always far in advance of the solution to both these enigmas as it would unfold out in the world, namely, at its own soggy rate. Without being able to articulate I knew I had solved them but not to my satisfaction precisely because the ingenuity of the solution shut me off from the event to which I wished and did not wish to be in thrall. Yet having solved all I was able to go back and mimic perplexity which was very much in keeping with the tone of the event—the child looking around, immediately noticing the hider, smiling. This was a member of that swelling species, single father, visiting his son on—well, when you are unemployed and fashionably so then every day is Sunday—single father, I could tell, from something about the way he looked to other people, not to me, for I was already delivered up to a story that made me invisible, but to the others, the nannies out with their charges, the businessmen resting on their worsted haunches, for some kind of confirmation, not that he was dutifully spending time with his kid as a good dad should and therefore only impersonating a good dad, but of something deeper, it needed to be much deeper, or else the anecdote would die, though why should I care since I was delivered up to a story impervious to anecdote. No, he sought confirmation that he was *in fact* with his child in the world, that this event was *in fact* real because enshrined in somebody's consciousness. And wasn't this what any story needs. Hadn't the passing of photo from Jamms to cop and back again required such confirmation. Hadn't that moment in the story—our story—collapsed precisely because I was, sole pivot, torn between a hunger to embody the confirmation of its unfolding and, as a character crucial to that unfolding, bestow the function on some other—some hovering witness—completely outside all unfolding? As I looked around it seemed few if any could give the kind of confirmation he was seeking, surely it had to do with the stupor peculiar to members of a crowd, of beings per se, unsure of what they are therefore of what they see, or if sure then gutturally resentful of such a surefooted seeing being visited upon them. I moved off, to a farther bench, further and further from father and child, who were now a pinpoint of shadow among the deeper shadows of the apartment buildings and literally stank of the past, not mine but Jamms's. Only now I was next to one of those city couples

one of those

city couples that proliferate especially during the weekday lunch hour on park benches. I moved quickly off but still within hearing distance for it was none other than Maggy and Jim. And even if it wasn't Maggy and Jim it still was for what she, the Maggy figure, was saying illuminated the Maggy/Jim dyad in such a way as to propel the story—our story—into dazzling clarity, or rather,

OR RATHER

into the possibility

of dazz

ling clarity.

It was Maggy and Jim because it had to be Maggy and Jim. For what this couple was managing to say advanced the story further than it had ever gone compliments of the good auspices of the real Maggy and Jim.

These were the real Maggy and Jim even if they could not confirm
definitively what the real Maggy and Jim were doing to at last propel the
story into a possibility of momentous clarity. "Even, Jim, if I have my
symptom, Jim you still love me, right?" Nod. This was a new, a fragile,
Maggy, a Maggy raw with need. "Even if I am not always the most
beautiful." Nod. "And even if one day I don't have my symptom anymore —" I turned away — from Maggy and Jim — for I was haunted by the
splendor of this final plea. Even if she had her symptom would he love her
and even if one day she didn't have her symptom — she, Maggy, it was
Maggy, was driven by anxiety to attempt the exhaustion of all pretexts for
anxiety though it was precisely the overwhelming fear of such exhaustion
that generated the most dazzling shifts of phrase. She was trying to eat up
and procure comfort against all conceivable pretexts for anxiety at the
same time that she dreaded coming to the end of all such pretexts. But
what fascinated me most about Maggy here and now, was that she was
no longer the substantial fleshly Maggy of Rhinebeck, New York, but the
fulcrumless puppet of endlessly proliferating possibilities on the level of
language. Here on this bench she had left the real world behind, or rather,
the twists and turns of her thought forever anticipating and attempting to
squelch a new cause for anxiety even if on the other side of the squelching
lay not ultimate security but a void more terrifying than any concrete
instance — the twists and turns of her thought in *relation to Jim* had forced
her to leave the real world — that is to say, the promptings of her personal
pathology — behind. There was no longer a one-to-one correspondence
between that pathology and her utterances, her elaboration of cases,
pretexts. I was a witness, I could confirm in any court of law that from
symptom as pretext for estrangement from Jim she had been driven to
absence of symptom as equivalent pretext for estrangement NOT because she lived, had ever lived, the possibility in her collisions with the
outside world but simply because the flow of the words twisting and
turning and writhing their ratiocinative calm directed where she must go
so as never to exhaust all pretexts for anxiety. For her there was no being
definitively consoled: the closest she came to consolation was being able
to go on asking for consolation through the elaboration of pretexts
without end. The terror for her, for Maggy , this new Maggy, Maggy
finally outside the Rhinebeck ambience, divested as it were of her earthly

envelope, was to run out of instances, possibilities, pretexts, formulations insuring notice from, conspicuity to, the other — Jim; proving that she had gotten, apotropaically, to the finish line though never, hopefully, the final finish, before him. For they were both, Maggy and Jim, this Maggy and Jim, the only Maggy and Jim, descending on her formulations though from different directions. And once she seized so she must assume on a dire formulation before him he had to acknowledge and defer to her priority by refraining from giving himself up to all that formulation evoked/invoked of contemptuous abandonment in pursuit of fleshlier flesh. "If one day you didn't have your symptom any more — " She shrank, she turned away, as if it was he who had broached this horrible possibility, horrible only because it would necessarily lead to her abandonment, her punishment, for throwing away or being divested of a vital prop. "No, no, you won't leave me," she murmured. "Even without the symptom, right?" She had tried to metabolize all possibilities before he got to them, before he could even begin to think of them. But even now, contemplating one possibility long after she had broached/appropriated it, he was managing to get to it before, long before, her. These possibilities, formulations, pretexts, had one trait in common: they were all too quickly not her own. She no longer spoke, this prospect of the absence of all symptoms terrified her beyond belief, thrust her into a world of pronged hallucination. "I think that under the circumstances this little trip will do me good." "With him "' she retorted. "And under what circumstances." I waited, beginning to loathe myself, for what were these: man, employed or unemployed, and his son; man and woman — Jim and Maggy — but specimens erected to baffle the story's course, the story in its nudity, story as the revelation of its own musculature. They began to walk back and forth over the sandy turf, trying so it seemed to escape from each other. But whether they were trying to escape or rejoin it simply could not be allowed to matter. They were an obstruction on the way to the story. As long as he was coupled to Maggy, he, Jim — though its protagonist — was nothing but an obstruction on the way to the story. Or had the story already just begun through them and them alone and should I then now deliver myself up to the delicate tracery of their footsteps. Two old crones, toothless and well-dressed, observed them with the irritable incomprehension of perfect comprehension, or rather, their perceptual apparatus, conjoint like the vasculature of Siamese twins, so ravenous, so prehensile, quickly became overrequisitioned with respect to the generation of ideas made to the measure of so much seeing and so this insufficiency of idea became the intrinsic ghastliness of the scene before them. With consummate ease they quickly went about confusing their impotence with the loathsomeness of the scene at hand.

When I arrived at his doorstep suddenly I did not want to arrive, I wanted to go on arriving indefinitely and I could only go on not arriving accumulating details such as those furnished by the playground, mere counterparts to his tales of tumorly woe. He had somehow managed to get there ahead of me; no sign of Maggy. He surprised me by asking very nicely if I wanted some coffee and a few of Maggy's famous sweet rolls. "Are they famous," I could not prevent myself asking. He explained that after baking them she had been obliged to trudge off to the state unemployment office to report an error in the computation of her biweekly benefits. Bessy was still up in Rhinebeck, at a tap dancing class. He seemed just a little too eager to explain their absence; as if I cared. On the open road I realized with a shudder how very little indeed, at this *juncture*, now there's a word to be grateful for and right on cue when I needed it to define, that is to say, mask the anguish overpowering me heartily. As we rode on—a car trip this time—Jamms grew more and more distant, every comment induced a shrug, and sometimes, even before I opened my mouth, he seemed so rapidly to anticipate the need for a shrug that the shrug was shrug less at what I was about—what I had— to say than at the always recurring and infinitely tedious possibility of being obliged to shrug it off. And then the next or at some future time I might expect the shrug to be against this instinct to shrug against the recurring need to shrug and so on and so forth into the vainglorious night of snuffling suburban foliage. And then a shrug against the need to shrug against the instinct to shrug against the need to shrug against. But after a certain point I knew I would have trouble justifying my articulation of a matter—an event—a fact—that was no longer one of even infinitesimal perceptual clarity but had instead become a havoc wreaked on the subsidence of that clarity. Here was articulation—utterance—enunciation—on the lookout for any opportunity to make a mockery of perception as scholarly reportage, as moments before it had been similarly vigilant in its effort to perplex and thwart poor Maggy on her voyage toward union with the fair Jim. Yet was it union she sought. Didn't her frantic elaboration of horrifying possibilities requiring incessant refutation in fact enable her to steer clear of the union her clutching groping inflections and gestures professed to crave. I was suffering as Maggy had suffered. We had much in common; she should have been invited along on this, perhaps our last voyage together. Turning to him with both hands on the steering wheel was equivalent to playing back the formulation: *a shrug less at what I was about — what I had — to say than at the always recurring...* What was the purpose of such bloody distinctions, hyperdiacritical marks lost in the sludge of a failed relation. What did such distinctions do for the story. Were they necessary to the story, our story? Were they, on the contrary, destructive to the story?

Jim shrugged subliminally as if he knew my eyes were upon him. How explain to the likes of Jim that I was driven to such distinctions *within the story* out of loathing of anything even faintly redolent of the delights of a normal life. And wasn't a normal life what Jamms was heading for once I was politely or not so politely dumped along the way? I could imagine him being felicitated on the birth of twins and smiling sheepishly rather than incense Maggy against him. So what recourse but to the elaboration of fine distinctions as straightforwardly outside the hysteria responsible for incessant regeneration of this ostensibly supremely natural craving for — the normal life. Enmeshed in the elaboration of fine distinctions I was by definition outside the hysterical craving for the blessed tranquillity of a normal life. Neither Jamms nor Maggy wanted such a life; simply they thought they should want it. Couldn't he find it in his heart to felicitate this going to fine distinctions as to rectification of a perilous situation: such entrenchment in fine distinctions surely made everybody feel happy, that is to say, nondiscriminatingly excluded from their elaboration everybody incapable of happiness on any front. My retreat to fine distinctions — my surrender to the unspeakable delight of their elaboration — was a way of shitting fairly and equally on everybody bound to yet refusing to do his or her duty by the story. For such a surrender left these everybodies out in the cold while I went about exalting and expanding their unanimously latent gravamen that by consorting with one I necessarily and mercilessly neglected another and, even more horrific, allowed the relation with that one to instantaneously evolve into the ultimate atrocity visited upon, perpetrated against, me. My relation with one or another was nothing but that one or another's vulturely exploitation of the manifold opportunities my surrender to that relation presented. Yes, this was the verdict of the hovering witness dormant in all the characters of the story so far and to come and by drowning myself in my addiction to fine distinctions I was tormenting all these hovering witnesses equally. My flagitiousness was too widely disseminated to be reducible to a localized imposed excruciation. To any of them, insanely jealous each of the other and of each other's claim upon my affections, I preferred my fine distinctions. Before he shrugged himself away forever couldn't Jamms discern, then, why I resorted to fine distinctions such as those clogging the drain of his shrug?

And yet, and yet, all this babble about addiction to fine distinctions torturing my congeners did not belong here. Or rather, I had the distinct impression that in thinking about fine distinctions and about the torture indiscriminately inflicted by my addiction to their elaboration—that in thinking about them I or rather somebody else—some hovering witness about to be born or annihilated—was thinking about something else and somebodies else, figures enmeshed in relations more primal and an addiction more unspeakable than that taking for its accessory a shrug, a smile, a hand on a steering wheel. I had the distinct impression that in going on about the dire virulence of my addiction I was in fact merely broadcasting the RADICAL DISJUNCTION between the innocuousness of such an entity and the tortures it was supposed to be inflicting right and left. Such a potency, such a virulence, belonged to some other addiction, not necessarily mine, most probably not mine, a hovering witness's then, whose story—a fragment of whose story—I was recounting in advance of its scheduled inundation of the only story that mattered—ours. And in recounting this witness's story so as to forestall any need on anybody's part—witness or no—to live it, to need to desire to live it, I was also of course righteously seizing on a golden opportunity to recruit its moments to the event at hand, that is, the trip out to the Island—an event surely and indefatigably in the service of another story—the only conceivable story—our story—and by recruiting thereby enrich it, in other words, barely sustain it, forever faltering into nonexistence. Perhaps one day Jamms might find it in his heart to enlighten me as to the nature of the real addiction lending its potency and virulence to the matter at hand. But I did not want in delivering myself up to mewlingly insatiable curiosity over some irretrievable thing-in-itself to lose sight of my only site: the story, which if it was to survive must derive its nourishments not from such things

     but rather

     BUT rather

but RATHER from the radical disjunctions between last-minute stand-ins for such things...in-themselves and the repercussions these last-minute stand-ins were recruited and required to account for.

     In short, he grew more and more impatient at having to sketch a whole shrug. He was in quest of an abbreviated form of the shrug running nevertheless the whole gamut of shruglike emotion. We stayed in one of the big chain hotels; on our second, no, our third hike, this time up a little path strewn with dead red berries and hints, here and there, of spectacularly reclusive avifauna, no longer able to contain myself I said, "What about our story," but as I spoke and in the midst of what I took to be my supreme nakedness I had the distinct or perhaps it is more accurate to say the contradistinct impression that I was stating what was ostensibly uppermost at a moment of least concern. Or perhaps it was only the alchemy of a stating that somehow cancelled the state stated or rendered it incompossible, immiscible rather, with the stating. I shuddered at the axiom I was proposing far down in my bowels, to wit, a state of soul, a velleity, a hunger, for story or other, and that state's utterance could not possibly occupy the same space at the same time. It seemed, then, that this moment, big with berries, was but the preliminary sketch of an impossible future, at some point in which I would ask about our story and know I was meaning what I said. He turned to me, never had contempt seemed so marked on his features, and said, "To hell with the story. After this little hike, I'm calling our little relation a dead issue." Maybe it was the unfamiliarity of the country air, the stench of dead leaves not quite done with dying, at any rate I could not tolerate *all this* and so I told myself I was back on the bench, in the playground, with father, son, lover, and lover whose symptom or eternal absence of same was still threatening to annihilate a relation not noteworthy for its tenderness. In short, I was catapulted back to that previous scene or rather OR RATHER to my failure to have actively utilized that previous scene as a crucial prophylactic element in our story to stave off just such impasses as this. I thought of the bench, of the missing slats, and tried to make myself wonder how many slats might be safely removed and the bench still retain its identity as bench, how far the concept of bench might be stretched against the absence of certain tiresome accessories. I tried to go on fixing not on Jamms but on the bench and all I had not noticed due to my preoccupation with our new life flowed back to me willy-nilly: the building across the way, perhaps a courthouse, adorned with mullioned mirrors that had managed to give a better account of the acacias screening me from the pointed finger of midday sun than they gave of themselves; a hydrant on which a derelict chose to sit briefly and for the duration of the sitting and perhaps shitting who's to say that that derelict without a pot to piss in in an extralegal sense did not forcibly annex the hydrant protruding from the calves of that building, maybe a courthouse, buses reflected in its mullioned mirrors long before their timorous advance guard of shadow over asphalt announced incursion; a shopping cart draped with what looked like old clothes, making it the property, logically, of some other derelict squatting at stool nearby, or rags, making it the property, logically, of some workman sunning himself, also nearby. And I went on hungering for what was taking shape so what if retrospectively as a perfect moment and vowed, before Jamms's receding rump, that if this moment could find it in its heart to be refunded I would live it differently, change my evil ways, barter blessing for injury or vice-versa and never again allow myself to indulge in the kind of stale reflection of which I had been guilty all the time that perfect moment was unfolding for I had come to realize — Jamms, stand still for the solemnity of the occasion — that far worse than this or that terrible event encroaching on the purity of the moment was the total absence of event, least in keeping with that purity and by allowing it to go its way unmolested to oblivion perpetrating the greatest molestation of all. No, no, no, I promised myself that never again would I tarnish the purity of such a moment with reflections on the dreaded undesirability of events infinitely less tarnishing and expressed calmly the hope that whoever was now — whatever was now — making

Jamms grimace in this way would ultimately hear and take pity and transport me back to that moment just before I encountered Jamms for what was sure to be the last time and all hell unleashed on my world through all his loathing refused to depict. "You are free to do as you like with the rest of dad's money, in fact, I will gladly string them along into thinking you are still about to land me, reel me in. They needn't know I intend never to go back and that I consider our relation officially at an end. Why am I not going back? I gave you my definition of the father/son relation quite some time ago, now go chase it, Rover, like an old pizza bone." He turned forward, then back, and proceeded on his way. Picking up a stone or was it a rock or a branch, a mere branch, no more than a twig, a petiole limp with gyration, it was once again with the sense that all was preliminary to a moment that might never have to arrive which moment, should it be somehow compelled to arrive, would require me—make it imperative for me—to pick up a stone and straining backward launch it yet, even under those strained circumstances, in nothing more than the vaguest general direction of Jamms. I was particularly struck by the tautness—the professed tautness—of his buttocks as he climbed without hesitation into the farthest reaches of what would soon be night. When I heard it hit his head I knew it to be more than stone, more than rock, yet less than twig. He fell backward and though he seemed to be falling into my arms there was a pleasure almost voluptuous in rejecting one who had made it almost a vocation to reject our beautiful story unfolding. "To hell with it," I whispered when, sure he could not hear, I let him down gently, let him somersault a few times, before searching for yet another stone, rock, twig, with which to pummel him further until a huge clot told me my work was done. This is our story, I heard myself whisper. I covered him with leaves. Were the trunks, sires of the leaves, feigning innocence of the mighty meaningfulness of this act and all that ringed it round of frustration, torment, unavowable sentiments of undying devotion tinged with obliterating servility and a slight tincture of rage at that servility, in looking away, from me, representative of big cities and highways. Or if not quite complicitous—accessory—to the act in their stance couldn't they be thought of as actively boldly shamelessly proclaiming that mighty meaningfulness in what was not a turning away but a turning toward, a

turning toward. The rugous boles knew very well what had transpired, what mighty meaningfulness had been afoot in breeding my act, or rather,
OR RATHER,
or rather, they knew insofar as they were connected with their roots, twigs, leaves. And suddenly I began to loathe myself with Jamms's loathing for always trying ever so hard to understand...myself, in and out of act. So that Jim was right after all, smelling dogshit somewhere or other, when he proclaimed this self-rehabilitating hunger to understand to be worse, far worse, than alcoholism, teetotalling, encopresis, or coprophagy with a twist of lemon. What was I — and now more than ever, if past, that is, was to shed light on present — but one in a catchcrop of quasi thinkers ever so earnestly — it was the earnestness that had to have turned his stomach for he could unfailingly sniff out the plea at the heart of the earnestness — and without even a demiurge to snicker at the futility of the task — struggling to *come to terms* with the universe. And yet the absence of a demiurge hardly engendered an indemnificatory pathos. No, no, no, no pathos, only stupidity and that in the idiotic look with which I regarded, or tried to regard, the space above or to the right or left of the dead body beneath the leaves, though not yet quite beneath the leaves, space comprising distant farmhouse passing itself off as village inn, pigeon-infested steeples, tree trunk, tree trunk, tree trunk, patch of sky, green arc of sky, yellows and pinks, flavors of mortality, odors of greenish bough. In my look at last I tried to signal and for Jim's immediate benefit an authentically skeptical curiosity concerning my concern, my deep concern, to understand at last the workings of a mighty meaningfulness spilling into and oozing out of my acts. Too late to pass muster in his eyes.

What had Jamms's dad said on his deathbed, *according to the dead man*: I fired her because she refused to clean my groin. I immediately hurried, though standing still, to appropriate this as my reason for having just killed Jamms. Yet...had I killed him? What hovering witness was nearby to confirm the act, ratify its substance? All of a sudden this having killed seemed hopelessly tenuous, it terrified me in its looming tenuity. If only I could be sure it had been done and done quickly then I could go about doing away with the signs. I looked around: nothing and no one, not even a patch of sky ravaged by pigeons stunned out of flight. It became clear to me no event is ever real in itself but only insofar as it is swept up and not quite dissolved in yet obliged to yoke itself to some other, possessed of no clearcut disaffinity for its mate but simply content to stew in its own specificity without any extraneous aid or opprobrium. I needed such an event to make my event real, to make it fall into time. I raised him, began transporting him into some little depression in the cliff overlooking the ocean. He resisted. And as I dragged huffing and puffing I felt hopeless, worse, infinitely vulnerable, as if this transport rendering me infinitely vulnerable would continue forever. As it was going on now so it would go on forever. Yet the minute I set him down—and he was set down faster than I might have imagined—to my satisfaction—set down in place and camouflaged though not smothered with several inches worth of peat, leafage, moss, lichen lard, and other anti-decidua, foully redolent of the great outdoors—I felt a resurgence of hope, I mean, I could begin to think about orienting myself toward the future. I was no longer in transition, marred by incompleteness, transit [the poor man's evolution] was permanently evicted from my life, I was not only outside this act—of laying him to rest—but outside all acts, complete, complete, no longer marred by the scandalous conspicuity of any act in process. Now I was complete, having found Jim his good-looking casket, his very own good-looking casket, as was consonant with a hallowed family tradition. And what was that casket after all but the nuptials of putrefactive country air, moxibustion of time, space, and the pockmarked leaves of autumn. The only problem was that all his dad's phrases—of which *good-looking casket* was but one of many stellar examples—his dad's comments—so many instantiations of story sabotage—threatened to come back and revile me, repel me, but with a carefully constructed, might I say even a calculated repulsiveness so that I would be ending up with a revulsion, a reviledness, that was not quite revulsion, reviledness, and more like a rare opportunity to exploit just the behavioral—that is to say, theatrical— stratagem to improve my appearance, ethically speaking. Recoiling repulsed from dad's excessiveness to my jaundiced eye I would end up *not so criminal* —newfound criminality instantly eclipsed by and transformed into concern over the unseemliness of all those little remarks made once in haste by tumor-ridden dad. Repudiating these instances I was becoming more than myself, refunded to myself but as more, far more, than myself, as when long long before the man in the delicatessen called me *son* and when I willingly, undemandingly, gave directions to a slob from the Midwest. So, as you may imagine, I actively encouraged memories of Jamms's dad's—now my dad's—reprobations of all those dedicated to his moribund well being so that I might glorify my very own abstention— estrangement—from such an attitude. For at this very moment, under the night sky unbroken and unsoftened by housefronts, I needed to feel estranged from something for this newborn act, this killing, put me too much in the heart of things, showed me too much at home with that heart's ways, inevitably and ubiquitously violent ways, and so I needed to impersonate—in order to save face with myself—someone not at home with those ways. I needed to feel myself withdrawing from the world in reviling contemplation of its lewdness. The dad's reprobation of his helpers was turning out to be a perfect embodiment of world from which to withdraw. For the duration of the withdrawing the dad's reprobation was the world entire, all of being. At first with all of nature on my side I had thought of not burying. Now I was glad I had since all of nature was not on my side, never would be. I looked around: to the west not only leading strings of the motherly setting sun but a field of what could pass for glowing wheat—the kind about which affluent urbanites are always babbling so as to appear interested in other than their only interest: bank account; to the east, a wigwam which became on my closer approach a little silo; to the south a little inn where Jim had seen fit to check his bags, not I, being instructed to await him at the local pharmacy [The Hippocratic Oaf]: why pay double if we, or rather he, would be using the room for only a day. To the north, woodland streaked every color of the spectrum of the emotions yet none straying very far from what could be deemed greenish. Could I leave without somehow implicating all this space, proliferation of leafy landscape, in my story, for at once it was clear the story was doomed to continue, with or without Jamms, though strictly speaking Jim was still very much in the story and perhaps the lesson to be learned though I was sick to death of lessons, hadn't my relation to Jim been one long lesson unlearned—what to do; what not to do, when it was a question of ruffled peacock feathers—perhaps the lesson to be learned was that the story was most progressing and Jim most in that story now that he was not cluttering and impeding, almost annihilating it with his bulk, his long lean dissatisfied talentless bulk. The story was now possible but only in the absence, the permanent absence, of its protagonist. Or was this a mere fantasm of the story-mongers. At any rate no

AT ANY RATE

no more vital energy to be eaten up wondering if he was going to fall short again and hinder the story's plowed progress. I tried to compare the present incident, Jim's murder, that is, with the incident concerning the photo and the cop and the beach. But it was unclear whether that incident was still, had it ever been, a paradigm, or even if not or no longer a paradigm could it still be adverted to as a paradigm against which the substantiality of any subsequent incident must be measured and determined, or could I safely shelve it as a mishap, a false start, a wretched little detour on the way west of elsewhere.

I had gone only a few steps when I found, or rather, lost myself, unable to remember whether I had buried him completely, even if at the same time I knew for a fact that I had not left him the slightest bit unburied. I had a very clear picture in my mind of the body completely smothered. This didn't matter, for the hunger to give free rein to certain emotions — fear, sorrow, dread — was greater than the certainty of having done what left no room for the free play of these emotions. Or perhaps it is incorrect to say that in spite of my certainty of having thoroughly buried him I was giving free rein to emotions consonant only with uncertainty. Rather: because of my certainty of having thoroughly buried him I was delivered up to the emotions consonant with uncertainty but in a form far more virulent because far less distracted by the circumstantial side effects of authentic uncertainty. I could not remember whether or not I had left a glove even if I knew I had not been wearing gloves for years. On a certain level the fact of not having worn gloves for years was irrelevant to this throbbing fear of giving myself away. But I refused to go back. Was my refusal to succumb to this demon seeding me with doubt — my refusal to return to the scene and confirm — sign of essential strength or of mere hyperrigidity incapable of altering its absence of course even in the name of maintaining the basal tone of structural integrity. I knew I was waiting for some future event to resolve the matter either by bringing forth that resolution in all its blindingly boorish lucidity or by saddling me with worries so overwhelming that my sudden indifference, my snoring abulia, in the face of a problem so tormenting but a short time before, would qualify as admission that I very well knew and had known all along no incriminating evidence of ineptitude had been left behind. I was waiting for the future to supersede this torment, this torment so intense precisely because it could not conceive of the future even if it was already deep within that future. I was able to torment myself about whether or not he had been sufficiently smothered precisely because I did not wish to exit from the sludge of the moment of smothering as eternal. For there was some kind of comfort staying in the moment, staying on alone in the moment, forever.

I made a detour en route to the ferry slip and through that detour superseded my torment. As the collapsed wavelets on the little stretch of beach between the stretch of waste where Jamms was buried and the port were absorbed immediately into the next wave forming rather than, still bobbing up and down, as that next wave fully formed broke against them, thereby allowing me to profit from the dialectic enrichment to be discerned in such a mechanism—as the collapsed wavelets were immediately absorbed I found myself able to say: I smothered Jamms completely, and, seconds after, I did not leave a glove behind. The momentousness of this event—the collapse, that is, of the wavelets, absorbed into their successor, immediately, obliterating the possibility of a delayed absorption although such delay conceivably could also contribute in its humble way to the formation of a successor—transformed me into another, somebody able to accept irritation from without (dialectic enrichment observed but ultimately withheld) without feeling sucked into indistinguishability from the tormentor, without needing to want to feel sucked in as a way out of isolation in separatedness from the torment source and by extension from all torment sources, to wit, the whole fucking ugly planet. And at the same time I felt that I had done *something* in relation to the story though still I was not sure if it was propulsive or obliterative: I had manufactured a radical disjunction between the proclaimed momentousness of this event transforming me into all I was not and enabling me to shed the noisome uncertainties that moored me to the recent past of smothering and brothering AND its essence. For how could an event so minuscule as the collapse of a wavelet be responsible for so momentous a transformation? As I entered the main street I made a

point of interrogating the sky or rather the line of sky between sky proper
and rooftops, there where sky was made almost shrilly crystalline in
contrast with rooftops vaguely illuminated by lower reaches but never
enough to mar their silhouetting. At one corner, just before I reached the
ferry, a tiny building turned its single column of windows to the absence
of traffic and passersby. Only a dog stopped to watch me watching and
so doing immediately transformed me into a prosperous proprietor
enjoying one last look at his place of business—"He goes to business," as
housewives in the outlying boroughs of New York are wont to say when
they are struggling to evoke an essential decency—before resuming the
small trek homeward. For said yokel must make sure all the lights are
extinguished before going home to tickle his wife's fancy. And lo and
behold he is suddenly struck by a certain luminous fizzle, the being
suddenly struck synonymous of course with a more than dormant
intention to reprimand the straggling lackey responsible, not that said
lackey has in actual fact done anything wrong for hadn't proud proprietor
been actively encouraging said lackey to strike up said fizzle before departing in order to ward off thugs, hoodlums, and competitors—no, no,
no, reprimand is being incubated simply toward keeping him on his toes
and at a distance by showing that he, proud proprietor, ever the proud
proprietor, is never never never never never to be assumed satisfied at a
job well done. I was emboldened to linger by Jamms's sudden death. The
phrase, *sudden death,* made me feel almost a pitying alarm and for Jim not
myself. Nevertheless I moved along. As at the slip I found myself behind
a beefy businessman I was put in mind not so much of Mr. Jamms as of
his uncollected aphorisms the most dazzling among which I certainly had
to number: I fired her because she wouldn't clean my groin, balls and all,
though I knew I was adding the very last phrase for effect. Suddenly I
realized [the air was thick with the factitiousness of self-discovery]: if
Jamms's dad had all along been an obstruction to our going and doing and
being then Jamms himself had been an even bigger obstruction—to my
undergoing of that prior obstruction as a way of being in, crucial to, the
story. Suddenly—why now, why now—it became clear, clear, clear,
clearer than clear, that the doings of Jamms's tumor-laden dad must not
necessarily be considered an obstruction to our story. Only Jamms's
telling, telling, telling, about the doings. His dad's obstructiveness and not

only to our story suddenly seemed crucial to my story. At any rate, the dad
had died, or was dying, soon would die, in rage and disgust and contempt
for the world in its fly-by-night ministrations best exemplified by the
timeworn smile on the face of the neighbor whose first nickel ever earned
was still and always would be glued to his hairy old butt—and was to be
congratulated for so dying if for no other reason than that I was plausibly
his truest heir, inheriting all that rage and disgust and smirking contempt
as only the truest scion, most authentic offshoot, might and must. Given
the (temporarily!) loathsome state of the planet Jamms, Sr., had been
correct in and true to his revulsion right up to the very bitter end and I was
elected to continue the tradition, even if, strictly speaking, I have starting
from this moment a deeprooted antipathy to reversals of the sort: And as
it later turned out, it was not A but B who turned out to be the true and
rightful heir, as it turned out. At any rate, I was the true scion and now
Jim was out of the picture I wasn't quite sure where the tellings about
mom and dad and the tumor-laden dawns and dusks stood in relation to
my—to our—story. It was as if with Jim's death these incidents were no
longer encapsulated in specimens—storylets—and were free to be absorbed into the bloodstream of my own story, presently being held in
escrow until such time as Jim was deemed worthy of reinstatement.

It was only when I arrived back at the hotel that I realized how
tired I was. The clerk on duty did not seem to recall that two of us had
checked in. I cashed a few of the travelers' checks pillaged from Jim's
person. With all this money on hand I had a right to a good dinner in the
hotel restaurant. The minute I was inside I wished I could be outside
looking in at this motley group seated about the Long Island fire in the
cozy twilight, every member of the nauseous agglomeration husbanding
a frozen smile vengefully worked into the physiognomic paste. The smiles
said: We are at peace, we focus on nothing but that peace, and yet through
the corners of their eyes—eyes all over their slack well-toned bodies—
supremely prosperous and supremely lean—they were alert to anything
that might dare to challenge, crowned by the flicker of the flames, this
delicate equilibrium within and among. I was unnerved and at the same
time fascinated by their ability, reflexively united against any threat to
that equilibrium, to converse without showing signs of obliteration
issuing from a suspicion that it had all been said and done before. Turning

away but reminding myself I was turning away as Jamms not myself made me feel stronger, but only for a moment, not strong enough certainly to enter the charmed circle, as Jamms would have done, but strong enough to move away without feeling pursued or denounced by conspiratorially discreet glances. But I do not wish it to be thought that the company ensconced around the fire consisted only of voraciously bland youngish islanders happy as fireflies in dogshit. No, there was an elderly man and woman arguing with no particular rancor. At any rate, I turned away. But did I have the right to turn away, in other words, could I muster enough reminiscences of anterior achievement, or at least risk-taking, to bolster the flamboyance of turning away as something more than flimsy presumption, pose—as something manly and more than justified by *all I had endured*.. Turning away I had difficulty reestablishing myself in the key of self-affirmation that had been, at least in accelerated retrospect, the pretext for the turning away. I thought of the murder and all the obstacles I had encountered en route to its consummation and concealment. Although wasn't concealment the essence of its consummation. I thought of all I had endured with—but no, it was Jamms, not I, who had endured his father's bellowing and anathematizing. I had endured nothing of that, except the telling, his.

She, the old woman, required that he, the old man, furnish examples to support so preposterous a point as he was making yet as he began to comply—the wrinkles on his face looked as if they were knotted into compliance—I saw her looking off, calculating, no longer thinking about him and all he said and did to irritate her in no very satisfactorily definable way. Did she know in advance there were no substantial—no conceivable—counterarguments. No, she was further off than that. Was she preparing a retort to what he had not even begun to elaborate? No, further off than that, clearly beyond her retort and any possible response to her retort, ruminating in a plane where no counterargument could caulk the wound that went deeper, far far far deeper, than its occasional manifestation in—suppuration into—disputatious chatter, occiput-deep in a primal puddle reflecting a firmament speckled with next week's shopping list or tomorrow's visit to the dentist. She was already living far in advance of the futility—albeit the necessary futility—of intermittent chatter permitting her to forget intermittently how she was tormented beyond the possibility of chatter ever to express. She was my Mr. Jamms: I hungered, as Jamms had hungered, to disgorge this anecdote centering around her recoil into rumination.

Suddenly NO

I was understanding NO NO NO

why all along Jamms NO.

I waited for the story-mongers and their cohorts, the meaning-mongers, to pass me by. They would do better on the rumps of a charming young couple at the table adjacent to the old folks'. This was obviously a first date and both were aware of the significance of the occasion. Scooping up her food and listening to him speak her consciousness was partitioned between the saying and the scooping. Or rather, her consciousness would have been so—justly—partitioned if the scooping had not been a way out of enduring the excruciation of the listening. When finally she looked up to meet his gaze and nod her understanding it was somehow, at least to me, a little—far too—belated, uncomfortably out of synchronization with the decisive moment allotted to looking up and ratifying the saying as food ideally fit for a listening. Or maybe it was I out of synchronization, *especially now that I had committed murder.* But was I *especially* out of synchronization *now?* Hadn't I always been a bit unsynchronized? Only now I owed it to the story, that was still in transit, to remind it of its essential building blocks, to quoin them to its superstructure with an allusive glue before they fell away to disrepair. And one of the essential building blocks—the crowning building block—was the murder. And so here I was giving life to the murder after the fact, like a good meaning-monger. But this was not to be spurned: An event is real to the extent that it can be referred back to. Called back. She was forced, the young girl, as she lifted her head at last from the crowded plate, to feel his quizzical scrutinizing, or rather

OR RATHER, to endure her own excruciated scrutinizing of a face that was appallingly or delightfully different from its voice or all too clear a reminder of that voice. By lifting up her head Maggy—she—Maggy—she—opened herself up to a maximal scrutiny at the moment long brewed and slated for her own maximal and optimal scrutiny of the face connected with the voice. At this moment long incubated and set aside precisely for a maximal scrutiny of the face belonging to the voice

that had been harassing and caressing her she found herself imperceptibly transformed into the target of scrutiny. Yes, yes, yes, this was the
meaning of the undulation passing over her face as she faced the
interlocutor I could not see, only hear, a mere soundtrack, to wit, the
instantaneous transformation of scrutinizer into scrutinized, of scrutiny
into scrutinizedness—this was the meaning of the undulation or rather,
this was the use of the meaning, correct or not, to perpetuate the
undulation, to allow me to hold on to, enshrine it, the undulation passing
across the face as it was lifted from the plate. But what did this undulation
have to do with the story, wasn't it as subversive of the story as Jim's
anecdotes had once been. What did her—Maggy's—her, not Maggy's—
her—undulation have to do with the story. She was now completely
delivered up to scrutiny, no longer protected by the scooping up of rice
and greens. She felt herself the target of scrutiny without having been able
to decide and decree when she would allow herself to be scrutinized,
much less make the scrutinizer a reciprocal target. She answered him
back but the conversation did little to distract attention—at least from my
perspective, that of hovering witness—from the essential spectacle: collision of two beings obliged to rummage in each other's particles. She was
given up to another undulation succeeding imperceptibly to the first,
perhaps the very same miraculously prolonged, at any rate enclosing a
shock of awareness that this scrutiny with which she had just collided had
been going on all through her scooping and chewing. The shock of
awareness was a retrospective modification of her past AND an interrogation of that modification. Had she in fact been scrutinized all through
her scooping and chewing. Was the retrospective modification of the past
that terrorized and enlightened her features an authentic revelation or the
perpetration of a distortion. Lifting up her head from her plate she had
been shocked by a collision with *him*—Jim—not Jim—Jim. The form of
the shock—the only bearable—conceivable—form of the shock was her
sudden awareness that she had been similarly scrutinized all through her
recent past of chewing and scooping even if she hadn't been. Even if she
hadn't been scrutinized all down the remote and recent past the only way
out of shock in the present, of amortizing that shock, was a subsequent
and simultaneous and retrospective shock of awareness that all her
comings and goings, chewings and doings in the past had been founded

foundering on an erroneous assumption, namely, that she had never been
scrutinized in the past but was on the contrary delivered up to a terrifying
freedom in deciding when and how to scrutinize. Shock in the present was
being   undergone as retrospective tabulation of innumerable errors
committed under a false sense of security in the past. Perhaps I too was
on the verge of a collision capable of demonstrating that unbeknownst to
me I had been scrutinized all down—all through—the murder and the
burial and the flight from the burial amid a maze of doubts—by some
hovering witness eager either for reward or alliance. Maybe I too would
soon be undergoing a collision so terrifyingly in and of the present that my
only lenitive would be a spasm of excruciatingly painful discovery
regarding delusional floundering in the past.

　　Yes, this was the meaning of the undulation for the story. It
simply foreshadowed some overwhelming shock of recognition regarding an irreparable lapse perpetrated in, against, the past. I waited. I
turned away from the young couple and the old. I did not want to focus
on all this indecipherability of glances. No, no, no, I had a story to contend
with, especially now that I was the legitimate heir to old man Jamms's
disgust inflected by especial contempt for his son. The undulation had
nothing to do with me, with the story, our story still our story. If only the
young man and woman had been Jim and Maggy, or Jim and Bessy, as
in the playground some other young man and woman had *turned out* to be
Jim and Maggy, more Jim and Maggy than Jim and Bessy could ever
have found the resources to be. I looked their way again through the
corner of my eye. But they were most emphatically not Jim and Maggy,
neither Jim and Bessy. And it was not even a question of one being
Maggy, and the other a perfect stranger or one being Jim and the other
a new unprepossessing face in the crowd. Neither together or separately
could they be taken for the characters crucial to prosecution of the story.
Although slowly but surely the more I looked in their direction or the
more I turned from them in disgust the more the elderly couple were
turning out to be none other than old man and old lady Jamms, in all their
autumnal glory. Yes, it was clear to me. And once again, as in the
playground, it was a case of these two—who were, oh yes, they absolutely
were—being far more old man and old lady Jamms than old man and old

lady Jamms themselves. In this cozy little island parlor they were allowing themselves to express all that for so long had been redirected elsewhere, in the name of good taste or dread of head nurses.

Every so often the young woman turned to me, out of desperation, I flattered myself but fleetingly only, as if still trying to prove that she could function as Maggy or Bessy, better than Maggy or Bessy at being Maggy or Bessy. I wanted to assure her she might turn out to be of more use to my story—our story—as other than either. But at this point I was not quite sure. She almost flung me her profile as she went on making a pretense of listening to the less than beloved, but a profile grotesquely overladen with the bric-a-brac generally associated with full face—two eyes, two nostrils, both breasts, jewels dangling and dazzling from all angles. She or the world through her was luring me toward a sense that I could capture all her aspects simultaneously. As I waited for my dinner—the illumination, I am convinced, would never have descended upon me otherwise—turned three quarters away from the others yet with the light fretting my contours in such a way that the infinity of angles of ill-will whence I was viewed were conflated into a unique and irreparable lump of lard fit for the fastidious delectation of these gourmands—it occurred to me that I was inheriting old man Jamms's rage and disgust *only if I wanted to*. One of this effervescing crew might any minute say as much and at the not so distant prospect I could feel my fists clenching. When I looked up again the happy souls were as grim in their pursuit of collective pleasure but it seemed as if I was observing them from another angle, all other angles at once, no. In fact it was the same, the very same, deadly vantage, forgive me. But for a moment I—or rather, the story-mongers seemed to haul me forward, promised me story and nothing but story (thus the leap from the modest, another angle, probably not the work of the story-mongers, to ALL OTHER ANGLES AT ONCE, very definitely their product in its impatient superbole, its eagerness to enliven the narrative stew) in exchange for—for— In fact it was the same, the very same—EVEN MORE LURIDLY THE SAME, no, no, no, more magma from the story-mongers' Vesuvius—vantage, for here they were and here was I, in this aggrandized alcove sipping iced water and waiting for the main course. There was a dead man in the woods. I turned away from the happy group. Then back. Then away. Then back again. Turning away and looking back for signs of conspicuous change in my absence was surely the stuff of which story armatures was made. Wasn't their collective gaze soliciting my oddity with renewed vigor. No, it was not. This was what I would have liked to see and what for not seeing I was afraid to be punished. Or maybe they were in fact soliciting with renewed vigor only the wan soft part of my soul which, in turning away however briefly, had forfeited all preparedness for seeing, in other words, contending with such solicitation. Nothing was making for change.

In my—in Jamms's—hotel room I threw myself on the bed, tried to think of what it meant *to throw oneself on a bed* in such circumstances. Sensing that such thoughts would not, surprisingly, torture me enough to stay awake and alert I rose, dragged myself to the bathroom sink. The story seemed to be a little in advance of my forebodings. I splashed my eyes with cold water, dragged myself, onward ever onward, to the window where down below a few trees adopted heartrending postures for the benefit of their insomniac human counterparts. Leaving at dawn with Jamms's single piece of luggage I noticed the desk clerk on duty had his nose in a book. He looked up and tried to smile for that, among other things, was what he was paid to do but the smile was preempted by a curious grimace at my luggage or at the hand holding the luggage. With my head slightly turned away I remarked that I had already paid through the next night. He nodded as if this had been so well understood even before I began to consider the possibility of letting it be known that, to be quite honest, he was more than a bit taken aback at having been accused, however unlocalizably, of entertaining even the shadowiest shadow of a doubt regarding this matter of my bankability. This, in any event, was how I articulated the nod to myself after a long enough period of suffering over its resistance to articulation as my resistance to its articulation. And now that it was articulated I couldn't help wondering whether this articulation was a mere makeshift, the quickest way to a hanging— camouflage of the nod's essential nature, essential non-nature. Yet wasn't I speaking of something other than a nod when I mentioned event inducing dread and craving with respect to the possible relief of articulation. I was speaking, I knew, of something(s) other than a nod, VASTLY DIFFERENT FROM—no, no, no, the story-mongers again, trying to puff up the facts at the slightest opportunity lest the story-to-be

lull itself back to prefetal sleep—something far different, there, that's better, from a nod yet to which I had access—the beginning of access—only through speculations about the nod. The clerk groped to conclude his farewell with my name. "Jamms," I murmured. "Mr. Jamms," wishing him a good day. Dragging myself and my luggage across the wide parking lot past what looked like a dog cemetery into a fast-food emporium with a salad bar where, in full regalia, an old dame insisted—against all odds—on treating the hard labor of overloading her paper plate with the high seriousness it most certainly deserved, I ended up sitting down with a hot tea and cheeseburger content to watch her return again and again and again, her plate piled always ever higher. A few local youngsters entered and proceeded to discuss who, in and out of their group, was homosexual and if so, with whom, who not, who pregnant, who not, who rich, who not, until, as if in response to some imperceptible call of the suburban wild they filed out, leaving me with the distinct—as opposed to the indistinct—impression that all vice is facultative and that given the slightest alteration in rainfall the cruelest sodomizing murderer would be instantaneously transformed into a solid stolid citizen (wife Patti; two kids, Russ and Gus) revolted by the merest hint of such proclivities as sodomy, as murder. With them went the youth I had never, except for these few minutes, had. With my suitcase I forced myself to walk through the town admiring the glow of a new life beginning. I mean, a new life had to be beginning. I thought about Jim's father dying, or rather, I thought of Jim's father as Jim might have thought of him, or rather, laughing to myself almost hysterically at the edge of a little lake, as Jim would have wanted me to be thinking of him, his father. The maudlin fulsomeness of *would have wanted me* induced no little delight. So I went about trying to think of the dad as he, Jamms, might have thought of him if he had been vastly different from himself, I went about trying to think of him dying in a hospital bed, dark, with the nurses coming and going against the drawn curtains. Toward late morning I was back on the platform. An elderly
      NO
      father with
NO his one-armed child, presumably born too late, were also going from suburbs back to big city. I wanted to get far from father and child as

quintessence of detail once again obstructing story. At the same time I needed these details, for unlike the story about to evolve they could never be relegated to the slagheap of paraphrase, the ghastly contemning simplification of summary. As much as I did not wish to be captured even more I did not want my story to be captured by paraphrase, summary. At the moment when my story—our story—was delivered up to details such as this encapsulating father and one-armed child it resisted simplification, paraphrase, annihilation. A detail—a specimen—cannot be paraphrased. In fact, the elderly father was planning under cover of all this hearty platform concern to ditch his remnant and wave goodbye with a relieved heart. I did not have to turn away and back to undergo this change in plans or in my perception of those plans. Maybe he, the father, was already busily anticipating all he would be able to do once divested of this mutilated simulacrum of what was after all—what with its bronzed hair, tasseled *and* perforated alligator shoes, and skin to match—so noble a template. Weren't his shifty boardroom eyes already clouded with the prospect of unavowable pleasures now there was no child's unquenchable need to take into consideration. But I resented him most for... having nothing to contribute to the story.

On the train I sat in front of a man and woman NO I was becoming Jamms, usurping his role of saboteur. Now it, the train, was rolling unwieldy details right in the direction of the story's increasing and exquisite momentum. But in this case I allow that I am justified in reporting what occurred for the woman was Bessy, yes, I am sure it was she. Their flirtation consisted primarily of the woman's—I mean Bessy's—the woman's—Bessy's—aggrandizing self-definition to greater and greater heights of which she was expertly prompted by the man's valorizing questions though for such a woman any question would have been valorizing. But in his case—he was different, vastly different, from Jim—the indefatigably self-effaced prompting assumed all the colors of cunning, expectant hovering, or was I simply unable to tolerate the possibility of smittenness. So there had been nothing to hope from Bessy, after all. Fell back and slept for what must have been hours, as I opened my eyes people were already hurrying toward their destination points in this clammy dead-of-winter aquarium. These others knew where they were going, knew beyond the shadow of a doubt. It suddenly occurred to me, now that the train was in the station, that I should run right back out to the Island and make sure the corpse was sufficiently buried under all that leafage. Jim was clearly not dead, dead only intermittently, and when dead, buried only intermittently. As I walked across the promenade separating long distance trains from actual subway, of a hot smelly pissy shitty immediacy in and off season, and between seasons too, *especially* between seasons, no, not especially, but what pungency, cogency, of vengeance to have been able unobstructedly to say, especially between seasons, and mean it—vengeance and on far more than that shitty immediacy—as I walked across the promenade toward the taxi ramp, no subways for me anymore, even if there was no guarantee of a fixed income and all I possessed were my travelers' checks, remnant of the Jammses last honorarium, and the key to the safe-deposit box on Lexington, I suddenly felt that Jamms was definitively dead and buried at last, incapable of doing me any harm, and it was then I wanted to weep. For the first time I wished to weep for Jamms. But there could be nothing of that kind for Jamms. Jamms never had had time to say, as old man Jamms had been able to say, Find me a good-looking casket. So what if it was just one phrase among so many others equally meaningless, such as, She refused to wash my groin, or, speaking of the relict-to-be, I'll strangle the bitch, or, speaking of his lawful issue, You've been going straight to hell over the last ten years, or, speaking once again of the lawful issue once said lawful issue seemed to be deciding to take mangy issue with so peremptory a verdict, Ah, so you haven't been going straight to hell over the last ten years: Good. Punishing myself for not having arranged for a good-looking casket I took the subway, risking murder, theft, rape. Drowsiness protected me, drowsiness like a wound that left me exhilaratedly wide open or like somebody else's wound leaving me, a mere bystander, callously closed. Back in my hotel room in the heart of town I called Maggy, what prompted me if not the fear that if not now then never. She sounded not so much as if she had been sleeping BUT RATHER

but rather
as if
she had been

trying desperately to sleep. Making this distinction soothed me. It was as if Maggy was now in my debt. "Hello," I said. She replied in kind but there was hesitation, crouching, expectation, wariness, behind the reply. She didn't trust me, didn't trust where her own expectation might lead her. "I'm calling to let you know I just got back, Jim has decided to stay out in the wilds for a time. He is quite taken with the landscape and relishes the privileges of anonymity." "He's seen it before," she said, less accusing than wondering. "I mean the landscape." As if she had just made a bid for more information I said wearily, as if engaged in a conversation with myself of which I was at liberty to allow only a fleeting privileged glimpse, "He's become extremely uncommunicative, far moodier than before." Her silence whimpered, at least to me, that her worst fears had been realized—of a veritable misalliance springing up [in the hinterlands, naturally; never would it have occurred in broad daylight with Maggy cracking the whip of a loving that is, premonitory, solicitude] between the tormented, brilliantly talented painter [What did she think of his apti- tudes by the way, I mean, when not as now obliged to exalt them so that another's absence of same might be all the more abased] and the parasite living from hand to mouth, or rather, from hand to foot-in-the-mouth. "That's rather odd," was all she said but, or do I flatter myself, this already involved a tremendous effort of weighing the terrible need to expel her immediate torment against that other need equally though differently compelling—to husband some dignity amidst leering hovering witnesses. She in her torment was managing to take the future survival beyond the shellshock intrinsic to being abandoned by one's own true love, into account. "That's odd," she went on, only now it sounded as if she was conferring with somebody in the background, probably Bessy, back from her train trip. It was difficult to hang up, tear myself away from Maggy's perplexity, partly because it was contagious and idiotically I was expect- ing her to quash that with which she had just infected me, partly because I had induced it, her perplexity, and therefore felt paternally linked to it, all down its lifespan, death, partly for both reasons, that is, if both do qualify as reasons, partly for NO

   No
   [the story-mong
   ers/the mean
   ing-mongers !]:

partly for neither—it was difficult, more than difficult, to hang up so that
I surprised no one more than myself hearing that self quietly say, "So, if
it's all right with you I'll be out tomorrow. Don't worry about letting me
in: Jim left—gave—me the keys." After the call I fell asleep instantly. For
once I had managed to tear myself away from her—our—perplexity, so
solid, so viscous, I could not bear to live in its absence. Up in Rhinebeck,
just before taking a taxi out to the house, I sought out some little
playground. For it was now a hallowed ritual to sit myself down in one
before visiting Jamms, living or dead. No mothers, children, just an old
mum, the old mum I might have had if I hadn't had the better good fortune
of turning out to be an orphan, giving orders to her superannuated son of
a bitch beside her on *their* bench, this one No with more NO far NO NO
far more slats than it—they—it—knew what to do with—orders having
something or other, mainly other, to do with calling a lawyer to arrange
for the opening up of a precariously perched safe-deposit box. Clearly,
the year of the safe-deposit box. I tore into my pocket at these words and
was relieved that the fatal key was still there. The son surprised me by
being as unlike the son Jamms as it was humanly possible to be, nailed as
he was to a strange grimacing calm that could not be accounted for by the
weather or by the scintillation of the pavement or by the presence or
absence of shops, gas stations, movie theaters. And suddenly remembering how Jamms had spoken to me looking over his cold shoulder as he
scaled the pebbly steeps—another paradigm, another paradigmatic moment
big with revelation but of what—remembering I knew suddenly what this
calm must signify: a keeping under control second by second, minute by
minute, of an infinite rage most afraid of letting go and thereby drowning
world upon world. So old mum went on expostulating her woes as if
daring anybody within ear- or buckshot to challenge this grumblingly
militant tone which she must justify to herself (nightly, between the
dentures and the talk shows) on two crumbly counts, namely, that she
was in excruciating pain and therefore not to be held accountable for no
real harm was meant, and what is more, intending to leave her vast and
ever-expanding fortune to the little shit cum cicisbeo and was consequently entitled to a certain truculence given all the fun he was doomed
no doubt to have squandering— the swag—once she was bottled under-
ground—and as old mum went on not so young son went on listening,

seeming to listen, rather, so that his real business of calling upon all things inanimate and animate but especially inanimate to witness such exemplary self-restraint in the face of recurrent downfall and decay might continue unremarked, that is to say, unreproached. Noting his real business alerted me to the fact that this was none other than Lou Testic, Jim's one old friend, at the height of less, far less, than his glory. What could account for this most radical of disjunctions between him, the boisterous heir to the blustering family fortune and him, companion to that fortune's last remnant. I was glad to have him under control. In his present state he could never be expected to drop in unannounced.

    I rang the bell even if I had the key, all of Jamms's keys. "Hello Maggy," I said, before she opened the door so that I would not be tempted to say it when face to face with her for what would her own reflect back but a ravaged sneering perception of this thoroughly unsatisfactory impersonation of one picking up casual odds and odds for a capricious acquaintance still very much alive though to not much more than his own whims. She stepped aside, a trifle ironically, though I was and continue to be hard put to locate the ironic trifle in the stepping aside—as if to say I had to free rein and who was she to stop my rummaging through his private effects now that he, Jim, had mandated me along these lines in perpetuity. She looked down at the floor, not away from but anywhere but at me, the source of all her sorrows. We moved *sadly* past the kitchen, with its refrigerator and several cutting boards. We regarded it both at the same time, or so I needed to believe, as if this was not a wretched little dump but the scene of so many heartwarming moments past all going to show that despite mutual loathing, self-loathing, and loathing of more, far more, than each other, than all others, than the world of grapplings and failings, plummetings and wizened writhings, we had unflaggingly managed to always induce some trickly spasm of communion in the vile bedrock of eternal opposedness and what is more with unflinching eyes wide open on the cutting edge of homicide, never more than a stone's throw southwest. In short, we trotted past the kitchen as a single organism, as a single organism is transfixed by an unchanging and unquenchable predator. I preceded her, though not from a wish to prevail, rather to spare her the painful effort of having to choose whether to stand forth, advance, draw back, grow dim, dimmer, sink—dimmest. I was taking the initiative, new for me, but I was a new man, or so the meaning-mongers wished me to believe in their wholehearted approval of this my singlehanded advancement of our story. Murder had transformed me into that new man, that man big with prospects illimitable. As morning rolled toward noon, and high noon at that, we managed not to get in each other's way as I prepared to extract, sort, gather, and hoard clothes and toiletries. "It must be freezing up there," she murmured, evidently elsewhere, equidistantly far from here and there, yet not yet far enough to be spared the quizzical despair that comes from undergoing in every fiber the heartless exultation of some opposing other. Though I was not heartless and certainly not exulting. I looked around the room for my mind was less on exultation than on the story and what could come of it, exultation or no exultation. At any rate, story or no story, we advanced, she, I, and the toiletries, into the heaps set aside for Jim's hinterland comfort. Here among the heaps it was definitively night. Only night could have created heaps so orderly, through premeditation of a wily, might I even go so far as to say a feathery, sort—the kind of sharpedged knowing that passes and not only among the dullwitted uninitiated—and to what?—for sheer aleatory frenzy. Yet I did not allow myself to be carried away by my own mastery as night's in creating the heap for already I had had—but when, story-mongers, when?—too much experience (retrospective modification perpetrated on the past: radical disjunction between this boast camouflaged by plaint: too much experience AND the actual facts of the case: no experience to speak of, much less remember, in this domain...of extrapolation) extrapolating erroneously from a little local success to universal victory. Careful, wise, prudent, therefore, was I as I gathered together the detritus of a life lived, bunched together with the pursestrings of night, still—a life lived as the father's life had been lived, tumored or tumorless it made no great difference in the end, lived first as fetus, then as chum, then as buddy, then as coworker, then as colleague, then as flunkey, then as head of household now as pretext for the torpid selfpitying wonderment of others. The heap naturally grew smaller as I drew in the other strings on the rucksack full of socks, belts, underwear, undershirts, sweaters, shirts. Spotting a tie, a spotted tie, half concealed by the heap, I looked at Maggy as if to say, Who dares conceal a spotted tie behind this massive heap of collectibles knowing my time is limited and the next train out the most pressing thing on my mind. She backed off, into

her own meditation. Wary of antagonizing her too much I said I might be back to claim more of same. Out on the street I felt stronger, sat down in a fast-food emporium with my cup of tea, sat down next to another NO
     mother and
     son NO, but a different NO NO NO NO NO
mother and son, deciphering, this doomed dyad, doomed, that is, to nonextinction, a letter from a relative, probably close, perhaps in Puerto Rico No. The son was NO

As I went about cleaning things up, getting things ready for Jim, Maggy strangely enough began talking and in a low voice, as if Bessy, not yet back from her train trip, might somewhere be listening. And all the time I, like a pregnant sow, was pointing elsewhere — sagittal cipher of a future making all such tabulation and inventory in the here and now futile and frightful. "At the height of our passion we went out to see his parents. It was a big family party. The master-of-ceremonies was a dwarflike creature with pointed ears and a pointedly distracted look as of a man of the cloth who, though scrupulously attentive to the vulgar little needs of his vulgar little flock, is under no illusions regarding their capacity for cognoscitive vastation. Seeing beyond the haymakers, the beneficently dire prophecies of his silence were more than borne out by the panic that ensued once the Swedish meatballs emerged, toothpicked of course, on heaped platters from the kitchen. Jim was frozen in contemptuous judgment whereas I proclaimed, even after the meatballs, my great willingness to participate." Then she seemed to turn in on herself, saying, "But this has always been my great great problem — proclamations of an overweening eagerness to participate in anything and everything when my truest sentiments lag behind. And so is it any wonder that, in dizzying fright, I fixed on and clung as if for dear life to any detail seemingly anodyne such as the long fingernails of that creature, in order to remain unengulfed by the totality of anomalies constituting this world, his world, though it was not in fact his world for haven't I just gotten through emphasizing his lofty peripherality studded with acrimonious judgments. But it was the world from which he had sprung. Yes, the horror is that no matter how much Jim repudiated and drew back from this world I went on thinking about it as irreparably his and reproached him for it in my heart and not always in my heart. When I told him about the dwarf he laughed, explaining that he was not in the least entranced by that creature but only by a frenzied intimidatedness driving me to reproach him, Jim, for its very existence. Filtered through my consciousness the dwarf began to take on life or rather not so much the dwarf but rather the dwarf/ consciousness (mine) dyad. Here I was pretending to be pulled inadvertently up short by a simple flaw—the dwarf's long fingernails—rather than by the whole landscape apparently embraced from the start in its totality but in fact not even barely digested and with its ostensibly single flaw in fact my only fulcrum, my only pivot, in disorienting revulsion. And buoyed up by this pretense—this DISJUNCTION between ostensible engagement and my true feelings—I went on expatiating on how the landscape—forever embraced in its totality—proved an ingrate and in perverse reaction against my heartwarming and unconditional welcome had yielded up a stumplike flaw. And Jim in turn raged against my fixation on this single flaw doing us both in, namely, the long fingernails of the dwarf, or rather, its, the fixation's, implicit claim that there was only this single flaw mangling my immaculate goodwill and thereby interfering with complete and utter immersion in a totality of landscape doings when in fact, in point of fact, in actual fact, no doing amid the totality spurred me to goodwill, and I was as far as always I had been from immersion. And he was right, oh how right he was, for still I feared being sucked in, doomed to the doom of this plaguey purlieu of the faithful contemned by its bellwether and rightly so given that their only thought was for smuggling yet a few more sausage crumbs into unlined pockets. So you see, maybe this, my pretense, my false claims, has driven Jim from me. Maybe if I had not reacted so falsely he would still be with me today."

I looked at her almost tenderly, not for the poignancy of her lacerated regret but for attempting without necessarily knowing she was attempting to advance the story, our story, to plausibilize its new direction adumbrated by Jim's death and meagre little resurrection among the heaps of underclothing. Her reminiscence if on one level an example of sabotage worthy of Jim's tumor-laden monologues in their heyday on another scattered much needed salt into the wound inflicted by the murder. Even if her interpretation of Jim's hasty retreat was a misinterpretation, on the level of advancing the story, soldering its moments one to the other, misinterpretation had the same absolute weight as an interpretation drunk on its own accuracy. She looked at me grudgingly, as if expecting me never to agree. "And if I'm not mistaken Mrs. Jamms came in *at that point* to invite us to a little after-gala repast. I of course thanked her for inviting us. She smiled. But then I made a fatal mistake: I misinterpreted her smile as a sign that I must now *enact my thanks* by kicking up my heels on the dance floor, which I promptly did, and with such alacrity the old girl was obliged to turn away in disgust. For she did not want signs of joy, only an assurance that we were joyful—joyed— thanks to her." I could not help feeling envious as I listened to Maggy for her anecdote clearly encapsulated a very radical disjunction, between saying and doing, having and saying: According to Maggy's anecdote, saying was a substitute for having and doing, a subreption of doing, an instant exorcism of such having and doing, of the need to desire to need to have and do, a pledge that loathed and disreputable having and doing would never take place thanks to the under-lock-and-key supervision almost rabbinical in its severity effected in the deceptive ease of the saying with its irrevocable mastery over the debasing tendency to have and do and incessant surveillance of the dangerous upsurge of all having and doing. And this radical disjunction even if it sabotaged her story, my story, our story, belonged to Maggy, was hers incontrovertibly, seemed NO

      better NO (down, you meaning-mongers!)
better than a story. "I learned the hard way," she went on, "there must be no manifestation of joy and so I kept my own counsel. Manifestation of joy such as I had just forced her to witness made Mrs. Jamms an accessory after the blessed event. She did smile a sickly smile though it was clear she smelled a trap—precisely because she smelled a trap—for her ambivalence—however she was rapid enough to be able to dissimulate and in some small way she must have been fascinated by the conventional image of unabashed joy I had managed to generate. Maybe she even wished to prolong that image even if she felt she was being forced to jump through the hoop of its bottomless pit to the rhythm of my bidding. But then she went back to remarking thereby trying to induce remarks on the high agreeableness of the proceedings as one more guarantee that the high agreeableness would never be enacted for remarking and enacting, as I have already pointed out, were mutually

exclusive. And if we had proceeded to enact the delight we were obliged to profess we felt she certainly would have had second thoughts about having invited us at all and procured us a rarefied whiff of all she was herself incapable of expropriating. But having nowhere to go in my discomfort and despair, I did what I often do, I prostrated myself before the dowager, told her she had been too too generous with her time and money and even with the dwarf's flock gyrating at once lewd and lumpishly around us the constriction of her physiognomy told me she had just taken me at my word and was oversecreting second thoughts about having been far far too generous for her own good, having perhaps thrown a bit too much caution to the four winds. After that visit I assailed Jim mercilessly, condemned him for the vileness of his origins. He would only grit his teeth. Maybe that is why he has finally run off to you. You can give him what I never could." The son, clean and "nicely-dressed", shrugged movingly when he could not decipher word, phrase, or whole sentence. The mother seemed to hang on his desultory decipherment not because she particularly idolized him, he was too dumpy for that, not that she loathed him, but simply because he knew how to read. As I watched him decipher the letter all the time munching at his sandwich without soiling himself—as I watched him decipher the words as he ate I felt that if I could understand, make myself understand, with or without the support of my heap of clothes no longer in a heap but carefully tucked away inside a rucksack—be made to understand how he was able to live serenely according to and within the contingency-laden solicitations of the moment, frequently at cross-purposes like eating and deciphering, without getting soiled precisely because NO

    NO precisely

because he did not permit his consciousness to circulate within the narrow defiles of a conceivable danger of getting soiled I would learn what living my story meant. As long as I did not think of him and his mother, that is, and the sandwich and the letter from Puerto Rico, as details to acquire against the grain of the story but rather BUT RATHER as constituents of a model, without any connection with story, to respect and emulate. Did they, the mother and son, belong to the story, in the story, were they the next turn in the bend of the story's only ostensible meandering. I did and did not wish to live as this son—so different from

filial Jim—lived. But to this way of living—of being—there was nothing
to oppose. There was nothing connected to my doings, my heap of doings,
to oppose to this simple rectitude completely unconscious of itself as
rectitude and therefore all the more correct. There was nothing to oppose
to this sample—this specimen—of rectitude. Yes yes yes mother and son
was a specimen. But wasn't I rabidly opposed to such specimens of the
middle class and its capacity to live its life, in other words, its own
excrement, patiently enduring the unendurable in the name of tiny
solatiums, flung peculiums compliments of master huffing and puffing at
the other end of the day's leash. Yet what is opposedness—opposition—
but a capsized hunger to participate obstructed by a deeper sense of the
impossibility of participation due to unavowable premonitions of inadequacy (claudication, undescended testicle, herniations where herniations
had no business to be, inspissated bile). But I needed something virulent
to oppose to this model, this specimen, calling across the centuries to some
other...specimen, what was it, yes, that of Jim's raging shame and shamed
rage in the face of Maggy's insistence on confronting the sacred irascibility of his mother. Jim had been unable to escape with his specimen intact.
I would escape with mine, or rather, OR RATHER,

with the specimen of my response to the specimen being visited
upon me in shape of the mother and son. Unlike Jim (ploy of the story-
mongers to cross invoke widely separated moments of the story in the
name of plausibilized self-referential compactness) I intended to escape
with my specimen though not for purposes of subsequent rehabilitation.
No one would manage to scrutinize this specimen in the name of
rehabilitation. Specimen opposedness would be extracted from this flow,
this sludge, rather, and sacrificed to the story. The story from this moment
on was to be the sum of such specimens of opposedness to everything
happening outside the story. The specimen mother/son unitedness in the
face of word from abroad—of world—or rather, my specimen opposedness to the spectacle of that specimen—would accrue to the story,
henceforward the story-to-be. Still I had nothing to oppose to the
specimen/spectacle. As long as it remained unopposed it froze me in the
tracks of my story-doing. Where was my *something* to oppose. But it was
unclear whether this something to oppose, this fruit of unendurable rage,
unendurable and unenduring, would function as a bona fide element in

the story-to-be, or if not *of* the story would somehow manage to constitute an auxiliary capable of keeping its—motor going at least until I could procure an authentic story element or until I could familiarize myself sufficiently with story anatomy to know whether or not a new element was, at this time, in this place, needed. So I began to dread that the story would, if unwilling to acknowledge its dependence on targets of loathing such as this, a mother/son dyad chewing the cud of its fixation on an elsewhere, roll over and die. Yet did fructive dependence on such targets necessarily require an overt acknowledgment of that dependence, which overt acknowledgment might in fact diminish the intensity of the specimens of opposedness induced by those targets. At any rate, in any case, at any event, how tell the real elements of this story dedicated to and transcendently about Jamms yet obliged to crawl forward without his participation, his incendiarily immodest presence, in quest of scraplike specimens capable of kindling a correspondent opposedness integrable later into the body of the story. Out in the wintry air, far from the mother and son, whom probably I would never see again, I could only wonder why I hadn't—or had I?—thought of taking them as they were, in toto and uncosmeticized, deep into the belly of the story-to- be. Why was I so fixed on the generation of a phantom opposedness comprising both them and my revolted consciousness of them? Weren't they as they were already a construction of my consciousness? Why dilute them further? Why macerate these angels of light? A leaf began to fall. As it fell I spotted a thought on the horizon rising to meet it, not to catch it, stave off its descent, carry it back to its node of origin, merely to meet it, perhaps annihilate it, according to the rescript of an arcane catoptrics. The leaf made its way toward me, cutting through the swath of the thought, smelling no doubt one more specimen of opposedness already consecrated in embryo to the rigors of the story-to-be and resenting such premature affiliation—made its way toward me in somersaulting spirals of reproach, its tang grimacing more wildly than a circus clown in the middle of Central Park's Bezhin Meadow. The leaf and the thought, presumably of the leaf, rising to meet and presumably annihilate it, and then the thought of the collision of leaf and thought and then the thought of the absurdity of a thought envisioning collision of leaf and thought— of anything and any other thing, in fact—here where all was harmony, preestablished or not, infinite and irrefragable and of no thing more redolent than of a ray of sunlight trapped inside the musculature of a public urinal puck ground down to exility by promiscuous trickles of acid longing—when I thought of all this and simultaneously of the burden of thinking, of having to think, of all this—the mindless pitiless untimely impingement of all this—of this thought, that, and the other—I naturally NATURALLY suspected that at long last things were at long last summating to a pitch whereby, in relation to which, mammoth reparation for services rendered always unremarked, much less remunerated—take, for example, my exemplary burial of the dead replete with posthumous scruples regarding the completeness of its execution—was about to devolve upon my atrophied shoulders and that at long last all acquaintances—and even those beings who were not even acquaintances—were not only participating but being recuperated as nothing less than depersonalized voices in that embodied hymn to my greater glory. I looked back on them without rancor for hadn't they all assisted in their way at the creation of that secondary sexual character most crucial to survival, namely, hunger or thirst to be other than one—I—was thereby guaranteeing a future of questing enrichment even if there was no place to put the enrichment and flex its muscles. Yet hardened by experience—with smothering leaves and refractory corpse parts—more than this mammoth reparation I wanted to parry the predicament indistinguishable from its hallucination—this thrust toward sublime and beautiful reconciliation with all my snivelling demons. So rather than goad ever onward this radical disjunction (between some tender meagre moment in its nudity and its expropriation as a source of tribulation so vast as to be conceivable only as the imminence of a mammoth reparation) I strove to stand absolutely still and respond to the fall of the leaf in itself rather than as the first of a multitude of such falls (coming! coming! coming?) at long last to sweep clean the slate of the irrelevant, that is to say, all that precedes a reparation as mammoth as it is apocalyptic.

This was where I was obliged to refrain from getting down on hands and knees to give thanks for the murder. For the murder kept me whole, sane, irrevocably stained I was in less danger of being swept off my feet at every turn by the hallucinatory prospect of an immaculate conception always as more, far more, than myself: as I had been swept off my feet by Jamms and to what purpose, after all. I was on the run, too. Therefore, not only was it too too late for such reveries but also there was no time. At the same time I could easily have rent my clothes for the impossibility of deciding whether or not it was in fact too late. So that—here under the falling leaves, no leaf—between joy at the murder's equilibratory effect and rage at uncertainty over whether or not such equilibration was indeed incompatible with persisting hallucinatory reveries concerning mammoth reparation/benediction—uncertainty over whether or not there was time for such reveries—and neither rage nor joy at this almost programmatic oscillation between rage and joy, joy and rage, raging joy and joyous rage—so that I was understandably inundated with not necessarily foulsmelling semen by the time I reached Penn Station.

Oddly enough I was sorry, supremely sorry, to be saying good-bye to Maggy. I realized it as I hailed a taxi. But hadn't I realized earlier, long before I decided to take a walk through Tribeca, Soho, then Chinatown, with my heap, that up in Rhinebeck things would have been far easier if I had been able to count on her active scrutiny all through my ransacking of the bedroom, all in the name of Jamms's well-being hundreds and hundreds of miles off. I called her from Canal Street in Chinatown. She seemed happy to be hearing from me or perhaps it was simply a question of my being able, when she was several times evidently on the verge of humiliating me, to buoy myself up by remembering not so much this tic or that gesture—how, for example, when furious he, Jamms **** or ++++—but rather that in comparison to what she knew, what she thought she knew—what they thought they were always knowing—all the Maggys of the world—I—I—I knew all. Not that I believed it derogated in the least from her perspicacity not to have the slightest inkling, how could she, yet at the same time it was most definitively as if she should, given that this modification of the cosmos was in some way basic to her well-being, only I through some fluke had managed to descend on that inkling first and therefore exclusively for all time since two beings cannot occupy the same *knowledge as destination* at the same or any other time. So I had an edge over her and reason to be happy for once in my life. Then I remembered what Jim had said or what I thought he had said or should have said or what I thought he thought his father should have said given everything else left said and unsaid on and off the

interminable deathbed, namely, that most people have no desire to have
an edge over their congeners especially if that edge means greater
originality, uniqueness — originality and uniqueness at any cost or even in
the absence of all additional cost. "Jim, I suppose, never told you what his
father said just before he died, I mean, just before we thought he was just
about to die. He was lying on his bed and on the walls the shadow of the
leaves played havoc with the little rotunda of light charily allotted by the
late afternoon. He asked Jim to get him pencil and paper. Are you
listening?" I assured her that I was; I was. "He enjoyed giving orders even
if his tone said it was excruciating to do so." I wanted or rather I felt I
should stop her. She was doing what Jim had done — introducing an
episode, an anecdote instead of letting the story of our telephone call
proceed. Yet could it have proceeded in the absence of such anecdotes. I
had to control myself, throttle the impulse to throttle her. She was doing
what he had done on countless occasions and, like him, purely to thwart
the dormant propulsion of the story, my story, our story, and I could only
loathe her for it even if I was in principal far more nauseated at the
prospect of a story in the nakedness of its succession of sharply delineated
events susceptible to the grotesque caricature of paraphrase — preeminently susceptible to the grossest adulteration compliments of language,
the contagious language of somebody else supremely sure he or she was
understanding perfectly, comprehending all inclusively, in other words,
whittling away to nothingness, getting it all under control, doing away
with it — the story, mine — once and for all and forever after — even if I was
nauseated by the prospect of a story dragging me, through its susceptibility to the corrosion of summarizing, epitomizing language — although
itself, story I mean, supposedly cut from the same stuff as nature and
therefore refractory to such a summarizing, a whittling down; too vast
and monolithic, again like nature, to be caught in the act of being itself,
to undergo the belittling differentiation of its parts: it had no parts; the
classification of its moments: it had none — even if I was nauseated by the
prospect of a story and its susceptibilities dragging me down to the point
where I must finish as little more than the butt-end of a self-satisfied
paraphrase, a tasseled and beribboned précis fit for the choicest archives
of proctology. At any rate she was introducing an irrelevant episode,
carrying on in the tradition of Jamms the prodigal son, hawking her set

piece, detail, chunk of surrogate duration advertising its own nullity, in other words, its refusal to be anything more than a pastime, obliging me at the same time to pass no other time but its own. At the same time I was fascinated by this ploy, more fascinated I might even say, by what was to come than I could ever be about some idiotic story line, so what if my own, progressing from A to B, then from C to D, with the briefest of stopovers purely for the sake of conspicuous consumption in this or that tenement boutique disintegrating with the twilight. I was fascinated by what was just about to unfold deep within such a shard of contextlessness digging roots ever deeper and deeper into its very absence of contextual topsoil. I could tell from the way she had begun that there was absolutely no interest here in getting inside the proverbial skin of the dying toward the tumor throbbing beneath the ribbons of the catafalque, no interest in proving—to some cattle car of spectators avid of enlightenment after a hefty dinner at the newest fashionable pre-theater-dinner emporium— that if you listen closely enough in the sickroom or the funeral home or out in the cemetery itself you are bound to be enlightened by the drizzle of mother earth on the good-looking casket in its last throes, no interest in proving death was edifying thereby confirming to these pre-theater-dinner piglets in their comfortable unavowed terror that nothing is wasted, everything so made to make sense ultimate, to engender and yield duty-free a meaning. Perhaps I was less interested in the shard to come than in its coldblooded intrusion on the story's progress, for this coldblood-ness was different from Jamms's in a way I had yet to particularize. Or perhaps it was only the story-, the meaning-mongers, encouraging me in this fine, in other words, nonexistent, distinction so that I might seem to be progressing, that is to say, changing, and the story in tandem. "The old man called for pen and pencil and made Jim write to an old friend. The usual salutation. Jim found it hard to write for he was struck almost dead by the hollow theatricality of the gesture but more so by the fact that his father, usually so mordantly intolerant of theatricality in others, was in this case blissfully unaware of his own. Yes: I know: the lack of awareness was of course the pathos: imagine this cold mocking being drawn toward a mode of behavior he instinctively reprobated. 'Dear X: It isn't going very good with me.'" There was a long pause. I waited: I was getting cold. As if sensing my impatience: "Then Mrs. Jamms entered, and in her panicked cheerful way, worse than any tirade, asked why he was writing that things were not going well with him. After all, he was getting better and better and better and better. And even if she was right, about his getting better and better if not better and better and better, let us assume for argument's sake that she was sublimely right, still it was not the moment for such rightness. This was rather the moment—the fall of the light and the lack of spring in the mattress and the thin ochrous liquid flowing from the convalescent's mouth and the smell as of rotting cheese in one corner of the sofa should have told her as much but, alas, poor lady, she was positively tone deaf to circumstances not of her own making— for accepting death globally whether or not death came, for living through all the stages of rage and resignation entailing whatever insatiable asslicking of the heavenly choir was appropriate to such a sequence though who's to say resignation so-called isn't always completely or in part suffused with a hortatory backdoor plea for reprieve as reward for all hope abandoned, isn't always more or less a vigilance of provisional good behavior with its thousand eyes focused exclusively on possible in- demnification for surfaces rended. At any rate old mamma Jamms proved once again tone deaf to circumstance, noisily intruding her intolerance of whatever had not been initiated compliments of her own panicky wiles. And there stood Jamms, pencil still in hand, with the dying rays making that pencil's shadow unnaturally long, longer than any catheter or pros- thesis, loathing now his father's peremptory theatricality not so much in itself—" Her voice grew almost inaudible as if she was instinctively apologizing for this incursion of fine distinction into what she knew I had hoped would be a mere chaos of meanings succeeding each other too quickly for sticky paraphrase so dear to once again those rollicking pre- theater-dinner invertebrates. " —not so much in itself as for provoking old mamma Jamms's panicking contempt. I know, I know, why should Jim have cared. Why should he have wished, I mean, to suppress an event simply because it induced the old girl's panic of contempt, how could he have allowed himself to be effected by the possibility of her panicking contempt to the point of wishing to suppress entirely the event that had induced it, and this a pain event, the prelude to a deathbed utterance. He simply could not tolerate the coexistence of her panic and the event inducing it, that is to say, all events. And since he could not obliterate the old girl he wished to obliterate all events reminding him of the old girl, or rather, making him custodian of her specimen responses to event. And why you might ask was it so difficult for Jim to tolerate — to curate — these specimens of raging panic deployed with a coating of self-defensive viciousness. At any rate it was far easier for him to respond in kind — with specimens of his own — than to go about his business of ministering to the needs of the dead man as she went about hers. He could not bear being saddled with her specimens lest they become assimilated to his own substance. At any rate, he had always been loathing life for dooming him to be the offspring of such a pair and this insurmountable loathing explains why he now wishes to be alone. He isn't running from me. He is running from his loathing. And if this is the case then I should understand, don't you think, and not harass him." I thought she was done at last though the minute I thought so I began to miss her perturbations and distractions and wondered how I might go about soliciting more. Incoherent, weeping bitterly, she added, "To think she was impatient of old man Jamms's theatrics when she herself waxes far more theatrical in her times of crisis. But she — and Jim has inherited this loathsome trait — has never been able to note incongruity, absurdity, dissonance, self-contradiction and nevertheless with true fervor embrace it as a lovable trait and not a betrayal of the spectator. There is never an abandoning of the self-protective stance of vicious ridicule in order to jump in and reassure the figure of absurdity for the figure in question — according to her — to both of them — is clearly in no need of reassurance since only unshakable self-assurance would permit itself the luxury of inducing in another that self-protective stance with panic at its core. Among the Jamms, absurdity — self-contradiction — as outcry — as heartrending vulnerability — must be punished for what it is — an inducer of disequilibrium, a taunt to raw nerves. I could have had more respect for Jamms jumping in to warehouse the old lady's tantrums — with a shrugging smile and a caress." I did not know what to say so I said, "Jamms had — has — a hard time warehousing specimens: his own or anybody else's."

The train trip out to the Island again was uneventful, as if it could have been in any way eventful. As the train pulled out of one station I noticed a man half-turned toward the waiting room waving goodbye to somebody in a car farther down. It was his being half-turned toward the waiting room that made this event memorable. I found a hotel, different from the first, but of the same breed. Before doing anything else I sat down at the desk and wrote Maggy a letter (the hotel very nicely procured me a typewriter) in which I, Jamms, explained how I had decided after much wrestling with myself to stay up here in this neck of the woods in order to sort out, on my easel of course, scrambled thoughts on those old chestnuts—warhorses—love, life, death. Rereading I decided that I very much liked the lumpishly casual sound of all this, clearly just what somebody like Jamms would write—and with just the right dash of failed humor—when trying to shirk the issue. I tried to put myself in a Jammsian trance by adding that the other, meaning me, had very nicely agreed to bring him, meaning Jamms, some of his belongings, for a small additional fee, of course: I was not his dad's emissary for nothing—and then make himself—myself—scarce. I thought of commenting in passing that I was not a bad sort, had some ingratiating characteristics. This seemed too risky only then I panicked thinking that any risk sidestepped would only rebound later to the essential futility of the project, itself a vast risk seeking sustenance from lesser yet still fecundating risks. So I went on a bit, mentioning his—my—ingratiating opinionatedness, yet not failing to point out that this was of course the quirk of one with no essential feeling for opinion—for the stuff of opinions—except insofar as hasty acquisition forestalled sodomization by somebody else's. "He is so abrupt and jerky when he holds forth—at once adamant and quizzical— concerning my work, for example, that I don't know whether to strangle him on the spot, making sure of course to bury him far far far from the little studio I have extemporized, or fall down in prostration before his rare and singularly unspotted idiocy—the kind they don't synthesize from scratch quite so meticulously any more." I liked the strangling touch. In my companion letter to the Jamms—at this point I was not quite sure who was still alive, who dead—I directed them to continue sending my checks to the bank at the corner of Lexington and Seventy-second where they kept one of their many safe-deposit boxes. I had no need of Jamms's allowance checks since I was still regularly receiving my stipend for services rendered. I mentioned that after my sojourn in the wilds I was thinking of moving semi-permanently to Europe since as they must know I had long been at loggerheads with the American experiment, that is to say, the American capitalist nightmare, just *the sort of thing* Jamms might say, one of many puerilities to which only one of his type could lend the appropriate panache. The striving to remain — and ultimate conviction of remaining — faithful to that panache allowed me to survive the excruciation of this letter writing. Being true to a model far outweighed the overrated pleasures of spontaneity. Oddly enough when most faithful to the Jammsian tone I also felt most original for at this stage — of what? of what? — the only conceivable originality was the originality of Jamms. My own originality, if such a beast might ever be deemed stalkable, had not yet begun to resonate at a frequency perceptible to self-love: would it ever? Toward dusk I returned the typewriter, lay back, slept. I dreamed and what I dreamed understandably made me a bit shaken. But when once again awake I was becalmed by the thought — no, the awareness — that in contradistinction to Jamms I was possessed of a calm, a chloroformed tact — especially when it was a question of contending with his parents to whom he invariably responded only on the one note of hysteria — that could almost taste its own intricacy. And hadn't Jamms always been most corralled within his own theater of protest. I forced myself to write more and more, describing my little excursions in search of the right light — bicycling very fast at night, for example, and being assaulted suddenly by dazzling clusters of lights, assuming as a result that I was about to descend on a good-sized town only to find myself immediately and once again deep within an abyss of blackness. Not that this was the case but I was after all practicing toward the story — our story — I might yet be living. And so I had to — I found myself having to — transmogrify what I saw — a cluster of lights, for example, standing in for nothing but themselves — into something I could with irascibility and confounded disappointment say I saw — a cluster of lights promising the imminence of the proverbial good-sized town — so as to be always aptly masking the simple hunger to tell, to describe, so patent, so naked, so destructible, so self-convicting. I was learning to hide the hunger to express and to seduce through what I expressed via an apparent irascibility toward and grave disappointment in what I expressed — an irascibility and disappointment ostensibly so absorbing I could hardly be accused of that most capital of sins — the hunger to express and by expressing fuse with the expressed as the most exquisite of seducers. It was as if all that came out came out in spite of me and when I was not looking or listening for all my looking and listening was a looking and listening elsewhere — at and to what excruciated and let me down a long way, far from any strategy of expression. In another letter I described how I had decided to take the Long Island Railroad out to the southernmost or northernmost or easternmost or westernmost tip of the land mass and how, the conductor announcing a delay, a slight delay, before the train could resume its trek, even before the words were completely out of his mouth, the train had begun moving. And conveniently taking my own befuddlement at this point in the letter for their uncomprehending outraged silence I proceeded with something to the effect of, Didn't they see: This radical disjunction between what I had heard (the conductor's warning) and what I immediately underwent (resumption of motion) was vital to *the kind of work I was trying to do out here.* I reminded them that after all I hated stories, had always hated stories, incessantly prey to caricatural paraphrase, existing only to be paraphrased. To break the chain of paraphrases, this was my aim. And how could anybody paraphrase the radical disjunction between what I had heard and subsequently/ simultaneously undergone. Of course, of course, I hastened to reassure them — reassure them! — the train had not immediately made its way again at a gallop. A gallop merely would have exaggerated and thereby obliterated the radical disjunction between sound and image — creating something storylike, an entertainment. No, while the conductor was still talking, the train began moving at a crawl. There were no sharp contrasts here to quicken the profiteering pulse of a Technicolor mogul.

I assured them, mom and dad, that crawl had suited and was continuing to suit me just fine. I spoke of my vision deep within my seat, to the effect that if such a radical disjunction between being and being had been visited upon me here, in a rickety suburban train, then there had to be numberless radical disjunctions elsewhere as well, ready like rats to propagate the bubonic plague of that anti-story that the world — from the opposite direction and for what it was worth — was rolling my way merismatic and explosive as a pomegranate. Of course I could not wonder in their presence why radical disjunctions were proliferating so superabundantly now whereas before the murder — In any case, were radical disjunctions proliferating more superabundantly now or was this one more bit of transparent propagandizing on the part of the story-mongers and meaning-mongers in behalf of the old virtues. On that same train I had listened in on the conversation of a hideous young couple. For purposes of popular consumption by Mr. and Mrs. Jamms, these were immediately transformed into Jim and Bessy, she clamoring for tenderness, he mercilessly diagnosing that clamor with the thousand eyes of retrospect. I explained to them—they did not like Bessy and would be glad of this sign of our relation's imminent dissolution—that with Bessy nothing was ever satisfactory, nothing ever acceptable, all a mere substanceless makeshift, a placeholder for the life to come, an interim biding time before the agape. As was consonant with their needs I left myself, the prodigal son, turned away and she, Bessy, gazing on alone at the colorless wash of the street invading the storefronts opposite my little cabin at the edge of the woods. I had to be grateful for the couple on the train, so like and yet so unlike train couples, to the extent that their chatter had allowed me to advance, that is to say, hasten the dissolution of, my relation to Bessy, especially since I had not seen nor had I any intention of seeing her again. To close my missive on a more optimistic note, though optimistic for whom I frankly don't know, I spoke of a few couples in the neighborhood who were doing everything under the sun to initiate an acquaintanceship, with Bessy and me. I liked the idea of Maggy's being mysteriously out of the picture, or rather, I liked my idea of the way it must resonate or fail to resonate in their consciousness. With delicious ease I was able to paint a Rockwellian portrait of myself emerging out of the rainy snow in my topcoat and putting my key in the door only to discover new friends Pam and Steve striving ever so desperately to attain the status of old friends, then to overcome momentary embarrassment threatening to overcome us all parenthesizing that embarrassment by drawing back slightly opening wide mouth, eyes, palms. Having once begun I had no great difficulty in going on to say how Betsy (sic) jumped into the fray thick with the suffocating stench of good cheer by telling me how she had just been telling Pam how much she agreed with her, Pam's, observation, that *things are becoming so expensive.* Now, with sodality reinforced and discomfort camouflaged to everybody's satisfaction, I am on the road to understanding how very much she and Pam have in common even if the best way to have something common in common (always and forever from the vantage, is there any other, of inauthenticity struggling to peddle itself as its fissureless opposite) is to be chewing on the cud of a common grievance. Understandably, then, in keeping with this thesis, there is a slight note of reproach in Betsy's tone since I insist on continuing (that is, according to her inflection's instantaneous construction as the steaks sizzle medium-rare) to like living here where things have become so expensive, Pam. More and more Betsy's reproachful tone is constructing me as more, far more, than merely liking to live here, in Shittsville, where things are becoming so expensive since Betsy needs to feel opposed to me if ever she is going to generate a bondedness to Pam. According to the nineteenth law of the middle class ass one must make the guest feel at home and what better way than through a phantom bondedness as sketched, for example, in the phrase: I feel like I've known you all my life, and founded on a mutual impatience with some third, also present. Having no particular affinity for said Pam—not, however, that they were not birds of a feather—Betsy was obliged to generate that affinity from scratch and in the only way she thought she knew how—through opposition to me. So I went along—I thought the Jammses would be pleased and revolted, in other words, mystified by an acquiescence that was so sublimely unlike me at my most usually sublime—allowing her to transform my liking for this my hometown and home base, to wit, Tittiesville, into a secondary sexual character, a symptom of obtuse maleness, which maleness—which symptom—had the execrable habit— always from the vantage of her hunger to appear to be authentically welded to the simpering Pam, wife of Bill, Bob, or Dick, or Pete, or Steve—of refusing to bubble up centrally from very heart of her exasperation over its dire centrality, dire, that is, until superseded by some other scrap in which she could dig her claws . Waiting for *my* steak I mismanaged a conspiratorial leer at Pam's hubby, Mike, since whether we liked it or not we had been assigned the role of "the men." And then came the interminable dinner itself, with Betsy, alias, the little woman, interminably waxing uncertain over the success of the steaks and the bird and Pam promising, in response to Betsy's frantic plea, to call and divulge her recipe for broached breast of poached roast. I flattered myself that the Jammses would never begin to be able to decipher my relation to the events described. The depiction deigned to allow them to live in hope but of what. Once I retrieved the small fortune in jewels and other knick-knacks reposing in the safe-deposit box—to say nothing of dependable checks from mom and pop for services unrendered—I took an apartment on the outermost fringes of—Desbrosses Street—Soho, landsend of my dreams. Just as I was about to depart on a small trip—to the Island, in fact, to ascertain whether Jamms was still buried—putting on my shoes and packing away the last pair of socks in an elasticized sidepocket of my green and blue valise the doorbell rang: Colletti. He quickly made his intentions known and I agreed to free-lance as his courier along the lines made half explicit during our long leisurely dinner in the hotel. Just as he was about to leave—my—our—story had made a quantum leap but in such a short time there was no way to undergo its rapidity—there was another ring at the door. The taxi service, but I hadn't had a chance to call the taxi service. Colletti agreed to wait in another room as much no doubt from fear of being seen in broad daylight as from intrinsic discretion. Opening I heard the unmistakable voice of...Lou Testic, Jim's bosom buddy, who was enjoying the dubious pleasure of seeing me sporting one of Jim's shirts and one of his jackets. I backed away and even if a little distance it was something I should never have done with somebody as blunt, monolithic, and mercurial. Before I could shut him out he was in, looking around. I asked how he had found me. He asked where Jamms was not, it seemed to me, because he wanted to know from the likes of me or expected to find out, again from the likes of me, but simply to bypass my question. He looked around and everything he looked at—How can I express it otherwise?—tallied with him as looker. Things having ignored me for so long came to life NO in NO his presence. No, no, no, this is not me speaking, this is the piecework of the story-mongers—the hunger of the story-mongers—striving to convince you, me, everybody, something is happening at last.

There was a one-to-one correspondence between Lou's look and the things he looked at, as there never was, could be, with Jim, Lou's long lost, especially now that the story-, I mean the meaning-, I mean the story—, I mean the meaning—mongers were pressuring me to create stark contrasts between elements of before and elements after the mur-der—stark contrasts are, of course, the poor man's radical disjunctions—so that I might give the impression—as one speaks of giving off a whiff—

that the story was advancing because I myself was changing or saddled with the changes of those around me. When Jamms had looked at an object and I followed the look — be it at vase or crematorium — the object was always already gone. Or on those rare occasions when having located and impaled the target of his gaze I turned back to Jim to invite him to join me in the gazing he was always no longer there and I was obliged to gaze on alone...at what was meaningless, worse than meaningless, since it existed only within the context — at the end of the leash — of his gaze. And there were times when I would look up, at a sunset or a derelict pissing at a hydrant, and I would know this, like all other sights, was meant for Jamms, or rather, OR RATHER, for his assimilation of its substance into a vital story element, yet Jamms was always elsewhere, even if right there beside me. This, then, was what Jamms should have been seeing, all this was meant for Jamms alone, this had no existence apart from Jamms, wedded as it was to if not his character then his particular momentary lines of force. So it all became, the sunset, the derelict, the piss, what he would have been seeing if he had deigned to see, if he had not incapacitated himself for seeing at the very moment when seeing was most crucial to the story's progress. And with time — I saw that now — or rather, the story-mongers wanted me to see that now — more and more of the landscape came to embody what Jamms would have been seeing if he hadn't been elsewhere though right beside me every time. And here was Testic come to remind me of all I had endured of an impossible sequestration of the landscape — meant for Jim and no one else yet ignored by same. So that when I was at last able to locate the targets — what should have been the targets — of his seeing — what after all did they turn out to be once they had sufficiently distracted my attention — once they had fastened on my gaze as on that of an inferior but passably glutinous surrogate — and my gaze on theirs — but pretexts for his flight not only from seeing but from being...inside, or even at the periphery of, the story. And once the target made contact with my glutinous under-belly — yes, yes, yes, I saw it now! — what did that target — whose collision with Jim Jamms had boded so mirifically for our story — come to but an illegible heap of shadows, an indistinguishable fusion of echoes, immi-nences, absences. What invariably began for Jamms's gaze as, say, a clearcut altercation between mother and son behind closed doors, or a

hovering derelict witness pissing against a hydrant, became, when de-
moted to quasi fusion with the glutinous inquietude of my own, a mere
trash of dissonances, not even. His gaze, its initial expropriative rapacity,
even quicker abdication of the spoils, left me a world without lever, a
world without orientation, fixed point, origin, for that origin was, should
have been, Jamms in relation to his objects. And here was his best buddy
Lou whose looking in a series of spurts made sure no spurted effort went
unlinked to some lucidly contoured being, that there was never any
question of a bystander's inheriting by default. Unlike Jim for whom
seeing was always a seeing postponed, postponed and not even in his own
name but in the name of another, in every sense less perspicacious—
another, that is to say, like me—yet whose inevitability of advent Jim's
every step announced therefore denounced. It took a bug like Lou—
vector of every disease known to man-beast yet always curiously unin-
fected himself—Hyperion's satyr—to alert me to the phenomenology of
Jim's seeings past. Or perhaps it is more correct to say that it took not Lou
but the story-mongers, the meaning-mongers, the hovering witnesses
always ready to shit in my face, to erect Lou as the instrument of a
delusional storylike propulsion forward. The story—according to the
story- , the meaning-, the story- , the meaning-mongers—was moving
forward since now I was afflicted with Lou's seeing and before I had been
afflicted with an entirely different—thanks of course to the retrospective
modification shed, induced, cast, by Lou's enlightening contrasting-
ness—kind of seeing—Jim's seeing as a nonseeing. Story or no story, I
may aver that it is sad, seeing all at once as another sees, from the comfort
of that ostensibly mutual seeing to be suddenly looking back to the
discovery that long before that other absconded with himself and has left
you, contextless, alone, to sustain the rapidly fading target of the seeing.
I looked Lou over and suddenly I knew—suddenly the story-mongers—
whom I ought to have considered my friends, my allies, why didn't I, why
did I go on insisting on striving to screw my despair to the sticking place
of a story unabetted by story-mongers—knew for me, knew through
me,—that *unlike Jim* he embodied all I loathed of life, death, and the daily
grind. "Where's Jamms," he repeated, I tried hard to extend and expand
my loathing thinking of him, Lou, daring to present himself on the eve of
my departure. Then I remembered what somebody significant said or

should have said if he hadn't been cut off by untimely death—wasn't it Colletti's twin brother Bertolazzi?—namely, that I would never accede to reality— if, that is, reality was to be rid of Lou forever and it was, no doubt about that—by thinking about him—by thinking him—in relation to the sinuosities of my character, my cravings, my frustrations. I would not accede to that blessed reality by nursing my contradictions—sometimes I loathed him, sometimes I did not, sometimes I almost liked him— through their so-called internal development, but only by colliding with all that was not me quintessentialized as those contradictions—by collid- ing, in short, with Lou.

So there was Lou Testic, simply being, and there was I, needing to loathe Lou in order to begin to be. The camel's hair coat, the tasseled loafers, the shoulder loops and upturned collar, these were all pretexts. I studied him, went over and over my loathing, stared back inventorying his ungainliness one more time as the sum total of *post-industrial* bric-a- brac. Once again I realized I would never survive this moment—even if Colletti was conveniently in the next room—going from strained con- sciousness of this to strained consciousness of that. He, Testic, induced a never-finishing flow of images designed to keep me busy within my own skull forever whereas more than ever I needed to abut on something outside myself, outside the ring of my contrariety, the contradictious musings up to now my mother's milk and stock-in-trade though I myself motherless and tradeless. Yet with every moment—and if I didn't act fast—it was becoming more and more difficult to abut—to conceive of abutting—up against him as something outside myself, something huge and alien, for whatever began as alien was necessarily instantly synony- mous with food for thought and puny self-transformation into self + thought. I had to go on trying to abut against him as something alien but not necessarily loathsome for the minute he was loathsome he was comprehensible, assimilable, and no longer outside myself. "Out camp- ing," I managed to say, "for a few days with a famous filmmaker who happens to—" I tried to laugh, rather to induce Testic's horsey laugh, instead he remained stonefaced and managed it in such a way as made it clear he was not used, didn't take kindly, to remaining stonefaced in the face of somebody else's laughter. "Decided a new slant on the landscape would be useful." "Magg told me he was thinking of moving to Europe."

As if reluctant to confirm what Testic with all his heart clearly wanted to believe was hearsay I turned away, murmuring, "He spoke of China." "What," the voice bellowed. "China. And Tibet. Mongolia." "Why China, I wonder." He looked me straight in the eye as Colletti entered, harder and harder he looked, in such a way as to suggest an unnatural relation between us. I did not answer the truculent challenge of perplexity still flushing his features as he turned to study *the other man* seated a little to my right. I seemed to recall Jim having told me Testic's father owned a vast corporation—based, wasn't that the phrase—somewhere-in-Virginia—and that Testic, Jr., already laid claim to a prominent position entitling him to strut into the premises every day around 10:30 A.M., after a hearty breakfast and some futile repartee with the first circle of female receptionists. The next minute I couldn't remember whether or not Jim had told me as much but looking hard and straight at Testic looking reprovingly at Colletti now sprawled coquettishly across my best ottoman as if it was a pulvinar and he the satyr god long awaited and only two minutes late the memory was stronger than memory—so strong it had to be diluted along the lines of something somebody or other must have told me in his, or my, half-sleep. As he started to speak of his dad's firm and of Jim's dad's firm and of how Jim would never have just packed up and made himself scarce I saw Colletti pick up a lamp—any lamp, I told myself, any lamp—but in this case it was by no stretch of the imagination just any lamp for this was the kind with a waferlike base and an interminable neck punctuated by so many joints that just when I was beginning to be convinced that Colletti was grasping it at the knee it began to sway in such a way as to suggest it was being clutched at the hip and by more than one fistful of fingers. Colletti was clearly brandishing the lamp and as Testic leaned over to examine what must have looked like one of Jim's slippers Colletti brought it down on his almost imperceptible bald spot. He looked up at me—not at Colletti—at the very moment the blood began to ooze as if to say, why now, when I was just getting warm, as if all this had been a game invented by Testic, Sr., as one more test of Testic, Jr.'s mettle preparatory to being deemed worthy of imperial accession to the headiest responsibility. For here lay one completely identified with the father, completely fused with the old ax, for it was not merely prohibited but inconceivable to see the world with other than fatherly eyes. As he lay there a bit declamatorily wallowing in his own blood I, in contrast NO, was no longer NO NO wallowing NO in the mire of my own contradictions NO. I had emerged from the rathole of those contradictions and come smack up against something truly outside it. He was no longer all I loathed, all I had no hope of ever not loathing. For I NO NO no NO loathed the story-mongers more: for attempting to make me believe I had achieved a breakthrough for and within the story. Wearing a fashionable camel's hair coat—sign in our day and age of leisurely sophistication as potency italicized from another epoch yet no less vital for all that—the epoch, in a word, of our forefathers—he was very much dead yet most dead in the sense NO NO

that his pretenses had been exposed as NO

incapable of saving him

NO NO from the very fate those pretenses had been wont most to scoff at.

But death had in fact done nothing to debunk those pretenses incarnated in tasseled loafer here, bristly shoulder loop, there. They were now, these pretenses, differently, perhaps even more powerfully, virulent. I tried to assist Colletti in raising him by his feet. When he began bleeding too profusely I turned away and would have dropped him, heavily, if Colletti had not rectified my ineptitude. There is no such thing as ineptitude, I heard myself say, there is only rage. I continued to turn away for there was nothing more to learn. Mistaking the lamp's hip for its wrist or rather OR RATHER achieving a universal conflation of both views—of all views—in a single gulp of seeing that was at the same time not a seeing handed down by the likes of Jamms—I had achieved my last, my final, perspective. Coming full circle my eye caught Testic's. Colletti had succeeded in dragging him a little closer to the front door. I waited. Something was wrong. Something was...interfering with my final perspective. Seeing the dead bulk, which might have been anybody's yet which was very much the particular dead bulk of this dead man, this flunkey, this silver-spooned offshoot of a proud man's contumely made me want to puke away what was proving to be nothing less than a...final perspective on my already final perspective, was effectuating, in other words, a by no means devoutly wished consummation above and beyond what had just a minute before appeared supremely refractory to further consummation, a retrospective modification of what moments before had passed for definitive and transcendent perspective. And all this because — and somehow, not because — the dead body was but a stand-in for the real cause of such a modification — a modification too grandiose to have coupled yet with a cause, — for the moment until further notice all this because I was all of a sudden annexed to my adnexa, namely, the sprawling bloodsoaked arms, legs, and other extremities of one Lionel Lou Testic of the Greenback Hampton Testics, thereby discovering so annexed the incompleteness, that is to say, the fraudulence of a prior vision. Yet I could not help feeling, knowing, and a — *the* — hovering witness — enemy to all story-mongers — a little to my right seemed to confirm as much — feeling, knowing, that what was here and now being deployed — over Lou's dead body, so to speak — was not the transcendence through retrospective modification of some prior vision but the radical disjunction between that transcendence and the state of affairs ostensibly responsible for its upsurge. There was no transcendence, there was no state of affairs responsible or not responsible, but there was — and always would NO — be — a radical disjunction between the transcendence and what was made — purposely slapdash (for in the slapdashery, the extemporization was the dramatic intensification — the very kernel — of the disjunction) — to appear to have produced it. Transformation and transcendence of a prior vision belonged to some other state of affairs — in Jamms's life, maybe — but something or someone had recruited it to this state of affairs — with mixed results. Mixed, perhaps, only because I seemed to be refusing to go on peddling the transcendence as directly inspired by the sight of the corpse, particularly, of so many arms, legs, fingers, toes, and other extremities. I looked at Lou's fingers, got closer and closer to the fingers, every look got me closer and closer. But rather than clarify the close-up completely obstructed and disoriented whatever didactic apperception was still to be had — took me further and further from the story that was unfolding. This close-up — closer and closer up — ostensibly a trustworthy agent of the story's unfolding, handmaiden of the story's native self-elucidation, was in actual fact far less an esemplasticizing flunkey than was commonly thought. What use to me were his nails in all their grimy avian detail. They merely forced a graceless exit from the story, our story, his and mine, while still at its very heart. But,

I thought, smelling Colletti's sweating breath on my neck, I can return to the close-up of the nails later though a close-up within a certain proximity is like any other close-up at that proximity so that nominally serving as diacritical advertisement of the narrative's uniqueness it in fact sends it back to the dedifferentiated slagheap whence it may or may not have failed to emerge. So much for a close-up of the murdered man's nails — so much for close-up and its overrated arabesques over story's corpse. I turned away from old Testic lest I start butchering his parts, all of which might now be deemed private. By now his head had stopped bleeding and for no reason at all, or so I flattered myself, I kicked him in the thigh. Once we had managed to get the body down the service elevator and into Colletti's car he drove off with an unnatural swiftness, heady, almost potable. I was fatigued by this *unexpected stroke of good luck* that was nothing more and nothing less than a stroke of havoc imposed on the bole of night gyrating toward day, a ploy of one of fate's innumerable fulsome flunkeys disarming the ever-imploding momentum of my sure-footed rage by introducing a little confusion over flow of flow in the normally immobile sludge. But, as we drove further and further into the country, there was no escaping this one more radical disjunction between what I had anticipated and what had befallen me through no special aptitude of my own — a surefooted getaway. One more radical disjunction between A and B to throw on the slagheap of such disjunctions. But surely all these disjunctions must be recuperated somewhere as *something* — some domain unchartable by my likes and likely to remain so. In some domain — the story's, the story's — never to know my hoofprint — doubtless I would heartily have rejoiced, even jubilated, over the plethora or even the direst dearth of radical disjunctions between, as now for example, what I had anticipated if anything and what I was presently living, or as elsewhere, what I saw and what I felt, heard and saw, saw and heard, heard and heard, underwent and retrospectively modified, farted and shat, belched and shat, shat and shat and shat/and shat. Where was that domain. Was that domain the story's and was Colletti escorting me there. And if so who was Colletti. The aim was to locate that domain. The radical disjunctions ordered me to locate that domain and suddenly it was as if only present circumstances stymied my encroachment on that domain. In other words, if only I could divest myself of this smelly camel-haired baggage and his tasseled loafers then there would be nothing, or less than little, keeping me from a domain where the production of radical disjunctions *between* was no longer a mere disorienting stunt but rather

BUT RATHER an arcaded infinitely advancing prospect of inexhaustible adventure. And I might work that adventure as I was working this corpse into its final resting place. In all my hurrying euphoria I failed at first to understand that Colletti was obliging me to drag him through the front door on the margin of what resembled a deserted woodland. For all the door's extreme narrowness and the operation's extreme clandestineness I tried all the time and as much as possible to avail myself of the circumambient odors in order to feed off the radical disjunction between what I smelled and what was on hand to smell and from there advance to the radical disjunction between what I thought I saw and what was on hand to be seen and between what I in fact saw and what I did not see but should have seen. I turned to Colletti to see if he was aware: wearing Testic's camel's hair coat he was sprawled on the back seat snoring. Clearly he was not aware the neighborhood was looking far different from what it had been when we first arrived. How could I begin to tell him that in every situation, however marginal, however benignly static, in which one begins by feeling supremely unique in one's estrangement there is always change, incessant change or the incessant illusion of same, so that invariably and inevitably one finds oneself in the presence of recruits even newer and is thereby obliged to take stock of one's newly devolved seniority and say something along the lines of, It seems things have gotten much fatter over here, or, if it is a parking lot or tenement block, The rules for taking them seem much less stringent nowadays. Yes, yes, that was it: I wanted to let Colletti know that the woodland's rules for *taking them in* seemed much less stringent now than when we had first arrived. But immediately I knew it was best I had no opportunity to speak since I would not have been reporting an authentic observation so much as testing how starkly I could wrench a simple situation to accommodate what was completely irrelevant and inappropriate to that situation, in order, or was I only flattering myself, that that situation, simple or not, might live a little distance as it had not managed to live up in Rhinebeck at the time of the parents' visit to the prodigal's homestead. As I dragged him I kept telling myself he was drunk and that I was merely assisting him, or rather, merely being of assistance, and so from time to time it was only natural that I shrug as if I was indeed dragging a drunk against my better judgment but in consonance with my unfaltering moral instincts. Who was I at this moment shrugging away my good intentions though persisting in them? Was I shrugging away intentions that were less good, was I impersonating such shrugging away, was I shrugging away the temptation to impersonate one carrying out such good intentions, was I shrugging away the imputation that I was impersonating one who carries out his good intentions? Or was I shrugging away the unintended intrusion of any *classification of* into this scene whatever its mission in the realm of vivid depiction. What made this onrush suddenly bearable was the sense that I was once again Mike — Pam's husband — friends of the Betsy and Jim I had created for the stupefaction of his parents. For though Mike began every day full of loathing yet once he was in the middle of the day's dawdling — meeting the tasks of the day in the order of their benevolent allocation by the day's flunkeys always the same flunkeys whatever the day dressed in a little brief authority — he, Mike by name, began to feel considerably better, less harassed by the fates knowing that he was doing, that is to say, suffering, all that it was humanly possible to suffer in the name of that worthy Puritan, Long James Betterlife, whatever he is, but of course he, Mike by name, knew him intimately for he had a brood comprising wife and brats and pets and a howling grandma and a dead father clamoring though not quite as loudly as grandma bellowing for his ration of ivy to camouflage at last all the headstone drivel piacularly concocted to accompany him on his passage to eternity. In the midst of such thoughts I thought it not inappropriate to open wide Testic's zipper and bring forth his miraculous member so that this might look like what the tabloids were all too prone to call a sex- , no, a sex-related, crime. Ah, the wonders of universal euphemism in the middle of moonless meditations, racked only by the absence of stormy cypresses, beech, and night's prosthetic claw. I was suddenly full of ideas, ideas for the future, for my future with Colletti, for the story I had no intention of abandoning to Jamms's ghost. But something in the corpse's by now rarefied demeanor — a sullen refusal to participate? — more specifically, the peculiar reluctance of his prick to get an ennobling whiff of the fresh air alerted me to the possibility that I might by some fluke be confusing the ebullition of ideas for the future with the mere impingement of a fresh and airily monolithic calm masquerading as a multitude. I looked around: there was much in the book of nature to inspire me. I looked at Testic beneath my feet: there too was a text to be read attentively. I kicked him, kicked him again, as if to atone, and his gnarled fingers — or rather, right down to his gnarled fingers he — seemed to say, You kick me because you are too obtuse not to take me at my face value of standing in the way of your story and I do stand in its way, no doubt about that. I knew I was able to begin thinking along these lines only because Colletti was suddenly nearby. I heard him say: "Don't kick him. I know: he stood in the way of your trip — of your personal evolution. Kicking him you sabotage his sabotage of that personal evolution. But watch out, watch out, for the imperceptible transition from kicking as a labor in the direction of personal evolution to kicking in its sabotage of all that sabotagingly stands in the way of said evolution becoming the biggest obstruction of and after all." Although I had stopped kicking I did not know what to say especially since once again *that feeling* was overcoming me, the newest of neophytes, the feeling that though completely estranged from these surroundings — as a new arrival with a new arrival's divine right to stand back diffidently revulsed by the great guffawing idiosyncrasies of the landscape already at home with itself and all that was not itself — there were even newer arrivals, newer than I, and with the right of the same inverse seniority to discreetly recoil from the easy flamboyance, the complacent roil and toil, of that landscape as now embodied in me, its well-nigh oldest denizen. Only Colletti was choosing not to recoil. Maybe Colletti was not among the newer recruits plighted to recoil. Maybe there were no newer recruits nor would there be any. Nevertheless I compelled myself to rejoice at the possibility of emergence of such recruits for on their possibility depended the resonance — the potency — the beauty of an instantaneous retrospective modification of the immediate past into a hotbed of one single sublime radical disjunction between a nonexistent mammoth duration spanning immediate past and immediate present and that duration's bringing forth my displacement to a point whence I was obliged — with apparent reluctance — to witness their — the recruits' — discreet recoil as I, raw recruit emeritus, had once, centuries — seconds — before, discreetly recoiled from the landscape I had become. Now I—but where was the duration to account for all this?—was the boldest manifestation of a landscape too much at home with itself and therefore unworthy of anything better than recoil from its complacent putrefaction. I had to go on believing in a distinct possibility of arrivals newer than I even if there was no viable localizable chunk of duration responsible for their presence—for my displacement to a vantage whence I might smell out that emerging presence. Here then was but another radical disjunction between what I was claiming to undergo and the circumstances that could be held accountable for such an undergoing as more than hallucinatory. But I was undergoing... Colletti or no Colletti, Testic or no Testic, this undeniable emergence of recruits rawer still than I, judging me as I had judged, that is to say, with the vertiginous well-being of those too overendowed with options to relish the prospect of setting foot in the durational sludge of space at any given point. As I lay him devoutly under a glaring absence of cypresses, beeches, birches, and guiding stars turning to Colletti and deducing that he was annoyed—was it taking too long, all this?—I could only rage that I had at every turn to apologize for the existence of my radical disjunctions—fierce partisan that I had become—and could not help wondering—as, looking down I saw his, Testic's, features suggesting beauty, or rather, OR RATHER

the equivocation of beauty usual in women or in beings of mixed racial heritage—I don't say he was a woman but his gestures, in death infinitely more expressive because far less profuse, evoked woman and not just woman but the most beautiful of women deserving to be viewed through a scrim of fishnets, ortolan feathers, chipmunk droppings and the like—in short, he was beautiful as only one aspiring to the condition of womanhood can be—and could not help wondering—looking up as I had just looked down—if there mightn't exist a domain in which justification of the existence of these radical disjunctions no longer would be necessary although I had to admit the precariousness of that existence contributed in no small part to their beauty, their potency. So there he was being laid to rest and madly gesticulating and I not knowing how to take it and receiving no help from Colletti, who seemed to be concerned about just one thing, my immediate availability for work, as they say in the smiling employment agencies up and down the midtown strip. "I don't know how to take it," I said, as we both covered Testic with dead leaves. "What,"

Colletti said, scraping a little of the landscape off his right foot for the Collettis of the world are perpetually at war with landscapes such as this. Just as well, I thought, there are no cypresses or beech. Those might prove the last straw. "His madly gesticulating," I replied. "I mean, I don't know how to take it so as not to became diagnosable myself according to specifications of the most recent straitjacket designed across the river and ready for shipment: fetishism, voyeurism, consumerism as fetishistic voyeurism." Colletti sighed, looking at his watch, as if to say, Where were the days when a blonde was just a blonde and not a cobra or a penis resartus. And at the same time—whatever the ultimate price in terms of diagnosis and internment—I wanted to go on looking at him, enjoying this rare expressivity of a being no longer aiming at expressivity. But was it becoming clear that only a story could provide the necessary framework, scrim, deodorant crucial to such enjoyment. Only a story—not a fire trap, mine field, of radical disjunctions—but a good old-fashioned story which I had just been spurning so heartlessly in the name of those disjunctions—could domesticate my looking into a leering gaping salivating looking common to stories—the right stories—but never common to the point of banality. So I ended up looking and wanting to go on looking and looking and looking at the same time as—destitute of—or rather, refractory to—stories, I was all too eager to bury the looking and keep on burying until the last gurgle of leaf gravel had scattered to the four winds the unstayed casket of his bones. Yet each time I was about to keep on burying I found a new appendage that enthralled. And so immediately I wanted to have done with it as if ablation of target of desire had ever succeeded in doing away with desire. But if I couldn't have a story in which to found and regulate my desire—although I had no guarantee the story wouldn't do the very opposite—then I needed somebody—Colletti, for example—through whose looking I could look, yes yes yes, this was the meaning of Colletti, and I had debouched upon it faster than the story- and meaning-mongers could have shoved it down my throat as a meaning good for the story and for my reputation as a teller and a meaner— somebody, I say, like Colletti or not like Colletti, through whose looking I could look, someone to incarnate the loathsome looker I was fast becoming, the hero of a shameless looking—and of everything that shamelessly succeeds to looking *of a certain   type*—I could never hoist myself up to become —someone —someone —someone enough like me to experience similar putrefactive fireworks of desire yet infinitely beyond me by virtue of an infinite distance of shamelessness from that desire. Only through him could my desire end up conceivable to a story. For if there was to be a story that story had to comprise —I don't say actively embrace —but surely comprise my desire. I began throwing more sand and gravel, even earthworms, but no longer as if fulfilling or striving to fulfill a story function —a STORY FUNCTION —but rather as if the sand and the gravel and the earthworms and the very twilight were the enhancing scrim between me and the target of my desire —of which scrim —dutiful fetishist that I was —I oft had been a-dreaming. The sand and the gravel and the dead leaves —these were not doing away with Testic —with Testic as target of desire —this had been my error in connection with NO NO

      this NO had NO NO no had been been error my with respect

      in connection with the Jamms burial —at least according to the story-and meaning-mongers always on the lookout —even at this terminal stage —for stark contrasts professing to encapsulate a change in behavior a NO

      a No a no

      growth

—this doing away with desire had been my gross error in the course of the Jamms burial —these were not doing away with Testic but RATHER

      But rather NO

bringing the target of desire to a fever pitch of desirability, enhancing each and every facet of its being for my slobbering delectation. Finally I kicked him in the jaw and called it a day, or rather a dusk, and trudged back to the car alone [for Colletti had clearly lost all patience] refusing to look over my shoulder since this precisely was what was expected of one in my battered shoes —as a function of my function in the story I wanted and did not want. On the way back Colletti instructed me regarding the importance, upon entering the apartment building, of chatting with the doorman or whoever else I could recruit to my garrulity —a garrulity he was careful to point out lifting his pinky from the steering wheel that was under no circumstances to stink of that corposant variety emblematic of the class of white Anglo-Saxon murderers between the ages of No, I must try to speak like somebody just a wee bit lonely though careful not to burden others with his loneliness though on the other hand never stooping to be catapulted to rapture at the triumph of that loneliness without bound. I did not know whether or not I should reveal to Colletti that for the first time in my life I was feeling triumph—or was this triumph simply another contraption of the meaning-mongers—for having done a deed without an assailing sense before, during, and/or after that it was far from the right moment with the point of the moment becoming not to do the deed but to get beyond the moment of its scandalous untimeliness, a moment incapacitated once and for all by my definitive sense of incapacitation. At no moment before, during, and after the deposition of Testic's corpse in the woods—I would gladly— ecstatically—have sworn to it— had I undergone the moment as a pressing need to get beyond the moment rendered unfit for perpetration of the act at hand since the actor was unfit. Yet the moment after I decided not to swear to all this I wondered if it was all true. Had it been true before, during, and after the burial. It didn't matter: true or not, it was true now, within the confines of Colletti's four-wheeler. Its untruth then had paved the way—had fought single-handedly—for its truth here and now. I agreed to meet with Colletti the following day. When I turned, just before reaching the elevator, I heard quicker—far quicker—than I saw one gumchewing neighbor say to another, "I just saw Teeeeeeena. She's due in October." About four in the afternoon of the following day I went out to meet Colletti: surely it was too early for there to be any news of the event in the papers. I was especially looking forward to the description of Testic's disarray replete with genitalia nodding like begonias at the four winds and to discreetly summarizing mention of the *possible sex-related crime.* We went to an insider's fast-food joint in China-town, I am tempted to say: At a neighboring table two men were speaking and then berate their peripherality to the story, our story—mine and Colletti's—unfolding at last. Only there were no two men speaking at a neighboring table at least not about what I wish to attribute to them out of fear, laziness, rage. For we were doing the speaking, Colletti and I, or rather Colletti and an acquaintance who managed to amble over between courses, and among whom I was able to interject a few rejoinders. Colletti's acquaintance argued for the edification of the working class after the revolution. The other, namely, Colletti, insisted that such edification was propaedeutic to said revolution's ultimate success, that said revolution was inconceivable without it. He looked at me as if suggesting that by transporting a little bag of pharmaceuticals from point A to point B surely I for one was undergoing edification. Both, at any rate, spoke of revolution as if it was inevitable, as if the country—fount of all injustice—could not go on proliferating fast-food emporia, tee shirts, video games, spinach pasta on the half shell, and condominium residences indefinitely. Suddenly I understood why we were in a fast-food emporium in Chinatown: this was a statement, a proclamation of aversion to an elsewhere. They both agreed about the revolution even if one had a stutter and the other did not; one sipped tea, the other coffee; one had fingernails rimmed with dirt, the other's manicured and appallingly clean; one had had a tumultuous adolescence, dermatologically speaking, whence at the age of, say, forty-four he had not quite recovered, the other's skin as smooth and complacent as a baby girl's. About the revolution they both agreed even if one was decidedly and incessantly x, the other starkly and defiantly b^x. The longer I sat the more profusely and complaisantly they went about spinning out for my pleasure oppositions that are the true stuff of drama, of story. But I had to work at extracting these oppositions beneath and around the corner from their consilience when it was a question of the revolution. Colletti said, "This simply can't continue. The prosperous middle- and upper classes will have to be overthrown not because they consummate themselves in their work at the expense of other classes—they don't—but because they are most grim, dogmatic, and shrill in their delusional insistence that the work 'fulfill'—to use a word I loathe above all others—in the same way as marriage, as life itself, must themselves fulfill. It is the doleful tenacity with which this class strives to realize its aim which is at the same time a processed and stultified aim—an aim appropriated from some computerized billboard scrawl—an ill-begotten aim—that signals a need for overthrow. Work is punishment, marriage the mere submission to a clot of tabus, —we cannot allow these cretins to go on producing and distributing such epochal ideas. But in fact they are not producing these ideas: they are merely disseminating gobbets of their own thralldom but to what—to whom—are they themselves—the so-called proprietors of the prevailing ideology (embodying their not so finely honed illusions about themselves: their minds ultimately as shapeless and colorless as their billboard bodies)—in thrall? Perhaps it is more accurate to say that the shreds of this prevailing ideology—that work can and should be 'fulfilling,' that marriage is an unabashed joy, that the body should run like a well-oiled machine,—are conceived and generated by them and them alone but in response to enthralling pressure exerted elsewhere by forces—beings?—over which and whom they cannot hope to have the least control. Nor do they seek that control. Their response to the unbearable pressure exerted to the left and the right of this ostensibly sublime and blithe manufacture of a useful ideology is—said manufacture."

I listened until I could no longer bear to listen for what I heard crying out from the depths—of one, of the other, of both—was some hungering claim to a name, the name of hero, the name of prophet, the name of shaman. And the right to the name could be demonstrated only through knowledge of...the story, their story, a story like the one that might have been had Jamms only participated— or rather through appropriation of the myth that sang the praises of—that is to say, constructed—their essential difference one from the other once and for all. But there was no difference, aside from the fingernails and the acne. But the myth sang of the difference and either's right to the name was clearly based on excruciated rehearsal of that myth. Here and now, at the table in this lowly Chinatown dive (Name: Sam Fuller's Lightning Louie) there was no difference between Colletti and...Colletti. Aside from the fingernails and the stinking chop suey breath and the texture of the skin and a host of even more exilious details belonging now exclusively to one, now exclusively to the other, they were indistinguishably welded beyond the differences that only affirmed their identity. Yet each hungered after the name and the name could only arise like the sun once they—one or the other or both—managed to tear himself free of this drama in which they were indistinguishable and scaled the pullulating foothills of a myth where they were safely sculpted as each other's negation. But here they were delaying, sipping tea, reordering egg rolls, having a world of trouble naming their myth for the revolution was not their myth—the revolution was a convenient evasion of the myth. But how could they be straightforward in their invocation of the myth when invocation would only kill the myth and killing the myth kill them as they needed to see themselves out

in the world. To name the myth, to adumbrate the myth, was to destroy
the myth as private property and yet only by reference to the myth could
each begin to begin to stake his claim to the name after which he panted
hopelessly and helplessly. So—I heard the story-mongers hot on my
trail—that was why Jamms had refused to participate in the construction
of our story—our myth—he had instinctively—heroically—rejected the
selfserving falseness of its construction of our vast and essential difference; this life-lie—at least for me, a life-lie—was far more excruciating to
him than the exposure of our essential sameness. The story's—the
myth's—glorification of our differentness—the polar opposition of which
Hollywood sagas are made—could only call attention to a far more
essential sameness. Mr. Naven—for this was the other man's name—
strove first it seemed to me to grapple with the problem of appropriating
the myth without exposing it—by discreetly mentioning certain details.
The middle class, he suggested, was trying with a grimness that gave new
meaning to the phrase, Procrustean bed and breakfast, to fulfill its ideal
with no point of application in the real world. Bed and breakfast, then,
were two such details capable of momentarily illuminating the firmament
of the myth without dragging it to earth and fettering it amidst the toils
of a chronology. For who was to say—me? Colletti? Naven?—that bed
came before breakfast or breakfast before bed. Colletti nodded but not so
much, it seemed to me, at the content of this pronouncement as at its
dazzling success as a sagittal figure (heralding though all the time
maintaining the secrecy) of the myth—the story. So, for the moment,
Naven had a more substantial claim to the name they were both seeking
though they were very quickly—again, so it seemed to me—sinking back
into the primeval sludge of their maimed sameness. And as much as I
wanted to I could not answer the question on which the success, that is
to say, the perpetuation, of all this speculation seemed to hinge, namely,
Why was it so crucial to shroud the myth—their story—in secrecy? Why
was the right to the name—of leader—or shaman—in part a function of
the sustentation of that secrecy? "This new grimness of conformity,"
Naven went on, "is more virulent, more loathsome, precisely because it
has the noxiousness of an ostensibly irrefutable and universal hunger for
everybody's health behind it. These new middlemen will do anything—
even—especially—if it means denying their selfhood—whatever that

is,—to conform to the specifications of fitness. Fitness, according to a certain exoteric billboard mold and modality, is infinitely more vital than selfhood achieved and sustained. Yes, yes, yes, they all—these middle-men—have a long, lonely, acrid and atavistic memory of individuality behind them: individuality has been tried and, sad—or rather, glad—to say, yielded nothing in the way of yield. For these worms individuality lies if anywhere in the praxis of a stringent—might I even say, an astringent—conformity. One reveals one's true stuff by showing how close one can come—ablating all protrusive and obstructing personal peculiarities—to a grim ideal, the more provenanceless and absolute the better. " So here were other details similarly skirted, glanced: billboard, health, astringent. Once again, there was no uniting them into a vulgar chronological sequence—bugbear of all stories—for future reference. The potency of these details as far as the story was concerned was their spontaneous dazzle, their polite fugacity. There was no hanging onto them as a permanent clue to the congealed identity of the myth of these two men, Colletti and Naven. So Naven had scored again, putting Colletti to shame, but only momentarily of course because they were beginning once more to look like NO NO

       even NO

       even MORE like each other than before.

I was about to nod into my coffee cup at this windowless portrait of fraternal rivalry—cup tepid and foul—when Colletti turned to me and seeming to completely abdicate all concern with achieving the name of shaman in the service of the revolution through tellingly precise and oblique allusion to the details of the story—the myth—of their totally phantom differentness, totally fictive polar oppugnancy, indicated that soon I should expect a visit from the police regarding one or both murders. "What do you mean: both murders," I said feebly. He did not bother answering. "Our men of the law, as you must know, are sensitive to fine distinctions that disrupt the norm. So that when you are asked— and of course you will be asked—what went on at the time of the murder do not advertise any disjunction between what you seemed to be living and what you really felt. There must never—do you hear, never—be any radical disjunction between your living and the posthumous report of the living that ends up shedding an entirely different light or rather soot on that living as the mere ghost of all it might have been, should have been, was soon to be but of course only in the course of the report denuded of and oblivious to all the contingencies that constitute so much of a living, satisfactory or not,—the posthumous report of the living that ends up trumpeting forth its mere inadequacy, bad smell, recuperated and reviled at last in the light, or rather the flutter, of another's understanding. There must never be any radical disjunctions—radical disjunctions are toys to be confined to solitary use—for their—the detectives'—eyes at least— between your living as having been a mere waiting out of its own futility toward the telling of such futility AND that telling as the only sign of life to be associated with you, a prime suspect. Yes, yes, yes, you must go, and rapidly, beyond this foppish taste for radical disjunctions between the content of your living at any given moment—at the time of a murder, for example—and that of the telling about the living—radical disjunctions between the pointlessness of the living and the pointing latent in the telling about the living. In short, let them think you have been living as you all along intended to be living. In short, don't try to make yourself interesting. If you are interesting you are most probably guilty."

The detectives did come, several days before news of Testic's retrieval appeared in the newspapers. I experienced a certain pleasure in the fact that having prepared myself for the occurrence of this latter event—newspaper mention of the murder—I was obliged when it did occur—to let it be swept away into an insignificance—a marginality— dictated by the unexpected upsurge of another, anterior, weightier, event, namely, arrival of the police.

This seemed very much in keeping with the self-preservational, or rather self-authenticating, techniques of the story comprising, among others, the need never to show its hand when the showing of that hand was anticipated but only when the attention of the spectator—the hovering witness—was elsewhere diverted. Along these lines the appearance of the news of Testic's disappearance and murder, when it did appear, was already a memory—a memory long before NO NO—it appeared—and therefore insusceptible to canvassing suspicions that it had been planted—constructed—at the appropriate moment in the story in order to advance that story. So the story was advancing precisely because nobody could accuse it of advancing—no hovering witness, for example.

Literally minutes before they came up I got a call from Colletti, for whom I had already completed two assignments and been, I had to admit, handsomely paid. "Look, he said, chewing gum at the same time, "you're in good shape. You've got nothing to worry about. Simply because you got me to drive you and *him* to the final resting place. You're all right because you implicated me. I don't mind being implicated—I relish it—for it's the easiest thing in the world for me to implicate in turn somebody else—like Naven, here. Right, Nave?" I heard a subdued grumbling, perhaps only a mumbling. There was a long silence: I was waiting for him to resume. "Why so glum? Oh, I see. Approaching the site: you're afraid somebody may have seen us approaching the site. I can assure you nobody was around long enough to witness the whole voyage—not even the whole approach to the final site. More than likely, some characters fringelike as yourself, caught mere fragments of the great nameless curve of your—our—delirious descent on that site. They may have stayed with you on that curve for as long as it took you to look up at a chestnut bough—remember, no cypresses, no beechen greens—since to some extent you were authentically interested in that bough—insofar, that is, as the interest sketched or began to sketch a character other than yourself—a character unlinked to the likes of...*him*. So you have absolutely nothing to worry about and anyway, didn't you delay your descent upon the final resting site, didn't you delay your progress so that the other fringe elements also about at that time of night could move on ahead and allow you a glimpse of their mien and posture? Oh no, but you didn't do that. You did not outsmart your pursuers—your hovering witnesses—how could you? I forgot: you had me along: I obstructed your progress. Why did you have me along then. Ah yes, of course, to implicate me, but even more, to have someone to drive you, to save, in other words, on gas. But this has done you in—this having me along to drive you. For alone—or rather, alone with Testic—you would have had greater mobility. I enhanced your conspicuity and, after all, a ride out to the woodlands is not that expensive." I did not know how to answer: before my eyes he was constructing a radical disjunction—the supreme radical disjunction—between the transparent meaning of a past incident in our story and all he was now making that meaning mean. So that I no longer knew what the incident meant and if I did not know what the incident meant how could

I retail it to the detectives about to arrive on the scene. What was the point although dimly I felt there was a point, to wit, to manage an accrual to the story itself if not to me. Yes, this radical disjunction *between* was in the service of the story, making sure the story was never what it seemed. But why was it important that the story never appear to be what it seemed and that it seem to be betrayed at every turn by its own elements. For in this case Colletti was introducing no new elements to deform that long trek into the woods. "I see, I see, you're upset, he said soothingly. "For I am coming at you from two directions *with the same datum*. At first I made you think your recruiting me to the cause of the premature burial of Testic was a sign of singleminded dedication to a central task whatever the threat — whatever the cost—to such peripheral perquisites as eating, sleeping, shitting—and now here I am suggesting that implicating me in the delivery of the body to its sculpted woodland home is a sign not of singleminded dedication to a central task but of simpleminded preoccupation with a peripheral one—namely, how to save a few cents on the way to the burial ground. At the height of your career—in the midst of unparalleled dangers—you could focus only on an exiguous—a negligible—fringe element: reasonably priced transport. And so I was recruited to salve your preoccupation and salvage that fringe element. Yes, yes, I come at you from two directions *with the same datum*. But this is to help you—to prepare you for the police, who are going to come at you from far more than two directions *with the same datum*. Just remember: a datum is never what it seems: it depends upon the schema with which it has the good or bad fortune to be united. Coppers aside, the best storytellers—for this is what you are driving at, isn't it—telling your story or having it told as you live it—are able to come at you—the liver, the spectator, the hovering witness—from *n* directions *with the same datum*. Stems from the old Leibnitzian saw: maximum of effects from a strict minimum of causes. Don't you see—don't you—if nothing in the story is what it seems—subject to retrospective modification whereby present determines past and future present—a state of affairs I managed to achieve in my depiction just now of our drive out into the woodlands— then we are at last outside of time. The difference between me and Jamms is that I can make my subversions—my radical disjunctions—work for the story. My radical disjunctions are not a simple and simpleminded bombardment. Mine are integral to the story. There is no story—our story—without these bombardments to extract that story from the sludge of a linear time casting it, the story, to the rhythm of death. And if I am able—as I was once again just now—to come at you from *n* directions *with the same datum*—the same story datum—then once again the story—through its datum—is outside of time—outside of space—for where in space is that datum if it is coming at you from so many directions at once?—and therefore we are outside time and outside space. Jamms bombarded your story because he could not allow himself to feel real in any story. His most salient trait was his unreality—as unreal as you may have always felt in his presence—his presence as absence—so unreal—even more so did he feel in the presence of his parents—the figures in the photograph, yes, I know about it—the cop to whom he handed it is a friend of mine, a dear friend, willing at a moment's notice to accept little favors—. I know, he was constantly defacing and dismissing them, the parents, but he was paralyzedly prostrate before them. And yet over and over this at once spontaneous and constructed unreality was the most virulent blow—there, I am constructing him retroactively, modifying retrospectively your sacrosanct image of the little bastard, merging present, past and future—the most virulent blow he was able to deal to those who, like you, craved his presence and more than his presence. This flaunting of an unreality that went far far beyond mere inadequacy was his most powerful weapon...against those committing the grave solecism of wanting to profit from his substantiality. He was consubstantial with nothing—never. And that is why he point blank refused my offer of employment that night in the hotel dining room. It was not because he yearned to be a shepherd in the morning, a cowboy at noon, a critic at dusk, a fire hydrant against which a derelict sagely and blissfully pisses at midnight—no, he was afraid of his inadequacy and he was afraid that once again here was someone wishing to profit from his nonexistent substantiality—profit, in this case of course, in the baldest way. But the police will be arriving shortly. But don't be afraid. Try to think that your most powerful weapons in your dealings with them *and with those like them* are the story data with which they may try to come at you from *n* different directions."

I waited for the detectives. I thought I might feel weak, exposed, but then surprisingly I was sucked up into the strength of a telling that had chosen to sweep aside the long-awaited mention of Testic's death in the tabloid of my choice in the name of making way for this new event. Such a telling but by whom—who was telling my story?—capable of casting away at the drop of a hat an event of mammoth proportions in the name of one even more mammoth, was clearly a telling with a terrible abundance at its disposal from innumerable sources it had most probably not even begun to tap. Nevertheless I still wanted to run off, pack my bags, and disappear. Every time I was about to run out, with or without my bags, it was as if somebody other than myself was compelling me to stay and listen and accept responsibility not so much for my act as for its aftermath.

"Where were you the night Mr. Lou Lionel Testic was killed," one of them asked. I was prepared to say I had been at the movies. This was my most watertight alibi since Colletti or Naven or both were prepared to support it. Subsidize it, was the phrase Naven had used as we emerged from the Chinatown dive. Yet I was reluctant to use it or any number like it—as if I must hoard it and its myriad for some other occasion—far direr, though what occasion could be direr?—or as if I must work with a minimum—a penury—of information lest I make myself too airtight too quickly. I had to remain forever tangent to the curve of their suspiciousness, their clinging refusal to let go of me— though they seemed on several occasions more than willing to depart— rather than catapult myself too immediately through a foolproof ingenuity buttressed by the even more NO ingenious alibis of cronies into a domain inaccessible to their sordid imputations. For their imputations— or rather, my proximity to those imputations, or rather, my sentient ever-palpitating proximity to those imputations—were now my only lever, fixed point, gauge, under the circumstances and not only those connected with murder. No, every aspect of my life, my being, required the lever, the foothold, the fulcrum that only the possible upsurge of new imputations at any moment could embody. In short, listening to them, watching even with eyes closed, I vowed never to venture out into or find myself deposited in those hinterlands where I was sure to feel myself free at last of their prongs, the termite art of their indagation. For they were sure at last to follow me and their setting foot in inaccessibility's domain would be purest proof that they were *even more intent* on driving me to the wall. So the more they sat and waited the more I felt constitutionally incapable of giving my plethora of alibis—even my single and supreme alibi—free play. My only integrity with respect to these interlopers was in paucity degree zero, the only way to feel strong in relation to what they had inevitably turned out to be was to be buoyed up and buttressed by the rage that came of restricting myself to the martyrdom of having not a single wormridden subterfuge to my name. The only strength, the only trustworthiness—as far as they were concerned (as if it was only as far as they were concerned)—was in impotence carefully calibrated against the lucid contour of their inquiry. Now that I was confronted with them the aim was no longer—had it ever been?—to gamble for freedom through a flaunted untouchability, a flaunted immunity dappled with alibis, but rather BUT RATHER

to hold on tight to the credulous terror generated by their menace and which said untouchability, said immunity, could only dispel, or rather, provoke to more wily, less easily identifiable, ploys. Now, now, and always, incessantly resuscitated terror was my only lifeline.

There seemed no way out of self-protective impotence until one of the two said, "This must be pretty hard on you: you were a friend of Testic's weren't you, I mean, aside from knowing him through Jamms." Suddenly there was a way out: a report on my wretchedness at Testic's loss, dear Testic, cut off in the bloom of uncouth youth. How maraud—through ostensible wretchedness at Testic's loss—with imperial calm the obscene chaos around me (comprising Testic's being more than his loss)—chaos triggered of course exclusively by this deeply unwelcome death—without becoming a target of the straitjacketing contempt, worse, mild-mannered irritation, of these arms of the law? How speak at last of life's loathsomeness—as Jamms, for example, might have spoken of it— it did not matter what suddenly accounted for this obsession not so much with life's loathsomeness as with the necessity of conveying the certainty of that loathsomeness—how speak of its certainty as the last surviving untainted diagnostician of that loathsomeness without being heard as innumerable ones heard before in homologous variants of the diagnostic impasse? Suddenly, there was less, far less, of a concern with proving my innocence and/or remaining tangent to the curve of the cops' suspicion as a way not only of keeping myself abreast of my status as criminal but of staying alive, in being, through them, the rise and fall of their deductions, and far far more of a concern with proving how loathsome I knew life to be without thereby making myself susceptible to their straitjacketing caricatural paraphrase meant for precinct files. They were seated far apart from each other. I told them Lou had turned up just when I was on the verge of a voyage. And I assured them I needed that voyage now more than ever. They asked me — or rather, the younger asked me — to keep in touch. At first they reacted with extreme impatience: every time I spoke of the voyage the younger turned away with revulsion. But then as the interview wore on and perhaps with my guilt becoming more and more of a settled, an irrevocable, thing they softened to my aspiration or perhaps it was never in the least a question of their softening but rather of my instinctively tempering mentions of that aspiration to the point of indecipherability in the face of a manifest indifference or raging jealousy. For wasn't I for all of their suspicions free to come and go as I chose still and they fettered servants of the state, enmeshed by a long praxis of self-abnegation in the name of such dubious joys as family, army, church, business. Again they asked what I had done the night of the murder. They explained that he had been found on a deserted country road. The younger now wandered about the room as the elder consecrated himself to questioning me more and more exhaustively about my whereabouts. He made the word resonate far beyond a particular moment in space and time. Yet I could not help fixing my attention on the one moving about the room casually examining the bric-a-brac and believing that without him present the interview might be going so much more smoothly. I watched the tensing of his buttocks under his rumpled trousers and wished him away. Yet could I speak of a phenomenon, this phenomenon, an interview with the police, for example, minus one of its elements, minus one or more of its elements as if it, they, were mere disposable excrescences. Would I be talking about the interview simply minus one of its elements — an officer — or would I be talking in fact about something of an entirely different species. And the very fact of talking even about something entirely different, wouldn't that drivelling luxury have been underwritten by not merely one but both officers, each in his niche. Yes, as he wandered about the apartment this younger arm of the law, this flunkey, seemed to be a mere contingency, disengageable, extirpable, at a moment's notice, from the scene, and without whom the interview would most certainly have proceeded more fluently, whatever that might end up meaning. But in fact—in actual fact, to be exact—and I was being convinced of this more and more, with each passing step skirting the bric-a-brac—there could be—could have been—no interview apart from this young officer, fixed or mobile, the interview had already gone too far to be conceivable as other than it was. The interview was inconceivable without either officer, I speak of the interview as I was now living it most intensely—most intensely not in responding to or shirking the questions of two high-wire flunkeys of the state but in imagining its modification to suit my fastidious fancies. Now I knew, was every minute knowing more and more, that my only and substantive foothold in fastidious reveries of interview overhaul was the interview itself, but flawlessly intact, and more especially, its two principals. The blessedly eternal rootedness of both, especially the younger, it was this made possible my not so daring little excursion into the domain of modification characterized in this case by excision of one or the other or both to suit the rigors of the season. But didn't this mean that the interview and/or its two participants were vital to my story, illustrating exemplarily what it meant for a story element to be a story element. I spoke of accompanying Testic to his car, the sky was starlit, we had both perhaps drunk a little too much, and here they were telling me Lou, old Lou, was dead. I spoke a little aggressively but made the aggressiveness seem to stem—successfully, I thought—from deepest grief. And they seemed to be accepting my grief. But again, were they learning to *accept me as I am* or an even faster learner than impersonator and having learned they were most appalled and enraged by any intrusion of self-affirmation—as when I spoke of the thirst for voyage—had I once again simply tempered my delivery, reduced, in other words, my being to a pinpoint of amicable grief molded to offend no one. Yet how could I ever measure to what degree I was muting myself in delicate response to their possible revulsion man to man and to what degree mouthing whatever I assumed it was most suitable for them to hear if I was to save my skin. And did I really care about measuring out varying degrees of accommodation to the slime-ridden requirements of the moment. In other words, was all this a real dilemma mirroring a painful reality or the mere impersonation of dilemma designed to tie a signposting knot in the story's turbulence and whose very existence more than compensated me for any incidental torment it embodied or exacerbated. What did all this matter: what truly mattered was that from this interview I had learned how to define a true story element as the incessantly intensified possibility of its elimination in the name of a smoother flow.

They kept returning to the subject of Jamms, what had made him retreat to the back woods. I explained that when I first came upon him—but I was quickly interrupted by the younger who suggested that when we first came upon each other I had represented or managed to represent—here a look at his colleague, since older, probably his superior, as if for approval at this insinuatingly fine distinction—in my stigmata derived from an uncomplaining arduous factory toil not a being but—was he being impertinent to suggest it?—but the dissolution of all beings, dissolution of all concepts of fungible being. Warming to the subject, especially as the younger increased his pace around the sofa, I in turn suggested that through our briefest of relations he had been able to divest himself of that scab of ideologies by which his life up to that point had been governed. And what were those ideologies, I could not refrain from asking, but a sum of misconstructions by which a privileged class—his— vindicated its values as the only conceivable values. It was through me that my friend—more privileged than ever I had been—learned how little will, consciousness, purpose—all that detritus of privileged class selfdramatization—actually counted within the system of concepts and values passed down to him by his eternally dying forbears. Until he met me, I explained, he had never perceived of the present order as the merest conduit through which some inevitable and better future order had first to pass. I taught him—but gently, gently, through example—that his fatuous sense of purpose, painterly or otherwise, did not determine the course of events in which his own—life events, that is—were enmeshed. "Rather, gentleman," I intoned, and the younger seemed to stop dead in his tracks under my reproduction of a little hunting scene, quite pastoral for all the grotesquerie of dying postures assumed by bloodied stags, "there are laws, freefloating, ubiquitous, powerful beyond a little brief despotism, governing the flow of movement—the sequence of historical events—each concrete and unrepeatable in such a way that all this protoplasm of volition, consciousness, artistic striving, high purpose, clean living and cleaner thinking, can ultimately be determined and classified only as its most putrid byproduct." There seemed to be a second stopping dead in their tracks even if they were already both quite still. "And you must believe me, gentlemen, it relieved him, Jamms, to know that his so-called commitment, to the cause of the work, was the toy not of his will but of stalking laws of historical movement ever onward, ever blindward toward an apotheosis of justice for all. In short, through me he learned that this craving to paint was but the alluvium of a particular historical moment and that these crises of election whereby every other moment he was chosen by and himself chose an artistic vocation counted in the long run for very little insofar as such crises embody nothing more than a puny disavowal, impotent flight, from the historical flow. My friend, alas, did not belong to the flow but he was willing to learn how to belong. Lou, on the other hand, had no desire to learn. I tried to educate him, encouraged him to say farewell to his wild reckless living, preoccupation with the dollar — his contempt and at the same time his...hunger for the common man." The younger said, only dutifully I thought, "What do you mean by his hunger for the common man." I demurred as if he was the first to use this phrase that was so distasteful to me. Finally I conceded, "Lou had a massive contempt for the workmen in his father's factory, for the working people he scrutinized in passing on his way home from work. They were all surface, they had no lives beyond that surface. They were merely bit players in the drama of his lumbering aggrandizement. He was, of course, at least when I came to know him — though can I say I ever knew him? — already aggrandized but he liked to play as if not quite there yet, at aggrandizement, I mean. It never occurred to him to conceptualize them as belonging to that class unprotected from the extremes of exploitation by any special qualification parrying replacement by others of equal strength. Guided by me, Jamms was able to begin to see himself as belonging to that class for isn't it true that all of us, you and I and the lamppost, belong to this class of classes, this class of supernumeraries, as it were, unprotected from extremest formulations of exploitation by any special qualification, any sterling credential that can appealing to the machine mentality make it stop dead in its tracks of shifting and rearranging. We are all fungible." They both looked at me as if in spite of themselves requesting me to make the deduction they had already made, namely, that if we are all fungible then I was the most fungible, absolutely uncaparisoned with any special talent, anything that might qualify as a special trait, charism, rebated erogation of the swamp and bayou gods. But did they also expect me to deduce from this deduction that I was thereby the most heroic of all. The total absence of any diacritical mark, as it were, on my human person, this was what had fascinated Jamms, put him into a trance, I won't go so far as to call it an erotic trance . . . I went on to say all this and, as they looked blessedly uncomprehending, even more. "Jamms—not Testic, of course, but Jamms—told me, when we were traveling on Long Island together—that having achieved the zero point of fungibility I had introduced a little much-needed mystery into his life . For moments at a time, contemplating my complete absence of marketable goods to differentiate me from the lowest common denominator of humanity, his hungers and petty cravings were swept up into my oceanic lack of differentiation from the great mass. He was able, he told me, in my presence, to foster the illusion of an enveloping mystery vaster than the recalcitrant toy to which those hungers and petty cravings recurringly reduced the world, thereby purging it of all mystery. And at the same time watching me struggle to survive and so gracefully and in the complete absence of any diacritical marks attractive to foremen and personnel managers he found himself pursued—as he had never been pursued—by an almost bilious comprehension of, that is, revulsion for, his diacritically marked cravings and hungers FASTER than he could take refuge in a delicious and disquieting estrangement born of the dislocation fostered by my mysteriously unclassifiable status. In short, my status was a thin status and the survival of one yoked to so thin a status was an eternal mystery, more than willing to assimilate him to its halflight in which all hungers and cravings are ablatedly grey—in which the real world's sharp contour—supreme and solitary source of nourishment for worldly hungers and cravings—is effaced. At the same time my struggle for survival despite the thinness of the status could only rouse him to a mimicking action—could only intimidate and spur him to action. He could no longer pretend his competitive spirit—that robbed the world of its halflight, of its mystery—had not understood the message of my struggle. His delicious sense of estranged veneration passed to envy. If the thinness of my status in itself escorted him out of the world—whose only spirit is that of competition, fratricidal mimesis—the unflagging struggle to survive amid all the absence of trappings such a status brought in its wake escorted him back, primed to fight in my mold. He began to understand that I was able to survive—bereft as I was—precisely because I was conscious—without said consciousness degenerating into a classifiable trait—a docketable piece of marketable goods—that my consciousness was determined by a flow of events inexorably outside myself. In this way I was spared all the poisons and purulences of that supreme bugbear of Jamms's nonexistence, namely, the arrogant insistence on a hallucinatory freedom decked out in all the spasms of will, purpose. I tried to convince him that once he had relinquished this insistence we both could struggle to achieve the struggle that would finish by transforming consciousness into—into—But he refused—refused to believe the machine is not the ideal toward which civilization is striving and it is possible to make that machine mentality stop dead in its tracks. He wanted proof and of course gentlemen I never pretended that what I was putting forth was a hypothesis susceptible of empirical confirmation, nay, nay, nay, it was but a pattern stripped bare by a flagrantly nonhistorical method, of gutter intuition, you might say." But they looked, both inspectors, older and younger, as if either they had heard all this before and what to me was new and refreshing—given all I had had to surmount to impersonate one likely to say it—on the verge of saying it—could, by other—should I say, opposing—forces be achieved any time they wished through a very banal shortcut of which I was expected to have not the dimmest untutored suspicion—as if either they had heard all this before or authentically and totally baffled by a dazzling newness of daring thetic contrariety they were merely pretending to be jaded. What did it matter: whatever I had constructed, invented, of their relation one to the other had spurred me to this presentation of a relation to Jim that hadn't but should have been. This sketch of our relation was not a sketch of theirs, the policemen's, each to the other, but a fantasy—with no connection either to them or to me and Jamms—spun out in the shadow of the courage lent me by the mere fact of their being... here. "These men and women on the early morning subways—the men and women Testic was wont to meet out of idle curiosity belong to a class that is a class in relation not to itself but to greed ineluctable, greed, greed, greed. I was beginning

to wean Jamms from that greed before he...went out into the hinterlands.
Testic, had he lived, would have proved a lost cause. But of course I am
sad to learn that he is dead." I looked out of the window. Were the eyes
of the detectives upon me? I did not care for NO

for the first NO

time NO NO (story-mongers hard at work)

the

first NO NO NO NO NO NO NO NO NO

TIME, in the shadow—the aftermath—the context—of a class that was
the dissolution of all classes—a universal class engulfing all sentient as
well as semi-sentient beings—the landscape was slowly beginning NO

to make sense, especially the dark walls abutting on vacant lots
used as parking spaces. In the upper reaches of one wall across the way—
how I hungered to be able to say, In the upper reaches of all walls—there
was a regular array of windows but further down, in the region of a particularly nondescript ochrous plaster, the kind that catches every rugous
inflection of midday urban sunshine, windows were very very few and far
between, as if the surface could no longer gather up enough strength to
exude these conduits. Somehow the stark opposition between upper
reaches saturated with windows and lower depths pierced by so few
delighted beyond any concern with the effect I was having on these two
dicks. But of course this stark opposition was conceivable only in the
context of a circumambient dissolution of all classes into the distillate of
a single class to which all belonged yet very very few had any consciousness of belonging. I turned back. Something was brewing, something
about to be poured forth. But I did not know how it would be poured forth
or when or by whom or by what. Yet there was a terrible hunger on
somebody or something's part to get it poured forth, over and done with,
even if strictly speaking there was nothing in the immediate circumstances of our condition to call it forth to be poured forth and yet it was
strictly speaking very much connected with immediate circumstances.
And at the same time it had, this latent mass waiting to be poured or to
pour itself forth, something of the quality of an intrusion, into immediate
circumstances, a prosthetic device, some adscititious being less than
beauteous called in but by whom to spur and goad the story onward or to
sabotage that movement ever onward. And but neither they—yet how did

I know?—nor I was willing or able to divest ourselves of this chunk coming from a long way off to annihilate and resuscitate: we were moving differently, smiling, stalking each other now, in the comforting shadow of this bulk soon to emerge. Maybe this hulk, this chunk, this bulk, had the peculiar ability common to its species of both propelling and obstructing the story, the story that was of course more significant than my living or dying, being taken into custody or allowed to go scot-free. Yet suddenly, or not so suddenly, as the first interview with the detectives was coming to a close, it was no longer a question of this bulk, though provoked by and yoked to it, being visited upon our confrontation here and now for it was conceivable said bulk could postpone its visitation or float forward forever latent without deigning to implicate any of us in its pertinence.

Something driving me back to the hotel dining room where Jamms, Colletti, and I had our abortive conversation, it was quite by chance that I heard two voices resembling those of the detectives on the other—most secluded—side of the salad bar. I had never really left that dining room, having never solved the desolation it continued—even now—to induce. Still I could not understand how I had lived through our meeting nor of what that living through consisted. I followed them down to the hotel lobby where they took their seat behind a leather-and-glass partition. The space of the hotel lobby was, like Soho, vast and, also like Soho, there was no assimilating it without participation in a story. At the moment I was not participating. And this was why I might get caught NO It had nothing NO to do with innocence or guilt or with some immiscible brew of the two: it NO had NO NO everything to do no with not being enmeshed in a story to carry me forward beyond innuendo, beyond imputation. The block was about to emerge from the undifferentiated mass of its own latency and overcome us both, detectives and me. Yet though the block—the hulk—the bulk—was at last emerging—here in the hotel lobby—it was emerging only tentatively, alighting, localizing itself in this somewhere—anywhere—as a pivot whence to assay other sites, more appropriate, more plausible, Its emergence here was a mere resting place, a mere pivot-point. And what if all the hulks constituting my story were mere pivot-points on their way elsewhere. I listened and listened to the exchange between them in the hope that that exchange might become paradigmatic, as that between Jamms and the cop when long long ago the photo changed hands. As I was not in this exchange there was still a possibility of its resonating paradigmatically. "Look," said what sounded like the elder, "she isn't trying to run you into the ground for your humble antecedents. Forget what that creep said about some class being the dissolution of all classes. She isn't trying to attack you when she points out that you seem to be quite content if and as she slides into the same decrepitation she associates with your mom, dad, aunts, uncles, and cousins, whose only fear from what you tell me is a shortfall in prune butter after the annual jamboree. She isn't attacking you. Her tirade is a mnemonic: she knows the only way you, an avowed solitary, can be made to remember the little house, the filthy little bedroom where somebody tried to be born but was ultimately more successful dying— filthy, mind you, not from the carousal of rats, mice, excrement, but effaced from too much uncontrollable scrubbing—she knows the only way to make you remember and cherish that whence you come and therefore what you are is to be seeming to reproach you mercilessly for allowing her to go the way of these mummies as the only way you wish to go so that remembering and cherishing is linked thereby to an unforgettable shudder. Like any loving wife, she wants you to get ahead in your chosen line of work and how can you possibly get ahead without—as a cop, I mean, obliged to deduce brutal truths from various cluelet configurations—having previously mastered your own... configuration. In short, her ostensible ranting and raving is crucial to your work, as crucial as a promotion." As the elder went on giving what seemed a fairly seamless account of the younger's marital plight I could not help feeling that this diagnosis belonged elsewhere—a bulk—a hulk—a land mass—that should have fallen into actuality elsewhere, long before, in a house out in Rhinebeck, for example, might with a little more skill and a little more planning—but on whose part?—have ended up belonging to Jamms or to his dad or to young Testic rotting in some morgue. Why should truths so clearly relevant to the turmoils of Jamms as I had known him, to Maggy as I knew her, be lavished here on a figure so marginal as the young police officer. It was only my suspect status that kept me from leaping up and strangling him on the spot for drawing to himself what ought to have been festering elsewhere.

I watched the guests come and go, I a guest no longer. None

seemed to belong to that class embodying the dissolution of all classes, except perhaps this or that little whore between fourteen and fifteen fishing for a visiting computer salesman between lunch and dinner. Watching them come and go I wondered, topologically speaking, if they mightn't be divisible—all of businessmandom—into those who sported shoes with ornamental tassels—as opposed to the starkly functional variety—and those who did not. Would such a partition cover all of businessmandom's being? Then it seemed more probable fixing on another accessory—raincoat shoulder loops—or one not visible to the naked eye. I craved that definitive cut in being, at least in the being of males, for that definitive cut, that division achieved at last of the whole male species, with eventual extension to the female and everything in between and on the fringes, into two classes, must reaffirm my lifelong anonymity since surely I belonged to neither having synthesized both from scratch.

"If," droned on the elder, as if sipping or yawning—doing something, at any rate, to give the impression that what he was saying came easy and was even easier tossed off—"you can only begin to grasp what your wife is trying to drum into that fat head of yours then I think you will be better able to understand our man. What she is trying—oh, little dear one—to let you know is that your long abstention from wanting, needing, hungering—after goods and not goods alone—is more than mere abstention. It is a purposeful defiance, withholding, denial, challenge—perverse contestation over the longest term of all she and the rest of the thinking goodish world have every reason to hold dear." When had I heard the phrase he was now intoning and where: Teeeeenneeennanana is due in October.

"You simply cannot expect her to want what you want, namely, not to want." I imagined the younger completely undone yet he came back with an exquisitely poised: "And how does all this connect with our man." He did not use the phrase contemptuously, as if under the duress of the other's prior, heuristic, determining use, but as if it was his, had always been his, even if it was not his, had become his, proving that he was a good subordinate for a good subordinate undergoes no shame or defiance appropriating the phraseology of his superiors, and as such would soon be rising to higher echelons. Although who's to say that the younger's *our man* was not the basest mockery of paraphrase—at the extremest occident from conversion's pinkish rising sun.

I too was waiting to discover how acceptance of the underlying futility of his wife's mnemonic tirade—enjoining acceptance and cultivation of his own foul roots—would enable him to penetrate to my depths. I held my breath, the block—the hulk—the slab—was more and more massively about to emerge, intolerable. They, because of my own laxity, my own eager acquiescence when long ago I had never left off complimenting myself for having managed to hobnob with the Jammses, senior and junior, they—this pair—had found a way to appropriate the bulk— the hulk—the slab—embodying the connection between Jamms's cultivation of his own foul roots and comprehension—the better to rid himself—of the parasite come originally and ostensibly to haul him back to his mom and dad; or the connection between Maggy's cultivation of her own foul roots (as laid bare by Bessy) and comprehension—the better to rid herself and Jamms and anybody else who cared to profit from the vastation—of the same foul parasite; or the connection between old man Jamms's cultivation—on his deathbed, no less—of his own foul roots and comprehension—the better to recall and dismiss—of the same foul parasite.

But the hulk did not emerge—fall—for the elder did not go on, go on, I mean, to explain, although I could not say that by not going on he made the other, the younger, stew thereby in his own juice, simply because I as disinterested and dispassionate auditor needed to feel that somebody must at this intolerable moment be stewing in his own juice. Yet just when I had given up all hope of a resumption, the elder said, "Your wife..." but now, long after they had first broached the subject of wives and roots and culprits inextricably bound up in a network of desires unquenchable and unspeakable—desires that seek victims only as a vengeance on the inadequacy of said victims to slake those desires, which wild-eyed perspicacity is afraid of nothing more than to be alone with itself and therefore seeks every chance it gets to lose itself in the futile ravings of the victim crowds—but now, long after, I had already ceased to expect anything in the way of enlightenment, even exposition, from these two—ceased to postpone hunger and thirst in the name of an enlightenment sure to abolish them forever. I had ceased to expect

anything in the way of enlightenment for I was in mourning—mourned
that enlightenment must come to me from them rather than from the likes
of Jamms and Maggy, or Jamms, Sr., and the Missus, or Jamms, Sr., and
Jamms, Jr., or Maggy and Bessy—any other dyad would have done,
would have resonated back into the story. I mourned that enlightenment
must come from my connection to them or their connection to me:
whatever the direction the connection was slapdash and marginal. And
yet even the mourning was marginal (or was this but another goad on the
part of the story-and meaning-mongers to organize—to unify—my
output by deeming it uniformly marginal). For there was no reason to
mourn now—yet—since the enlightenment hadn't begun, strictly speaking, and who knows how dazzling, even useful, once it had begun. Once
again—once again—once again—more propagandizing for the ubiquity
of motifs—of meanings—compliments of their mongers—once again, as
with the appearance of a mention of Testic's death in everybody's favorite
tabloid—once again, a less than blessed event was taking place long after
the death of expectation and if on the one hand I could not rise up and
applaud now that the elder was about to resume—to escort us both into
the realm of enlightenment—on the other I could barely restrain myself
from jumping for joy at an event, any event, electing to miss its beat,
refusing to coincide with expectation, refusing to descend like a testicle
at its rightful moment, refusing to bend to the world's decree that it elapse.
For in some way I felt I—no, not I—but the event, the event, ostensibly
foiling the smug expectations of the story, in fact was working harder NO
than ever for its upkeep and propagation. I began to detest the elder, more
heartily and harrowingly than I had detested his sidekick prowling inside
my apartment. For he was about to embark on another scheme to
facilitate prowling. With his prowling so near I feared—despite all the
money coming in compliments of the expertise of Colletti and Naven,
Certified Public Accountants,—becoming a worker once more, that is to
say, one thoroughly unprotected against extremes of exploitation by any
negotiable qualification, that is to say, gimmick or simian quirk—wasn't
I, after all, the quintessential man without a qualification—unprotected
against extirpations—subrogations—of the most elemental kind—therefore always obliged to make it a point to pay extra attention especially
when I had absolutely no desire to pay attention. This was my post on the

assembly line of being, I was hired to listen, to eavesdrop against the
calamity of ineptitude unmasked. To tremble in my shoes as I struggled
to catch a glimpse of the detritus they were planning to turn me into, this
was my task but hardly a marketable one. And it suddenly became clear
as I waited for him—for them—to begin that whatever role I ended up
playing in this little affair—and this little affair was clearly no longer
indistinguishable from my relation to Jamms and the string of crimes it
had engendered but rather the sum of those crimes as insertable into the
agenda, the itinerary, of the two detective grenadiers—even if this little
affair would never, or so I flattered myself, have gotten off the ground
without the sponsorship of my transgressions—what the women's maga-
zines ought to call *larger-than-life emotions in action*—whatever role I ended
up playing and however global and irreparable my sponsorship those
who came after would be sure to concur that in actual fact I had been
washed away and very early on in an overall operation to which my crimes
were only a minuscule goad, spur, prick. And all this stemmed from the
fact that I was a fungible being—the most fungible of beings open to
exploitation from all directions. Yet even if I was convinced the elder's
speech would trigger my downfall there could be a pleasant surprise in
store. Hadn't Aesop said salvation comes from the direction we least
expect it. I stopped short. "Your wife," the elder continued, and it was as
if I had been instantaneously inserted—me and all my fungibilities—into
their improvisational science of crime and retribution and so inserted (I
was concurrently aware of the radical disjunction between a simple,
"Your wife," and the expansive and irrefutable discovery to which it had
just appeared to give rise) obliged—or was it the crimes rather than I
myself—to answer certain questions but in a language—of crime and
retribution—at once immemorially codified and sublimely improvisational—in a language supremely alien to me, them—questions that had
never been put to me, to them, could never be put outside the realm of
their science. Or maybe these very questions and answers had been put
to my crimes all along and were seamlessly incorporated in the text only
I did not know how to translate out. What to me had been the mere stuff
and nonsense of daily life was to these clowns of great pitch and moment.
They were able to construct a vocation over the corpse of the very
paltriness I had seen fit to throw away or rather reinvest as an excess in

the crime itself without considering how to parasitize it across a lifetime's brooding. But maybe, when all was said and done, it was best that my crimes and everything leading up to a life of crime(s) were incorporated in their museum of facts. For that museum had no beginning nor end and was therefore suitable—the supreme excipient—for the kind of criminal self-examination that over and over and over seeks to be electrified by its own nullity and thereby baffle its fate. Whereas if left to their own devices those crimes seeking to expropriate, store, and then dehisce the momentum of a universal knowing yet handicapped by a allotted fixed span would simply shrivel up aghast at the unendurable disjunction between knowing's time needed and knowing's time allotted.

I listened. They pooled what they already knew: the facts of the case: corpse found on quasi country road, disappearance of the other friend, quasi painter—the facts of the case came into view and as they came revealed themselves to be quite different from what they were as long as I hoarded them from the world. On their own once more, yanked free of the context, however shaky, my presence had lent them, they were understandably ripe for vengeful misinterpretation by all the forces of interrogation currently on the prowl. But I will say this for both of them, they spoke *within the facts*, were wary of absolutes. They did not then exploit my fungibility with abstract constructions designed to mask that exploitation. I was still impatient to know to what degree the younger's understanding of his wife's loathing of his roots could authorize and facilitate his comprehension of my strategies.

"You see," said the younger suddenly, "I am a man afflicted, a slob of time, neither its carcass, as some may think, nor, as others, its eunuch, but somehow and somewhere redolent of a eunuch's carcass and therefore not in the least a eunuch for whenever a eunuch is relegated to the status of carcass he simultaneously transcends the ignominy indissolubly bound to the status—the being—of eunuch. He at once achieves the dignity of insentient things. At any rate, as you know better than anybody, being my colleague, I'm a poor slobbering slob foundering on the shoals of barbed domesticity. Family man, that most hateful of animals—a good and proper specimen incessantly bombarded with plaints from depending malcontents. There is, for example"—and here he took what I presumed was a deep breath—"the old dad forever on the verge of submitting to the rigorous ablative regimen that may or may not soften his peduncle and then there is the wife—mine—with the obligatory sis and sis's obligatory husband laying perfervid and porcine and incessant claim to the salary forever on the rise and prospects proliferating everywhere and visible—everywhere, to say nothing of sis's mother-in-law furnishing such an altogether astonishing contrast to wife's—cantankerous and stalwartly withering away in her exurb incapable of passing for even a slum and whom I—he—the family man—is trying in vain to wean from this diaristic communication of her ills. And of course there are the kids who what with all the turmoil despotically inflecting their desires unsurprisingly require—demand—the attention of experts. For there is turmoil, don't you know, since the wife cannot refrain from depicting in bottomless depth of detail the comings, goings, and comings without goings, of the far more fortunate myriads wont and absolutely within their rights to proclaim the world their confectionary, and the husband in turn cannot easily refrain every now and then from a shaman-like outburst of envious rage, raging envy, truculence, and other imperial afflictions triggered by a whiff of these invidious comparisons even if rattled off in all the innocence of tabletalk. And yet the husband is envious not so much of sis or the mother-in-law's confectionary or the neighbor's cantankerous proclamation of prospects forever on the rise as of—envy itself—that, through thick and thin, continues to elude him. Not that he is indentured to some higher calling. At any rate—finally—husband makes a point of denouncing some small detail prescinded from the flow of other lives by which the little woman has shown herself to be particularly smitten at which point wife forbearingly informs him that it is not this detail or that detail that in raising a vicarious rapture stretches her desolation but rather this, the whole, namely, and in short, the aimless little life he, the husband, the insignificant little functionary/flunktionary, is trying surreptitiously, covertly, and maybe even clandestinely and perhaps in collusion with the old granny (whose gout, loneliness, niggardly self-abnegation, frugal meals, earnest repudiation of new brindled bedsheets, polyester trousers ravaged right up the buttocks—whose accessories and memorabilia and anathemabilia—are nothing less than a purposeful construction, an imposed paradigm, sly prophecy, slyer ukase, of how things will, must turn out for the offshoots specifically her *bru*)—the aimless little life he—with or without the gramp or granny functioning as grey eminence—is plotting to substitute for her steely dreams for their future. At which point that is always the same point she, the little woman, a granny soon herself, grows more and more despairing and despairingly vindictive for it is never—less than ever—clear, at least to her, whether he, I, the husband, is simply a simpleminded ambitiousless shard of state machinery jetsam or whether this his refusal to make his way and by extension their way in the ranks is a diabolically premeditated torture perpetrated in coldest blood against one—namely, she—deemed peremptorily and without appeal unworthy of the solatiums that devolve even upon fishwives. It is never clear to her whether—given my roots, my origins—I am simply the way I am or whether that way has out of the blue been willed purposefully to punish—to abolish—her. "Perhaps," suggested the elder, the wiser, "it has something to do with *her* forbears." Oh, how I wished I could have been hearing this very conversation long before, but between, say, Jamms, Sr., and Jamms, Jr., regarding, say, Maggy or Bessy. What a spur to the advancement—the enrichment—of the story—our story—*that* might have been. To think that all this excavation was now being squandered on marginals. "I thought of that," said the other. "For as you may or may not know he, the pater, is not only a general but also head of one of the multinational corporations presently carving up the planet—you know, the kind that underwrites the Masterpiece Theater concept of advanced art while inciting hoodlums to squelch all efforts of the Third, Fourth, and Fifth worlds to reclaim land, sea, sky, what is rightfully theirs. In short, a heavyweight and hard act to swallow." "Talk to her, talk to her," said the elder, "for by *talking to her*—reopening negotiations, I presume—you will simultaneously be talking to the case or rather for advancement of the case. For, as I have already indicated—in my nuncupative memo dated April 1—by reminding you of your slime and that of your forbears she is doing your dirty work, or at least part of it, spurring—nay, enabling—you to recuperate all you pretermit and might otherwise apply to the case at hand. Her rage and resentment is a mnemonic." "No," said the other, "through invidious comparison she exasperates and punishes me. This is retaliation for what she takes to be the perversity of my choice. She isn't helping me become a better policeman: she's depleting me. Yet when I point out that she too has been guilty of certain choices she bristles—this is intolerable—this is hitting well below the belt—this she can and will not endure—this countervailing caterwauling adversion to her own choices is a colossal and unforgivable lack of consideration on the monster's part. For everybody knows she never had any choice where I was concerned. She cannot be taken to task for choosing or not choosing since her choices were inevitable given the glaring penury of my own—ensuing from my own. Everybody knows through my negligence, my failure, she was denied the luxury of choice: my pitiable choices bequeathed her nothing but the impossibility of choice, choice amputated through tandemness to me and my vagaries. She had and has no choice, only the haphazard suturing of the gaping wound left by my choices. My failure to have chosen correctly—me, upon whom a truly embarrassing plethora of authentic choices—despite the penury of my antecedents, the purulence of my roots, the squalid machinations of the gramps and granny—had once and still devolves—and through no real effort of my own—through my devastated and devastating failure to strut wisely in the corridors of that plethora it was I who had compelled—is compelling—her—railroading her—to the only conceivable choice."

I listened hard, trying to make connections to my own plight. Yet I couldn't help thinking that if only Jamms were here, to profit from such scalding self-commentary...in the name of his relations with Maggy, Bessy, his mother, his dead dad. This was all meant for Jim, a running commentary on the torment he had never met head-on, much less vanquished. And what if he had managed to vanquish that torment: we might still be together, within—on the threshold—of the story. There were no connections here, to my own plight. One of the two, I couldn't tell which, breathed deep, deeper NO

than I NO no NO

ever heard a man NO NO NO

breathe. "In fact," the younger continued, "what is most disturbing is this." He handed the other a sheet of paper for I heard it rustle. "Effective today," intoned the other, "Tim Shhitnik—" "The husband of sis," the younger explained. "—is hereby promoted to the position of associate director in charge of operations insofar as said operations redound to sales force and computed marketability. In this position Jim (sic) will be responsible for coordinating merchandizing with the joint sales force efforts of the expanding promotional underbelly to meet the ever-growing ever-glowing need of the customer. Jim joined the force in 19— as mid-Atlantic commandeer of sales forces and was instantaneously promoted to the second round of field sales managerial solicitation and thence ever onward, ever upward, beyond sales, beyond reprehensibility. Pete will report to Frank Frankfurt. These new assignments of Bill to deputy sales coordinator and Tim to deputy coordinator of sales and Frank to under-deputy of sales and coordination and miscellaneous realignments cannot fail to have an exciting effect on the strengthening of promotion, marketing, and sales in conjunction with the joint activity of the vice-president in charge of liaisonizing all subfields. We look forward to real successful superspecial teamwork. Let us all wish them all the very best of luck." The elder said: "I suspect the murderer—our Soho friend—comes from a background very similar to your own. Now, then, try to put yourself in the position of Testic—attaching himself casually to our friend—and of Jamms—who also attached himself, far more com-pletely, of course—poor dead Jamms, yes, I am sure Jamms is dead—put yourself in their position attaching themselves then realizing whence he hails, our Soho friend, I mean. Especially with Jamms the painter's financial prospects becoming more and more obscure, as it were. Didn't the old man threaten to cut him off if he went on pursuing this activity. Clearly Jamms—and Testic—but more especially Jamms—must have felt—" The elder cleared his throat. "But I'll let you tell me what clearly Jamms must have felt." A long silence. "Surely you know. You just don't want to know you know. Say it: say it: think back to your wife and to her loathing of your simpleminded roots and failure to extricate yourself from them to her satisfaction. All right: Jamms felt the young man's—our friend's—shabby background was a vectored—a sagittal—repudiation of all the comforts and exquisite pleasures he loved and loathed. He must have felt that background—for all its marginality at least as far as Jamms's own interests were concerned—was a lasting tribute to our friend's ability to have pulled himself free of its—the background's— marl and morass as well as—remember the hovering ghastliness of the background's marginality, the ultimate impertinence of its perduring in the rigors of its slime—the inevitable endpoint—untimely reminder—of his—Jamms's—own downward path to obfuscating penury since it was very likely he was as talentless as his father's unceasing pleas that he rejoin the family business suggested. It suddenly must have been as if our Soho friend, our exhibit A, B, and C, had constructed said past purely as hovering punishment for Jamms who never knew quite what to do with his own. And so Jamms had to kill the lingering temptation—but to what?—embodied in the other's—our Soho friend's—past. For this was clearly, teleologically, what he must become. The stronger our Soho friend proved himself the weaker Jamms must become. Jamms had no choice but to become the other's quondam landscape—that landscape whence the other had freed himself. Just as your wife is afraid of becoming your landscape—the landscape you simultaneously embody and transcend—all that impinges on and feeds the laches of inertia, an almost sensuous lack of will directed toward objects but those always the wrong objects. For the message of your inertia—thoroughly innnocuous in its own medium, of course, but hypervirulent elsewhere—is that she is distinctly unworthy of anything better than your putrid purlieus can offer and must continue to be purposefully, meticulously, with the greatest malignancy of ostensibly offhand organizational skill, dragged down by you and your forbears to the level of those purlieus—that landscape—that neighborhood, in the topological sense—whence you managed to spring the leak that persists in being you." I was carried away by the elder's music as if it was less an analysis than an adolescent revery shot through with orgasms. "Just as the state embodies the irreconcilability of all classes, so Jamms planned murder as a similar epitaph on irreconcilable differences that plagued and at the same time of course created—weren't the irreconcilable differences precisely the erotic spur—thorn—in one side, at least?—created his relation to our young man. Sensing Jamms's murderous intentions our Soho pal who, as a member of the class of supreme fungibles, constitutionally loathes ambiguity, took the decisive step and murdered first. Jamms lies elsewhere." Suddenly he, the elder, added a phrase that seemed—oh no, I did not want it to—to vitiate all he or I or both of us together had striven to create of virile ratiocination. Slimily he smuggled in, "You know, I forgot to mention the chief says we should always be ready to answer the phones at a moment's notice. And make sure somebody is covering if we aren't personally there to—" Then, with nauseatingly reassuring and self-assuring conciliatory playfulness—as if he was the last man in the world to secrete the functionary's panic conveyed in his previous remark, "But, we're in good shape." His tone indicated that he had begun to smell without necessarily knowing he had begun to smell the self-derogation inseparable from such a plea, however veiled, however offhand. The other must have motioned for I could see the top of a waiter's skull over the partition. I had needed without knowing I needed to believe this elder's crystalline perspicacity *where everything connected with human nature was concerned* exempted him from petty concerns with the otiose machinations of higher-ups. "So that," he continued, "it is definitely a class-related, perhaps even a race-related, murder. He—Jamms—felt raw shame before this being, this figure disfigured—this embodiment of the dissolution of all classes—of exploitability rarefied beyond computation. Far more than Testic—whose murder, I am convinced, was a distraction concocted to throw us off the scent." So here was one of the detectives mourning for the marginality of the Testic murder—so much violence, so much of the violence of ambiguity invested in so porcine a specimen—as I was mourning. Yet unlike me the elder was going beyond his mourning—beyond the marginality—by decreeing the marginal to be just that and nothing more. With Jamms, he was back in the center of things and I was back with him, more so than the younger, I felt. It was unjust: I deserved to be the elder's partner. "How do you know our little Soho friend started out as a bona fide worker, a member of the working class." "He does work—he did, at any rate. His hands show it. And at any rate"—with a rising rage of contempt that was new, at least in my experience, to his dealings with his comrade—"this is not a hypothesis and as such susceptible to confirmation through laborious experimentation out in the field of the lower depths where such a specimen is most at home—but a pattern flayed bare, sucked dry, through a spasm of intuition. I repeat: Jamms was tormented—tormented—tormented—by the exploitability, the infinite exploitability of this child of the working class exalted—in Jamms's eyes at least—through having absolutely no special qualification to hinder or even delay usurpation by some slightly less fungible—we measure here in momentary terms—other. And I further contend, much, I am sure, to your chagrin, that he was most tormented in his tormented torment by this—this total absence of any special qualification. This became for him—Jamms, I mean—a, let us say, not so secondary sexual character. He, Jamms, found himself totally dazzled by this preeminently fungible other saddled with the supremest secondary sexual character: total absence of marketability, negotiability, which total absence became for him, our man Jamms, the most powerful—aromatic—erotic—of all traits—as explicit and unlocalizable a proclamation of virility as a particular distribution of chest or pubic hair. Something inside wanted to grovel before this proclamation irresistibly sensuous everywhere yet localizable nowhere. Jamms became obsessed with a man unprotected from extremes of exploitation by any special qualification able to stymie subrogation by some superior being reducible to only a hair's breadth greater skill. Our Soho pal's predicament—absence of all negotiable qualification—was for Jamms, a son of the idling class, a trait—a trait almost constructed—rather than some something that had willy-nilly devolved on the unsuspecting victim. Jamms pursued the other's plight as if it was a manufactured trait." Suddenly they were silent. Just when he was about to elaborate on Jamms's doomed pursuit of my beauty. I began to be afraid, in the silence, that I had done something wrong, something to give me away, something connected either with Jamms or Testic or Maggy/Bessy. But still in the silence I could not move, could not begin to react to rectify the lapse sketched by this vaguest of spasms, this thought without notochord, as it were. I remained immobilized in relation to the not-so-distant point on the horizon embodying lapse, myself as mere scandalous outcome of that lapse. Then I listened to the silence, in other words, I strove, right there in the hotel lobby, under the potted palms and in the shadow of the piano bar, to let it make use of me no longer as breeding ground for spasms that set me stalking strange wares. Making a stalwart forthright effort to listen to the silence I found myself beginning to begin to learn how to loathe these its progenitors. And buoyed up by this new loathing—of silence and those who manufactured it for purposes of microenvironmental pollution—I was able to rise up though sitting still to confront the act that had led me to think I had given myself away for good. Loathing propelled me to confront this transvestitial vision of a self-indicting act without any special qualifications for indictment. Loathing set me free of a memory that would never take shape, could never take

shape, had no existence apart from its collaboration with a judging silence
that threatened to overwhelm all instinct for self-preservation. Good.
There had been nothing in my relations with Jamms, Testic, Maggy,
living or dead, to give me away to these thugs. I rose, almost conspicu-
ously, not caring whether or not they saw me, they did not, they went on
talking, I heard their voices well out into the night, their blemished
mellow voices beneath the sallow lighting. And though I did not in fact
hear their voices well out into the night as I have just stated it seemed at
the moment of stating, that is to say, of having nothing further to state,
that it was a perfectly legitimate way of prolonging the stating without
cheatingly recruiting odds and ends from outside the strict domain of the
immediate stating. Prolonging the stating I subserved the story—I
muffled a transition, giveaway of story facticity. For on leaving the hotel
lobby I did something unusual: I took the subway back to my apartment.
Across from me NO NO NO

     sat NO a couple NO no

     :

     :

he was reading the newspaper, the stock page, to be exact, and she
attended to the business of ruminating as he went about making comments on the order of, *P* went up three points, no, closed at 3.141659...
And she—Maggy—not Maggy—should have been Maggy—must be
Maggy no, not Maggy—Bessy—Mrs. Jamms, Sr.—no, not Bessy nor
Jamms nor Maggy, least of all Maggy—nodded, though she seemed to be
nodding about something entirely unrelated even if she was certainly
with him in spirit. And then he gave her another figure and another after
that and then they chatted about the raincoat he had had to return before
George's party *out on the Island* and then he spoke—or so I had to believe—
desperately had to believe—about the tasseled loafers purchased just
recently or suddenly returned several years before. And then he spoke or
rather his Neanderthalian visage spoke of the hard day at the office and
what the boss had said to suggest that the fall of the debentures and
dividends might be his, my man's, fault. And not so suddenly I was
loathing him, my man, with renewed though not necessarily infinitely
renewable vigor. For he was clearly the Mike or Steve or Rhonda or Pam
I had written about to the Jammses—the Bill and Bob and Will and

Ralph I had taken to impersonating in the wee hours that in my case descended at all hours — but by expropriating and swathing himself all at once in their raiment of banality he was cutting me off from its supply of usable tics so that I was fast developing the sense that I could no longer hope to reinhabit that banality as if it was my very own glorious invention in whose one-to-one correspondence with the things of the meaty little world I might and might not, as it suited me, choose to believe. He, this usurper, and during the briefest of smelly little subway treks, had managed to establish some kind of inviolable herringbone relation with my Mikes and my Steves and my Bills and my Franks or rather with the serrated edge connecting their outermost points thereby leaving me to stew at last in a verjuice all my own.

And yet he insisted on remaining such a marginal figure in my drama [radical disjunction between length of time he has actually been on the scene and expectations madly agglomerating in spite of though as if commersurate with that length]. Then the girl friend — for clearly neither could have tolerated all that had developed or failed to develop without the certainty of refuge available though not necessarily to both at the same time in the roomy folds of that postmodern pulvinar known as, The Girl Friend — alive with facial tics that stung the spectator and were frequently impossible to distinguish from the simplest ripple of well-behaved delight at finding herself right smack in the line of fire of her man's delusions of grandeur — to have and to hold on to for dear life — then the girl friend began speaking — Had she observed certain changes in his inflection alerting — alarming — her to the need to resettle him double-quick within her purlieus? — of how earlier that day a crowd had congregated around an office building — not hers, she hastened to add, meaning, I presume, the one in which she passed her days, but one a little further off. For two drug addicts had taken it upon themselves to engage in a halfhearted battle, one advancing halfheartedly on the other and slapping him straight away. But although the crowd stood by watching dully, bovinely, with a bovineness that was the most NO NO criminal thing NO of all , this halfhearted battle was not the target of its concern, assuming it, the crowd, could be cowed into concern about anything besides feeding time. And even if she — the girl friend — with her tics and related spasms of deference — revolted me completely — especially since she too insisted on remaining marginal to my story—insisted on refusing to prove herself to be Maggy or Bessy or even old lady Jamms—even if she revolted me completely I was suddenly assaulted by a certain slant of light in the vicinity of the area she was not so much describing as skirting on her way back to her man's dazzling and ultimately tutelary inattention, purest sign of purest virility. Yet there I was hungering more and more for the slant that the two of us, so I wanted to think, had collaborated squarely in creating from scratch, or rather,

OR RATHER, wresting from some typically ungainly mass of visitors to the human condition itself ungainly and even—especially NO—under the best of circumstances. But did I hunger for the slant only insofar as it remained brief, nay, ephemeral? Now he, the virile one virile primarily though not primordially through apish inattention, was again looking away, clearly preoccupied with other matters though the speeding subway car could not strictly speaking be held accountable for such other matters and he was certainly not clever enough to invent a topic of reflection as ponderous as, say, the motives for his slouched withdrawal from things of the world. Her chatter was precisely the background—the context—needed if he was, and he was, to begin to preoccupy himself with defense against the hoard of faces, mine included, that impinged. Her chatter cushioned his elaboration of stratagems of defense. Or maybe it was her chatter as purest evocation-in-flight of, from, herself, that self he too wished at all costs to avoid much as despite himself he also wanted nothing more and nothing less than to settle down with—it—her—Sallie—since after all he had a penis and she a clitoris and never the twain shall be kept apart by the puniest enemies of connubial bliss—maybe it was her chatter as purest evocation of her being that tormented him to the point where he must look away, leaving me with the ungrateful task of ascribing such an insidious, essentially feminine ploy to the vagaries of virility at its superfetatory peak yet who's to blame him since the purest instantiation of any being's quiddity is always an occasion for alarm. And for him it was—this instantiation—though never raising its voice above a babble or a barnyard cackle—a tocsin of impossible solicitation, a straw breaking his camel's back. So he found himself looking around in order to be looking away rather than because her chatter furnished the context—the background—of courage within—against—which to defend himself against the world impinging at long last and at that very moment when the rush hour crowd seems deceptively to be attenuating and is in point of fact mounting ever writhing toward intimations of apocalypse. Not so very virile after all.

Yet what did this couple mean? How did they figure in the story, the story that Jamms had been to my unforgiving chagrin so often interrupting? Where were they in the story? Were they in the same plane as for example the detectives, or at least one, presuming these two functionaries functioned in different planes for all their professions of adhesion? Or were they entrenched, was that the word, in the plane that claimed the younger detective's wife as one of its most celebrated denizens? Or were they both—or only one—in the plane of the cantankerous old granny whose poverty and afflictions were, according to the younger detective's wife, nothing but a ploy oriented prophetically toward her own abasement? And the detectives, if they were floating in the same plane, was that in fact the story's plane? The slant of sun wrested from the midday crowd congregated about Sallie's place of employment—that slant of sun was certainly conducive to a story—was most definitely a narrative slant yet very much inaccessible. Too bad because I could smell the story unfolding along the length of such a slant. The story I ought to have lived belonged to—was decreed by—such a slant. Thinking of that slant I felt at least for a split second inserted within story time. But the slant was gone. Perhaps these two had nothing to do with my story. They would never turn themselves over to a story to wither away in its depths as tactfully as a rose petal or as a leg of lamb—the kind that is vended, frozen, by vagrants at midnight to unsuspecting passersby on Manhattan sidestreets. I mourned their loss. Catching the tail-end of his camel's hair topcoat as I emerged from the car—though not into sunlight—I mourned that he was not Testic. Why hadn't I noted the startling resemblance before? If only I had encountered him, with or without his sweetheart, earlier—but on the same moving subway car—and not as himself but as Testic who was after all more he than he himself—if only I had encountered him earlier, before the murder of Testic, so that to my fear of Testic's unmasking of my unnatural acts I might have added rage at his—Testic II's—monolithic preoccupation with the things of the world at the very moment when—on a moving subway train no less—his dearly beloved was crying out in the name of a little tenderness, already deictically distilled into her exquisite depiction of a ray of afternoon sun wending its way among masses of flesh avid and yet too bovine to be avid of thrill—if only I had encountered him then. Having encountered him however it was now impossible to accept Testic's death as a fait accompli. It had to be revised: he should have died hereafter, for here he was, or rather, there he had been, but a minute before, on a moving subway train whence I had just alighted, neither sadder nor wiser. There he had been, Testic Testicized far beyond the powers of the original. There still had to be a way to force the original Testic, dead or not, to absorb this brute's traits and thereby pave the way for a murder of far greater resonance. But to whom? To hovering witnesses? It was only now—in the wake of this brute more Testicized than Testic himself—that legitimate reasons for murdering Testic were accumulating. Yet shouldn't I be rejoicing at the radical disjunction between a murder and its original motives retrospectively modified into a startling penury by the sudden overflow of motives awful and authentic? If I was to get on with my story I had to take its moments as they came without crying over the spilt milk of their untimeliness. As I walked away from the station I tried to focus on Sallie and her man as having triggered a positive event...even if said event would have re-dounded far more to the credit of my failed relation to Testic—even if for all intents and purposes said event belonged with—to—Testic and this pair the unsightly artifacts—ventifacts—of Testic's failed appropriation. If only I had been able to kill Testic—a Testic refracting this one additional event that cast such a definitive light on, say, his vulgar acquisitiveness and thereby on my righteous fury in doing away with him—it—once and for all.

When I got back to Desbrosses Street there was Maggy: I greeted her in a way I tried very hard to render quizzical so as to shift the burden of absurd discomfort onto her—not that I necessarily felt burdened but there was a freefloating burden somewhere in our vicinity whether or not either of us was at this very moment collapsing under it. "Where is Jim," she asked threateningly at first. Then I saw she was quite simply absorbed, utterly, into the hopelessness of a sorrow not quite—not yet—free of petulance. "Traveling, I guess," I returned, motioning her to the very seat Colletti had lollingly occupied the night of *the Testic murder*. I was afraid that by speaking too loudly, honoring her question too explicitly, I would change its direction, restructure it and thereby awaken her to its contiguous more incendiary implications. "He's traveling, I explained, didn't I," repeated with a certain irritation went if not a long way then some toward proving—most of all to myself and mainly through the manly inflection that took me by surprise—that I had no reason to defend, forfend, kowtow, hurriedly gather the loose ends of inference to satisfy some other's doomed demand for coherence. "He's gone, for good. I know he's gone. I drove him away for you see when he spoke of how he loathed his forbears and how their world was a dead, a loathsome, thing—" I listened though suddenly flooded with the greatest difficulty tolerating her, tolerating life as it ebbed and flowed through her, tolerating the ebb and flow of the radical disjunctions her chatter seemed nimbly if chaotically to sketch and then dispel and of which she or what she went on trying or over and over again failed miserably to say was always one of the terms. As I listened—tried not to listen—I had, in short, the delirious sensation of losing a veritable superfetation of disjunctions—for the story—the story—the story—even faster than she, fount and source and fertilizing matrix, produced them. She—or rather her babble—obstructed my path toward the breeding ground of *the very disjunctions I needed* if the story was to get off the ground at the same time that that babble was their supreme source. "I know you don't believe ours was an ideal relation: there was Bessy, for example. And apart from Bessy I was always terrified of the silences between us even if I know every great artist is a willful *perpetrator* of silence. But I couldn't keep myself from madly interpreting what he never even deigned to begin to formulate, thereby producing time and again a misinterpretation that becoming a pretext for even greater rage in defiance dutifully widened the already spacious distance between us." I asked her how it had become established between them that it was she must save him from himself, dredge his swamps, and yet always with such a momentous backwash of ingratitude for services rendered. "You mean," she continued, but not with the eagerness I was expecting, "when did it become established between us—for something is always quickly enough established in any relation—that I must cancel myself completely. And yet strange to say I have been buoyed up, even strengthened, by the excruciating and exquisite pain of knowing how far and how often he fell short of being able to endure my passion. How often did I give myself up to awaiting his return for I knew with the waiting my character was forming as little puddles form in mudflats—as little hollows are sucked out in the cheeks of the greyish dunes. You see, he took me into the current, the chilly current, and his warming paddle strokes smashing and reconstituting the blue above the peevish cries of those in whose name I was being abandoned became the unison of a creature's—my—ability to sustain the pitch of recoil, the unbearable tension of love folding back on itself. The light ended, his other engagements began. Over and over and over." "Other engagements," I prompted. "Oh—he was no partisan of the lichen-encrusted nooks of childhood, of the family. There was not a single simple contortion of its landscape that managed to fill him with hope." I could not bear to go on listening. And yet, she was simply being Maggy, persisting in the being that was Maggy. Yet I could not help taking this sublime example of conation in full bloom as proof of a malignant intention, serpentine self-promotion gone deliriously foul. I asked myself, why should Maggy not be Maggy, why should she be expected to do something that was not in the interest of her being Maggy even if there was the dimmest chance that so doing—so striving—and with all her heart and soul to be nothing less than other—anything other—than Maggy might represent the bland beginning of a step forward, a crucial step forward, in other words, out of that morass of always sidestepped fructification mossily contingent on the wan intermingling of radical disjunctions miasmic as snouts.

Like all its Maggys—she and the world were out of joint. Between her expectations and world availabilities there was a radical disjunction, a ghastly rift. Yet as long as she remained unconscious of the rift she could go on striving to be Maggy and thereby heal the immedicable rift. I was expecting her to long to stand outside the rift—to be on the lookout for rifts derivable from *the rift* and cultivating thereby acquire them. Yet what was to be gained from noting such radical disjunctions when they broke—as a dam breaks; when they fell—as night falls; when they hatched—as death hatches. She embodied—loomed big with her embodiment of—radical disjunctions and as long as she managed to go on embodying without becoming conscious of all she embodied she would bloom. I no longer bloomed—never had bloomed—so here I was collecting radical disjunctions in the hope they might lay bare the notochord of a story never to be. Taking her hat and coat though I had given no sign that I wished her to go Maggy said: "Now I understand why he felt compelled to ridicule all that is decent and pure. Because unlike you and me"—I resented her lumping us together—"he could envision a future where even what is decent and pure is improved, shorn of its stigmata. And he was one of those rare beings willing and able to relinquish the possibility of pleasure in the name of that future."

Going down for a bite to eat in the local gourmet eatery after this by-and-large pointless interview with the fair Maggy who had limped away, as usual—as usual?—with her head between her knees or tail between her legs—all suspiciousness lulled at last to a long wan silent bewailing of what so beautifully might have been, between her and Jamms—no doubt aggravated by so many evidences—if what my eyes were now drinking in was any indication—all around her, in parks and on grassy urban slopes, at the entrances to office buildings and on the stools of coffee shops of just this thing she had *all her life been searching for*—going down for a bite to eat—I did not feel like cooking—I suddenly remembered the stock-quotation reader's girl friend depicting the crowd in front of *her* building, its fretwork afflicted with a specific slant of sun, and for a moment stopping dead in my tracks for all who cared to see I panicked for the fugitiveness of the crowd and for the fugitiveness of the specific slant of sun even more—dying away both in the flesh and in her inchoate depiction ravaged by big bald (he was not bald) bold boyfriend's patent and crucial lack of interest.

Sitting down in what after two or three visits now qualified, at least in my eyes, as my usual booth and having ordered my usual—juice, toast, coffee—I suddenly heard a pair of familiar voices engaged in murmured debate. One—who?—said to the other: "This seems to me eminently a crime of the sexual variety. And I hold fast to my thesis no matter what the myrmidons and janissaries of our imbecilic chief may decline to say. Take Maggy, or rather, la Maggy,—the other girl—the concubine—seems to have skipped town—all-American girl, coed and gum chewer with artistic aspiration entangled somewhere with her pony tail—with her 'you guys' and even better 'hey, you guys' and even better, the last said with torpid men ace rather than breezy self-introduction—and all the other detritus of mass culture corroding the tartar already deep within her blushing gums. At any rate, I have no alternative but to assume that both men—we give these two the benefit of the doubt—were in love with her. Rather: both 'men' were 'in love' with her. This, of course, is what the context dictated. Yet, yet, yet, the gap between context and truth which gap may at any moment still burst makes for the unfathomable itch in my vitals that makes for unsatisfactory, that is to say, unending, analysis. In short, I cannot—since falling in love with Maggy is what the context demanded—make up my mind whether they actually believed same or merely wanted others to believe it. At any rate, one thing has always bothered me." Long pause. Longer pause. Long pause. Longish pause. "Shoot," said the other but after so protracted an interval that the saying was by no means the communication of the desire etched into the word, i.e., Shoot, but rather a broad advertisement of the radical disjunction— yes, the radical disjunction—between ostensible desire and mode of its profession. "I have always wondered," muttered the other, loftily striving to ignore this radical disjunction rapidly staining the fabric of his inflec- tion, "whether—" Never had I felt NO NO

no so grateful NO

toward anybody NO as I did now toward he—the one—who— elder or younger—had had the audacity—the foresight—to introduce a radical disjunction—so perfectly formed a radical disjunction—into the proceedings, into the...story.

Never NO

Never no

Never NO

in the whole course of my feverish history NO

had I felt so sure of the crucialness of radical disjunctions to the evolution—to the possibility—of a story as I did now. He who had just introduced so purely formed a radical disjunction had proved—was still proving—that I was on the right track and that I must go on seeking these nuggets for all I—and they—were worth to the story. I tried briefly to imagine what their murmured debate might have been without this ghastly and protracted interval before the descent of the signal, Shoot. I tried to imagine the debate proceeding without obstruction, delay, unmentionable postponements and crisscrossing of messages. "—whether two entities like those with whom for better or worse we are now confronted, two stooges like this Jamms and his nelly—whether they might not conceivably share a simultaneous paroxysm of lust for the same fellow entity out there, say, the redblooded all-American girl or rather feel a need to share such a paroxysm and managing to generate said paroxysm a need to go on needing to share what at this stage of the proceedings may be characterized as a discreet augmentation of lowminded virile lust such as was undergone, evinced, and slaked—all in one gulp—between man and buffalo, buffalo and tarantula, on the great plains—whether they might not share a simultaneous orgasm without there accruing thereby, syllogistically as it were, unto their differently flabby surfaces—now composite, now conjoint—the abhorred stigmata—yeah, even in this day and age—of the sodomist or pederast. In other words, can this shared simultaneous craving for the same target—which craving has for so long been celebrated in song, dance, and other folkloric recrements—still qualify—and to hell with diagnostic testing and even worse diagnostic testing services—when we get right down to it, that is, if we wish to get right down to it, as true-blue all-American heterosexual desire. Is it simply that in the face of said indisputably true-blue all-American authentic heterosexual craving like naturally and necessarily inclines to, nay, craves, the proximity of like as buffer in the face of dazzling unlike-therefore-unknown without anything untoward and scandalous necessarily devolving upon said craving. In other words, is it simply, this secondary—this epinosic craving, that for the comfort derivable only from like, like unto like, and that like confronting the same unknown yet with the unknown for all that no less passionately craved for and in its own skin and without the slightest intimation of a diminution in or deflection from that unknown—target of primordial craving, to wit, the big blowsy apple-cheeked blonde. Isn't it simply, then, a case of redblooded all-American craving becoming augmented through proximity to its like—forget, then, the need for comfort, mutual comfort in the face of the unknown—a mere pretext facilitating the proximity that automatically induces a gigantic growth spurt of craving in the proximates. Is then, oh cursed spite! the craving of craving for contact with—proximity to—a homologous craving more primordial than the initial craving craving the proximity? So that—oh God, what am I saying my God can I be saying this?—and in the broad daylight of a downtown coffee shop!—in this case the craving for the redblooded, all-American female, the role expropriated—once again, in this case—by the unsuspecting and deliciously obtuse Maggy—this craving becomes nothing more, compliments of my lowminded prestidigitation, than that for a supervenient thrift shop decoy hastily recruited to serve as pretext and camouflage for the shameless slobbering salivating connectedness of like to like, in this case Jamms and his crony, our two entities, which connectedness—as the shameless longing for connectedness—has of course now gone far far beyond—a simple hunger for security and support in the face of the ostensibly beloved unknown. Or can it be—can it still be—that the secondary craving for security on the part of both parties facing a vast unknown although not for all that any less purely and virilely and redbloodedly craved target, namely, the fair—fairest Maggy—promoted from thrift shop decoy to vamp and muse, reinstated, as it were, in said capacity and from whose breezy purlieus she had never in fact really and truly strayed—at least from the perspective of true believers in authentic redblooded all-American virile lust—can it be that this secondary craving for security from the vastness—the vast and overwhelming authenticity of the primordial— the very craving we moments ago had the impudence to call into question—that this hunger, this craving, not for Maggy but for security from the overwhelming terror indissolubly bound to such a craving for such an unexceptionable Maggy among Maggys—can it be that this craving, this hunger, wandered off into a metamorphosis of itself, a volte-face, a transmogrification. Can it not be that the friction generated separately but equally in Jamms and his crony—our little Soho pal—from skirting grazing yet nevertheless overwhelming contact with the likes of Maggy Kindlingwood somehow managed to become friction of a completely different sort, that is to say, a friction about itself, kindled from its own impossibility, friction most if excruciatedly enhanced from growing consciousness—just below the peak of the pubic escutcheon—of itself as a thing apart, from the housing body, from the receiving body—that is, a thing apart with its own life, deaths, pulsion, and always a little in advance or in lag of the phenomenon—I mean the target—I mean the Maggy—that gave rise to it in the first place, in short, a friction dangerously contemplative of itself as falling due but falling short. And from here, oh curse the day, it is but a skip and a jump to friction of another species entirely, in other words, from friction in friction with itself—forever before the mirror of its own hysteresis—is born a friction between two frictions—between the frictions of two likes—one embodying the dissolution of all classes and too majestic in his degree-zero fungibility to think about being proud of it and the other slobbering now in some ditch or alleyway adjacent to the latest art gallery cum boutique cum gourmet delicatessen to grab Soho by its powdered fanny—is born a friction between two males, who, though initially and sincerely in quest of their heart's desire—the delicious and delightful female—became enamored of their own infatuation—each first of his own in itself and then of his own as deplorable and grotesque homolog of the other's and vice-versa. So that each ends—ended—up enamored of infatuation—no longer of his in itself but as the slightly mocking mirror of the other's, automatically his better's. From the moment desire smells itself in the other it recoils from itself and flies to the other, or rather, it recoils from the object—in this case, the fair and red-blooded Maggy—that had the temerity to provoke a desire—a hunger—a craving—that was not unique and therefore could not accrue to personal uniqueness—it recoils from the object and falls back on itself or rather itself as situated in the other. Since desire has found itself indistinguishable from the other's it will perversely—voluptuously—yield itself up to—lose itself in—the other. Appalled by its own lack of uniqueness—its ununiqueness—desire's only painkiller is prostration before—fusion with—its nearest though not yet dearest homolog. Each discovered separately—in lag and in advance of the other—that his desire for her could not pierce Maggy's veil and that at any rate such desire must never be thought of as unique since the other desired homologously. So the two men began to hit it off, slowly forgetting Maggy, for she had to be done away with as too lancinating a reminder of a desire that having failed in its bid for uniqueness now was foreclosed. But their desire—for each other—soon surpassed any residual craving for uniqueness—dread and shame at the intensity of this passion quickly overcame, rendered illegible the craving. Wouldn't have surprised me if they had both done Maggy in—and Bessy too, and for the same reason. Better, of course, for Jamms and his pal—now our pal—if they had never stumbled on this kind of desire. Nobody ever said life was inconceivable without this kind of desire. For example, yesterday, as I was coming up from or going down to the subway I espied a couple leaning against—making their very own—a pole. The husband/lover was reading the stock page while his wife/girlfriend avidly imbibed his obiter dicta even if every so often her physiognomy disintegrated into a diffident crystal of ticlike doings mimicking both the preliminary symptoms and aftereffects of love, disillusionment, regret, remorse, loss, despair, death, resurrection. These two, surely, have never known the excruciation of the kind of desire I was talking about a moment ago. And I for one don't see why our little subway thermocouple should be ashamed of its modest joys and sorrows, the little nudgings and penetrations subsequent to a good little Saturday night dinner once the dishes are cleared away for the future hired help. But I am by no means the first to speak of little lovebirds conjugating fiercely under the bedsheets, ours." Deep sigh, mine or theirs, who's to say amid so much blinding enlightenment cutting one off from any clearcut relation to a clearcut sensorium and its fluctuating testimony. "You are asking," began the other, "why I wish to pounce on and loathe their conjugating along with related humble pleasures. I am holding myself in reserve." "For what." "I am presenting a flawless inde-cipherability for purposes of—of—" As the younger groped for the right words I could not help mourning the allocation of this little conflict to the dyad disporting before me rather than to, for example, Jamms and I at the height of our intimacy, or to Jamms and Maggy, or to Jamms and Bessy. " —of something better than a story—something better than an anecdote susceptible to the kind of cheap paraphrase you practice. Edd, you've been a cop far too long. Your imagery is a debased imagery—a copper's imagery." Leaning back and sniffing my grapefruit juice I could smell only the glass, that had been incompletely washed or washed too well, leaving a sour deodorizing after whiff that took me back to the remote hinterlands of a grief I wanted to believe dead without knowing of course that I was inhabited either by such a grief or such a want. Was it my hunger for meanings taking over and, for the NO

　　　　　first time No

without the assistance of the meaning-mongers: at any rate, in my hunger for meanings—however inept, however blatant and indiscreet, I was discerning that the opposite of what the elder cop anticipated had

occurred: through his intuitive understanding, that is to say, feverish
middle-class dread, of the Jamms/non-Jamms relation—in other words,
our relation—the younger cop had ended up with no other alternative
than to come to treasure a relation— that, to his wife—blissfully bereft of
the species of desire he was made to understand had been ravaging the
other—our—dyad. Rather than apply his reluctant comprehension of his
wife's discontent to the investigation and thereby reify and perpetuate
that discontent, the younger chose, was choosing—against his far more
instinctive comprehension of the sinuous relation between two men,
amorously entwined against their better judgment—to move in the opposite direction, that is to say, out of the realm of amorous sinuosities
between and among like to like and back to bovine and this time definitive
pacification of wifely discontent—over origins—similar to mine—if I had
had any—replete with pavement-encrusting dogshit, black-eyed squir-
rels, ambulances fibrillating in readiness at every streetcorner as if every
streetcorner were the very bottom of the bottomless sea, storefront
headstone salesmen just back from the Florida beachfront slums, prosti-
tutes roving under the anxiously curious eye of the very old and very
debilitated refusing not to be incapable of budging against the onslaught
of such newer immigrant wavelets, delicatessens clutching to their
marinated bosoms the last of the neighborhood refuse, namely, palsied
superannuated shoeshine boys, retired obese assistant automobile me-
chanics and clerk/typists (before they were rechristened assistant admin-
istrative assistants and spared being left to stew beneath the brinish haze
of the label's slash), and schizophrenic daughters of the local quidnunc
regiment estranged from husbands and children without the least visible
regret and milking the severance for all it was worth in the arms of the old
mom and pop at once wholly, partially, and by no means responsible for
such a state of affairs—he was choosing to pacify, placate, quell, and
quash—the safest, always the safest, road—in the hope that out of that
pacification transcendence of all discontent—hers, his, and the lamppost's—most of all the lamppost's—might be born. I could see that he was
ready to sacrifice discontent even as mere and monumental mnemonic—
lest he forget the sacredness of his origins—for anybody's origins are
sacred—and retreat to the origins is cure for all ills—he was ready to
sacrifice even the mnemonic-laden facets of her discontent if it could

yield—the sacrifice—a little peace and quiet. This was the meaning I suddenly deduced—interpretation I suddenly put—on the turn their conversation had now taken. Yet I loathed myself for extracting a meaning from what bloody well intended to proceed without one, more particularly, a meaning of the form most acceptable to the meaning-mongers, namely, not A, but rather B, where A is the expected, the anticipated, the relished, the blessed, the vulnerary meaning.

I did not know what they intended to do with me: after so frequently catching them by chance in these little out of the way places, landmarks of a life wretched and miserable, neither did I know whether or not to take my trip as planned—a trip postponed since the unexpected arrival of Testic on the scene of my regeneration. Colletti had many lucrative new projects waiting for me on a group of islands not far from Miami: hadn't one of the two mentioned the Miami slums? Clearly they must believe Jamms had wished to kill his lover in a fit of class-related sex-related despair—in a fit of envious prostration before all he, the lover, was that Jamms was not, could never be, and what that lover was was precisely nothing, fungibility degree zero, at least according to the detectives chewing their late-night cud. Sensing the imminence of death the lover had acted out of the instinct of self-preservation, strongest in nonbeings. I packed my bags, filled with Colletti's instructions regarding where to encounter Naven and his band of merry macaques and headed south. On the train I vowed that I would not allow myself to be distracted by the circumambient dyads sure to abound, the relevance of whose dialogue to a life that might have been—a story that might have been—only would make me mourn. And I was sick of mourning. I was on holiday. Here, then, was the clue to safety—to innocence, in other words, the appearance of innocence, namely, to concentrate on the story in its purity. But it was no longer clear what and where that story: wasn't, for example, my story very much bound up with the girl on the subway dutifully upholding the divagations of her stock-page-devouring paramour, or rather,

OR RATHER, with the crowd that had seen fit to congregate in front of *her* building in the city's financial district thereby impeding the passage of a ray of hazy autumn sunlight toward. And if the story was very much bound up with that girl and her ray of sun weren't those elements already embedded in the story—hadn't I already grafted those sequestra onto the dismembered degenerating corpse of the story so that in fact the story consisted of nothing so much as spasms of failed, or rather, pretermitted annexation—so that in fact—in actual fact—in point of fact—the story comprised nothing so much as colossal inattention to its own omnivorousness. The story was the sum of its missed spasms. Missed sum of its spasms.

On the train a woman NO
NO NO NO NO NO said to another NO
NO NO NO across the aisle: "They don't want me to undergo surgery." I tried to stop my ears against her flagrant flaunting of an uncanny resemblance to old lady Jamms. These were old lady Jamms's lines being mouthed by a third-rate impostor deriving most pleasure not from her flounderings quasi-Thespian but rather from this implicit demonstration of how thematic scar tissue vital to the story corpse could at the drop of a hat be mercilessly squandered on marginals—supernumeraries—with already far too much fat on their bones. I tricked her: I listened to her as old lady Jamms relishing Jamms's rhadamanthine embodiment of filial responsibility. Or rather, I tried so to listen. Until I remembered that in Jamms's case, what little filial responsibility there was was utterly severed from compassion—had never been anything more than a chimney sweep's appetency for discharging his function under the sootiest and most starless of hollow groined vaults. Yet here was the old granny—old lady Jamms—no, not old lady Jamms—captioning Jamms's—no, not Jamms's—activities under completely divergent—completely...disjunctive—lines. Here was a mother talking about her son—here was something relevant to the story of Jamms and me—but there was no relating it to that story. No relating it, that is, until I began to relish the radical disjunction between affectionate—almost startled—boasting on the part of a dowager AND the actual facts of the case as skirted by that dowager. Not that it was a question of irony—of the old girl's blindness transmitting a message, according to the specifications of realistic drama, to some hovering witness and spectator eager to suck up all he could of the foibles and fancies of man in the raw. I did not wish to begin to relish *it*—the radical disjunction—as an ironic moment on one character's road to enlightenment or further blindness as

ultimate irretrievability. "He doesn't want me to undergo surgery." I was beginning to relish — I was fascinated by — all the words — the inflection as much as or even more than the words — adumbrated of a lovingly protective — supererogatorily protective — function being exercised by the son — by the likes of Jamms — a function shot through — as the words and inflection also made clear — by a strong sense of aggressive opinion-atedness and dour — even dire — suspiciousness in the face of the world's far too free and easily quacklike ways with a remedy here, a prescription there — a function scandalously alien to Jamms wherever ma and pa Jamms had been concerned. And yet the relish — the beginning of relish — did not stem from the sharp contrast between a mother's delusion and the hard facts of her case. The relish was for the form of the old lady's expression, or rather, for the interpretation to which that expressive form gave rise in me — an interpretation that encompassed, so I thought, not only the old lady's world view — her perspective on being — but all perspectives — any possible perspective. As far as I was concerned — as far as my relish was concerned — this old lady had severed the connection of her perspective on being with the actual, incidentally ironic, and reversing facts of her particular case — in being — long before...she ever started ruminating on the delirious dutifulness of her beloved son. The radical disjunction between the old lady's vision of her son's devout — almost dour — solicitude and the actual facts of the case was not the source and target of the fascination subsequent to what her utterance/inflection induced in me of a craving for interpretation — interpretation of how beings — all beings — manage to exist — to subsist on their perspectives, justified or not. And who's is justified, by the way? The radical disjunction was the driving force, the power behind the throne, the bedrock, the subsoil, the archeus, the potentiality and possibility of this utterance-as-royal-road-to-exploration-investigation-of-her — therefore anybody's — being — as-a-perspective founded-on-grounded-in-consciousness-as-nec-essary-delusion.The radical disjunction between her motherly fantasies and the fetid filial facts of the case was not, I repeat, the lodestone of my relish. The stark beauty of this radical disjunction — assuming she was still Mrs. Jamms and the scion in question Jim Jamms — stemmed from its laying bare as for prosectomy in the amphitheatre one particular con-sciousness's construction of its relation to the world of facts — one particular consciousness's means for holding on for dear life—one particular consciousness's evocation—invocation—through words and sounds of some strongly desired relation to the world of facts. The words and sounds propelled me to find my own words—story words—for what those—her—the old lady's—sounds and words, words and sounds—challengingly set forth of struggle toward some perspective on being. The existence of a radical disjunction between what was out there and what the words/sounds said was out there intensified and excruciated my task—and the relish of my task.

So was I seeking these radical disjunctions for the story. Or was I seeking them to subserve another task. And did I know I was seeking them to subserve that other task: to accumulate—before my capture—as many instances as possible of other creatures formulating their perspectives on being—beaming their words and sounds on the no longer starless vault. Radical disjunction had no relation to story: radical disjunction between consciousness and what was in actual fact out there for consciousness subsisted to permit the spectacular clarity of a perforce moribund perception of the trajectory of consciousness. The old lady's being—"My son won't allow..."—the old lady's perspective—"My children would never permit..."—had, compliments of a radical disjunction, been illuminated with that spectacular clarity.

In particular, the radical disjunction I had just discerned—was discerning—to be the foundation of the pathos inherent in her—in anybody's—perceiving—stating—uttering—living through consciousness and always in lag of these radical disjunction(s) abounding. More and more, as the train moved, and even when it stopped for what seemed like the rest of the my life, I was fascinated by this old battleaxe's vainglorious and at the same time supremely humble insistence on attributing to him—the son—Jamms—always Jamms—to his comatose and grudgingly minimal dutifulness a pugnacious and impassioned forthrightness on her behalf and her behalf only. Had Jamms been comatose and grudgingly dutiful only or had he also—or rather—been downright abusive and negligent. At any rate, the radical disjunction between downright abusiveness/venal negligence and this simpering strutting vision of filial conscientiousness was not—would never be—as interesting as that between a seamless fissureless unsmiling uncompassionating affectless conscientiousness and whatever was conjured up, for me, for her, by the sedately boastful: "My three daughters and seven sons, among whom triplets and quadruplets, would never let me undergo surgery." For it was the radical disjunction between affectless conscientiousness and whatever was conjured — for her — for me — for me as she — FOR ME AS SHE — in — by — the phrase: "My eleven sons and thirteen   daughters would never allow me to undergo surgery," that furnished — embodied — the springboard for a perspective of dazzling devastated clarity on her consciousness — on the birth and death of her consciousness as birth and death of everybody's — anybody's — consciousness. For the radical disjunction between downright abusiveness/venal negligence and whatever was conjured for her by the phrase: "My twelve sons and three daughters-in-law, of which two sets of quadruplets," was too saturated with obvious bellicose irony to qualify as authentic window on the world of her consciousness dawning — consciousness aborning — bringing to birth its version of reality and to hell with things as they are. And didn't her perception of that reality somehow modify that reality — somehow shift it ever so slightly in the direction of her aspiration? As the train picked up speed — heading south, forever heading south — and even when it refused to pick up speed — I grew more and more fascinated not by the landscape without — all withered dugs of what had once been exalted as the military/industrial complex but rather BUT RATHER by this *landscape of a soul* expertly sketched by the words/sounds of an old woman, also heading south, this figured slab of being... this figured slab of being subtended by, "My young ones don't want me to undergo surgery." I left the mass of crags, crisscrossing depot lines, unsmiling livestock, billboard torsos above freight cars abandoned forever all to their witches' sabbath.

Suddenly all the polite letters written to the Jammses in an effort to do my duty — effort accelerated when from time to time I sensed how their seamless impersonalness transformed me into more of a being impervious to the trickle of time and ooze of space — had delivered me over to the caption her utterance [the weighted average of its inexhaustible variants] had become. I was within its frame. I was the Jamms who would never permit her — especially on a train heading south past the withered dugs of billboards, livestock torsos, and crags of crisscrossing depot lines — to undergo surgery. Hearing and feeling myself encapsulated within the frame of her utterance—ground down to embody whatever that utterance-as-caption evoked in her consciousness—in hers as mine—and at the same time outwittingly outside the frame she or anybody else might take it into their...consciousnesses—theirs as mine—to provide for my stultification beyond appeal I was put in mind of the two detectives and how they might now find it much easier to apprehend me since I was localizable. Whether inside or without I was referred to the frame spontaneously generated by the caption into which her utterance had been transformed. It was not quite clear who was within or without—whether I, Jamms, Jamms as I, I as Jamms, or simply every last scion of this tenacious old witch with all of whom I had just established so fusingly tenacious an affinity. If this proud old granny, prosthetized beyond recognition and yet still very much headmistress of her faculties, was able, by encapsulating either me or Jamms or some irredeemable hybrid in her telling, to pass herself off as one not merely beloved but dearly beloved of her offspring, then surely these two arms of the law would have no trouble ultimately encapsulating me in any well-tested hypothesis aiming to pass me off as a murderer. If I was placeable inside the frame of her utterance as caption then surely these two hefty cops could find a way...On some level, always traveling south, I was aware of the defective logic sabotaging such a supposition although on another—what other?—level I was willing to sacrifice logic—and the painfulness of its consequences—to such a surefooted acquisition. The correlation between the old girl's techniques of capture and the detectives' made me less of a stranger to the world. It shrank that world to manageable proportions.

I descended on the first in a chain of sunny little islands all owned by Colletti off the Florida coast, took a room in a hotel, strolled along the beach, some of the bronzed or bronzing torsos momentarily attracted me, only for a moment, then I moved on. These might have become targets of desire—whatever that was, is—only I did not know how to begin to desire, to be one, once begun, with that desire; to propel forward the story of that desire. Armed with my money I felt less awkward about chatting with the other guests, feigning interest in what Jamms would have deemed not altogether unjustly their petty sickening lives. All the time chatting and shaking my head significantly I told myself: This is health, at which point I felt a profound—or perhaps a quite shallow—desire to laugh, or rather, OR RATHER, to run back to Jamms with but another specimen of the world's fatuity—namely myself on the verge of chatting laughter. One night at dinner a middle-aged doctor vacationing with wife and teenaged daughter—he should have been Colletti or Naven or a cross between the two—but he was neither—never would he be either, I cursed him, cursed him for his supremely miscellaneous robustness—delivered an impromptu speech on health. The gist, that health is worldly success, no substitute for social accreditation of one's struggles day in day out. Each and every tooth and nostril proclaimed: I am a physician. I must know. I could not help feeling his fertility was if not directed at then prompted by my stance or absence of identifiable same, especially since he began his tirade at the very moment I chose to proffer the butter dish with bubbling affability to his *lovely wife and daughter*. He went on reminding me of Colletti, or rather, of what Colletti might have done with such an opportunity. The more he spoke the more I...felt like Jamms, as one of his type must be inclined to look upon or be unable to look upon the likes of Jamms. I was Jamms in his presence insofar and as long as he sustained what seemed—felt—like the fever pitch of an incapacity to even begin to comprehend, apprehend, conceive of Jamms. Hadn't old lady Jamms spoken of such a scotoma-ridden character? Not that he seemed jealous of my attentions for in some way he loathed the pair—I was sure of it—but as his little speech already incontestably demonstrated, at least as far as I was concerned, he found those attentions simply too perfect, too—sunburnt, to qualify as manifestations of health. "Beware of those," he bellowed, "for whom health is but another change of stance, dilettantes of the affections. Beware of them, I say. Beware their ancient airs and graces, say I. Many I know who search for health and when they find it, when at last they are able to extricate themselves from the tics and compulsions that made them unhappy and unhealthy, then they are appalled at how health turns out to be as tedious as—no, far more tedious than—illness. And when one thinks of how much effort they have probably invested in remedies—pharmaceuticals—drugs—drugs—drugs— breeding of course their own enervation and the consequent need for counter-remedies, all putatively aimed at nullifying the status of being set apart and estranged, then, then— The trouble with these folks is that they pursue—hound—health with a sullen hunger: they want to get to health before the madness of its pursuit stigmatizes them beyond appeal. And I tend to feel — I do not feel, I tend to feel — that this impatience to get to and beyond appeal is very much correlated with the certainty that in their case health can never hope to be all they must hope it to be. In other words, these creatures are striving to arrive not so much at health as at some remedy-clogged relation to health nullifying the omnipresent feeling that health is simply one more loathsome posture, among many." He kept looking at me as if I was very much to blame for being me. I tried to return his gaze and at the same time affirm an affability that was more than a mere tic subject to disintegration at the slightest whim of a ticlike aspersion. After the speech, he paid no further attention to me. It was only later when I had at last managed to disentangle myself from wife and daughter, whose sense of my value seemed strangely to have expanded as a result of that oration not quite directed my way and from their point of view that was no point of view no doubt nowhere at all, that I could begin to feel he had done me good. Or am I, was I, simply doing the dirty work of the meaning-mongers faster than ever they could do their own. Statement — affirmation — of meaning had intervened to banish forever the possibility of a slow and authentic secretion — a slow progress — a slow evolution — a slow deflagration — of essential meaning from the still glowing embers of encounter. For slow secretion in casting me inexorably to its rhythm would have hindered escape at a moment's notice. Or was I simply afraid that left to its own devices the encounter would secrete no meaning whatsoever.

And NO

for the first time NO NO NO NO

in a NO

long time for the first time in a long time (or is this yet another self-blinding against the conceivable torment, agony, of finding no meaning in present doings so that I am obliged to fabricate one all the time maintaining ostensible surprise at this artifice or against the panicked anticipation of some inexorable meaning taking snakelike its sweet time in affirming itself and to my utter ruin) I felt myself to be on the track of my story as the best of all possible stories for no story that is not concurrently the best of all possible stories is worth subserving. This encounter with the doctor, who clearly disapproved of my drug-running,

even if contradictorily he was renting the flashiest suite in a hotel financed
by Colletti and Company,—this encounter as once before with a policeman, the policeman, was putting me back on the track of the story. Yet
as I put out the light in my luxurious penthouse suite with the island's
gracious and hospitable billions dying like flies below I wondered: Was
all I had imbibed of the doctor's affinities and disavowals essential to the
story's unfolding or so much irrelevance to be chewed up and discarded
before the story could even begin to think about beginning all over again.
Or was this the nature of any authentic story element compossible with
all other authentic story elements residing in the best of all possible story
universes—had I in fact pinpointed the essential nature of any true story
element, namely, its being undergoable only as an obstruction to what
could not even begin to think about existing in the absence of such
obstructions, namely, the story—its being undergoable only as an obstruction that had necessarily to be undergone by the story as an essential
rite of passage—undergone, assimilated, and then spewed forth before
the story could begin...to acquire the true story elements, specifically, the
analogous other ostensibly non-story elements to be analogously undergone and spewed out to validation in its, the story's domain—as if there
was any other domain except the story's, as if such spewing out—spewing
forth—could actually take place outside the story domain, validatingly or
otherwise, as if the spewed and the spewing were not inextricably bound
up with authentic story life cycle and metabolism from the very moment
an ostensible outcast element was rendered distinct by story's overly—
inauthentically fastidious repudiation of anything not its own, not of its
own, as if story grew fat on anything except what was not its own, of its
own. Eventually I hoped, enough spewed spewings would sketch a story,
the story, the story poor Jamms—I liked this sanctimonious slant—did
not live to see aborning.

I knew I would see him, the doctor, again. For the way he had
insisted on his diagnosis in the face of my refusal to dissimulate or mitigate
its essential target, namely, my affability, and the way wife and daughter
unknowingly and concurrently collaborated in my advertisement of that
target—clearly, all these elements constituted a paradigm worthy of
comparison with that concocted on the beach, long ago, by—or rather,
from the likes of Jim, the cop, the photo, a hovering witness, and me. In

the morning—mornings—I took a stroll along the beach, this, a different beach, waiting for some word from the New York police. They had my address. I studied the sea, waiting. I tried to go on studying the sea as if studying the sea belonged completely to the story Jamms might have lived if he had been here in my place. For a little distance I was able to live a story unharassed by story elements—for as long, that is, as I could muster the slackness to impersonate Jamms. The doctor kept looking at me and from all directions as if I was Jamms and he, the doctor, at home with his slightly or markedly disapproving incomprehension of such a specimen. Just when I felt myself getting quite comfortable with this story blissfully destitute of story elements I noted NO

    no

    NO

a defective-looking woman pushing a man in a wheelchair (dark glasses, convulsions of body in time to music evidently transmitted through fashionably minute earphones). A helicopter wading overhead made not a bit of difference even if I could not quite say what the entity was with respect to which it made not a bit of difference. Then she stopped, letting go of the wheelchair, to raise her socks. Otherwise I would never have noticed that she wore socks. I waited, was waiting, far more intensely, so it seemed, than I knew myself to wait for the mail, for the police, for the doctor, that old gasbag. But as I waited for the woman to raise her socks— which waiting completely supplanted the other waiting(s)—and extricate herself thereby from a situation that only rendered her more defective, almost a psychopath, I knew I had become—for all spectators—the two of us now a story element—a failed story element— indistinguishable from her grotesqueness, or rather my waiting had become indistinguishable from that grotesqueness to the extent that the waiting, such as it was, could be characterized with no danger of caricature as a spellbound gaping contorted by a succession of wasteful and overlapping thrusts to bring socks out of reach of sand. Every movement—hers or mine, who could tell—gave new meaning to the innocuous expression, wide of the mark. Each thrust was wider of the mark than both its predecessor and successor. Observing her—becoming she—I became, in turn, as clumsy, absurd, unappetizing, absurd, absurd, absurd, as she and in my case it was far direr for I could only—

inevitably—embody the general idea of absurdity. But what did this little paroxysmic fusion with the infinite augur for the story, for my safety, inside or without the story. Was it completely irrelevant, did it belong in its peculiarly marginal way, was the ostensible marginality the tactic of essential building block wary of losing its place. I could not make up my mind as I stood waiting long after the socks were raised and/or the woman gone with her charge. My waiting was still a waiting for the woman to pull up her socks.

These denizens peculiar to a resort community, people like the doctor and his wife and their daughter, were completely oblivious to the slow and inexorable momentum of the masses around them. I, in contrast, could smell them, recusant and miserable, awaiting a mere signal from their leaders to throw off their chains and expropriate all state machinery in behalf of an ultimate statelessness infinitely distant from their present dystopia where no artisan could hope to flourish, to be a shepherd at dawn, a revenant at nine, a cowpoke at noon, a slowpoke at the stroke of four, a declaimer at dusk, a sleeper at bedtime. On one of my strolls I passed a hotel even more luxurious than that chosen for me by the highly accommodating tourist bureau *recommended by friends*—whom with a little effort I might manage to make pass for friends if and when I returned to my darling little apartment near Soho. Every door had its doorman, each solitary and proud in sunny splendor, I speak of the doors. Yet going down a sidestreet I very quickly found myself, as if with no further ado, in the heart of the seamier—perhaps the seamiest—section—seamier or seamiest proving beyond the shadow of a doubt except to those who must insist on holding on at all costs and for dear life to its little outpouchings of local color that this was not just another resort with *thousands in help* emerging every dawn from the woodwork to fulfill their serverly function with a smile, with a smile, have a good evening, with a smile. No, this was very much a teeming, swarming, pullulating mountain of miserables. Suddenly I recognized one of the doormen from the luxury hotel with a doorman at every portal in the act of purchasing a soft drink at a grocery not fifty paces away on the other side of the street. Turning to go he tucked his purchase deeper inside his paper bag: I watched as he struggled to twist off the cap on the store's doorway gadget set aside for that purpose. The cap tinkled onto the pavement. I waited to see if he would pick it up.

If he stopped to stoop this would increase his doormanly pathos and thereby enhance the beauty of the image invoked by the caption: Doorman off duty for a few minutes. Instead he let it flow away into the gutter, proving revolution was near. Outside his cubicle without walls where he was obliged to refer to every frump one third his age as Mrs. So-and-Shit he was no longer a docile delicate wounded creature. I kept my eyes on him as he walked off: he noticed my looking and seemed heartily surprised by it. If I could make the target of my gaze one who was officially outside being and knew he was officially outside then my looking was a defective looking and I was as marginal as he. I got on a public bus that took me deeper and deeper into the heart of the slums. Large numbers got on at subsequent stops with the look of those used to being pushed and shoved and who having learned in this destructive element to immerse themselves always await the definitive shove that will push them definitively deep into the safety of the conveyance's bowels. I descended at a plaza of dirty sand far from any visible arm of the sea. In a little pizza joint that could very well have been flown over whole from Lexington and Seventy-ninth I ordered a hot tea with milk and sat down. The owner's wife had to run out for milk. Waiting I watched the owner and what looked like his old mother read a letter. The son—who was a son very different , —vastly different—from that other son who long ago had attempted to decipher—*his* mother also standing or sitting by—a comparable letter—said, "It was always far more painful to hear him babble on and on about our folklore and how that folklore should suffice to our misery. For you, mamma, were in a certain sense to that manure born and you dutifully made it your business never to transcend it lest you betray your ancestors. Whereas he, under your influence, had slowly and rigidly to construct this sort of smallmindedness and at the same time — and most of all in his own eyes—affirm it as his very own. Of course, in those last days he had very little else to do since all authentic emotion—remember the time he gathered us to his deathbed and you balked at such an absurd display—it was an absurd display—but such absurd displays are one of the few rights of the dying—all authentic and legitimate emotion was outlawed as an offense against your equilibrium. When I began to hear him mouthing the kind of drivel you have long been known to specialize in it was not only as if he was sinking away from me like sand beneath the receding pedestal of the tide but also as if all of being was — taking the cue from his righteous self-obliteration — metamorphosing into something grotesquely other than itself and therefore thenceforth unavailable for comment regarding my true state, my true destiny. Now I know why I must overturn the powers that be and obliterate those forces that have turned this island into a haven for cocaine pontiffs and fascist murderers. He killed himself under your reign and we — our people — are being asked to do the same only we are not even being asked. With each smile we darken the authorizing signature on our death warrant." Bovine, the old woman said, "You have changed a lot since you went away." This exchange clearly belonged to Jamms and the old lady. Only I was realizing what the story — our story — had so desperately to express could never come from its legitimate denizens — Jim and old lady Jamms were as of this moment legitimate denizens of the story's kingdom — but from watery simulacra of those denizens residing on the margin of the kingdom. It was hard for me to determine whether the old woman was being poisonously accusatory or simply vending the fruit of spontaneous and impartial contemplation. Perhaps the time for all rancor between mother and son was passed. He turned away exasperated though this did not necessarily mean she had been accusatory. He, the young man, might be exasperated for any number of reasons, justified or not, just as for any number of reasons they were taking, now that my order was brought, no further notice of me even if what they were saying was decidedly not for customer consumption, even compromising, as if once I had paid or stated my order paid for or not I no longer existed. I did not know if I should go on listening or whether exit from this situation that had nothing to do with my story. Clearly this descent into the slums represented a flight from story, from privity of plight. Sitting here I sickened myself tabulating the delight I experienced watching the scene between old mom and son unfold. And when I thought of running from the sickening induced by the scene to the sickening to be induced by that from which this scene represented an escape there was no prospective diminution in sickening, it did not matter where I was, who I was. "This is an about-face," said the old woman, tone still indecipherable. Stamping his foot over and over the young man, long before the stamping was done, said, "It isn't an about-face. Immediately, imperceptibly, as he was dying, I knew the futility of all prior preoccupations compared to the revolution—our revolution. Subliminally I switched into a new mode." He cleared his throat: "My new, my present, mode." "Then his death, or rather, his getting ready to die, was nothing more than the long-awaited signal you needed to become yourself. Before his dying all you were was a writhing lying in wait to become yourself." He stripped in front of her, revealing a discreet—a tasteful—distribution of chest, pubic, thigh hair, donned his uniform with a theatrical flourish of hostility. The old woman shifted her posture to show, so it seemed to me, that she was willing if not quite able to change her tune. Turning suddenly toward me, still waiting for the milk in my tea, he said, "Here mamma, is the son you always wanted. He stands erect in Bermuda shorts and two-tone loafers and he even sports a bowtie as a signal hint of iconoclasm. But is he really willing and able to smash the icons in their niches. Oh, how I loathe him—loathe his kind—not for his love of money nor for his discontinuous love of the sublime and beautiful but rather for his pompous advertisement of the torment induced by the conflict among these conflicting little loves—as if he expected the whole world to fall in love with the unflinching integrity he ascribes to that torment. Look at him. And I loathe him for being able—to which, once again, his bowtie attests with such sly panache—to reconcile such torments though perhaps it is fallacious to speak of reconciliation where there was no prior conflict. What we have here is a case of reconciliation where there was no prior conflict: isn't that wonderful. Just as the state was erected over the irreconcilability of classes so too this fool is erected over the irreconcilability of his torments—the forced and failed irreconcilability, that is." I let him speak for didn't his speech promise that my excursion into these depths no longer would be irrelevant to my story. He was on the verge of being of my story, a denizen.

So here I was, far from the *resort community* I had paid so much to see at last, waiting for the stimuli crucial and appropriate to my story's unfolding and then, with these stimuli arising—it did not matter in the least if these stimuli were not the right stimuli for it was conceivable I might have the very same reaction against the appropriate stimuli,—with these stimuli arising as now, appropriate or inappropriate, here I was raging against them for obscuring the story's true form or marring the life beyond the story. There was no story, I saw it in a flash, only a waiting for

the story or for a life beyond the story either or both adumbrated by rage
at the stimuli obscuring the rudiments of that story or of that life. At the
same time I was always rushing out toward contact with those entities —
such as the young man or rather, his tirade against me — that in making
me sick at heart pandered to a need to believe in the fiction that my story
was contingent solely on transformation of the antitypy intrinsic to such
shreds. This, then, was the story, namely, the delusion that story was
dependent on collision after collision with shreds of a certain species
counterpoint out there. This was the story, a sequence of incompossible
collisions perhaps not entirely bereft of compossibility but only in another
world, another story, none that I could conceive, much less live. Here I
was, in the midst of the slums — a child of the slums — inventing once again
as if it was brand new the sickening task of seeking out those who could
find it in their hearts only to loathe and ridicule my impersonations of
whatever I apperceived the moment demanded that I be. Why must I seek
out these situations that only confirmed my permanent state of abeyance
and attempt to construct them faster than they managed to unroll on their
own steam. Perhaps if I had not provoked this situation's unrolling — but
of what did such provocation consist? — a young man might never have
taken it into his head to denounce me in front of his old mom, or granny,
so that in the middle of their fiercest enmity discovering a common enemy
they were reconciled after all these years. And here I was smothering
abeyance with — in — a new kind of abeyance dependent on an impossible
retraction for humiliation avidly provoked. But as there seemed no
possibility of a retraction from this young revolutionary I told myself I
needed such humiliation for the work at hand, as cement, gristle, parget,
caulking, grout. So that to the humiliation oozing from collision with
entities in situ I had no need to add the humiliation of having been
humiliated in vain.

All at once I stopped dead seeing the young man and his mom and
his hairy groin as story elements. The sense of being in abeyance
vanished. But I sought to sustain the feeling of no longer waiting — a
rejuvenating feeling of total absence of abeyance — at the same time that
I continued hunting for story elements without finding any. Or I would
have been slaked by a feeling of the intensest abeyance — the most
tortured being kept waiting — in the total absence of any interest in story

and story elements OR amid a veritable plethora of story elements. I would go on hunting for story elements as long as a sense of abeyance — interim — incompleteness — set in amid a plethora of elements or amid a total indifference to the conceivability of story elements OR as long as total freedom from an abeyance-laden malaise set in amid a glaring absence of story elements. For then my hunting would be embodying the radical disjunctions that are consecrated, so I was discovering, to leading a life of their own, namely, that of the story they decree to mask their incompossibility. And perhaps one day I might achieve that transcendence — the state I had NO

No all my life NO

been seeking — comprising a crying need for a story and a total indifference to its absence — crying need for the story amid a plethora of story elements and total indifference to its absence, even amid the most glaring paucity of such elements. This was something to hope — to labor — for. This was something of a consummation. I stood up, the young man was gone, the granny snoring, some unspoken law of the *barrio* prohibiting further intrusion of customers at this hour. I was still waiting for a story or for a life beyond the story. The story was asleep and no way to wake it. One night after dinner the doctor and I took a walk. He announced that he was indeed Doctor Scotoma against whom old lady Jamms had once ranted. He announced that my affability poorly concealed a void and in my even more poorly concealed rage at that void it was not inconceivable that I might take to murder. I thought of pushing him into the water at the moment when a wave of no common density was menacing the shore. I hurriedly tried to collect the facts on which he based his diagnosis. The facts, whatever they were, for I had no way now of retracing them, under no circumstances merited such a conclusion — such a verdict — even — especially — if said conclusion was a mere paraphrase of all the facts divulged. For having spoken or snorted or farted my facts — whether through my gait, strut, posture, finger placement, blinks per millisecond — I was beyond them irretrievably and therefore forever incommensurate with the diagnosis to which somebody else's detritus had given rise. Thanks to having spoken I was beyond relevance to his diagnosis yet here he was, though I was elsewhere, attempting to force me to recall what had been annihilated through utterance of some sort. He did not understand that once uttered the facts of the case died a peaceful death. And here he was trying to urge me backward, maybe he was working for the police — the two detectives' chief—the one, in fact, who had urged them to keep an eye on the phones—imagining that the sea air or the night air or the sluggishness subsequent to a good dinner must loosen my tongue. Returning to my room I was intercepted with a message from the police in New York. Clipped to the message was an envelope bearing the return address of Mrs. Jamms. Her letter described how she was now obliged to go looking for a headstone for her husband's grave alone. She knew he was not long for this vale of tears. The salesman had tried to rush her but she refused to be rushed insisting that the following words be inscribed under the dates: I could not make them out, or rather, I made out enough to be charmed by my presumptuous but quickly and deftly constructed radical disjunction between the banal little phrase itself and prior sentiments and behavior disqualifying for forthright participation in the tender regrets evoked by such a phrase. Yet once again — I had learned this on the train heading south, among marginal elements whose significance — crucialness — to the story — the real story — was only now being learned—it was not the ironical contrast between phrase and all it evoked AND facts of the case refusing to be retrospectively modified by such an evocation—it was not the ironical contrast that charmed—it was not the radical disjunction (between aspiration and reality) in-itself that made for this closest I would ever come to delight but rather

    BUT RATHER

the radical disjunction as window on the pathos of consciousness — anybody's: of perception—anybody's—as necessary ineluctable misperception of the facts of the case. What charmed was, in the chilly beam of the radical disjunction, to be witness to—confronted with—this dawning of her consciousness on a reality that had never existed—would never exist—and yet, as evoked in the sound of—the interstices among—the words to be inscribed on the headstone, did magically exist. What charmed—charmed—charmed—as much, for example, as the sight of Soho townhousefronts crepuscularly inscribed against the silhouetting sky—was this attendance upon the spectacular clarity of a dawning of consciousness unobstructed by fidelity—thralldom—to an already existing and veridical state of affairs—unassailable facts of a case—hers—

theirs—the Jammses—for there were none. In her case, the dawning of consciousness—that he was forever in her heart or forever her beloved or something of the sort—was bringing forth a consciousness unimpeded— a consciousness *in its purest state*—because unobstructed by preoccupation with target—there was none, the target itself indistinguishable from the consciousness awakened by the sound in the sense and the sense in the sound of the phrase shortly to be consigned to his, old man Jamms's, headstone.

During our subsequent walks I made no effort to kill the doctor, I did not even begin to make gestures construable as hotly denying any intention to murder. I thought that in the course of many solitary walks he would mellow toward the idiosyncrasies that enraged and whose only solace was diagnosis. Instead he became, as the sea rose, more and more virulently opposed to my very being—a being beyond the diversion—the mitigation—of idiosyncrasy. Strangely he announced as we sat among the shoals that he was in excruciating pain—the death of a— He stopped short but suddenly I knew who he was, Testic, père, come hunting his only son's murderer. Above the surf's roar he tried to explain that amid excruciating pain conscious evocation of an even more overwhelming and tormenting period went only just so far in quelling the excruciation. He was always trying now, always trying hard, he said, to remember just how miserable he had been when he first heard the bad news that—but he was always immediately overcome by the wiliness as it were of a present excruciation completely insusceptible to alleviation through memory of still having A (a lenitive, wife, for example, or daughter) or of having at last gotten rid or free of B (an irritant). There was no way, he went on, of adding A to the present torment, the present excruciation, call it x, or of subtracting B from that same x, in order to arrive at an $A + x$ or $x - B$ decidedly less mordant than x in its unity even if he knew that subtraction of A or accrual of B must certainly induce an excruciation so-much vaster. There was—with tears in his eyes—simply no way of contrasting the old excruciation with the new so that the latter profited immensely by the contrast. "I'll find his killer," he murmured, looking me straight in the eye. Some time before A had been added to x and B subtracted and though at the time the operation was intelligible— palpable—in its repercussions the results were now irretrievable and the operation itself irreversible, reduced to a mere erosion of its heyday. He shrugged and shrugged and shrugged, listening to the surf as he — we — lingered near a broken shelf of slimy invertebrates. And it was hard to say whether he shrugged against the content of his speech or against the remote possibility of my taking heed, that is to say, confessing. I looked him straight in the eye, confessing nothing. If I was his blind spot he was mine. Were we in the story, he and I, and if so, speaking relevantly to the story's needs, and if yes, and even if yes and no, where should I situate the shrug, I mean in relation to the story's progress ever onward and upward.

There was a couple talking nearby. I did not want to watch them talk and become entangled in the mere detail of their talk as a flight from story. The woman

NO was quite obviously entranced with the male's

NO plumage NO

the male obviously and obtrusively successful according to the world's terms if, that is, the blazer, white trousers, tasseled loafers, chain presuming to flatter and contain an abundantly hairy chest so as to be flattered in turn and the ensemble governed by the almost deliriously tasteful caprice of a pink sport shirt with the obligatory Gila monster envenoming the left breast pocket — if that is, these accessories emblematic of exclusive membership in — in — were to be believed and they were, at least by the lady friend. I pitied her, listening, wanted to rush out to save her from her credulity. She embodied, like me — like Jamms's Soho friend — the dissolution of all classes though without the stench of potency consequent to such a dissolution. Drinking in every word as if holy writ she clearly would never acquire — like the young man ranting his full before a bodega granny — the consolation of a nihilistic rage should the speaker decide to drop her. Only a matter of time before he did. And when he did she would not, alas, be numbered among those who manage to abscond with some shred by which — absconding or shred — they transcend participation in the universal credulity that decrees that such a Gila monster is the embodiment of social excellence. She had, this creature, nothing to live for beyond belief in this her Testic — her inflexible standard of how life must be lived in the world through, for example, the excretion of a chitchat and chat chat so molded — before excretion, of course — as to become the true — the only — measure of one's worth or at the very least

a gateway to some future expansive triumph of that worth, temporarily
latent. Yet how did I know she had nothing to live for? How did I know
I knew what to make of this event? And what was the event? The event
was clearly not quite the lady listening. The event, I saw it now, on the
beach, pursued by a grieving father, was situated somewhat closer to
home, somewhere in the vicinity of my noting and then leaping out to
expropriate the poor lady listening in order that that listening might be
deformed to correspond to my own sense of what listening must be. The
event was no longer her listening but an effort to make that listening my
own or rather my embattled estrangement from a listening decreed to be
and yet not quite my own. At any rate he strove to move away from her
and eventually they both disappeared amid flaws of rack almost as
tropically pink as his shirt though of course far less tasteful. It occurred
to me—as Testic, père went on eyeing me—that if only I could sequester
the presumption of my panic in isolating details, potential story elements,
before those details were saddled with and marred by that panic's bias
toward their essence I might end up living my story after all. I had to be
faster than the presumption of my panic in living among and sequestering
events. But the presence of Testic, père only exacerbated that panic that
threw me ever more headlong into the deformation of event. "My son used
to contradict me at every turn. Lou his name was. And I in turn
contradicted him at every turn. But now he is dead I find myself adopting
all the tics and points of view I repudiated in his lifetime precisely because
it is no longer a question of his appropriating a possibility—a course of
action long before I have made up my mind whether or not I might have
wanted independently to espouse that possibility. For when he was alive
how could I ever know that I would have espoused that possibility
independently of his espousing it. For when he was alive espousing *his*
possibility was always synonymous with giving him the malevolent
satisfaction of thinking I accepted my being as a being molded and
ravaged by the kind of being some prior choosing had allocated to my
capacity for immersion. I never considered thrashing my way past
thralldom to a being of my own. Lou completely overwhelmed me—flesh
of my flesh, loin of my loin—during his lifetime my being was always a
being because of/in spite of his ineptitude and injustice. But now that he
is gone, one with the waves and the rheumy rack, watch me with veritable

avidity acquire and succumb to those tics of jovial expansiveness that at every turn heretofore I spurned, for to have given way to them then, when Lou was alive, could only have been interpreted as a doing his bidding, natural spontaneity reduced to a wan mimicry. But if now I adopt his tics of jovial expansiveness I am no closer to authentic expansiveness—of which, and I am not saying this because Lou happens to be my son, he was an undisputed master—it is simply that after so much mourning, excruciation, torment, there is a craving to express for it is of the nature of man to express, to want to express and yet—thank heaven—it is no longer a question of my expressing first in imitation of his—Lou's—need always to have been expressing first not as I once so desperately wished to believe from despotism but from a gushing spontaneity in love with life that waits for no permission, no sanction, no...paradigm—it is not a question of my expressing first for now it is obviously I who am expressing first and feeling an authentic craving to express—and for once not because Lou has just chosen or not chosen to express always before me—it is only natural—it is only fitting—that I struggle to express with what is nearest to hand, namely, the interiorized paradigm for so long loathed and held in abeyance, comprising as my very own the very gestures—wrinkly, crepitant, shrill—always so strenuously, vociferously repudiated before. But now, of course, they are coming, these gestures, from me, not from him, and therefore there is no longer any fear of giving, through wan mimicry, satisfaction onto my lord and master and favorite son which giving satisfaction implies nothing so starkly and scandalously as that abased and obliterated one accepts one's fate, one's fate as it is, must be; one's being, as a being allocated, as a second thought, by another. For one of my ilk as I once was being was inconceivable as anything but a being handed down from another. And now that he is one with the sands there is no longer any need to reject the hand-me-down. So slowly you find me metamorphosing into the pitiful little ape of his ostensibly most loathed gestures—I speak of the man you killed—appropriating as my very dearest own what was his yet not even suspecting I am a thief, too obtuse to recognize larceny in all its glory, in its fullest bloom. Who then is the greater culprit, you or I? Who is the biggest perpetrator where my son is concerned?" I looked him straight in the eye. He met me without flinching. "I have been in communication with the police. They are obviously very proud of their theories where you are concerned. I don't pay much heed to their theories. As far as I can see, your relation with people is founded on a crying need, itself founded and foundering on a retaliatory rage antedating all conceivable provocation, for the other to evince a more and more extreme form of what you leap to construe as repudiation of your way of life specifically through ostensibly casual description of their or some other's way. You almost always—you must recognize this—goad, prick, spur, gudgeon, dupe, trepan, that other into ultimately thinking of you, their other, as a mere gateway, limit, threshold, to a better, a far better, version of your present self, mere embryon of vaster improvements, cipher of its own infinite amelioration, as it were, although it is never clear whether improvement consists of a mere quantitative enhancement of your properties or of a qualitative leap into alien terrain. You must recognize that you are the deceiver, the gay deceiver, leading them on to foresee in you the possibility—through your transformation—of their own infinite advancement. And why do you always end up in this predicament—goading the other? Isn't it because you are simply incapable of affirming yourself against the very natural affirmation of others? The self-proclamation that for them is birth, construction, enhancement, is for you annihilation, death. You can only suggest the achievement that leads to self-proclamation in the hope of bringing them to the verge of naming it—though the naming itself is a form of death." Looking at the waves he took out a little notebook to scribble what looked like a hieroglyph. "Frankly," he added, and his "frankly" made me quiver, "I do believe such a state of affairs cannot endure indefinitely and what is more it did not endure indefinitely. In short, one does his cohort in. One can take just so much strategizing across one's being as the map of an infinite, in other words impossible, self-improvement. One can go on just so long hungering to be named in one's infinite achievement and dreading that name. My son Lou was, I am sure, always the first to explore alien terrain. He was always, I am sure, the first to come back and tell you he had, for example, visited a port and found it sad. A bit sad, might be the phrase. The next day you probably ventured out—avid, I might add—though avid not for sun and sea but for the bit of terrain marred and erected by the phrase, a bit sad. You did not know how you expected to react, all you knew was that you were

ravenous to react—against Lou's reacting—to somehow trample and
surpass Lou's primary reaction as if it was, this primary reaction, his very
body and soul laid out flat across the port. You probably felt big and
brave, flamboyant and temerarious, a grade A stravaiger, forgetting that
it was thanks to Lou's primary venture that the port existed at all, carved
out of being. But you felt an infinite power emanating from the sense that
you were already pivoted, that your explorations had a fixed point
whence the tributaries were innumerable—which fixed point might be
easily marred and capsized and reviled, in the small, in the small, of
course, for in the large you desperately needed the pivot of the cohort's
primary verdict—you needed the already known, cradling the wary
traveler. But you got tired after a while of being always initially *and*
definitively surpassed and so you decided to kill your model. In short, in
short, in short"—he repeated the phrase as if intending to drive me mad—
"one does the cohort in, no matter who or what he is, better if he has a little
money and a camel's hair coat and a pair of tasseled loafers and an
identification bracelet purchased in Venice. But excuse me, excuse me,
excuse me," he said, waxing compassionate rather than apologetic, "if I
seem more diagrammatic than discursive, if I seem to be trying to capture
and formulate your reaction to an event—a state of affairs—long before
I have even begun to sketch that event—that state of affairs." He gave me
an idea. "I did not know your son, or rather, I knew him barely, through
Jim Jamms, the painter. In short, there is no state of affairs capable of
drawing both Testic—I mean, your son, Lou—and myself into its orbit.
But I can of course understand your eagerness to create an event—any
event—a state of affairs—any state of affairs—that plausibilizes the capture of his murderer. But the true event is not that against which you say
I react. The true event is your excoriation, destruction, annihilation of me
in advance of any event in which I might figure. The event, my good
doctor, the state of affairs, is not one encapsulating my relation to your
son, Lou, for there is no such event, or rather, there is such an event only
insofar as it constitutes the minimalized pretext for this relation—this
depiction—on your part of a strong man's fixed point—pivot—remorse-
lessly parasitized by the likes of me. You have tried to construct before my
very eyes a so-called unhealthy reaction to your son culminating in
murder, behaving as if you are concerned only with the unhealthiness of

that reaction rather than with the plausibility of a state of affairs on whose skewed adroit construction your indictment of the unhealthiness—the mammoth unhealthiness—hinges. There is no event—no state of affairs—where your son and I are concerned. It is your outraged reaction against the state of affairs that has created—plausibilized—the state of affairs, your recoil from the unhealthiness of my reaction has created that reaction so that in the long run and even in the short nothing is created, or rather, nothing beyond your proclaimed public disapproval of a phantom. You have created just enough of a situation to establish my motive in murdering your son." He did not seem to be following me: "Now I know exactly what happened and I intend to inform the police: You found—child of the gutter that you are—your old pal Testic quite easy to manipulate. After having drawn up a calculus of all situations capable of inducing his disapproval or repudiation or what you might construe as such, after generating those situations over and over from scratch—for your own viewing pleasure—the scratch, I say, of a tranquillity, a blessed domesticity—for I am under no illusions with regard to the nature of your friendship—that so easily might have been yours forever—you simply could no longer survive the shock of your own potency, your ability to manhandle your cohort, to govern the rhythm of his disapproval. His disapproval was of course the obligagory grit in your erotic machine. So what you began trying was to formulate and capture his reaction to your latest outrage long before you had even begun to sketch it, or rather, you sketched just enough—through gesture—through the obscene gestures of those you must have recruited to enliven your own—to plausibilize your indictment of the kind of reaction that judging from past experience it might very well induce in one of Lou's character. You needed just enough of an excuse for a plausible anticipation of that kind of reaction to elucidate and feed your hunger to indict it. And you supplied the shred of an excuse in the form of a minimalized pretext cum state of affairs replete with degenerates, hermaphrodites, jaded scion of the filthy rich, etc. You were never interested in his reaction, always predictable and traditional—the reaction, we might say, of the traditional theatergoer. What you craved was dissection of your own hunger for that traditional reaction embodying the kind of validation from which you—a less traditional man of the theater, or so you think—wished to free yourself.

No, no, no, you created—fed him—situations—states of affairs—shredded tableaux vivants—not because you were particularly interested in living them—and certainly not with the likes of my son—but in order to . dissect and flay your own impatient hunger for what was certain, from him, to be a traditional, in other words tripe-laden, response—reaction—to—being in—the situation. The flaying of your own impatient hunger for this—traditional tripe-laden reaction—your hunger caught in the act before it or its satisfaction could feed any further the excruciating and intolerable sham of the situation—this was to be the theatrical event as far as you were concerned. You were never interested in Lou's reaction to situations—to life itself. You were interested in analyzing—denigrating and thereby (since we are in the world of the theater) exalting—your hunger for that reaction." "And you are doing exactly what you accuse me of doing. You are busy formulating my reaction to a given situation before you have even begun sketching that situation." "When you were with my son Lou you were interested in one thing and one thing only: to produce a situation, or rather, situation after situation, that could be depended on to flay your impatient hunger for Lou's tradition-laden response—to expose hunger and response as symptoms of a bloated global inauthenticity with respect to which you had appointed yourself avenging angel. And this inauthenticity was of course very much bound up with the hunger to elicit not only the proper tradition-ridden response from my son but via that tradition-ridden response the adulation of millions of hovering witnesses. The situation under consideration, as it were, became—becomes—nothing more than a pretext—caught on the wing—for excoriating your own base use of such a situation—for eliciting the adulatory grief and joy of the millions. And through this excoriation of your own base use of millions you of course hoped to reach an even wider audience—billions. So that the situation—the procession of situations—events—states of affairs—never comprised in the least your relation to your cohort or bed companion or his to you or even such mighty and minute things as wavelets falling over rocks but rather your attempt through its—the situation's—shreds to induce that particular tradition-laden response capable of highlighting most glaringly—most scandalously—excoriating most trenchantly—with most dazzling analytic brilliance—your hunger for that particular tradition-laden response as pathway to the adulation of millions. For you were — are — convinced that by excoriating that hunger you open yourself up to the adulation as I just said of...billions. You pretended with my poor son to be *in the situation* when you were always very much on the fringe peeping in so as to be ready at a moment's notice to seize his reaction (tradition-ridden, tradition-laden) as your personal property, your personal...specimen. He should have known that you would never give him what he sought because like all pygmies you cannot bear to prostrate yourself in front of a superior soul. From the minute you are able to identify the rapture that superior soul induces you feel capable of trampling and discarding it. Anything his uniqueness — anything his beauty — induced in you was immediately discardable, jettisoned in the name of your need to travel light. Instinctively loathing and misprizing anything connected with your own depths you understandably felt authorized to misprize my son's uniqueness as indistinguishable from the stirrings it produced in those depths." We walked onward. "As long as you were with him you produced nothing but a bare minimum of situation — propless, without localizable decor — necessary for luring him into your glaring absence of such depths." I could only wonder if the story was not in fact homologous: a bare minimum of shreds needed to produce reactions of a certain type but in, from, whom. And assuming that in spite of every conceivable drawback and contretemps the story never stopped advancing on its own extinction how isolate that minimum of shreds producing through thick and thin the requisite propulsive spasms... Without being aware we seemed to have come full circle for here, in hotel's backyard, playground of the idle rich, were wife and daughter — Testic's dear sister and dearer mother — a bit too zealously, at least for my taste or absence of same, waving to catch our attention as they sat sipping some concoction that looked, from the way it was packaged — we inhabit the golden — copper — age of the package — with ribbons and shards of tropical garnish — like one of the supreme specialties of the house. Onward and onward and onward went our walking though we were very much standing still before the venerable wife and daughter, the little ladies, proclaiming through every glance, every shift in posture, their adoration of this the man of the house back home in —. It was their adoration NO

that made me realize NO NO NO NO for the

NO first
NO
NO
first no no time

that much as I might detest his huge income, white shoes, white belt, blazer, sideburns, tinted glasses, impeccable gold rims, auburny tresses combed dutifully over and athwart bulbous bald spot, silk socks, —much as I might very well detest all these appurtenances signifying wealth, leisure, hard work deserving of a playing dutifully at leisure, good citizenry enjoying the fringe benefits of the good citizen — much as I might detest the fact that he was impeccably, ruddily clean, looking as if every sparse hair on his body had been individually bathed and powdered —I had still to recognize the doctor was a storyteller—he too was a story-teller—striving to construct his story as he went along as I mine and so why not, even if neither of us would ever consider officially stooping to the ignominy of a full-fledged pooling of efforts, each try imbibing those characteristic features of the other's production in such a way as to embellish and festoon his own. Here was one—and who would have thought it from the way he dressed—looked—spoke—at least at table for out in the windy sea air his tone, I had to admit, participated in a ruddier more all-embracing element and to spellbinding effect—here was one, a grade-A storyteller who rather than concentrate on constructing situations of a plausible grandeur or a plausible pathos or plausible palette worthy of sunset preferred to smoke out and flay—the flaying then becoming the true situation—the hunger to embark on construction of such situations. The situation then became—did the situations, if any, constituting my story line meet these exalted specifications?—that is, if I understood him properly and I think I did, not the plausible specimen regurgitated oh so infinitely many times before but whatever prospect of undying adulation drove him to collude with his colleagues and witnesses—whatever prospect of apotheosis drove him to embark at any given moment on—in—pursuit of a situation familiar and reassuring for all its trappings of crisis and hysteria because concocted of the basest stuffs of traditional artifice. And so the rage of ingenuity usually lavished by storytellers on the erection of the key situation was instead in his case not lavished but rather squandered amid curses and guffaws on straightforward interrogation of the need to erect—to have erected—in the name of inducing a specific time-honored reaction among colleagues and witnesses productive of undying fame—that situation. So that the key situation for him—my pursuer, Testic's father, the good doctor—though hadn't Testic remarked that his father was a leading industrialist?—was not the key—the parent—situation never come to birth—but the sum of whatever byproducts and end results could be claimed and retrieved from the restless, ever restless, raging interrogation of the hunger for that key—that parent—situation never come to birth. Here was the born storyteller, here was one who, though his primary impulse was lyrical—though his primary aim was to win over his opponents—all those he despised and who prodigally returned the favor in kind—to rapture faster than they might succeed in branding and loathing him for the overtness of that effort—here was one, then, who, whatever the primary impulse, was plighted secondarily, tertiarily, and so on and so forth, to the far more supreme task of interrogating that impulse, that aim, thereby gelding all its—the impulse's, the aim's—future attempts to inform, generate, saturate, obliterate, a plausible situation able through the basest artifice of winning the hearts of the millions, better, billions. For if done properly didn't such gelding interrogation promise the undying love of trillions? Here was one, in other words, the good doctor, yet who would ever have dreamed it to be so? who, completely unfazed by a petty capacity for situation construction not much different from the most banausic of talents—construction of scrimshaw situations, that is, assured of achieving a desired, that is to say, a tired, that is to say, an infinitely repeatable and always calculable effect—preferred instead to unleash—to lavish—his savagery on the hunger—the drama—behind this puny need to create the ostensible drama—the plausible situations. He was most create, most himself—whatever that was—putting far from his hunger but close to his unflinching scrutiny—what the latter easily identified as—through made-to-order regurgitation of a situation already known—too well known albeit bedecked with a thrift shop bric-a-brac denotative of novelty—identified as a loving relation with the spectator—the hovering witness. Yes, he had come to recognize that this hunger to be admired and applauded was the strongest component of what he had long before repudiated as his personality and so his most fetching effects of fertile research were now understandably pivoted about situations on the verge of being but never quite erected to procure the admiration and applause. His most fetching contortions were generated by—in—spasms aimed at catching base attempts to generate such situations in the act. I was beginning to see him differently and truth be told to like what I saw. So what if he went on daring to plaster me with all sorts of traits and tics designed not so much to clarify my plight as keep its construed contagion at a distance—from him and his loved ones. Hadn't old lady Jamms spoke of a certain tendency to scotoma on the part of the old family doctor? So what if his construction of my being threatened to tarnish the image I was needing so desperately to cultivate and convey if I was to survive the prying of the detectives. Hadn't old lady Jamms attempted to encourage her son—to train him—to make use of these scotomata, to transform them into a concentrated nisus, motor, lever, hub, refractor, through and by which to more than view—to live—the world—to use the blind spot, the falsified conception of himself, as a cudgel with which to wreak havoc on the stuff of being. Yes, I could see that to be the doctor's solitary blind spot—he saw to the kernel of truth in everything else—surf, gusts, sand—was to be blessed—singled out for election, was certainly more helpful than to be properly named and filed away for proper naming is indistinguishable from annihilation. I was his blind spot—he was still convinced I had killed his son or that at the last moment I had recoiled from that inevitability. Consequently, I had something to work for—or rather, the delusion of working toward his enlightenment or greater benightedness—and this delusion could then be depended upon to mask my efforts in behalf of something wider, far far wider, than whether or not he saw me as I truly was. Before we parted and in front of wife and daughter he remarked that I was obviously living in the shadow of a terrible memory. "Memory of a symptom unleashed upon the world." "And the world became blood and decay," I added, turning to the space between wife and daughter, at first smirkingly and then, as the words came like wave upon wave, with greater and greater somber delight in their accuracy. I was about to admit that I was obliged to provoke over and over that terrible hunger—that terrible symptom—so that I was not overwhelmed by the sense—equally terrible—of having trespassed for nothing, gratuitously, in an absence of all hunger. For once the hunger

was slaked and the symptom appeased—as after the murder of his son—
then all I tended to remember was the superfetatory grimness of the
trespass and nothing of the stark urgency of the hunger—the symptom—
the symptomatic hunger to survive that necessitated the trespass. But it
was best I admitted nothing. It was best I was not tempted to allow myself
to be carried away by this good fellowship, all too drearily typical of the
verge of departure, into baring my deepest pulsions. He would be sure to
make the necessary connection of trespass—symptom—symptomatic
hunger—with his son's murder. I announced that soon I would be
leaving—question of a little financial matter to clear up. I held forth on the
cruel urgency of having to leave this world behind but then I stopped,
stopped defending my going, I was not being attacked, so why, so how,
defend, how defend when one's interlocutor and entourage are not only
not attacking but if they were to take it into their head to attack would
make it their business to be speaking always to a space a little to the right
or left of the one one might have very well occupied if only one had not
been definitively worn down too many times by the expectation of just
such a speaking, to right or left. I moved slowly away, in the greenish air,
though by moving away I was clearly inviting him to maraud me, resume
his diagnosis, catch me in a contradiction sure to blow me to kingdom
come, but this time he refused, did me instead a far greater disservice by
diagnosing everything around me, everything I was about to leave behind
forever, a world he too found strange though so much better able to
survive the assault of its dregs. I was about to commend his being as if it
was the impeccable cut of a tailor-made garment, though it was probably
the slant and fall of the light that was, after all and all things considered,
no better than a miserly dilution through scrim after scrim after scrim.
The sea was dead, time to return to my room and pack for the detectives
calling me homeward. Walking to the elevator with him was like undergoing a visitation not that he embodied the visitation, oh no, rather his
presence—he waddled, yes indeed, I saw it now—somehow permitted
the visitation—struggling as it emerged to draw off all sense of shame into
its poison, known conversationally as sense of self. And I was aston-
ished—in the astonishment was the beginning of strength—at how for so
long I had tried in vain to fight off this shame. I fought to keep the
visitation. For didn't I need a strong sense of self in confronting the

detectives once more? I tried to prepare myself in the suturing presence of this man—this being—who at once exalted and repudiated me on all fronts, those facing and not facing the greenish air of the sea. "Going back," he murmured. "To face the music," even more inaudibly. Was it with a hint of sorrow: I nodded, more at the closing elevator doors than at him. His wife emerged from shadow and said, "I have to go back too." This image of his wife emerging from shadow...did not matter, knew it did not matter, awaiting as it was the complement with which it had nothing in common so that from the nuptials might be born neither image nor non-image but rather some belated alluvium of the moment. Two day laters I arrived back in New York: in Penn Station sometimes—depending on my position in space and time—the odor of no longer freshly baked doughnuts overcame that of piss emanating from the sprawled vagrants and sometimes not. Sometimes there was an odor of piss overcoming doughnut and sometimes of doughnut overcoming piss and sometimes there was an overcoming neither by one nor the other but rather a simple cohabitation that drove me to the verge of fainting. A woman was screaming at her husband, evidently tardy, as their child stood by embarrassed. Theirs was the life I had missed, true life, enemy to the story, true or not, for such a life could not be disfigured into the moments synonymous with the intelligible unfolding of a story; such a life—so monolithic an embodiment of reality—could not be expected to resolve itself into the dew of incident succeeding upon incident. I missed the sea, maybe not, maybe my fear of contending once again with the detectives was now undergone as a nostalgia for the striped red and blue. I didn't remember my bedroom window giving on a parking lot where strange outcries could be heard, worse, their direst implications undergone, at all hours of the night. I decided to take a room for just one night in the hotel where Jamms, Colletti, and I had staged our interview. As I rode up in the elevator with my overnight bag, shoulder-looped raincoat, and tasseled loafers, a woman, young but prematurely aged, got in at some intermediate floor. She wore a fur coat draped around her pretty bare shoulders and putting her hand on my thigh asked if before reaching my floor I mightn't like what she referred to as a little *****. I looked around apprehensively: as if addressing what she had seen many times before on many many faces said, "I can stop this machine any time I want: I'm a friend of the manager." The curve of her naked thigh through a slit in the fur was lacerating especially after the painful discovery that I too had a thigh which painful discovery retrospectively unearthed and framed — even more painful — a blithe prior unconsciousness of that thigh. I changed my position in the elevator so as to be able to stumble on that thigh — hers — from another position. I was less lacerated by the thigh *presented* from this other position. And yet, as I wandered from position to position (radical disjunction between the wandering and the amount of time actually available for such a wandering) in the last analysis the superfetation of perspectives always less virulent did little to diminish the thigh's initial shock of virulence. The initial perspective of the initial thigh was as haunting as ever, as indifferent as ever to my fascinated slobbering before its broad autonomy. Just before the phone rang — I had left a brief message of greeting at the precinct — I became entranced or convinced myself I was becoming entranced with the blue of the sky through huddling budding branches. I submitted to a delirium which is the closest my kind ever comes to hope — to happiness — a feeling that was best left, however, to die untenanted since there was no foreseeing it — especially with the police on their way — translated into concrete action. When they arrived I was more myself than Jamms, all the swagger and aplomb of the painterly Jamms seemed gone, forever. Perhaps I could reappropriate it gradually when all this was over but in stepwise increments. The younger said, "You hurried back. You hurried back." I waited. He looked as if he had prepared something to say, suggested still only dimly by present circumstances though not quite plausibilized, at least not as much as he would like, and he was trying to intimidate me into making the move that would provide the pretext for intrusion of this prepared shred. He was close, I could sniff him sniffing, though not close enough, and daring me to step away from the having hurried back. "You hurried back, hurried back, afraid we would think you had done wrong or afraid to have left some telltale sign of wrongdoing." He was even closer now. "But of course all this hurry, or rather, terror that we might find a name for the hurry is conceivable only within the context of an otherwise spotless past and present. The life chronology is spotless but for this one telltale stain. So you are running back here less to save yourself than to somehow resurrect the spotlessness. Or so you would have us believe." He looked at his comrade: he must feel he was hypnotizing me most skillfully by keeping his eye on his comrade. I looked away, raged, wanted to know more, much more, about this being in quest of a spotless past, though I did not want to seem to be trying to extract more information. The figure who had hurried back—me and not me—was legitimated by my credulity but differently, or so I needed to think, from the way he had intended. They asked why I had moved from my apartment. I explained that I was here in the hotel for only a night or two: crossing a parking lot on which here too my window gave was a man holding a package. He looked inside as he walked, stopping short rummaged with two fingers of the same hand, middle and fore- , I think, then doubled up and hurried back in the direction whence he had come. And this image—of a man hurrying back—coming toward me at so crucial a juncture in my own life—this image spilling the exhilarating transparency of unambiguous meaning halfway out of its backside—filled me with the joy that comes of at last adhering to the world through collaboration in the extraction of meaning against all odds as they might be, for example, contrived by the alternately tightlipped and venomously loquacious speculations of a younger policeman trying to *make his name in the company* over my dead body. This image—with its powerful because easily extractable meaning leaking out its backside—this phenomenon—seemed powerful enough to obliterate the image—story event—deduction—he—the younger, always the younger, with his discontented wife—was trying to impose on me. I hid behind the image or rather behind my adherence to the image or rather behind my interpretation of that image as it went about fighting off my oppressor with its lucidity. Had I ever known—participated in—such images with Jamms. They left, I watched them go, cross the parking lot, and all of life as I was now doomed to know it seemed to ooze away with them, as through a beveled wound. It grew dark in my room and I welcomed—as I never NO

NO never had in my own apartment NO—
the decorous combat of light and shadow, the zones of unexpectedly chirping luminosity in those areas—every room has them—engendered by one surface steering prophylactically clear of another. I indulged myself by going for a walk in the rain, under trees whose leaves cast shadows that were gustily insatiable of whatever asphalt has to offer of

porosity and glint. The younger must be calculating on a remorse more aesthetic than ethical to do me in. Now that the hunger to kill had been satisfied I must, according to him, be haunted by the sheer gratuitousness of the act(s). And what was this gratuitousness, as far as I was concerned, but an enormous blot on a hitherto unblemished past. And so he was counting on my purposefully resuscitating the symptom—the hunger—in order to remind myself—even if such a reminder ultimately handed me over to the authorities—its devastations had all been grounded in necessity. He was counting on my renewal of contact with the symptom—the hunger—to kill—as my sole means of intoxicating myself against the torment of sheer gratuitousness. In the domain of the hunger there was no room for gratuitousness—for thought of gratuitousness—even if the hunger—the symptom—was in the large no less gratuitous for all that. Who did he imagine would be my next victim when I began once more striving to stave off the horror-inducing aftertaste of symptom's gratuitousness through further embranglement in its meshes. They were both counting, I suddenly decided under a sudden and insidious drizzle, on the monumental parapraxis of an attempt to stave off aftertaste, aftermath, of symptomal gratuitousness with yet another interpellation of its—symptom's—ironclad necessity. They were both counting on my failure once—as now—the symptom was dimmed and slaked—to perceive just how near it still was even if there were no immediate signs simply because I happened to have been let down in a kind of sunlit clearing, spent and trembling, from whose vantage symptoms must necessarily have all the consistency of hobgoblins. They were both counting on inevitable relapse in the face of my overweening terror of the void—a void festooned with the gratuitous havoc wreaked by its—the symptom's—low disregard for things like rectitude and order—left by its imaginary extinction and inveigling me into presuming there was absolutely nothing worse than such terror, least of all the symptom's resurgence as a means of reestablishing contact with the certainty of its coercive necessity. Or perhaps they assumed I would want to reestablish contact with the symptom—the hunger—in order to examine—explore it—as a specimen—either of gratuitousness or non-gratuitousness. Return to the symptom, then, was a return to experiment, or so they must think I thought. Inevitably, then, I would stumble and fall through a combination of authentic symptomal hunger renewing itself and a lazy accidie-ridden craving to test and challenge and berate and punish its —the symptom's— sheer gratuitousness, its scandalous lack of any core of driving necessity. Back in the bosom of the symptom they would be able to trap me. Not here, through mere chitchat, but back at the scene of the crime, the scene being the symptom. And no doubt they were also counting on my lack of imagination, my refusal to believe that even if once craved—as the only conceivable testing ground of its iron-clad necessity or rather of the ironclad necessity of the act to which it had given rise—the symptom could be staved off, gratuitous or not, through manly praxis. They were counting, I knew, I knew, on my belief that the symptom—the hunger— the craving—the need to kill—was supremely resistant to any kind of characterologic insect repellent. They were counting on my vision of the symptom as forever imposed from without.

The next time the police called on me only the elder arrived. It was easier in the presence of one and that the elder's—the fact that I was installed once again in my apartment also helped—to announce that I was planning another voyage. I asked where his companion was keeping himself, knowing he must bristle at so flagrant an effort to change the subject yet not caring. "Home," he replied, "with the wife." "She must be charming," I said, "for he is quite attractive." The elder shrugged but not slackly. "She tries to disseminate hope," he remarked taking a seat. "She is always trying to disseminate hope and in many ways is always disseminating hope even if in many ways dissemination of hope is but an exasperated outcry not so veiledly soliciting consensual zeal regarding her right to hope, to go on hoping, assailed incessantly as she is by her own nameless demons, for a better future, their better future, lest that future shrivel up and take the form prophesied by the demons—hers and in a mimicking but no less—perhaps far more—malevolent manner his—to whose ranks, by the way, I have been relegated. His demons wish her well by and large only she has needed to warp them into perfectly well-behaved little simulacra of her own. For she has found that it is easier to denounce his—her demons' ubiquity do not allow much of a foothold in denunciation. When all is said and done perhaps we may most accurately say she is convinced she is disseminating hope especially in the wake of his widening lag. To a certain extent she is correct: he is losing hope." He

looked at me piercingly as if to say, If you do not confess and fast he'll lose
not only his wife but his promotion. I thought of Maggy. As far as I was
concerned she was far more suited for the role of the wife. "Oh, it is no
accident that she married my young partner. For she must have known
that in the presence of his undemandingness, which at the beginning of
any relation is never interpreted as a diabolic wet blanket thrown on all
one's hopes for the future but a beautifully uncircumscribed arena of
freedom in which hope may ripen at its own rate and with no verdicts of
inadequacy and ineptitude—however justified—tossed into the pit to
confound and disorient the ripener—she must have known that in the
presence of his undemandingness, his sheer indifference to the needs of
the world—need to need and need to desire to need—she could quin-
tessentially flower until, that is, it became necessary for him plausibly to
assume the role of one or all of her demons consecrated to the capsizing
of achievements so dearly won. So in the gradual deployment of her latent
skills and desire for skill stronger than any skill he began to shrink
understandably obliged to interpret all this ubiquitous alacrity of hope as
nothing more than an excruciated impatience of vengeful mortification
pent up through eons and taking as target: How they—the demons—now
the old—now the new, namely, he, his family, his humble antecedents,
and I, the elder colleague, the mentor, the bad influence through my
merest presence on the scene—how they—the demons—could dare, had
dared, could go on daring, having dared might take it into their skulls to
go on daring—to brainwash her into believing she was not entitled to
enjoy those fruits of somebody's labor they themselves consumed as a
matter of bloody course. Don't you see, long before he ever met her—long
before she ever met herself—she had been castrated in her need, her right
to desire to need, and now, thanks to the breathing space permitted her
by his genial ease—which she was soon to insist on interpreting as
indifference, abandonment—she was able to achieve the erection of her
phallus of desire in no small measure engorged by a hunger for revenge—
a retroactive exasperation—for having dutifully allowed a terrified credulity in the face of her—yes her and hers alone—demons' strictures—
strictures as governing structure—to interfere for so long with engorge-
ment and erection of that desire to need to need. Sensing that it was not
so much the ridicule and contempt of her demons but her own willing

credulity responsible for so much stunting of the desire to need only increased her rage toward the most flagrant demon of them all—him— who had somehow or other—especially over the millennia when he was not known to her or she to him—managed to feed and enforce that credulity and was therefore retrospectively and prospectively respon- sible for all her misery—responsible beyond the pinpointing of mere responsibility. In the shadow of his support, the wide circle of enfran- chisement implied by his own repudiation of the desire to need to need— in the shadow of this subvention she has been able promptly to forget why and when she had ever been credulously intimidated by her multifarious demons. The temerariousness induced by his propinquity has allowed her to cut the cables connecting her to intimidation and now she finds she has only curses for the gratuitousness—yes, the pure gratuitousness"—was he eyeing me more and more suspiciously, or rather, with a triumph that proclaimed the need for suspiciousness was at an end?—"of that mutilat- ing intimidation. His—her eternal tormentor's—subvention has permit- ted—is permitting—her to undergo the wild freedom of confusing sub- sidizer with tormentors past and in this way she is spared having to contend with the apparent gratuitousness in—alienness of—a prior self's lacerated credulity. So we are dealing here once again"—again, he seemed to be eyeing me suspiciously—"with a case of the phantom gratuitousness of authentic essence resolved through resuscitation of tormentors past as benefactors present. Haunted by a sense of the gratuitousness of torments past—this sense of gratuitousness possible, of course, only in the shadow of authentic security furnished by an authentic mentor which security has for better or worse permitted her—permits her—to undergo infirmity past as incomprehensible and alien, uncon- nected with any microenvironmental or behavioral or characterological necessity—she decides—has decided—to kill her ostensible tormentor— actually her benefactor—subsidizer—whose only crime has been to show her a dazzling alternative to the intimidation she once unremittingly knew—but slowly, little by little, as we have seen. And this is why it is so important for us to extract a confession from the murderer of Testic and/ or Jamms—we are sure Jamms also is dead. For once we, or rather he— all the credit must go to him—has extracted this confession the tenor of his conjugal hell must necessarily change for the better. That is, if he

himself has not been too irreversibly worn down by his wife's vindictive-
ness. Do you understand what it means to be worn down by another's
vision of gratuitous suffering? Rather than face and scuttle the flotsam of
her past she prefers to go on holding him responsible for continuing to
pull—and from the outset, from the outset, from the outset and well
before that—the strings of her debilitating credulity—for now, in the
comforting shadow of his emboldening subvention when she summons
forth—as a lark—sweet remembrance of that credulity it seems—severed from a context of abuse and abasing intimidation—so easily done
away with, so easily excised, and knowing it now—only now—so easily
excisable how can she not give way to tormenting herself, in other words,
him, for not having done away with it then, way back then, from the very
start, long before the very start began to start, and thereby sidestepping
all that ensued of torment, torment, torment. Yes, my partner, gentlest of
men, is responsible for damning not only her past but her future too,
through his otiosity, venomous perversity, in refusing to budge from the
site where his slumridden forbears oh so complacently and wallowingly
and a trifle belligerently insist on carrying on to this day. Isn't it likely,
then, that Jamms or Testic became the target of your vengefulness along
the same lines? Or perhaps feeling yourself to be the target of their
vengefulness along these same lines you decided to strike first. Unlike my
partner you refused to go on turning and turning and turning the other
cheek. I applaud you for your audacity. Like you with respect to those
swells, Testic and Jamms, my poor partner came to his wife, so he
thought, completely divested—expressly or not—of his past, his past
roots, experiencing such a denudation as a gift, a homage to her supreme
influence and importance. But like Testic and Jamms she smelled them
out—she smoked them out—these severed roots and reproached him for
not sharing them with her at the same time that these very roots were
dragged through the streets as embodying a decree—no less heinous for
being veiled—that she follow in the footsteps of all they deployed of
degradation, abasement, mire. And he, my poor partner, has been
consistently hard pressed to respond to these particularly harsh accusa-
tions that are, in some measure, cries for reassurance. You see, my
assistant's—I mean my colleague's—wife, like all little bourgeois ladies—
excuse me for 'assistant'—he was never my assistant—term is degrading,

far more degrading, than her maltreatment of same—like all little bourgeois ladies at the drop of a hat tended and tends to interpret every state
of affairs as a crowding her out and finding this possibility unbearable
makes it a habit of soothing herself by taking her interpretation to its
extreme point in order that she may be heard and understood. For if she
in any way acknowledges the tentativeness—that is to say, the delusional
nature—of her formulation she may not be heard at all. So she exagger-
ates—as Jamms and Testic must have exaggerated so that their venality
and hysteria might be heard above the level of your transcendent
equanimity—of which they were both so enamored. And my assistant, I
mean my colleague, being highly suggestible for all his pretenses of a
bovine placidity, takes the extreme formulation—highly tentative, extreme only, remember, for purposes of audibility—for the definitive
verdict on a phenomenon he is not even sure exists but which all of a
sudden exists incontestably and in its most extreme form. And this is what
occurred as a result of the Testic case or the Jamms case. As a result of
his total immersion in the facts of the case—or absence of same—she has
consistently felt crowded out even if on the success of his performance in
these cases hinges not merely the success but the possibility of their future
together. Perhaps as a result of her gnawing resentment he—in other
words, we—have not been placing the emphasis where we should or
might have. But of course we cannot excise her more and less than
marginal participation in the investigation as if it were—her participation—an easily expendable contingency. At any rate, whether or not her
verdict—her extreme formulation—concerning the case is true or not
he—driving force in the unfolding of the case—has been willy-nilly
overcome by the force of her delivery synonymous now—whether we like
it or not—with final and definitive and irrevocable perception of things
as they were meant to evolve. And what does he do, my partner, my
cowering partner? He succumbs. How? By raging and rebelling—
inwardly, of course—against the inevitable. And of course there are two
currents in the course of his rage. On the one hand he feels powerless
against her formulation of their predicament—which is now indistinguishable from the predicament of the case—to the extent that he allows
himself to undergo that formulation as definitive and immutable and irrevocable. On the other, he is enraged that she has, once again, quite

obviously—quite venomously—sidestepped by jettisoning or vice-versa the more obvious, less extreme, ultimately truer formulation. Yet because of his own constitutional revulsion for the obvious—to say nothing of his paralysis in the face of her infinitely potent delivery of extreme formulations—less obvious—less true—because of his own constitutional revulsion in the face of the obvious and his even greater revulsion in the face of stating the obvious he is the last man in the world to easily appropriate the more obvious, the more true and present it in his own—in our—in the case's defense. In other words, all he would have to say is something like, Of course we will not end up like Testic and Jamms. Or, Of course my slum-ridden relation of whom you are so fond will never end up like Testic and Jamms. Or, of course we will have our charming little suburban villa somewhere on a hilltop smothered in yellow Tuscan roses whose heady profusion is, as everybody knows, reminiscent of the best Broadway boutiques. That is all he is required to say. In fact, if only he were able to do what I have learned to do only through bitter experience, namely, to take this kind of extreme formulation in this case, hers, his wife's—like the extreme formulation of a detective accusing an innocent suspect of murder"—Was he staring at me piteously?—"as a test prompting and tempting him to manfully take possession of the more obvious and true and by formulating it straightforwardly at last divest himself of the last shadow hanging over the paralysis he calls his life. But as I have indicated, he is no friend to the obvious, most true or only more. And as he loathes the obvious—frequently the first refuge of scoundrels—and is at the same time mesmerized by the urgency of her formulation of its polar opposite— as he is tragically caught in dread in the face *both* of her distorted presentation of their life and by extension of the case—our case—your case—a presentation transmogrified into a feeble frightened anamorphic outcry for reassurance Byzantine in its mendacities *and* of his own extreme loathing of the obvious—his tendency to undergo sodomization by the merest proximity of the obvious—is it any wonder he ends up a walking shadow. On the one hand he believes what her outcry tells him about their life together—about the case—for he is a susceptible soul— susceptible to phenomena and what phenomenon more virulent and unrelenting than her utterance—her delivery. On the other hand though he suspects that her utterance is a delirious falsification he is powerless in the face of his only weapon—the countering utterance of the opposing obvious. He is afraid—and that is his failing not only as detective but as man—man among men and man among women—of what will happen if he sets foot in the obvious." He rose. "But this is why somebody like my partner becomes a cop: Investigation—unrelenting and bombarded by revilement—is an element alien to his own. In the case, therefore, he is far from himself, forever on the high seas, forever taking more than he is able to give back in coherence and lucidity. A partner like mine was created not once and for all but is created anew at every moment. To say nothing of his spontaneous sympathy for the most obvious suspect." He fell. He rose again. "And how can he not sympathize being one who knows better than anyone that life imprisons and sodomizes when it senses the dimmest penchant for captivity—taking out of storage her long hard dick and thrusting it in, over and over and over again, rupturing time after time until there is only a kind of bloody ichor of anal resistance oozing from the psychic pores for the kind of captive we are talking about, you and I, I mean, never really submits even if, out of habit, and long before he smells the flab of the engorged organ, the flayed buttocks are squarely bared. But why do I go on boring you with these tales of domestic woe, especially now, when you have very kindly agreed to keep us posted regarding your whereabouts. Apparently Mrs. Jamms will be calling upon you shortly regarding the disappearance of her son. Old man Testic just committed suicide. Old man Jamms has also died recently but of natural causes."

The next day after receiving a telegram I prepared to *fly out for the funeral*, the expression buoyed me up, of old man Jamms, dead at last. As I prepared to leave, packing and dressing, I felt I was doing his bidding in participating in the scenario—the anecdote—Jamms had resolutely forsworn to the bitter end. I moved gingerly, wishing to remain unswervingly tangent to the curve of those sensations and sentiments Jamms would have been sure to undergo on this occasion and which the occasion though still embryonic was already abetting. After an only partially successful bowel movement I finished dressing, not feeling in the least like grieving, only a boundless exhilaration as if the haze shrouding all the skyscrapers up and down Sixth Avenue had been scraped away forever. Boundless exhilaration yet no channel for its exercise except grief. And yet no desire to grieve. In the funeral parlor NO

          there was NO NO NO NO NO NO NO NO NO
an obligation to grieve as one by one fat people presented themselves
expecting me to bury my tears in their flab. NO. Untrue. None of them
cared whether or not I was grieving because they were all too busy
looking painedly appropriate to the occasion. So I was — I am — obliged
to relinquish this false meaning, this stillbirth of the meaning-mongers.
Yet just when I was — am — about to relinquish what seemed like the only
conceivable meaning consilient with a chain of events I find that relin-
quishment is debouching on another a better, meaning, even if this
second, ostensibly better, meaning is yet another hysterical heightening
of possible meaning lest the event obliged — if it is to exist — to mean — lest
the event be lost through a penury of meaning, worn-out and factitious,
like all meaning. But I found — find — that the second meaning: That I did
not have to grieve because the others were all too busy wondering
whether they themselves looked sufficiently grieving, is superior to the
first: Even if I felt no hunger there was an obligation to grieve as fat people
came up one after the other expecting me to bury my tears in their flab.
For the first meaning tried — tries — to win me for me a certain worn out
heroism. I am he — Jamms or other — who, in the midst of a perfect fealty
to the spontaneity of his own feelings, or rather absence of same, is
solicited from all directions to blubber the inauthentic gestures appropriate to the vicinity of death.

          Before the mourners arrived, Mrs. Jamms requested that I take
a look in the coffin, a good-looking one, to be sure, to make sure it was
truly he, her husband, father of Jim. And it was he, fully dressed, cheeks
sunken even further than during the interminable death throes. The hat
on the head produced an ungainly pathos, and since nobody else claimed
the right to have a peek, became our little secret, ours alone. I subtracted
the hat: without it he was as if just laid out. But with the hat he was as if
presenting himself or as if being presented by another but according to his
very own specifications making a point of surviving him or as if presenting that other's claim to having done a good job in presenting him as that
other had assumed — with a few helpful hints from the dear undeparted —
he would have wished to present himself. Yes, yes, yes, the hat made it
clear that he was presenting not himself but somebody's conception of
that self. The sunken cheeks under the hat implied the beginning of, or

rather preparation for, a little speech. The hat confirmed the streetwise acuity in eloquence of somebody forever on the go. This final dress rehearsal was presenting him as he wished to be remembered and I—not Jamms—had been chosen to undergo his crucial vulnerability in attempting such a presentation—vulnerability, that is, from the vantage of my power to accept or reject or reject on any number of levels: I had it in my power to reject the finished product with hat or the absurdity of his attempting to present a finished product at all. I experienced the hemorrhoidal surge of my only partially successful bowel movement at the moment when the man of the cloth imported and primed for the occasion—the occasion being an eulogy for somebody he did not know from Adam—spoke of the good god breathing life into the immortal clay or clay into the immortal strife or foreclosing at last the clay of mortal strife. As Jamms I thought, Maybe I will come to love in death this man whose recoil from what I needed to take to be my uncompromising strangeness shifted to amazed contempt for—against—what showed no signs of abatement. As Jamms, though Jamms had not been present, I thought back to the moment when I knew for certain he was dead even if at first the end seemed no more final than the end of yet another bout, paroxysm of breaths spaced more and more widely in the name of self-conservation. I vowed to return again and again to this ultimate moment so as, participating in its ultimacy, to buoy myself up against such petty irritants as the now almost daily visits of the detectives. I looked at Mrs. Jamms, separated from me by several pews. She looked as if she was still questioning her man's dying tics and symptoms as if they had been fabricated purposely to torment and perplex her—as if these tics were gratuitous and therefore excisable and solely, singlehandedly, responsible for exacerbating—nay, inventing—a situation that otherwise would have been indistinguishable from the everyday, the normal. She begrudged him his tics. I looked forward to looking back—as Jamms, always as Jamms—on the especially enraging memory of his making, toward the end and beyond, absolutely no effort to differentiate the two of us, mother and son, as if the imminence of death loaned him the effrontery to state his real perception, namely, that we were, had all along been, indistinguishable: an indistinguishable—a detestable—dyad fit only for the tergiversations of the nosocomial hell. Clearly he had never even dimly perceived the seismic, magma-laden repercussions of my efforts to distinguish myself from her, to construct of her a being my loathing could self-protectingly speak to without—as she leaped toward every word—a diminution in self-respect. Passing on the way out I took a last look at the bloated fingers and toes that suggested the ideal proband's habitus, moral type, vastly different from the one I—Jamms—had all along known—a type less severe, alertly judging. I vowed to remember the bloating as his only way of restraining his contempt toward me. I vowed to remember—as Jamms, as Jamms—the temporary jolt of exultation—where was it, in the hospital elevator I think, at the very moment when the orderly bringing dinner to the terminal ward pushed from him the tiered trays on casters as both an expression of contempt for what he was obliged to do day in, day out, *and* a mere and mammoth display of aesthetic prowess—when I realized he was too far gone—but was he ever too far gone?—to scrutinize what until the very end he insisted was my ever-widening, ever-descending ineptitude rendered even more intolerable by my artistic—my painterly—pretensions. So here I was, exiting from the funeral parlor, seeking to extract jolts—instances—shards of meaning to buoy up my future at the same time that I heartily rejected the bugbear of pasteurized meaning. The cleric smiled at me. The unearthly resignation of which he had so casually and confidently spoken, what had it been for old man Jamms but a minute-to-minute shift from decubitus to decubitus in the name of a little less anguish here, there, and anywhere. His resignation had been sheer exhaustion, sheerer disgust. I too was seeking something sheer—something to override this quizzical hunger for self-saleable memories. At the grave Mrs. Jamms turned to me and said, "It's a disgrace that Jim is not here." Back at the family apartment I asked her if she would mind my taking a walk. I took a walk as Jamms might have taken a walk. I saw my father hiding behind a tree. "So you are working," he said. For he had expected me to be drowning. "How do you like it?" he asked. "It pays the rent," I replied. "I'm not long for this world," answered the father—his—his father, "so there is not much point any more in talking about likes and dislikes." Slowly he emerged, head first. At first I could not place him, then it came to me, this was the father, long lost and no doubt as grimly uxorious as ever. Here was the father, as uncomprehending as he always

had been and as usual on the verge of taking me to task. Yet what was
there to comprehend after all: after all, I was respectably, respectfully,
dressed, returning so dressed at twilight it was obvious I was employed
even though from the little spots on my cravat it was even more obvious —
there it was, that damned highlighting of meaning again — highlighting at
the price of total falsification or shifting of vital accent — even more
obvious — that I was not earning a princely wage. The father — his — was
now completely emerged from the trunk, all its boughs bare except for a
few highest twigs rattling their scarred, in other words, holed, lobes.
"What is it?" I asked at last. "What do you want of me? Isn't it enough I
earn my bread? How can anyone impugn me now?" I thought of moving
on, not so much refusing as failing to acknowledge the encounter
stretched to the breaking point. I threw my back against a bench, one in
a conclave that faced the water, looked up at the sky smeared purple pink
meaning the sun had just set. The — his — my — the — father said, "So what
do you have planned for New Year's Eve." "Don't do anything." My
father looked away as if to say, This is the sort of asinine remark I would
have fought my way into in earlier days but now I refrain, on the margin
of the fray that could have been I wave the banner of exemplary self-
restraint. There was doubtless so much he could have rehearsed with
respect to a son who finishes his day if not his days on a bench in the public
domain. With a grudging sense of the punily inevitable, and just before
descending the broad flight of wooden steps to the water's edge with a
step surprisingly jaunty that did not however (Go from me at last,
meaning-mongers with your too fine qualifications!) belie his age, my
father dug into his top coat pocket and pulled out an envelope. Here, said
his gesture, take it. Instead of a check or a few timeworn bills there was
a photograph, just legible in the near dead light. A little boy standing in
front of a storefront next to his dad almost completely cut out of the frame.
A boy and his truncated dad and the storefront beyond and behind
furnishing just that indispensable shred of context that could hardly fail
to bring a sting to the canthi. Looked at it, stone dead, then tore it up,
couldn't tear it up fast enough, faster than meaning could prevail upon me
to stop or slow down or applaud its most clearcut and irrefutable
resurrection in my very frenzy to parry its blows. Disliking superabun-
dance almost as much as disorder I threw every last shred into a

conveniently placed trash basket lined with plastic. I descended the steps to join the old guy. "What was that all about," I dared to venture in a tone that, completely alien, fascinated me completely. The old guy shrugged: "I've decided not to saddle myself with trash any longer."

Packing and preparing for my first European trip—Mrs. Jamms had promised me a generous little annuity for all my services to the clan—the journey whence—in conformity with the elder's request—I would always be accessible either by phone or wire—so that in my mind's eye the voyage quickly superseded—transcended—hoodwinked—its own image to end up as nothing better than a supererogatory form of accessibility to the powers that be—as I packed and prepared I suffocated now and again at the palpableness of this failed image—generated by the elder's apparent affection—of myself as one with whom there could never be any question of her easily going on communicating. I went outside to clear my mind. Wearing a scarf though the weather was quite warm I heard somebody behind me say: Look at that guy. I was at once constructed and demolished as a being. Taken seriously for the first time as a *guy*, as an entity, I was fleeringly castigated for the absurdity of my scarf. I felt as if I was living in the shadow of Jamms, as if he had come back to question my right to live. I returned to my packing. The more I packed the more what I might call the aggregative faculty triumphed over the jettisoning to which I was normally prone. Matter and material which I had haphazardly acquired all down my acquaintanceship with Jim and beyond and of which haphazard acquisition I did not wish to be reminded—as it jarred with a certain slender conception of myself that I cultivated intermittently as being very much in the Soho style—such matter and material were no longer incompatible with the conception and began to be welcomed by faculties and fibers I had never dreamed I comprised. These materials and matter were no longer obstructions to departure but nodal points of my being to be retained at all cost. Their profusion was to be savored as a robust and hearty stew is savored by the weary traveler. I wanted to throw everything I owned into the stew and thereby enhance the tender flavor of its scalding endproduct that was fast becoming my heart's desire. In short, I could not bring myself to flee myself and those endproducts. I'll stay behind, I said, as if to a dear friend. Inevitably Maggy called. Hearing her make a special effort to be pleasant

I felt guilty to be making her behave in a way so much against her grain, she who had never made any secret of detesting me. Sounding a bit out of breath she explained that Mrs. Jamms had hired a detective who would be arriving shortly in New York. It seemed she had received a particularly vicious and at the same time strangely acute anonymous letter suggesting that Jim had been murdered, imagine, that the killer belonged to the species that sees in the symptom—the craving to kill—only a nonself, a self inimical to the true self's ideals. For a being of this kind, once the vile act was done and the symptom gratified—in other words, once such a being had finished being itself—all that was not itself and could never have any truck with that foul sty of a self instantaneously became its truest expression. Once done with being itself the sick and sickened self consecrated itself to a single task: disentangling from the tissue of its essential flawlessness, spotlessness, purity, foraging strands of a symptom's damned gratuitousness and irrelevance. And how did the damned being set about—set foot in the shallows of—the task: through another surrender to the symptom—the craving to kill—once again a mere irrelevance on the way to the true, the unlocalizable, the eternally voided, self. Apparently Mrs. Jamms was convinced that Jamms was dead and that she might be the next victim. I decided to call Mrs. Jamms. Answering the phone herself she sounded half-asleep, unguarded. Yet instead of taking this unguardedness at face-value—as evidence of her growing terror and feeling of defenselessness—I converted it into still another inflection of her querulous but wily potency. Her drowsiness, her queasiness, was the primordial sign not of confusion but of a special form of shrewdness made exquisitely to the measure of what had managed to erect its feelers. Her drowsiness, queasiness, and terrified disgust was an indictment of the world that succeeded, at least in my eyes—ears—in vanquishing it. I apologized for calling *this late.* She said, "That's all right. I wanted to get up." This was less a statement about herself than a slithering disgruntled challenge, a spasm of her erectile tissue preparing to meet, that is, outwit, a world that was disappointing on so many counts and fronts. "I wanted to get up," meant—I was sure of it—that she, Mrs. Jamms, had been mistreated—jilted, as it were—too many times by the world and at this point had no intention of letting it slip by when it had once again so much to answer for. Her statement—"I wanted to get up"—

was not a statement about herself but a verdict on the state, that is to say, the failure, of the world. She confirmed that she was indeed coming to New York with *her* detective. Before she arrived Maggy dropped by. "This is a terrible throwback to the time of Jim's childhood," she concluded, if I may abridge her babble. "Once again he becomes an enigma for those responsible for his being so. They—the Jammses never discovered what haunted him—and here they are again, or rather, here she is again, following this time the stipulations of detectives rather than rehabilitators as she tries to track him down, not sure she wants to find him after all given the string of crimes that populate his absence but compelled nevertheless to go on searching for this child they quickly grew to loathe as the embodiment of all they loathed in each other." I invited her to stay in my apartment while Mrs. Jamms was in town. At a certain point I excused myself to take a piss. The stream, double at first, quickly folded back on itself. The mixture of hope and terror with which I greeted the phenomenon quickly fizzled to disappointment, subsided to relief. I could not fix the meaning—the meaning-mongers clearly would have nothing to do with me under these circumstances—of this phenomenon though incontestably it seemed not only to belong to but to propel my story forward, perhaps too late.

The day scheduled for the arrival of Mrs. Jamms and her flunkey, Maggy took it into her head to continue the analysis commenced the day I invited her to stay in my apartment. She preferred a hotel but not the one where Colletti and I had weathered the storm of Jamms's blatant disaffection. "I'm not surprised he's disappeared. Too long he lived in the shadow of their wounds. Now, with the elder dead he is probably feeling the only peace he has ever known. He is alive—I know he is—and Jamms, Sr., for all his contempt, is dead. Toward the end Sr. told him he had been going downhill all his life. Yet Jamms told me—perhaps to comfort himself—that the utterance itself was far less painful than the ease with which the corpse relinquished it—seemed to retract—at the feeblest protest from its subject, target. You remember him sitting in front of his easel that cold winter day up in Rhinebeck, cursing life, cursing death, yet compelled to try to depict—to get under the sallow skin of— this old man's dying, death, resurrection in inspissated bile, and at the same time hating—infinitely more than he hated the old man" (Was

Maggy under the spell of the meaning-mongers here?) " — the compulsion to depict. For wasn't this what all his Soho patrons expected of him if they were to take him seriously enough to sponsor his exertions — this effort of imaginative reconstruction of what the other corpse — the corpse other than oneself — happens at any given moment to be feeling. Wasn't he at this *crucial juncture* — this one among too many accreditedly solemn ages of man — supposed to come out and dutifully insinuate himself beneath the cancerous lesions of another's universal rage at having been obliged to live through them all? Yet that cold winter day — you must remember — dear friend that you were — are — there was no imaginative sympathy of this type to be had and all he had managed was a positive recoil from the loathsome possibility of sickening prostration — opportunistic to the core — before the multifarious forms of life and death — more particularly, life in death. For to Jamms this sort of prostration had nothing to do with sympathetic affinity and everything to do with a cleancut touristic antiseptically quarantined delight at a sideshow preconizing somebody's recurring failure to *learn from experience*. You remember too how the old man's death began not with the death spasms — not with Jim's first appearance in the hospital room — but with reappearance after reappearance inducing only outraged consternation. Old man Jamms had been used to obliterating his each and every posture and here was Jim coming back over and over to the same posture of condolence and never obliterated — never allowing himself to be obliterated — in the unexploitative manifestation of his decency. He simply couldn't fathom this new Jamms surviving the repetitions of his act unless such repetition regularly transformed him into other than himself. So that on every occasion of recurring decency it had to be a different Jamms, Jr., according to an excruciated Jamms, Sr. For Jamms, Jr., as Jamms, Sr., envisioned him — needed to envision him so that his own strength might remain intact for that strength was a contingent strength feeding off constructed contrast — was constitutionally incapable of achieving an act's repetition, an act's recurrence, since he was always annihilated in Jamms, Sr.'s, contempt before any act — much less its repetition — was even halfway begun. So old man Jamms dying on his hospital bed had no alternative but to believe it was always the same Jim and the same visit visited upon him time and again. Time, therefore, stood still for old man Jamms and it is from the moment that time stood still that I date his deterioration. So that never forget for old man Jamms dying the visits of his son were always the same visit and never a sum of discernibles with each acting as kind of delirious commentary on not so much the old man's illness as on Jamms's ability, in sequence, to contend with it, triumph over it by stepping up his solicitude in direct proportion to the old man's irascibility. But maybe old man Jamms was glad at last to be yielded up to Jamms's greater strength or rather endurance. Through unending repetition of the act of visitation Jamms— my Jamms—felt the slag of personality—all that was, in other words, gratuitous—sink to the bottom of the flask of the act. Repetition of the act smelted away all characterologic details routinely susceptible to intimidation, especially by the likes of a Jamms, Sr. But Jamms refused to build a story around his repeated returns. No matter how much and how often I reminded him that he had so much to be proud of in and through his repeated returns he refused to undergo those repeated returns as building blocks of a story but rather as a repeatedly renewed consternation on the part of something or other toward the ways of the son in the face of whatever more advanced stage of decomposition the father still was able to attain and, sorcererlike, to impose. Yes, Jim was always—did I ever mention it?—an enemy of stories or rather of the form stories are in our time expected to take."

Once Mrs. Jamms and the detective were inside I became uncomfortable, somehow I was waiting for Maggy to defend me, or rather, defend the situation, give it a caption that would isolate me from all accusers living and dead. As she did not speak I said finally, " Maggy feels Jim may have disappeared to induce his mother to go looking for him...in the old way." The detective, a nice youngish man, dutifully said, "What do you mean, the old way." I sighed deeply, not, I hoped, as if I was taken aback or stalling but rather because preternatural lucidity is always painful. As if drugged old lady Jamms said, "When he was a child we looked for him, looked for the real Jim, but the search seemed to capitalize only on pinpointing our ineptitude. And so my husband grew to hate him. Yes, he hated his own son." Her self-absorption burned like an inner light. She handed a photograph of Jamms to the detective: it looked as if it was about to crumble to dust. Now and then I smiled at her but she did not return my smile, looked away, doubtless to underline motherly alarm. While the detective and Maggy chatted briefly in a corner she said, pacing, "What about you. What have you been doing." She spoke not accusingly but mechanically as if driven by a desire to mask pain at any price. At first I did not know how to respond, felt walled in as never before, surprised myself nevertheless by being able to say, "Trying to locate him best way I know how, Mrs. Jamms." Finally the detective began to speak to .me, adopting a particularly feeling air, at which I feelingly lashed back. He thought or needed to think or needed to make me think he thought I was wedded to the story of my grief. For the present he refused to show he thought I might not be so wedded. The mother shook her head as I spoke. And then after the question of Jamms's whereabouts and his possible connection with Testic, living or dead, had been tossed about long enough to qualify as having been thoroughly exhausted the detective suddenly came at Jim from another direction. He was speaking of Jamms in a tone that implied his was a reality vaster than anybody's present and therefore infinitely more worthy of respect, and that his flight was not an ignominious hegira into parts unknown but contrary to all our babble's crippled evocation of little more than its own invidious atrophy Jamms—to whose density we could never hope to aspire—had managed simply to go on about his business whatever that might be and leave others, insignificant others, to their haggling and paltering and cavilling and equivocating about the ever more remote possibility of his continued existence elsewhere. Jamms, I saw, was being created—after all this chaffering about his continued existence and possible guilt—anew compliments of a detective's mindless and respectful naming as a kind of inadvertent verdict on all the prior drivel that had attempted, perhaps inadvertently also, to reduce him, Jim Jamms, to nothingness, to contaminate him with the frustrated insignificance of those creatures left behind, namely, us, yet all too vociferous in their hunger to comprehend and track down. Out of all the gabble Jim Jamms was being born, as an entity, yet more than an entity, elusive, impalpable yet terrifyingly real and triumphant. And his savior was the detective whose naming had become Jamms's unwitting champion. Naming Jamms— calling him Jamms—according to our specifications—he showed that he—Jamms—was not only not undone by all the previous haggling but loftily inaccessible still. Jamms had left us behind. We envied his absence, which the detective's remark—his uttering the name, *Jamms*—restored and made excruciatingly real to us. The detective did not know Jamms, he simply had a hunger to name him as the others were naming him, wanted to see if he could name him as the others named him, see if his naming could survive the demolition effected by discussions like this. The naming of Jamms by his pursuer revealed an ungovernable affinity. But I had to remind myself not only that Jamms was dead but that the detective's resuscitational strategies, however impassioned, did not mean he would not go on to hunt him down and destroy him.

The detective was in a sense saving the day and saving Jamms's image from the heap. And when he said the name, Jamms, Jim Jamms, his mother—though she too was a Jamms and though Jim was her son—responded as if she had never quite made the connection between the name, *Jim Jamms,* and what it professed to signify. Yes, I wanted to cry, though more for myself than for Jamms, the correspondence between *Jamms* and Jamms was always contingent, postponed, forestalled, made contingent ostensibly on the quality of his exploits but in actual fact yoked to nothing more and nothing less than the fluctuation of your own self-loathing and even graver than self-loathing your self-incredulity and so this extension of yourself, this Jamms, this excrescence, who never had the decency—until now—to disappear definitively like other well-bred excrescences, this Jamms was never quite Jamms. Whereas the detective, without even knowing him, merely hearing about him, had managed to create him from scratch on the level of the name. Perhaps he had undergone an infirmity in his most precious core—*his* sense of being nameable—when he heard us taking the name of Jamms in vain. At any rate on the level of the name and far more than the name Jamms was suddenly concrete and beautiful, as beautiful as when he had handed the cop, a different cop, the photograph of the mother and father. Onward and onward we burrowed, ever inward yet forever adhesive to the surface of things.

When the detective began questioning me at length Maggy inexplicably burst in, as if she was trying to protect me, as if I was suddenly too fragile a spirit to be tormented with such questions. Mrs. Jamms sighed deeply out of the blue announcing to no one in particular, "I think I'll be going back soon. Nothing to keep me here now." Now she had begun, Maggy couldn't stop. She spoke of how Jim must be rotting somewhere, how a life — any life — is simply not long enough to fabricate the shred of meaning necessary for its vindication and of how this — this — without knowing it she was looking for the term, radical disjunction — was the most insidious — and the most glorious, I would have added — of all. She explained that she was not thinking of the others, she was thinking of Jamms, for the others, unlike Jamms, were used to scraping and liking the taste of shit. They succumbed, these others, from any angle and to them always was vouchsafed a signification they could taste, more pungent than all their failures bred over a lifetime. I looked to the detective. Once again he seemed to be naming Jamms and this mindless naming both cut through and reestablished the primacy of the obscuring bulk, namely Jamms. All roads led to Jamms. The infernal glamor of a teleology was suddenly available but only to the space between corpse and commodity. Jamms was present, an available thing, to be pawed and complimented for this glamor of an implied teleology. The walls were crumbling down not on his corpse but on us, those who had come to watch its plowed progress toward a light we could parasitize without undergoing the inconveniences of its wayward motion. Thanks to the detective, Jim's bulk no longer threatened to invalidate assumptions contrivable only in the pure light of breath coming from orifices about to be sealed off. As I waited for the interrogation to continue — Would Maggy never stop bellowing? — I noted that it was possible without dying to diminish the distance between self and eternity. For after being badmouthed by the solicitude of all present Jamms had acceded to a being named by the detective — who had never made his acquaintance — with *deep and abiding* respect, or rather with a quiet resurrectionary acceptation that trivialized all questions of respect, bypassed the quibblers, retroactively quibblers through this quiet naming as deep and abiding respect that placed him — Jim — Jim Jamms — outside time and space. Because this vaguest of image pictures of Jamms induced by the naming simply did not care one way or the other about how we, the quibblers, the friends of the family drowning in our own literalness, were taking him. The naming of Jamms by the detective had produced — went on producing — an image picture — again, of Jamms — even if the detective had not functioned on the level of the picture but rather on that of the sheerest naming. He had

functioned within the narrowest defiles of the sheerest naming for that
was all he knew of Jamms. Yet I, as listener, was compelled, reflexively,
to summon up—forth—that image—that image necessarily of somebody
who simply did not care one way or the other whether he was summoned
up—forth—or not. So busy was he elsewhere. So busy was he elsewhere.
The naming imposed Jamms's blissful indifference on me faster than its
image picture could become an object, that is to say, a target, for the harsh
judgment born always of envy and bewilderment, that is to say, of even
the slenderest cathexis.

On the verge of leaving Mrs. Jamms turned to me and asked,
"Wherever he is, do you think he misses his father." Here old man Jamms
was being summoned up—forth—as Jamms had been summoned by the
detective's naming of the name. But the summoning was an altogether
different summoning. This image picture was of the father, old man
Jamms, going about his business being very much dead and in spite of
himself at the same time becoming—in spite not only of himself but of the
cemetery and the coffin and the nurses refusing to wash his groin—a
solicitor of opinion, of valorization, on the order of a contestant awaiting
the deciding vote yet unaware that he is awaiting. Whereas the image
picture of Jamms as glancingly evoked by—in—the detective's naming
of the name—*Jamms*—had always managed—still managed—to remain
completely indifferent to whatever the bewilderment and envy consequent to even the slimmest cathexis might construct of a verdict. Jim,
unlike the dead father as evoked by the relict mother, was outside day,
outside night, outside the too intense green of powdery asphalt, outside
verdict and quibbling diagnosis, yet without ever having to play dead
whereas

whereas NO NO
whereas
the old dad lying
in fact dead
in his coffin,
a goodlooking coffin with his hat on
jauntily as it were according to accepted funeral protocol with respect to
the posthumous jaunty, was very much on trial, quivering amid the
prospect of possible repudiation by the wormy cluster of maligning

survivors. "I'm sure he misses him very much," I said, trying to murmur incoherently. The detective now resumed. He asked me about Jamms and once again I was compelled to accept him, Jamms, in a different light, not as a culprit or non-culprit or victim or charlatan, but as a sprite, at once oafish and elfin, who, thanks to all this chat and drivel about culprits, had been inspirited and able finally to elude its clutching pincers and launch and land beautifully into a world where we could never begin to hope to stalk him. And all this through the detective's fumbling naming, invoking him from another direction, as it were, as one no longer on trial, as one whose innocence or guilt was no longer the prime issue. Instead the issue had become our, the survivors', futility and impotence in the face of Jamms's having managed to take flight and through that flight compel us to attempt to occupy the space of his vacancy. "What exactly did he do?" the detective asked when Mrs. Jamms was gone. Here he was trying to indict his absence yet here was that absence going on blithely in the face of indictment. Could Jamms himself have answered the question: What Jamms did—had always done—was mystify. His absence at the same time made matters worse and did the questioner in, for absence plus already implacable unseizability is a mixture far headier than fear of un-masking. I said nothing. The question was now about the detective's earthbound inability to seize Jim. The question demonstrated, for those who cared to comprehend, that he was always incommensurate with whatever chanced—dared—to be said about him. The detective's words evoked the triumph of Jamms over words and their potential ability to corral and appraise him. Here was Jamms, dead like his father before or after him, yet simply floated away, to be contained by no box of mixed walnut and beech fine- or coarser grained, just enough of him evoked by the detective's word chain to pinpoint his unlocalizability. I thought he would leap at my throat to punish me for that unlocalizability. Instead he said: "Jamms just went out, it seems, like a light." I was enraged by the cloudy panes that obstructed my view of the sunset over cherished Soho rooftops. All of a sudden, with the detective staring me down and Maggy impatient to initiate another tirade, I could not ingest the fructiveness of this particular vantage on the dying beams. This was no longer—as on countless other evenings—a view perfect in itself but a maddening poorer version of the better sketched by its blinding inadequacy. Just as I caught myself thinking it was impossible to manifest greater indifference to *my* possible innocence or guilt than that manifested by the detective, the phone rang: Mrs. Jamms was inviting all of us to dinner. "It's on me," she proclaimed, as if the definitive disappearance of her only son was somehow liberating. An unctuous waiter ground pepper for us from an enormous brown contraption, wielding it like firehose *and* sawed-off shotgun. In front of the apartment building across the street from the restaurant a young man in T-shirt and variegated Bermudas closed the trunk of his car while holding in his free hand several shirts on cellophane-shrouded hangers...a young man like unto Jamms living the story we might have lived together. The detective said we should not give up hope but was not particularly convincing. *I couldn't help thinking* he did not very much intend to be since his main concern, at certain moments, was to somehow underplay the heaping portions of shellfish he was intent upon bringing to his pudgy lips wet with red wine. Nobody listened, everybody—as in any family, I presume, having had blessedly little truck with that item—just as intent on camouflaging as gracefully as possible his or her main concern, which was getting enough to eat and getting that enough to his or her mouth with greatest dispatch. It was hunger-inducing weather, after all, a brisk little frost chiseling the skyscrapers and standardizing the pace of passersby. Everybody skidded in and out of his own thoughts circumscribed and circumvented by Jamms's absence. By the end of the meal I was convinced the detective intended to take me into custody for the murder of both Jamms and Testic, maybe even of old man Jamms.

I said, "I could use a walk." I smiled at the ashtray in the middle of the table, intrigued by the smile, especially as I knew all eyes were upon me—it—kernellike nisus and driving force behind this pure impersonation of one who is always making it a habit of smiling with unassessing wonderment at the things of the world and, better yet, looks forward to an unclouded future of such wonderment. I felt calmer as the dinner approached its close either because I was about to get away from the detective or because I was closer to our next interview where there was no doubt I would be able to rectify my inculpating errors perpetrated so lavishly here and now. Looking at him I felt that the true ground of my anguish was not the imminent next interview but its not materializing fast enough for the taste of a hunger to state my case at last. "Couldn't you show him around on your walk," Mrs. Jamms suggested in what seemed a mewling tone. I looked at her, for I was having great difficulty in believing my ears. For some reason, she was so terrified of my walk that she had no recourse but to assign him, her flunkey, as watchdog. Unable to control myself—all that shellfish, red wine, ground pepper—I heard myself—saw myself—found myself—growing more and more truculently apologetic, more and more bullyingly self-deprecating for daring to suggest that I wished to walk off all that damned good food. How dare I. On and on I went, as if by formulating the grossest paraphrase of what I perceived to be her raging fear and tremulous disapprobation I must induce a total retraction of her request, or better yet and far more to the point, of her rage and fear and trembling and disapprobation. A retraction of fear. By suggesting that the detective accompany me on my walk she was drawing the most radical though not necessarily the most implausible conclusions from its lack of avowed purpose. I was not sure what these most radical conclusions were but I knew that unbeknownst to her her raging panic had drawn them all. Standing there, about to leave, unable to leave, I was suddenly aware of the grossest implications of that purpose deferred even if they might reduce to nothing more than its conspicuity for her—for others—for all others hot or not so hot on my trail. But there was no understanding the conspicuity, at least at present, since the walk, this going, this intention without a purpose somewhere latent in a proclamation that would brook no gainsay, was precisely a flight from conspicuity. Her raging panic in seeming to subside to mere anxiety was now first making me aware of the implications of my purpose in an evening walk even if those implications had not been included in its original design. There was no telling what the walk might become once I hit the cold and lonely, hot and attractive streets. There was no telling what might ensue if I allowed myself at last to meet up with my own kind. But wasn't meeting up at last with my own kind the very best remedy against the grossest implications of an unspeakable (especially at the dinner table) purpose? Wasn't it precisely my own kind, whatever that was, who could most be depended on to cancel—by having already and long before expropriated—the inexorability of that purpose? Weren't they most likely to enact in my stead leaving me free to go about the better business of remaining unenacted, purposeless, in other words blissfully incomprehensible, to myself. So on I went with my self-deprecating phrases, bullyings on the order of, "I know I'm an absolute monster wanting to walk my full after being cooped up for so long. " I was still expecting her, somebody—even at an adjacent table—to recant or retract, to wooingly collude with my construction of her request as an absurd and colossal upsurge of unjustifiable panic. None moved. None spoke. I was being, fat sweaty beast that I was, put on the hot seat and made to see my purpose—my act—act-to be—act-to-be even if I was already neck deep in its mud—from without, outside myself, as object, entity, correlative and target of a hot hysteria that long ago had left mere matronly disapprobation far behind. And this excruciated. If the pur-pose—act—grosser—grossest—implications were fixable and conspicu-ous then I too—progenitor or vector—was also fixable, fixed, conspicu-ous, in other words, verdicted, diagnosed, stashed away for imminent sentencing, earmarked for obliteration and not necessarily on my own terms. I made as if to go, then stayed, stamping my foot and muttering under my breath. I was staying because afraid of her fear of my going, afraid of what her fear sketched of a gradual annihilating surrender to the law/lure of the streets, that world outside boundaries not so informally set by grieving mom and attentive flunkey. Even if it would appear that my fear of her fear must be linked to something infinitely greater than anything conceivable to her perception—or mine, for that matter. "I know I should stay," I blundered on, "hanging on your every word, your every clue, but the fact remains..." She and the detective—less Maggy—looked anguished, neither was hearing me. Didn't she know that my desire to escape was in the service of my—of our—mine and Jamms's—story? And here she was standing in the way of that story's unfolding. Unless she knew something I didn't, something on the order of the desire to escape being nothing more and nothing less than a symptom of the desire to escape the story—our story—unfolding at last here and now, at the dinner table, among mom, arm of the law, and grieving girlfriend. Yet watching her—the detestable trembling of her jowls—it became clear that everything—truth and falsehood—was being subordinated to her need to transmute my act—my purpose—its grosser and grossest impli-cations—into the outpouching of desire as symptom so that this newly defined symptom—this bias—this slant—might imbricate with and thereby provide solace or at least distraction to her own. She was making my desire for the streets imbricate, interlock, engage, with her panic. My symptom was being made to nourish her own. And all along I had been trying to browbeat her into retraction of her panic—her symptom—when there was absolutely no possibility of a retraction as long as that retraction remained strictly dependent on an (impossible) reduction in her panic. I tried again: "I know I'm detestable: leaving you like this. Instead I should take all of you in my arms and comfort you..." Oddly enough as I went on speaking a shiver of unanimous accord passed through them all. Somewhere in the course of bullyingly exaggerating—caricaturing—their expectation of a solace—a seamless deference—somewhere in the course of attempting to make that expectation ridiculous in order to procure a retraction I had managed to produce a completely plausible and undistorted conspectus of what from their perspective was needed and required, quite legitimately, from me. If I too was a lover of Jim as every gesture clearly claimed then what was more natural than that I should spontaneously renounce my plans for an evening walk and weepingly—comfortingly—enfold them all in my arms. In its very passage the statement—in other words, the bullying exaggeration hungering for collusion in its conception—begging for retraction—of what was really too too ridiculously excessive for words—in its very passage the statement had died as bullying exaggeration and been reborn (birth weight and filiation still unknown) as a passionately straightforward paraphrase of what circumstances demanded and had all along demanded. I myself began in fact to feel the nostalgic dimness of cravings for what I had no intention, under any circumstances, of providing. At any rate—as all further stabs died on my lips—I had came to recognize there was no bullying her—them—into retraction of what I had striven in vain to portray as absurdity pure and simple nor bullying—or rather, intoxicating—myself into an unwavering belief in that absurdity. Yes, yes, yes, I had tried—been trying—to save face behind the peddling of a radical disjunction not in the least radical. Bullying exaggeration had been founded and propagated on the basis of an ostensibly radical disjunction between what I had every right to be and what—failed amanuensis of their implicit requirements—vociferating self-deprecation made me out

to be purely for purposes of demonstrating how unfair those requirements were, how unfair and absurd and grotesque. Only my heuristic
specimen had managed to explode in my face. I had turned out to be
exactly what—in order to expose and cure the grossness of their expectations—I pretended to have become. I had believed in enlightenment
through a heuristic technique at work in the creation of still another
radical disjunction. There was no radical disjunction *between:* I reduced
simply to one of the terms, was as bad as it said. All along I should have
been doing what grossly vociferating bullying exaggeration said—para-
phrasing their absurd requirements—I should have been doing. No one
spoke. I came quickly to the conclusion or rather my utterance—
outflow—came even more quickly to the conclusion—reborn, transmogrified in midstream—that what her panic had implied and ultimately
demanded was exactly what she, a dowager non pareil, was entitled to.
There was no shaming her to a sense of the absurdity of her expectations
simply because there was no absurdity. She had every right to expect me
to stay put slobbering a boundless love for my victim and my victim's
victims.

      There was nothing more to say, to be said, and it was precisely at
this moment my heart beat
     faster no NO NO
     than it NO
had ever beat, for I wanted us all to go at last beyond this startlingly
complete absence of story—whether endemic to the situation—to circumstances—or contrived by premeditated and predigested paraphernalia—
something about desire for a walk and the lure of the streets and panic
consequent to gross vociferating expectations of undying love—waiting
in the wings for circumstances exactly like these on which to unleash
themselves—to the real thing, the story at last, the story inside the story
of the desire for a walk and the panic of her symptom imbricating with my
own and the dependability of my own kind in expropriating my unspeakable muddiness of purpose—the story beyond that story, the story I had
craved during every moment of our—Jamms's and my—life together and
whose potentially boundless space he had managed to defile over and
over with the effluvium of anecdote—concerning fathers and sons, for
example. I was hoping, now that all predigested and prefabricated

material had been used up—or rendered unusable by what had just occurred—Had the previous scene been a tissue of prefabrications or did it qualify as an utterly spontaneous clot in the flow of such prefabrications forever waiting in the wings of the story?—I was hoping something exceptional though by no means gratuitous might settle on us at last, something generated purely by the poverty of the situation yet in itself by no stretch of the imagination—or whatever faculty attended to such specimens—poor or shabby. But nothing came, all played out, no story unfolding unprepense within the space we all shared. I waited as Mrs. Jamms went on sitting where she had always been sitting daring me still to step out the door and the detective waited looking now and again at his watch and Maggy now and again sighed deeply at a life with Jim slipping through her fingers.

Then, afraid the detective might call me a murderer point blank I announced, but not just to him, "I am grateful to you, heartily grateful, do you hear, because you have taken the trouble to point to my desire—not to go—not to go for a walk—but to stay behind and offer comfort. You especially, Mrs. Jamms, pointed to that desire—your panic pointed to and painted that desire, that is to say you, or rather your panic, induced a desire up to this moment I was not quite sure I had. Or rather, you pointed with your panic to the language of desire—desire to conform to your expectations—and thereby made that desire conceivable should it after all be latent. I am just afraid that having located—that is to say, induced—my desire—as one induces labor—that you now feel more than ever entitled—entitled—entitled—" "Is this desire so degrading?" asked the detective. Not looking at him—hungering suddenly for the young man in the Bermuda shorts and the overabundance of newly pressed shirts—I replied, "I'm just afraid that surrendering to my desire to share anecdotes of the life Jamms and I lived together"—here I involuntarily turned to Maggy—I couldn't help wanting to torment the poor girl—"afraid that stepping into the warm bath of anecdote—anecdotes that trace my inconsolable rage at Jim's loss to its source—I run the risk at the end of anecdote and unbeknownst to myself—this is the crucial qualifying phrase—unbeknownst to myself—of coming out of the sharing and the telling and the stepping—that are mine and least of all mine—and finding—again, unbeknownst to myself—that the sacred rage has been mitigated irrevocably. And without that rage how I can begin to assist you in finding him." Mrs. Jamms shook her head as if at my naïveté in expecting to find him." I began to snivel—advisedly. "I would literally tuck him in. You know how, when you are tucking a child in, it will mutter some phrase it has heard during the day, some phrase that, with a child's instinct for the scandalous, it knows it is not supposed to know yet and so it goes on repeating the phrase slowly, solemnly, slyly, provokingly, yet with a kind of exaggerated gaucheness to avoid being reproached as for an incontestably clear and rapid utterance it would have every reason to expect to be. Jamms, for example, would mutter, Despair, or, Humiliation, as if he had recently heard these words for the very first time and was wondering if they might have any relation to him. So I made it a point on those occasions of taking him in hand, as it were, and telling him that if he was speaking these words, naming these names, then he was obviously flailingly and thrashingly hungry to fight back, speak up, and not allow himself to become the target of everybody's frustrations. Mind you, I was not advising him—nobody had the right to advise him for or against—I simply deployed the options—for his information, as it were, so that during that next moment of truth when yet another art world lackey tried to foist off his own incompetence on this uniquely gifted being Jamms—the uniquely gifted being in question—would be able to recall that he alone was responsible for his fate, that is, for canceling the specious version the lackey was trying to impose. Once under the covers he thanked me, he did, he did. 'You' he would say, 'you have pointed to my hunger.' Just as I was saying a moment ago to all of you. For the rehabilitation effected by friendship and something more than friendship is contagious, infects the world. 'You pointed to my hunger,' he would say, 'found words for the hunger. Even if you did not find the exact words, refused the exact words, in the name of tact perhaps, nevertheless your chatter somehow made it clear there were words—not too few and not too many—for what I did not yet know, did not want to know, yet hungered to know. You somehow implied the words were in abeyance yet at my immediate disposal should I create the crucial moment when it becomes necessary to fight back, fight back, dimly, then less dimly, then boldly. For too long, you imply, I chose not to create that crucial moment, pretended it would never arise . So that' —and here, I must admit, he brought tears to my eyes"—it was becoming easier to stay, behind, to give them what they needed, to renounce the street, lure of the street, especially with their eyes fixed so entrancedly upon me—but it was not by me they were entranced—their entrancement was in the service of Jim's resurrection—"'even if you think of me as a proven and absurd flunkey of the art world and what is worse a flunkey who needs advice somehow you have helped strengthen me beyond preoccupation with the humiliation attendant on requiring advice at my advanced age.' So you see, his dilemma becomes not merely serviceable but phraseable: Could he profit from my good advice before the very stark fact of requiring advice demolished him. Could he arm himself with all I suggested faster than he was done in by his sense (misguided) of my subjacent conviction of his futility—his flunkeyed futility—in requiring—and at his advanced age—any advice at all." All the time I spoke Mrs. Jamms shook her head as if to say, Do you still intend after all this to take a walk. And my endless pacing as I talked said, Yes, yes, yes. "We should meet again," the detective said. We met later that week in the office of the other two. In the labyrinth of precinct cubicles their colleagues were dictating into tiny machines only their reports sounded like mere random reflections on the state of the planet, such as I might have been supremely capable of at that moment, so lucid my terror and my impatience with terror. And this planet on which they were reporting, was it anything like the one I knew, that is to say, did it boast grand hotels with fulsome receptionists sporting the same worn boutonnière of a welcoming smile for the delectation of the same vagrants; sidestreets off the noisy main thoroughfares sloping toward sunset above rivers contaminated each in its unique way; flunkeys and lackeys peddling the same unendurable shop talk striving with all its might to pass for authentic engagement; men with vaginas and women with flabby penises parading in the broad daylight of their bad conscience wares no longer enjoying the same demand as in their demented, that is to say, nonexistent, youth. I fought against a terrible passivity that could not be mistaken for a desire to get some sleep. The elder said, "My colleague," meaning presumably the younger, "thinks you are trying to protect Jamms. Even if—following his dad's lead—seeing how easy it was to exploit you he began squeezing heftier and heftier assignments into smaller and smaller intervals to the point where he would have to kill you if he was not to be completely undone by your perfect willingness to succumb and be abused. We know he had you doing his dirty work for a big time crook named Colletti." I smiled sadly, as if to say, Such a thought is unworthy of my friend. The younger looked as if he was about to open his mouth. Hastily, the elder said—speaking now directly to Mrs. Jamms's man on the job—"It's best I speak. My partner partisanizes too much with Jamms. As with Jamms and his painterly stimuli, in his dependence on clues he often forgets to stand up for his rights—as if he has none until he has transformed one—a clue, I mean—into a nail in somebody's coffin. Yet when they come, the clues, they are merely undergone as obstructions to the true form, the true life, of the case infinitely greater than the sum of its clues. He waits for his clues every waking moment and when they arrive they are lived as obstructions to a life beyond the case." Looking now directly at me. "No, he is not at all interested in you—he is interested in the life beyond you and your kind. He is yet to be at home, my partner, in the desolation induced by the refusal of clues to present themselves at once and in all their doleful glory. I apologize for my partner: he created you too fast. He couldn't wait for you to arrive in your innocence. He created you too fast and thereby created you in guilt. But, as I say, he partisanized too strongly with Jim Jamms." I smelled a trap. I was afraid to be hurried off into a cell and interrogated: about my favorite flower, for example, me who loathed flowers; about the make of my car, me who knew nothing about advanced technology; about whether I sucked pussy or cock, me who loathed the ostensible holiness of any body. I was suddenly afraid of suffering to the point where I became nothing more or less than the avatar of a mere ability to survive a wee bit beyond the inconceivability of torture chambers, especially those designed to effect the purest of rehabilitations thanks mainly to smokescreen walls permitting a one-way visibility so that during a particularly instructive session the rehabilitee can—at the behest of a buzzer—exiting make way for the crucial commentary of those expert judges inside the smoke, inside the smoke. There was a phone call, presumably from their chief, for both came to attention. When the younger had gone, his partner added, "He tried to stand back from you, as from an embodied flaw. He has tried all along to stand back compassionately from men and their puny defense of their flaws. But this telescopic vision, it soon loses track of and interest in itself and the globally incisive compassionation reveals itself to be nothing more than simple dullness and fatigue, self-preoccupation failing to expand to dimensions of universal lifeblood." The third detective, Mrs. Jamms's flunkey, cleared his throat and said, "According to Maggy—the painter's girlfriend—when he was little they were always dragging him around from rehabilitation center to rehabilitation center. They would all sit in a room, almost completely dark, and speak their piece. And the mediator would attempt to help them before the buzzer rang. The buzzer ringing meant either that she, the mediator, had mediated inadequately or that the problem was itself insoluble but not uninteresting, at least from the perspective of the diagnosticians invisible but rampant beyond the smokescreen. Yes, this was their fate—as propositi. Their problem was insoluble in direct proportion to its interest for the community of mediators. On the basis of the conference inside the room—between mediator and her judges—they might—this family of probands—be temporarily evicted into the twilight of the landing until the damage they had done— each to the others—could be properly formulated." I resented this, Jim's, relation to his family, so easily recuperated into a story line. Even an idiot like Mrs. Jamms's detective could make the story flow without too much trouble. This was what I had sought for the two of us—to tell my—our— story as I—we—lived it, to live it as a telling, to tell the story before I lived it, before it could be corroded, rendered illegible by the living, by those paid to practice a deriding corrosive paraphrase on the margin of the living. "So I guess," continued the hired gun, "we shouldn't be very surprised Jim has disappeared for good given all he has endured. For when you spend your life going from rehabilitator to rehabilitator—when you allow yourself to become embrangled within the defiles of rehabilitation—there is no getting out for you are always seeking clarification from some new clown regarding the last verdict, the last diagnosis, even if at the time of that last diagnosis you were reminded oh so sententiously, pietistically, that any attempt to deform their irreproachable good intentions into the malleability of a verdict, a diagnosis, would constitute one further proof of grievous affliction and that, perhaps, the most definitive. According to Maggy all Jamms learned was that progress is a delusion and a breeding ground for more grievous delusion. And no matter how internecine the warfare among rehabilitators A, B, and C all striving toward Jamms's rebirth — as we are striving though in vain — it was never a question of x, where $x = A$, B, or C, feeling accused when the infallible testing devices devised by y, where $y = A$, B, or C, $y \neq x$, exposed the poor progress of Jamms while under his or her care, the care, that is, of x. No matter how much A, B, and C might loathe and impugn each other's tactics questions of ineptitude and maladroitness always bypassed these tactics and rebounded inevitably to — were invariably laid at the doorstep of — the case, the Jamms case, embodiment and vector of ineptitude." I couldn't help wondering if this wasn't a warning directed my way: in this case too my accusers, A, B, and C, or X, Y, and Z, would never be proven wrong even if their hypotheses were diametrically opposed. "And of course Mr. and Mrs. Jamms, though particularly aggressive in other spheres — papa Jamms, for example, in the business sphere, and mamma Jamms in the good works and gardening spheres — never dared voice their unspeakable fear that it was not so much Jamms who was afflicted as the rehabilitator of the moment requiring — for vocational purposes — a specimen of a specific type that corresponded or better yet could be made to correspond to a certain paradigm and on whose materialization and transmogrification depended said rehabilitator's tempestuous pas- sage into the ranks of full-fledged expert in contradistinction to snivelling trainee. And so what was more obvious than that said snivelling trainee would do all he or she could to hold on to Jim for dear life lest his or her apprenticeship be pulled out, like a cheap rug, from under. So on they went, the Jammses, sitting in dark rooms, waiting for buzzers indicating that enough raw meat was now available to the fangs of these gently advising carnivores squatting on their expert haunches on the other side of being. So on they went hoping to discover the cause or at least the signs of his — Jim's — affliction and always being told, or better yet, made to feel, that this vulgarity of eagerness for discrete signs was the single greatest proof of their offspring's predisposition to affliction. So now you can see why Jim disappeared and why the Jammses succumbed so easily to that disappearance. For it recapitulates, summarizes, apotheosizes a childhood that was also their childhood." Now that the hired gun was finished the elder, an old friend of sorts, said — he didn't have to turn to me, he was looking straight at me — "Aren't you scheduling a trip? You're a free man, you know. Case closed." I could not speak, became dour. I could see they took my dourness for a lack of enthusiasm. I was not dour because I was not looking forward to my trip. I was dour because they were expecting me to explain the overwhelming enthusiasm they had just led me to discover. I was dour because I was expected to put the story of my trip from me and before them. Long before I could call it my own the trip—my enthusiasm over the trip—the sudden departure—was no longer of me but in a potential telling apart, far away, from me. His question about this event—this story—took it from me, ripped it from my womb, in advance of birth, simultaneously transforming it—unique beyond uniqueness—into one of infinite facsimiles: somebody's—some ass's pleasure trip. Inside me it had been immense, contourless, therefore non-existent. Outside—thanks to his inhumane obstetrics—it existed at last but was no longer mine.

　　Shaking hands with an effusiveness I did not in the least feel—I hated them both—the younger cop too, if he had been present—I took my leave, though it was not really mine to take. In the little park outside the precinct house, a semicircle of benches deliciously delivered up to a blaze of noonday sun was proscriptively fenced off into a zone of reconstruction. So that I was forced to wander about in search of some at least partially illuminated stump. A few workaday world lunchers were sitting on the steps of a monument but the monument was too smeared with filth to justify my approach. From where I ultimately sat—well outside the pretty little park—the covers on a row of motorcycles were to be observed rippling in a complete absence of wind. How discern the logic inherent in the transition from a ragged puffing outward to a gradual subsiding still rabid, from time to time, with upsurges? How explain the shift from paroxysmic puffing outward to the pure poise without benefit of discernible transition of uncreased unrippling stillness? Sometimes a diffuse and global puffing outward would be crossed by a ripple only the slightest effort on my part to appropriate the organic interrelation of these events was perceptual torture. And yet it seemed to me that if only I could found the structure comprising these events and defining their interrelation— for the row of motorcycle covers was a single organism—then at last I would find myself talking about myself, or rather, about something larger, much larger, than myself, the story inside the story of all possible stories about myself. An old man passed swinging his cane: a little thrust and then a wider thrust, both in a forward direction, not quite dead north, then back, another little thrust forward, wider thrust forward, then back. I tried to link movement of cane with movement of feet, capture and master the wider system comprising—hoarding—the logic inside their interrelation. More perceptual torture. But then it came to me again—but had it ever come to me before quite like this?—perhaps it had come to Jamms quite—just—like this—that my being able to go on with the stories that evicted me from their absence of womb did not depend on my successfully completing such exertions as these. There was more to be gained—for the story—for the stories—from striving to understand why I sought to feel canceled—disqualified—without the fruit presumably to be extracted from such exertions. A family with its bags from a fast-food joint were making noisy motions of trying to fit into the little space left on my sunless stump, they wanted me to move, to move on, I was immediately enraged by their polite impatience of wanting, picked up my leavings, left, I had been about to leave anyway, in search of a sunnier spot—a spot where sun, crucial to everybody's well-being, would be uniformly distributed over my bulk.

I loathed myself for fixing once again on the motorcycle covers when there was so much else to consider: my trip, for example. Were these covers—this detail—at the core of my story of the trip or merely a convenient pretext for flight from the fear—the panic—that such a story might turn out to be incommensurate with any detail's lucid—or, to judge from all the previous huffing and puffing in a complete absence of wind, not so lucid—contour? Was such a detail at the heart of the story-to-be—a new story purified of precinct, purified of Jamms—or was it, having managed to pillage all pith of latent commitment to truth—a story truth—now too vast to be blissfully reducible to this detail or that and therefore denuded of any intrinsic merit. Though how debate the merit of what had succeeded in completely overwhelming me—as up to now no story had.

I had strongly resented the encroachment of the smiling fast-food family on my sunny stump. Yet looking back—at them, at the complete success of their encroachment—I could only marvel at ever having thought the story of stump life, bleeding out of the story of the precinct and into that of the trip-to-be, perfectible, conceivable, without it.

Books from **Four Walls Eight Windows**

Algren, Nelson. **Never Come Morning**. pb: $7.95

Anderson, Sherwood. **The Triumph of the Egg**. pb: $8.95

Bachmann, Stephen, ed. **Preach Liberty: A Progressive's Bible** pb: $10.95

Boetie, Dugmore. **Familiarity Is the Kingdom of the Lost**. pb: $6.95

Brodsky, Michael. **Dyad**. cl: $23.95, pb: $11.95

Brodsky, Michael. **X in Paris**. pb: $9.95

Brodsky, Michael. **Xman**. cl: $21.95, pb: $11.95

Codrescu, Andrei, ed. **American Poetry Since 1970 : Up Late**. 2nd ed.
cl: $25.95, pb: $14.95

David, Kati. **A Child's War: Fifteen Children Tell Their Stories**. cl: $17.95

Dubuffet, Jean. **Asphyxiating Culture and Other Writings**. cl: $17.95

Hoffman, Abbie.
**The Best of Abbie Hoffman: Selections from "Revolution for the Hell
of It," "Woodstock Nation" and "Steal This Book"**. cl: $21.95

Howard-Howard, Margo (with Abbe Michaels). **I Was a White Slave in Harlem**.
pb: $12.95

Johnson, Phyllis, and Martin, David, eds.
Frontline Southern Africa: Destructive Engagement. cl: $23.95, pb: $14.95

Jones, E.P. **Where Is Home? Living Through Foster Care**. cl: $17.95

Martin, Augustine, ed.
Forgiveness: Ireland's Best Contemporary Short Stories.
cl: $25.95, pb: $12.95

Null, Gary. **The Egg Project: Gary Null's Guide to Good Eating**.
cl: $21.95, pb: $12.95

Santos, Rosario, ed.
And We Sold the Rain: Contemporary Fiction from Central America.
cl: $18.95, pb: $9.9.5

Schultz, John. **No One Was Killed**. pb: $9.95

Sokolov, Sasha. **A School for Fools**. pb: $9.95

Wasserman, Harvey. **Harvey Wasserman's History of the United States**.
pb: $6.95

Zerden, Sheldon. **The Best of Health**. cl:$23.95, pb: $12.95

To order, send check or money order to Four Walls Eight Windows, P.O. Box 548, Village Station, New York, N.Y. 10014, or call 1-800-835-2246, ext. 123. Add $2.50 postage and handling for the first book and 50¢ for each additional book.